seven

by James Durose-Rayner

New Generation Publishing

James Durose-Rayner

'ITV 7' is the follow up story to
'I Am Sam'

Cover: 'See Emily Play'
by Tim D'Addio

With special thanks to Jon Sammels, Frank McLintock, Stevie Kell, Kevin Whitcher, Gary Lawrence, Brian Allan and several lovely people on Twitter who have made ITV 7 possible

Part of the football? A tale of two seasons and of what should have been. Long before Arsenal had Arsène Wenger at the helm the club had chased the League and F.A Cup Double on numerous occasions, sometimes lifting one trophy but not the other.

There were also two post-war and two pre-Wenger seasons, where the club had changed both its philosophy and dynamics and where they had looked odds on to take both trophies; however, due to the the board's parsimony, severe mis-management, squabbling off the field and injuries on it, both seasons imploded, so much so it would take many, many years to repair.

These were the 1958/59 and the 1972/73 seasons. During the 1958/59 season, Arsenal lost their way prior to the Christmas period, suffering a 4-1 home defeat to tenth-placed Blackpool whilst two more 2-1 defeats followed – the first at home to a soon-to-be-relegated Aston Villa and then to an injury-ravaged and much-depleted Preston North End, a side who had even had to blood 16-year old reserve goalkeeper John Barton, before they had their misery compounded further after visiting Kenilworth Road on Boxing Day, to be at the other end of a 6-3 hammering from Luton Town.

That period during the season cost them the title, as did passing on the chance to sign Gordon Banks in December, 1958 along with their manager's stubborn refusal to go head-to-head with Everton for Celtic's Bobby Collins.

As for the F.A Cup, and with no big teams left in it,

Arsenal had made it to the Fifth Round stages to be drawn at home against Division Two opposition that was Sheffield United. First, they drew 2-2 at Highbury and then crashed out in the replay after a fog-bound tie in front of nearly 50,000 at the three-sided Bramall Lane – a match where goalkeeper Jack Kelsey broke his arm with five minutes on the clock and where Danny Clapton got injured after 43 minutes, forcing Arsenal to play out the game with nine men and going on to lose 3-0.

The club tried to turn their season around with brilliant displays such as the 4-1 away win at White Hart Lane, where Arsenal – again played out the game with nine men after Len Julians had been given his marching orders after clattering Spurs' Maurice Norman, and at home to Manchester United, where, in front of just under 70,000 they halted United's 12-game unbeaten run by winning the match 3-2.

A similar occurrence happened in 1972/73, where they were not only chasing the Double, but the Treble, and with few big sides left in the League Cup they met Norwich City at home, where stand-in goalkeeper Geoff Barnett produced a stinker during a 3-0 mauling by The Canaries. Four days later Arsenal would go the Baseball Ground with Bob Wilson between the sticks, who himself knocked out a similar performance to that of his understudy, and where Brian Clough's men – Alan Hinton especially – mercilessly tore Arsenal to shreds, hammering them 5-0, and even having a legitimate goal ruled out.

Just prior to those two games Arsenal had passed up on the chance to sign the £200,000-valued, 23-year-old Peter Shilton – ex-Arsenal player from the 1958/59 season and manager of Leicester City, Jimmy Bloomfield was open to a part-exchange deal where Arsenal would get Shilton, and they in return would get Eddie Kelly, however what history will tell you is that the deal never happened.

Again, the club tried to turn their season around, going away to Anfield and producing a brilliant display to knock Liverpool off the top of the league with both Alan Ball and John Radford scoring in front of the Kop. However it wasn't to be, and as good as Arsenal could perform, injuries and mis-management played a huge part in their downfall, the club fighting through a F.A Cup Quarter Final tie against a brilliant Chelsea side only to get knocked out in the F.A Cup semi-final – again against Division Two opposition that was Sunderland, before going to Elland Road on the final day of the season, to be on the end of a 6-1 mauling by Leeds United.

Post-1958/59 season Arsenal looked in great shape, the purchase of Mel Charles providing the catalyst for what they saw as a great future; however, manager George Swindin had sold captain Dave Bowen and bought badly – missing out on several great players.

Post-1972/73 it looked the same, however during that season, manager Bertie Mee had taken a wrecking ball to the squad, offloading players such as John Roberts, Peter Marinello and George Graham, and come 28th April, 1973 he made what was possibly considered his worst-ever mistake and sold captain Frank McLintock to QPR. The club used the money from the sale of McLintock, for Sunderland's 23-year old midfielder, Brian Chambers who went on to play just one league game for Arsenal. As for McLintock – he went on to help a resurgent QPR to come within a whisker of the title.

During that season there were several good players available who could have come to Arsenal; however, the club never moved for the likes of Stan Bowles, Dave Thomas, Frank Worthington, David Nish, Lou Macari, Graeme Souness, Martin Buchan, Terry McDermott, David Johnson and Gordon McQueen. And if you want to really bitch about 'What if's?' – there was always Harry Redknapp.

As for bolstering Arsenal's assault on both fronts, Mee had already bought Jeff Blockley from Coventry, who proved as successful a purchase as either Igor Stepanovs or Sebastian Squillaci but just to prove how small-time Arsenal could be, in early 1973 Mee approached Bob Stokoe to get both Sunderland's Keith

Coleman and Richie Pitt on loan, the latter of who made his debut in the reserves before being recalled by his club, and who would rather strangely go on to play against Arsenal in his clubs 2-1 F.A Cup Semi Final win, whilst Coleman would break his leg in a reserve game before Sunderland eventually shipped him out to West Ham United for £20,000 come September 1973.

Of what was left of 'Mee's Arsenal', two-cap Scottish international midfielder and £150,000 signing from Hibernian Alex Cropley told Graham Spiers of the *Scottish Herald*, "I was being pursued by Chelsea and Arsenal and when Bertie Mee eventually signed me I felt that I had joined a lesser team in terms of ability. There was no doubt in my mind that the Hibs side I had just left was much better."

However, football is only part of the story.

Now let us fill in a few gaps.

Contents

Chapter 1

Jeanette's Tales – Take 1

Where do I start?

Sammy was born in early August, a week or so early and both parents and of course the grandparents were truly happy. The joy expressed at the 7lb 2oz bundle by Emily's mum, or my children's new Granny Sil' could have been multiplied by a thousand. If you wanted to see the ultimate in both happiness and pride you need look no further, as Sil' was without doubt the proudest grandmother on the planet.

As for me, I had mixed emotions. I had been clinging on to Lee for months; however, he was now well and truly Emily's. I was his second phone call from hospital. "Hiya Jeanette – Emily has just had a baby boy." The emotion he showed was reminiscent of when I'd had ours.

"Will you let the kids know they've got a baby brother," he added.

He broke my heart. He always did, and I spent the next hour in the bathroom crying. I knew as soon as I'd first seen him with her that I'd never ever get him back. You just know these things. The thing is with Emily – or M rather, as that is what she prefers to be called, is that she is clever – not just academically clever, but clever, clever. She saw what she wanted and got it. Me, I had it all and lost it.

The children were ecstatic at the news. Their dad was their hero and it was always, 'Dad this and dad that' and it was even worse when he got with Emily. It was then 'Dad and M this and dad and M that'.

I thought when Nicole had kicked him out that we'd get back together. He stayed at the house for three days and I honestly thought he would come back for good. Life is all about timing and I missed the opportunity. We had stood on the landing, and I knew he was all over the place. I kissed him on the cheek and he told me that he loved me. It could have been more than that, but at times I am such a stubborn cow. That was the moment and the timing was right. If I would have made myself more available at that point in time, just maybe – just maybe – the whole story could have changed. However, I didn't and he married M, and now they had Sammy.

He is a great friend and the greatest father ever. He always complements me, always provides for us and, and get this – he always tell me that he loves me, and M knows this and she is okay with it. As I said Emily is extremely clever, and a lot more so than me. I was too controlling and possessive and, that being the case I screamed, shouted and bossed him around for fear of losing him.

His mother – Rosemary – or Rose rather – used to tell me that I'd lose him if I didn't calm my temper. Lee never thought it, but my mother and dad loved him; however, my mother soon changed her tune after I told her what he had done, although dad didn't. My dad blamed me, but Dad's mum and dad – my grandma and granddad, were Greek – and that being the case he's a bit old school in his thinking that if the man strays, then the woman can't be doing her job right. To some extent he was right – I didn't. However, Emily is clever – she did.

I make it sound like I don't like M. It is true that I didn't – I hated her, but I was wrong. I'm wrong on lots of things, but my problem is that half the time I won't admit it. The first time I saw her was with Nicole. My first impression was that she looked about twenty-years-old and possessed a smile that you wouldn't believe. The thing was that Nicole looked almost identical, was it not for the fact that Nicole was slightly taller and had brown eyes.

Nicole loved him and it was her life's mission to hang on to him like no other, even though M was carrying his child. Nicole tried to do what it took and grabbed, scratched and fought for his love; however, M didn't. She was just there. Lee was never one for drama, even though is life is one bloody drama, and while Emily sat on the casting couch Nicole gave it her best shot and went after the BAFTA. "I just love him so much," she had said.

I knew she did and I told him.

"Marry Nicole – she loves you," I'd said. I also told him that M was no good or words to that effect. Again – I thought I was right, but I wasn't.

"Jeanette – just butt out," my dad always told me. "Half the time your mouth clicks into gear before your brain does."

I take after my mother for that, although Lee never pulled neither me nor her on it, and believe me when I say it, my mother was never one to mince her words.

The first time I saw M to speak to on her own, my mood towards her changed. My feelings didn't as I still hated her guts. The night before, she had gone back to her and her husband's house on Tuskar Street to retrieve some of her things, and her husband wouldn't let her leave. Lee made sure he did, however – and as he always did, he went about it in an arse-around-face way, and as her husband was some martial arts expert and he ended up taking a slap – not that he didn't deserve it, of course – he did. I gave Emily a forthright summary of my then-estranged husband, so much so I thought she would have packed her bags and left. However, she didn't, and she just thanked me for my honesty and aplogised for the fact that she was there and I wasn't. Well, I think she did? It certainly seemed that way, anyway. She also passed comment on our children saying how lovely they were and how much they look like me. She also said something nice to me which still stays with me to this day. "I can see why Lee still loves you, I really can."

I got home and I cried my eyes out. How could I compete with that? I rued the day when we stood on the landing and I kissed his cheek. That was the moment. Emily would have known what to do and she would have done it. My obstinate nature possibly robbed me of another go with him.

I do have Paul, although Paul is certainly no Lee. Lee would have you think that I'm some shelf-stacker in Sainsbury's which is certainly not the case. I'm an assistant manager and moonlight between of one of the local stores off the A100 south of London Bridge and one over near Chelsea Bridge. I met Paul at a birthday party of a girl who works in the Chelsea Bridge store and he asked me out. Whereas Lee would have you on the edge of your seat wondering what he was going to do next, Paul does not and you're sat waiting for the moment when he's going to explode into life. He never does though.

"So long as he's good with the kids and he's nice with you, then I don't have a problem," Lee told me.

It was another one of those moments when I cried my eyes out. I was jealous of him with women – why wasn't he jealous when it came to me? And it's me who's always telling him to grow up. It's a strange one, that?

Paul hated Lee, but not so much now. Lee looks like a Premier League footballer whereas Paul does not, although Lee says that Paul reminds of him of a guy out of Monty Python, which, when I told Paul, he got the right hump.

"He reminds me of Michael Palin," he had said.

"Bollocks, Lee," was my rather apt reply, but believe me I was on Google and YouTube half the night, and you know something – he was dead right. He does. Lee's like that – he has some magnetic charm, which has you scurrying about after his every word – every word, that is except Arsenal. I hated Arsenal, not because of the club, but because I was jealous of him loving them. Since we split up the only Arsenal mate of Lee's I kept in touch

4

with was Stevie Kell and that is mainly because his wife Jane took sides. Steve is some executive on the Supporters Club and is as batty about the club as Lee, although Steve is a die-hard fan who goes to every match whereas Lee hits and misses matches and kicks over the TV when he watches them on Sky.

I had to hold his hand watching them against Barcelona in the Champions League Final. For most of the match he was in awe and then when Thierry Henry and Freddy Ljungberg missed a couple of chances he went berserk but that was nothing compared to when Barcelona scored two goals right at the end. And he calls me premenstrual! M, on the other hand knows he loves Arsenal and while he's at a match she'll listen to BBC Radio 5 live for any news and converse with him about it. Like I said, Emily is clever.

The downside of Sammy being born – which sounds really horrible when I say it like that, as he is such a lovely little boy, was the timing of the birth as it was just as a big deal with ITV was being put together and Lee had not been there to manage it. Lee's business partner is or was Sooty; or 'Uncle Sooty' if you were my children. Sooty was on the scene the second time I met Lee and he ended up seeing Libby, as Lib and I went to University together, but I'll get on to that in a bit. When I first knew Lee he was working with Sooty and a lad called Yusef on some iffy DVD business. Well, a very iffy DVD business if I'm being honest. Lee would never tell you this but he always surrounds himself by people he can rely on and the fact that Yusef thought he was Bangladesh's answer to James Bond tells its own story. He shot a man outside a bar in south London a few years ago and the other year the police came calling, and that being the case he left the country. Lee is in denial about him as between them they made a hell of a lot of money, but after marrying me he and Sooty went legitimate. Yusef – or 'Uncle Bondy' if you're talking to my children – did not, and made his living selling drugs even though to this day Lee will swear blind that is not the case. Nevertheless Yusef never misses neither mine nor the kid's birthday and he always sends presents. Sooty loves Lee as does Libby, although the latter once confided in me one night while she was drunk that she would have done anything to be me. It was a bit of a haze but I think it was more to do with the fact that she would have liked to be with Lee rather than her actually being me, although the subject was never brought up again.

Sooty ran the business as a managing director of sorts with Lee as its creative director, with Sooty always having to dog Lee to do this that and the other. Libby was even worse, and when we split up he had been spending money like it was going out of fashion, and it was her who had tried getting him to curb it. Not that it really did however – that would come when M arrived on the scene.

M had problems having Sammy and it knocked her for six. She's only tiny and it was thought that a caesarean would have been a more viable option of having him, which I was told by her afterwards that a C-section would have "Most definitely" been the right way. That being the case, Lee spent a lot of time at the hospital and during that time Sooty was left to his own devices, which I got to know about firstly by M's dad – Mike, who is one of the nicest people you could ever wish to meet. Saying that, so is his wife Sil'. Apparently Eddie Mardell, who was working for Lee and who, at that point I had only met a few times, had told Mike that something was going down at the office. He was right, and when I asked Sooty about it, he clammed up. However, Libby didn't. The woman who had been preaching to Lee about how not to do this, that and the other was the subject of some lawsuit – from a personal point of view as opposed to corporate, and they were both in trouble and needed cash quickly. It also turned out that they'd had an offer for the business which was too good to turn down. I initially went crackers with Libby but once she told me that it was a problem with the house down Holland Park that they had inherited I calmed down a bit.

Lee was philosophical about it all and never panicked. He probably would have done if he'd have still been with me as I'd have given him my run-of-the-mill twenty questions followed by another twenty or thirty and nagged him like hell. I will admit – I nag, and as Lee will admit – he hates being nagged. Emily is clever, she never ever nags.

M phoned me from hospital and asked if I would fetch the children to see their baby brother. I have to admit, I always thought there was something underlying to everything she did, but there never was, as you will see; but if going to their wedding was hard it was nothing compared to when we visited her in hospital and she passed Sammy over to me whilst both my kids snuggled up to her on the bed. Lee took a photo of me, and that photograph has since been framed and sits on top of a piano in their house. M doesn't do envy – well if she does, she certainly doesn't show it. "Do you think he looks like Jamie?" she had asked.

"I do," I'd replied.

He did. Sammy looked exactly like my two, but he had blue eyes whereas both mine had brown. I held him for a good thirty minutes and every emotion went through me, with the one main thought being, *I wish he would have been mine*. Lee was a great father and I knew that this little lad would have everything, however what was to come knocked me for six and it came direct from M. "We'd like you and Paul to be godparents," she had said.

I couldn't fathom her out at all and I immediately looked here, there and everywhere for that underlying objective or ulterior motive, but there wasn't one. "I really want him to grow up close to his brother and sister and you'd be a brilliant auntie," she had said. "You really would."

Between them they had offered me a part of their life and there was no way on earth that I was going to pass it up, although I did ask if they were sure?

"I'm very sure," smiled M.

I felt like crying my eyes out, but I didn't. I waited until I got home to do that. What is even stranger is that they had included Paul and he was totally gobsmacked.

My mother said that they were playing with my emotions, but I knew Lee wouldn't do that – why? Because he loved me.

Back to M's father, Mike. "So what does it mean?" he had asked on hearing that the business had been sold. "Is he out of work?"

I told him that people like Lee would never be out of work but what I wasn't to know is how mad the next few months would be and how it would all pan out – but more to the point, how I would regret not kissing him properly on the landing. That was a huge, huge mistake.

Chapter 2

Out of Work

Emily had known all week that something was going down at work. She had got to know me better than me, and although she knew something wasn't right, she was always there for me, lovingly concerned and inquisitive, but certainly never, ever opinionated. Perfection is what I had married and that perfection sat in front of me listening as I told her, "The company has been sold – I tried to stop it but it's gone."

I had. I didn't want it to go, but my 48% wasn't enough and Sooty's 48% plus Libby's and Big Decker's firms, two and two respectively made it unanimous. I was out of work.

"They've sold it?" she asked. "How?"

I tried to explain how it worked and that a huge sports media company had come in and made a play for us – the Sammy project along with the documentaries on our take on the failed World Cup of 1970 plus the deceit regarding the Munich 1958 tragedy had made people sit up and take us very seriously – that and the fact that we had got a regular four hours a week with ITV.

"As part of the deal," I added. "I can't set up a sports media company for three years."

She had seen me serious, but not quite like this.

"So, what will you do, love?" she asked.

I gave a shrug of my shoulders. I didn't know. Part of my life had just been taken from me.

"We'll be okay for money, though," I said. "I think we did okay."

I'd just had the firm who had bought us out send £6.8 million pounds into my bank account along with a one-off payment of £400,000, which was my year's salary paid up in full.

Emily nearly fell off her chair when I told her. And then I got a massive love off her. I take that back – I got a really massive love off her.

"You know you'll definitely not be able to claim dole?" she smiled whilst wiping her eyes.

She then faxed the story over to the *Liverpool Echo*, or she may as well have done because she was on the phone half the night to her parents, although at that time she never mentioned any amount of money – just that it was "Really a lot."

There was another downside to this – their Stuart, or 'Our Stuart' rather, as that was how I am always referred to by him and young Lucy – as 'Our Lee'.

I needed to see him, and the next day I did.

Me, M and the new addition drove up to Birkenhead where we were greeted as we always were with an affection like no other and this is where I got Stuart sat down along with his mum and dad, and strangely his granddad, who had made a point in going around to his daughter's house for only the third time in twenty years.

I had got Libby to get Stuart enrolled in a two-year course at the City of Liverpool College; however, my promise of a job was looking bleak – to him that was, and not necessarily to me.

"I thought I would be working with you and Sooty down in London?" was the first thing he had said.

He was right, I had promised him exactly that.

"Do you trust me?" I asked him.

He nodded.

"Well I am saying this – and in front of your mum, dad and granddad so they can call me on it if they like – I will never, ever let you down."

I could see his mum's bottom lip wobbling and I could also see how proud his Granddad Bill was at what I had just said.

"Stick with me, because I reckon something really good is going to come out of all this," I added.

I then let him know that I had got him in to see an old mate of mine – Scott Tighe or 'Tigger' rather, who was working for BBC Radio Merseyside, and who said that on his two days off from college he could work at their offices on Hanover Street in Liverpool.

"You will be paid," I said. "Not by them, but through a new company I've just formed."

I noticed a bit of a smile on his face.

"I want you with me," I said. "However, it's really, really important that you learn."

"Have you got anything in mind that you are going to do, love?" asked his mum who was now picking up her only grandchild as it had started crying.

Both Emily and the baby weren't sleeping very well. In fact he wasn't doing anything rather well – with the exception of the crying, that is.

"I'm taking two or three weeks out to help your M with laddo," I said. "And then I'll decide where I go from there."

I could see her father pondering and I knew exactly what the pondering was all about.

"So, did you do okay out of all this?" he asked.

I knew he was going to ask me that, however the last thing that I had wanted to do was mention the £7.2 million, therefore I didn't – Emily did however – and to a rather gobsmacked audience, and that being the case the room was in total shock.

"They really paid you that much?" asked Sil'.

"They had paid me exactly that much," I replied, though I was quieter than usual, and Sil' certainly picked up on it.

"I'm a bit upset that a lot of this was done behind my back and while your Emily was in hospital," I said. "That and the fact that I'd got the backing of a major TV station and that it now looks like I have used them to generate the sale of our company – and that being the case, they'll probably never touch me again."

They listened, but I don't think they understood. In fact, I knew they didn't understand.

"It's a loyalty thing, mam," said Emily, whilst smiling over at me.

"Things will become clearer in a few weeks," I said.

Her dad couldn't understand it, as the money aspect of it was clouding the overall situation. We didn't stop over as we now had the *addition*, and that being the case we drove back down to London.

A few days went past, and I tried doing my bit with the baby, but I had to admit, he wasn't the most pleasurable of blokes, and the incessant wailing and bawling took its toll on us both.

"He's a bit of a misery guts, isn't he?" Emily had said as she peered over into his buggy at the sight of Horrid Henry grimacing back up at her.

"A bit?" I replied. "I would mind but he just whines for the sake of it. It's like having Michael Owen in the house."

I knew that I should continue as I had been doing, and like I always did. I was getting up early, having my jog around the block and I always came in to a house smelling of coffee with Sky Sports on TV and Emily either feeding Herbert, or on her laptop – but always smiling.

I'd had a bit of a 'pet idea' of the colourisation of monochrome footage and had sought some advice from a kid I know nicknamed 'Froggy' on the subject a couple of years ago, as he had a side-line in recreating colour photographs from black and white. I'd dabbled with it a bit but it was dead time consuming. It may have took Sammy (Jon Sammels) just short of 20 seconds to bend the ball away from Alex Stepney from 35 yards for the 1970 Goal of the Season; however, it took me about seven weeks to colourise it and the end product looked shit.

"I think it looks great," said Emily.

"Well, the red shirts look good," she added.

Mmm. Maybe film colourisation wasn't my forte, I thought. Nevertheless, I now had plenty of time on my hands to try and master the art.

A few days passed and out of the blue I had an email from some lady at NBC sounding me out about being a guest pundit for one of the weekend's games. It was definitely David Beckham related, but for the life of me I couldn't understand how as no-one knew me from Adam – and the general consensus regarding punditry is that ex-players are better; which, although I can see where they are coming from, is in itself a load of rubbish. It's the same with sports journalists – a lot of them actually believe the hype that surrounds them, yet there are much better football bloggers around – one of whom I was in daily contact with.

"Do you fancy a weekend in New York?" I asked.

Emily looked at me, a bit puzzled.

"NBC have asked if I'll be a pundit on one of next weekend's games."

"That's great," she beamed. "But what about Sammy?"

That was easy – Take him with us or let his grandparents look after him, and I told her so.

"My mam would definitely like that," she said.

I knew they would.

"You ask them," Emily said. "They would really like it if you did."

Therefore I did – sort of.

"Hiya Sil', I've got some business over in New York next weekend," I said before I got to asking the question; however, I noticed a bit of an undercurrent which suggested that things weren't well up on The Wirral and during the couple of minutes of chit-chat I hung fire on asking them and instead hit it from another angle. "Do you and Mike fancy coming? Everything is laid on."

I looked over at Emily who sort of looked back at me dumbfounded and shrugged her shoulders.

"Your mum isn't saying a deal," I told her. Well she wasn't at that moment, but she was ten seconds later and then Emily couldn't get her off the phone.

"What did you ask her that for?" M asked me afterwards.

"They've looked after me from day one of me meeting them, so why not give a bit back?"

They had – they were great people, and not only did they love me, they treat my two kids like they were their own.

There was a bit more to this NBC thing, as I was to find out, when some vice president from Fox Sports emailed me – and then phoned me, and then NBC phoned me and then Fox Sports phoned me again. This New York thing would transpire into something substantial and it turned out that they wanted someone to run their football channel – well, soccer channel actually.

"I think they are angling to offer me a job," I said.

Football had become quite big over in The States, but the reality was that the country had no history in the game. Saying that, it didn't stop them beating us 1-0 in the 1950 World Cup in Brazil or successfully hosting the self-same competition in 1994 – something which an ex-Leyton Orient and West Ham United player helped the country to achieve, although I'll get on to that in a bit.

"What – they said that?" asked M.

"More or less," I replied.

Emily was a bit quiet when I told her.

"I'll go anywhere with you," she said. "You know that."

I did, however I also had other things in my life as well as Emily and the soon-to-be rusk munching-cum-screaming machine, and that was my other two kids and their mum – and of course Emily's family, who were now mine.

"We have to keep an open mind," I told her.

I got a smile back, but I could hear her mind ticking away in the background.

My days during my three-week sabbatical were being taken up by pushing Sammy around Regent's Park and Highbury Fields and a lot of reading and research – The Football Betting Scandal of 1964, in particular as I found that fascinating and the 1958/59 season where both Arsenal and Tottenham had rather defining seasons in that Arsenal were being heavily tipped to win the league and cup and Tottenham were staring down the barrel of a gun at relegation. How the next few years would pan out would be incredible – but certainly not for the Arsenal supporter!

As for Emily – she was back into doing her music lessons and trying her level best to tone up her stomach, firstly by afternoon sessions of 'Bums and Tums' and then a bit of work at the gym, none of which she particularly enjoyed. I was sick of having to look at her stomach – well, I wasn't – It was just that I was always being asked to see if I could tell a difference after every session. I certainly could after every session in the bedroom – not that I ever minded though.

Jeanette delighted in the fact that I was at home and that I would be able to pick up both my kids from school, but she knew that even if I hadn't been at home, Emily would have more than helped out.

Ever since she had first met my two kids she had driven them here, there and everywhere. The kids loved Emily's mini – The 'Bulletproof Bomb' as she had labelled it to them, however Sammy coming into the world had made things a bit crowded.

"I think I'll have to get rid of it," she said. "It's getting a bit cramped."

I thought that the first time I got in it, and even more so when we tried a bit of a special cuddle during the first few months of our relationship, though I never told her so.

I ended up taking her to a car showroom where she said goodbye to the Bulletproof Bomb which she didn't particularly enjoy and said hello to a black Range Rover that

I bought her, which she totally did – and which both kids thought was fantastic – Obviously thinking that it was some gangster rapper's car.

"What are you going to call it M?" my daughter had asked.

"I don't know," she replied smiling. "What about 'Chuga-boom' or the 'Mean Machine'?"

"The Mean Machine," both my kids replied.

So there it was.

She'd only had the frigging Mean Machine a couple of hours when the AA had to be called out.

"I forgot it was a diesel," she had said.

I forgave her the first time, but I had to call her on it when she did again three days later. But as dippy as she could be, you just had to love her. As for my lad – He was as obstinate as the proverbial family dog, and he wouldn't get out of the thing.

Emily's mum and dad were on the phone on a daily basis, as were both her grandparents and they always enquired into what I was doing.

"He's been researching something on Sheffield Wednesday's in the sixties," Emily told her gran.

Ten minutes later her granddad was on the phone to me wanting to know the ins and outs of what I was doing, and I did of course ask him about it.

"The three Sheffield players were the real fall-guys – one of them had just won the league with Everton," said Bill before asking, "So what are you planning to do – a documentary?"

I explained that I was just researching it, however I did admit that I had also been sourcing film footage.

"Jimmy Gauld was a right snake in it all," Bill added. "He ruined their careers and Sheffield Wednesday had a really good team back then with some great players – Johnny Fantham – now he was class."

I was already aware of most of the things he was telling me, but I just enjoyed listening to him and as I was talking,

Jeanette called in at the house – at first I thought it was something to do with the kids, which I suppose it was, but in reality it was more to do with me. Well, me and going to New York, really.

"So these people have offered you a job?" she asked.

"No," I replied. "They are sounding me out about a job."

"That's the same, isn't it," she quipped.

I told her it definitely wasn't the same and that it was a case of them needing to know more about me and that's why they had asked me over to do a bit of punditry. I knew from that moment onwards that she would dig her heels in and try to make Emily do the same. They had got to be like best friends and some form of a conspiracy was set in motion that was to even involve Granny Sil' stopping talking to me – even though my thirteen-year old sister-in-law and best friend, Lucy always gave me the heads-up, continually revealing what was being said west of the River Mersey.

"Our M and Jeanette said that if everyone doesn't talk to you, that you won't go," she had whispered.

"Don't you want me to go?" I had asked her.

"Not if I can't come with you, I don't," she had said.

It was nice to feel wanted.

Before the trip to New York Emily's parents came down unannounced – not that I ever minded – I loved seeing them, and the sight of Granny Sil' juggling the baby when I walked in cheered me up no end as that day in particular had been a fairly shitty one if I'm being honest. I had been in with a corporate law firm half the afternoon – the same company that had acted for me on the sale of the company, but that wasn't the real reason – and as we sat around the breakfast bar talking, I mentioned that Sooty had just landed a job.

"Nubeon Entertainment," I said. "He starts next week."

"That's interesting," said M.

"It is," I replied. "It's one of those adult entertainment companies."

Neither Mike nor Sil' had any idea what I was on about but Emily did and wasted no time in telling them.

"What pornography?" asked Mike.

I nodded and told them he'd dropped the role of development director on £99,000 a year with incentives plus a car.

It was then the kids' Granddad Mike inquired further. "So what will he sort of be doing?" he asked.

"I'm not sure offhand," I said. "But it's a sort of fetishist company."

That got Emily's interest, although I wasn't to know that wholeheartedly until a few hours later when I firstly had to tell her every detail and then beat her off with a horse whip.

"It's a sort of a play on the dirty old man and the pretty young girl thing – more 'arty' than anything," I said.

"Old man thing?" Mike asked, looking rather intrigued.

"I wouldn't get too excited, Mike," I told him. "I think you're a bit too good-looking and not quite old enough."

The look I got back off him was a bit strange.

"I reckon Bill could make it through to the interview stage, though," I winked.

The look I then got back off him, Sil and Emily' was even stranger. Even Horrible Herbert was shocked and he was only a few weeks old.

Although I was happy for Sooty, it did mean that for the first time ever that I was on my own – in business that was, as my life outside of that was as good as you could get. Well, it would have been if it wasn't for the continual grimacing coming from the whinging, whining and shitting machine that was my second son.

"I can't recall my other two whining like that," I told Sil', whilst peering over at him.

"He takes after his mum," said Sil'. "She was a right miserable little bugger."

"You never told me that," exclaimed her daughter – sort of shocked.

"You were," added Sil'. "I used to leave you outside the shops in your pram hoping that somebody would take you."

"Mam, that's horrid," Emily said.

"It is – It was only your gran and granddad that made me go back for you," she added.

I looked over at a rather shocked wife who I could have never ever imagined looking miserable – well, apart from when she had to do the ironing that is!

"I love you," I told her.

"Thank you," she said. "I'm glad someone does."

Mike and Sil' being down gave us some respite, and we managed to get an hour out and we went to the bar off Euston Road that played the indie music – our bar – the bar where we got to know so much about each other. It was as good as it was the first time we had ever been there, but little did I know at the time that this bar would play a huge part in defining our lives.

Chapter 3

Jeanette's Tales – Take 2

We had been to New York a few times both before and after we had been married. I loved it; however, I totally hated it when I knew Lee had got a job offer over there.

"Let him go," my mother had told me, which was nothing to what Paul had said – so much so he walked out of my life for three days.

I had gone off on one, and I remember ringing up M, Sil' and Mike - and even M's grandfather, who is a really nice old gent who doted on my two kids. However, if I'm honest his wife Edie was and still is to an extent, extremely wary of me. In fact I knew that she had labelled me 'Miss Holly Go not so lightly' as a reference to me both having a look of Audrey Hepburn and of course the fact that I was still part of Lee's life. I also knew that she and Emily were very close, so much so she was highly protective of her granddaughter's newfound life. I wasn't upset, more touched by the fact that she thought I posed a problem. It was nice being the *other woman* for a change.

Sil' and Mike were very appreciative of me forewarning them and even asked me my advice. "Your M knows him a lot better than me," I had told them. She probably didn't as such, she just knew how to play him better than me! "But whatever you do, don't nag him or opinionise."

Sil' used to call nearly every day – firstly it was to talk to the kids, but as time went on it was more reconnaissance which metamorphosed into a very nice friendship, and which was something which my mother hated.

"What are you talking to them for?" she would ask.

"Why not?" I'd replied. "They dote on the kids and they are very nice people."

I think jealousy played its part in my mother's appraisal of them as Jamie wouldn't shut up about his Granddad Mike and Granny Sil', and my daughter, Harmony, thought that their Lucy was the greatest auntie in the world – an auntie who she regarded as a big sister, that is. The whole family were really nice, including Stuart who looked up to Lee as though he was god and I even think that is understating it a bit.

After Sammy was born I spoke more and more frequently with M and we set up a few unwritten rules, one of which was that we would keep the conversations between ourselves as exactly that and when in front of either Lee or Paul talking about our past life together was a no-go area, which was hard considering I'd intimately known Lee for around eleven years. I got to know a lot about Emily, too and one of the things that I could never get my head around was why there was such an age gap between her and their Stuart.

"My mam got pregnant with me when she was fourteen," M explained. "That's why I'm so close with my gran as she helped bring me up."

The obvious question was then raised regarding Mike being her dad, and he was. Mike was also fourteen years old and what was even stranger that they had stayed together all these years, although the relationship between Mike and Bill was never the best – but saying that, Lee had indirectly helped get them talking. That's what I meant by him possessing some magnetic charm, something which he had used on Paul time and time again. Libby wrongly described Paul as some insecure mammy's boy after he'd walked out in a huff. Lee was always the topic of conversation and me going batty about him going to New York and saying, "After all we've been through and now he's on about leaving us," wasn't perhaps the best thing to say to him.

My daughter gave me a reality check when she said, "Dad won't leave us – ever."

I told Sil' what she had said and Sil' replied, "You know something love – I believe her."

We spent the next twenty minutes on the phone crying our eyes out. I could have never been that close with my mother, and I could fully understand why Lee loved them all so much.

M never ever ragged him about it and told him that she'd follow him anywhere, however, she also told me that me and the kids were her ace card, which was something else which put another lump in my throat.

I could say that I never chased after Paul like I chased after Lee. I liked Paul but I not like I loved Lee, although I often told Paul I loved him. Every time Lee came to pick up the kids he'd have me on tenterhooks. I'd put my make-up on and dress up for him, just to get a kiss on the cheek and then see him drive off. It drove me insane – so much so I used to bitch him like hell just to keep him for five minutes longer. I'd gone to the effort of looking good for what? A kiss on the cheek and then my life was empty. Then Paul got it in the neck. Paul always got it in the neck and he never deserved it, however that was me.

Lee always stood there and took it but I think that stemmed from his mum, Rose. He said he couldn't wait to leave home, left and then spent the rest of his life trying to win her favour, which was a strange one in itself. Emily asked a lot of questions about his mum, but that was M for you. She always asked a lot of questions!

I once part-told her the story of how we met and the fact that Lee could have had anyone but he chose me. A few girls from university had gone up to Libby's in Derby and we ended up going out for the night. We were in some bar and in he walked with Yusef – or Bondy rather, and straightaway he saw me. I was supposedly engaged at the time but he came over and asked what we were all drinking and told me that I looked beautiful. He bought us all drinks – and there were around seven or eight of us and that was it. He left me hanging there. Where was the rest of the chat up line? Why didn't he ask me out? It drove me crackers. I was supposedly beautiful yet he was more preoccupied in talking to Bondy. I couldn't have that so I marched over to him and tapped him on the shoulder. "So I'm beautiful and that's it?" I said.

He had a smile that lit up the place. "Your ring is nice," he winked.

I'll tell you something, that engagement ring was off my finger in next to no time and I made sure that I got his phone number. I don't like talking about sex as such but he was someone you just didn't say no to and when I finally tracked him down he was living in a big rented place in Muswell Hill in London and all it had in it was a bed, TV and sofa and there were what seemed like millions of DVDs piled up everywhere.

"We had a date, remember?" I said as I stood at his door.

"Did we?" he replied.

"Well, can I come in or what?" I asked.

He needed pre-empting all the bloody time, that was unless he wanted sex which happened not straightaway as such, but a damn sight sooner than I'd anticipated. "You're supposed to phone me and arrange a date, take me out and wine and dine me and then take me home and try it on," I said. His arse-around-face way of doing things involved me nagging him over the phone for a date then driving down from Birmingham University in my best clothes and on getting in his house being slung over the settee for ten minutes followed by ten minutes on the toilet and then as soon as I got back in the room he told me he had to shoot out somewhere and that he'd be back in a few minutes. Being a nosy cow I had a look around the place – and it was then I decided that he needed a woman in his life and that woman would definitely be me, so I gave it a bit of a spring clean, but rather than mess up my best clothes I did it in my underwear which I must say didn't go unnoticed – by Sooty that is who walked into the house without knocking and carrying a big DVD cutter.

"Are you the maid?" he asked.

"Hardly," I replied, before asking the question of, "And who the hell are you?"

Then Lee came in carrying another big DVD cutter. "I see you've made yourself at home," he smiled before introducing me to Sooty.... and then Bondy who walked in carrying box full of DVD's and by that time I was over the embarrassment of being half-undressed, however what happened next was nice. He took me into the West End we watched some show at The Apollo before he wined and dined me at some lovely restaurant. I'd say I fell in love with him then, but that would be a lie. I fell in love with him as soon as I saw him. I got him, but I didn't know how to keep him. I was never brilliant at sex so that was an angle that could have certainly been improved upon. He told me not to worry about it and I spent the next eleven years worrying about it. Being that they mass-produced DVD's there was always some porn knocking about his house and on getting back to my dorm I watched one. Well I didn't – I watched about a dozen and I couldn't believe what the women in them did and I had to call him on it. I did, and called him a dirty pervert.

"But you love me?" he asked.

"Yes," I said.

The next thing I knew I was dressed up like a dog's dinner, driving back down to Muswell Hill in the middle of the night and knocking him up.

"Wow, you look good," he had said.

I huffed and puffed and told him that I'd felt a right idiot, and even more so as I'd had to fill up the car at Newport Pagnell Services on the M1 as Libby had been using it to see her parents in Derby and that being the case she had used half my petrol. "They were loads of people looking at me," I said.

He had the smile of smiles, and even when he told me that I shouldn't have gone to all the trouble of dressing up for him and that I should have called first as he had a woman in, I still loved him.

"You what?" I snapped before marching up the wooden hill with the intention of dragging some bit of skirt out of the bedroom and gouging her eyes out.

"What's the matter love?" the woman said, on me entering the fray like some woman possessed. "Are you the maid?"

It was his bloody grandma – his dad's mum – and here was I dressed like some slapper out of one of his bloody porn flicks. I could have ate myself. He made me a coffee and we ate cheese and toast in front of the fire and talked all night. We managed sex a couple of times as well, one of which his grandma walked in on us, which if I was embarrassed before was nothing compared to how I felt at that precise moment.

"My nan won't mind," he said.

"Yeh but I bloody well do," I replied.

Little did I know I had just boarded a rollercoaster and me dropping out of university to go and live with him was another thing that totally upset my mother, but not as much as it did my ex-boyfriend who made it his life's mission to kill Lee. However, Bondy was at the house when he came calling. As I said, life is all about timing and Yusef wiped the floor with him.

ITV seven

Chapter 4

New York

The planned trip to New York had to be put back a bit as we needed a passport for Sammy, which created a lot of problems as for some reason there had been backlog upon backlog of passport applications, and even though the trip had been put back a few times, we ran out of time – so much so that it was looking like I would have to go out on my own, and that is when my ex-wife came to the rescue.

"If you're struggling, I wouldn't mind looking after Sammy," Jeanette had said, whilst holding him during a conversation with Emily after one of my daughter's music lessons. "He would be really well looked after."

"You don't have to tell me that," Emily had replied.

I didn't get to know about this until about eight o'clock that night as I had been to look at a huge warehouse off Bounds Green Road along with an architect mate of mine, who was a season ticket holder in Block 16 of the East Stand at The Emirates.

"A warehouse?" Emily said shrugging her shoulders as she passed me a prawn, crayfish and couscous salad.

"I might need somewhere to work," I told her. "And I could rent out space."

"What about New York?" she asked.

I told her I liked having options, which made her smile.

"I can't believe our life," she said. "It's great."

I knew it was, but it's always best never to get too

complacent – you have to evolve with the times and the timer on my clock had been ticking since the birth of Sammy – a total of five weeks had passed and it looked like I was going to New York on my own, which I certainly didn't fancy. That was until Emily told me what Jeanette had said.

"And she's okay with that?" I inquired.

"She's more than okay with that," Emily replied. "She was on the verge of ecstatic when I asked her if she was sure."

I rang Jeanette and what Emily had relayed was spot on, therefore I let NBC know that I would be over in New York for the Arsenal versus Manchester City game, whilst Emily did no more and booked us to fly out of Heathrow and into JFK – First Class on British Airways and at the expense of NBC... eventually! She then let her mum and dad know that they had to get the early morning train down from Lime Street, however something had happened that had put a damper on the trip for them – and although it was something that I had noticed previously, it was also something that I wasn't to get to know about until we were actually in New York.

Emily had dropped Sammy off at Jeanette's, which had been a wrench in itself, as he had been gurgling and coy-coying when she left.

"All you've done is complain about him whining – then you get a couple of days off and you can't leave him?"

"I miss him," she said.

"I frigging don't," I replied. "I'd hate to think how he'd be, stuck on a plane for nearly seven hours."

"He was dead cute when I left him," she said.

"Yeh – that's to make you feel guilty," I told her. "He'll be wailing like a banshee by now – she'll be a nervous wreck by the time we get back."

"He right likes her," she twanged.

"It must be us he hates then," I replied.

We picked Mike and Sil' up from the concourse at Euston Station, and although Sil' was as chatty as ever – Mike wasn't.

"Are you okay, dad?" Emily asked.

He said he was, but she knew he wasn't.

Now Emily had her Mean Machine we drove straight out to Heathrow and being as we were in First Class we were able to dump the vehicle more or less on site and drag our cases into the airport. The flight itself was a non-event as I was oblivious for about five hours of it only to be awoken by Emily sound asleep and drooling on my shoulder.

"You've both been flat-out," said Sil' smiling over.

"It's laddo," I said straightening myself up and summoning one of the stewardesses for a soda water. "He's been a right handful – We're both knackered."

"He's gorgeous," said Sil'.

"'You both okay?" I asked.

I didn't get an answer, but I got another smile.

On touchdown we were picked up by a limousine and taken to the Warldorf Astoria. I had done New York loads of times, however my new wife and parents had not, and the New York thing hit them straight away.

"I could definitely live here," said M.

"Me too," said Sil'.

Mike appeared in awe of everything around him and said very little. That was until we had checked into the hotel and been shown to our rooms – which I have to say were extremely good.

"What d'yer reckon, mam?" Emily twanged.

"I can't believe it, love," Sil' replied looking at the suite we had been put in.

I had a meeting pencilled in and had to leave more or less immediately and I told them that I would be about a couple of hours, which transpired into five. NBC played hardball and knew exactly what they wanted and I immediately had the feeling that no one would ever piss them about – and that included me.

"So, what do you reckon the score will be tomorrow?" asked the vice-president.

That was an easy question to answer.

"Manchester City will definitely score – probably from a breakaway," I said. "Pelligrini can read Wenger like a book and knows he'll push his team up too far and the quick Spanish lads and Sergio Aguero will have them panicking."

"Do you think Manchester City will win?" he asked.

"If I was a betting man," I said. "I'd bet on a score draw – one-all or two-all."

"And you would say this on national TV if you were asked the same question?" he asked.

"I'll always try and be honest," I replied.

That seemed to impress him.

I got dropped off at the hotel to find Mike sat in one of its bars.

"Hiya Mike, where are the girls?" I asked him.

He explained that their Emily was getting changed and Sil' was in their room talking to Edie and the kids on the phone. "They've just been to look at where the Twin Towers were," he added.

"Didn't you go?" I asked.

He shook his head. "I had a wander over to Central Park and had a beer in a bar."

It was then that he relayed to me the fact that he was working his notice. The firm he worked for had lost the contract at one of the quays, which meant he would be out of work in two weeks' time.

"Try to see it as one door opening, Mike," I told him. "And not the other way around."

He just gave me a look as if he didn't understand me.

"You're a talented guy with a trade who is definitely a bit of a workaholic," I added. "Anything you put your mind to, you can do."

"It's okay for you, lad," he said. "I don't have your gift of the gab."

"It's not a bullshit thing, Mike," I told him. "You know how good you are and what you're capable of – just look at the people around you who look up to you."

"Are you one of them?" he asked.

"Fucking too true," I replied. "I think you're a brilliant bloke."

I wasn't lying either.

"So what would you do if you were in my position?" he asked me.

"I can't tell you what to do," I said. "But if it was me – I'd set up on my own."

"You need money for that," he said.

"How much?" I asked.

He gave me a shrug of his shoulders to tell me that he didn't know and it was then I told him about the warehouse off Bounds Green Road that was basically a huge building that was being developed into several business units – that was, until the developer had gone under.

"It needs a hundred grand plus to finish it," I told him. "Half of that is labour costs – It's yours if you want it."

"What do you want a warehouse for?" he asked.

"I thought this conversation was about you?" I asked, whilst at the same time winking at him.

He gave me a smile back, but said very little.

"I need a place to work," I told him. "I've got an architect drawing up some plans as we speak."

"What about New York?" he asked.

"Mike – They'd have to make me one hell of an offer to leave you all."

I wasn't wrong.

The very next day – Sorry, very early next day due to the five hour time difference, NBC gave me the red carpet treatment and sat me in a studio prior to the Arsenal versus Manchester City game and I got interviewed by the host of the show – the anchor man – however this was no amiable Ron Burgundy character but someone who thought I was in for his job, and the barbed comments I initially got aimed at me were totally uncalled for, especially how he spoke my name.

"Hiya folks," he stated in his exaggerated manner. "Today as a special guest we have a Mister Lee Janes – who is some hot-shot sports producer from Eng-er-land."

Straightaway he was at me, and when I was in mid-flow continually interrupting me.

"Listen – If you want to be the star of the show – great – but don't keep interrupting me halfway through answering one of your idiotic questions," I told him. On air as well – It may have made great TV, but it totally and utterly pissed him off.

"So the score, Lee?"

I told him exactly what I told the vice-president the day before, and suggested that Manchester City would score first – more than likely from a breakaway.

"You mean a swift counter," he smirked.

"Yeh a counter attack," I said. "Arsenal will push up far too much and the quick breaking forwards of city will utilise the space on the flanks with both Jesus Navas and David Silva."

"Do you rate Manchester City?" he asked.

"They are the English champions," I replied. "That tells you of their pedigree."

"Yeh, but they are not as good as say Real Madrid or Bayern Munich, are they?"

"I don't think if Madrid or Munich played in the Premier league that they would be quite as convincing as they are in their own countries – And this game today will be a draw. Possibly two goals apiece."

My number had come in and for as much as I hated seeing Manchester City equalise in the dying minutes of the match to make it 2-2 – It certainly separated the men from the boys and the vice-president treat me like his long-lost son and introduced me to everyone and anyone. However, Fox Sports had also seen my performance and by the time I'd got back to the hotel I was the focus of some five-man entourage in suits who had been aimlessly conversing with my wife and her parents – about me.

I shook a few hands and we did the introductions and then for the next for two-and-a-half hours they sounded me out, part of which I had Mike sit in on, just in case I missed anything – certainly the job offer of $2.1 million per year wasn't one of those things.

"Jesus Christ," he said on coming out of the meeting shaking his head. "I've never seen anything like that before. That was one hell of a job offer."

It was, but I repeated what I had said earlier – in that they would have to offer me a hell of a lot of money to leave everything that I had in the UK.

"You don't seem fazed by all this," Mike told me.

I wasn't and when I told Emily it had her head in bit of a spin – and even though we got a cab into Little Italy and ate some overpriced tomato sauce and pasta type jollop on Mulberry Street and against a backdrop of Frankie Valli, Frank Sinatra, Matt Monroe and in one instance Rosemary Clooney, she was still in a mild state of shock. Not quite as much as her father when he saw the bill and the 15% service charge that got chucked on top of it, however.

On getting back to the hotel room I collapsed on the bed – It had been a great day.

"What are yer going to do?" Emily twanged as she climbed on to the bed and sat at the side of me with her legs crossed.

"We have everything at home," I said.

"It's a lot of money," she said.

"It is a lot of money," I agreed.

I got a cuddle and the next thing I knew it was morning and not only did I have Emily brushing her teeth whilst both laughing and talking to Jeanette on face time via her mobile phone, I had Sil' in the room ironing one of my shirts. I checked my watch which told me it was time to get up and looked around for my missing father-in-law.

"What's Mike doing?" I asked.

"He went out to the Twin Towers site," said Sil'.

That was good news as yesterday he was feeling more than a bit sorry for himself.

Emily threw me her mobile. "The children want to speak with you," she smiled.

"Yeh – what are you both up to?" I asked.

"Dad, when can I play football with our Sammy?" asked my lad.

"When he can walk, I suppose," I replied.

"When is that?"

"Probably three weeks on Thursday," I lied.

"How old was I when I could walk?" he asked.

"About ten or eleven months, I think."

"How old was I when I could talk?" he asked.

"When you were three because everyone talked for you and now you're making up for lost time and have never shut up since – You're a right motor mouth."

I could see him laughing at the other end of the phone.

I spoke to Jeanette who told me that the baby had been as "Good as gold."

"What, really?" I asked.

"Yeh, he's a really nice little lad," she replied.

I relayed that little snippet of information to Emily who told me that she had already been told.

"They took him up to Jeanette's mam's last night – he never cried once," Emily added. "I think you're right – he hates our guts."

Me and M spent a bit of quality time together and we told Sil' that we would meet her and Mike at the Staten Island Ferry at around two o'clock to go and see the Statue of Liberty, however the vice-president of NBC had other ideas and I along with Emily got invited for dinner in the Astoria where they threw me a potential carrot of a three-year deal of $1.5 million per year to chew over, however this one had a much better job title.

"Thank you so much for the offer," I told them, "However I would need to speak with my wife and family about it over the next couple of days."

That being the case, they offered to extend our stay in New York, however that wasn't going to happen, and although I thanked them for their offer I told them that I had things in the UK that needed my attention.

"You must be really important," Emily whispered to me.

"Not really," I replied. "I'm just in the right place at the right time – a bit like when I met you."

I could tell she liked that, by the way I got a squeeze and a cuddle.

"I could live here yer know," she twanged. "That's if you want."

I told her that I knew that, and I thanked her for it.

New York had been an experience, but London beckoned as there was nothing more important than my kids, and something was to happen that would change the course of all our lives – it was only small – but as I have said in the past, it is the small things that matter.

I had kept in regular contact with Sooty; however, things had been a bit strained, and they would become more so before I knew what the real problem was.

I'd tried haranguing him into kicking up a new company, but he said that we had been lucky in that we had got as far as we had and told me "no". I didn't really understand what he meant as we had always made money in everything that we had done, and if I'm honest I wasn't just taken aback, I was also a little hurt.

"He probably didn't mean it like that love," Emily had told me.

She was probably right – Sooty was always a nice kid and had always been the meticulous one, and where as I waited to see what came along, he jumped into the first job that was offered. Or that's what I thought. I was nearly right, but not quite.

The house that he and Libby had in Holland Park was as good as you could get, however as I've said previously, it had been handed down to Libby through some Will and Probate stuff which both related to her uncle and which I didn't fully understand. What I sort of did, was that this had been rigorously contested some twenty-one months later by a female member of her family who used some top London legal firm to act on her behalf. The upshot was that this member of her family had a case – either take it through the courts and possibly lose the house or pay her a one-off payment of x amount of cash – which in this instance was quite a bit. This was the reason they needed the sale of the company, however I still never got told that from either Sooty or Lib, which on one hand I partly understood as it was them who always bollocked me for my errant lifestyle, yet on the other I could not because I loved them – It was Jeanette who had told me.

Emily picked up Sammy from Jeanette's and once she got the little bundle of misery home we stood over the crib and looked at his not so angelic face.

"He doesn't look right happy," stated his mum.

She was right.

"Are you sure he's mine?" I asked.

"I'm not sure if he's even mine," she replied.

"Your mum and dad did say he's like you," I said.

"Yeh but my mam and dad don't really like me," she lied.

"That is a total lie," I said.

"I know – I'm dead sorry for having rubbish genes."

The thing was – she actually meant it.

We slung Horrible Herbert in bed with us and for once he slept all night. He made up for it the next morning by squealing like a pig until his milk was heated up, but at least we copped a good night's sleep. I'd have been wrong to think we had turned a corner though.

I sounded out Mike as regards the warehouse and I must admit, he sounded dead up for it and mentioned that he'd come down within the next couple of days. However, my life was like some gossip column and someone had let the cat out of the bag about what happened in New York, which I'll get on to in a bit.

James Durose-Rayner

Chapter 5

Jeanette's Tales – Take 3

When Lee and Emily were invited over to New York they had problems with getting Sammy a passport. As I was his 'Auntie Jeanette' I offered to have him, and I honestly couldn't believe it when they asked me if I was sure? Was I sure? I was very, very sure and I must have spent hours looking at him as he both slept and whilst he sat in his chair being entertained by his elder brother and sister – and for two days he was all ours.

My mother being my mother wasted no time in wanting to hold him and feed him, which Harmony duly noted was a bit hypocritical to say the least and said as much. "Why does Grandma Kate want to hold our Sammy when she doesn't like dad?" she asked me.

My mother hit her with a rather astute reply. "I held both you and your brother and you were both your dad's children."

That got her thinking. "Yeh but we were mum's kids – our Sammy is dad and M's."

She certainly didn't have an answer for that one. "So this New York job," my mother said. "Do you think he'll take it?"

"I don't think so," I replied.

"That's a shame," she said.

"Well just think if he did – you'd have nothing to talk about," I told her.

She was the same when we were courting. She hated the fact that I'd allegedly thrown everything away and moved in with him and even though she was fond of Lee she tried her damnedest to put the spoke in at every opportunity, not that it ever did, however.

"He wants to get a job," she'd say.

"He's got a job," I'd tell her, but because he wasn't clocking on at a factory or going to work in a suit it wasn't a proper job, however it didn't stop her from hanging on to his every word and action when he told her what he did do.

"So it's illegal?" she asked.

"Very," he told her. "But if I get caught I'll blame your Jeanette as it's her bank accounts where all the money goes."

"I believe you," she said.

What was going to happen shocked us all in that both he and Sooty wanted to make DVD's from scratch and toyed with a load of ideas – one weekend in particular springs to mind when Libby came down to see me. She couldn't believe the surroundings she was in as the money they were earning was unbelievable. I was sometimes banking over £15,000 a day and Lee told both me and Lib that once he had saved quarter of a million he would go legit.

"What and you'd pass up on making all this money?" Lib asked.

"I can't marry Jeanette and have kids while I'm doing stuff like this," he told her. "There has to be an end at some point."

Pride at that statement was the only thing I could describe. Here was my great-looking boyfriend earning all this money and letting me buy whatever I wanted and all he wanted to do was give it away in order to settle down with me.

However that end would come sooner rather than later as Yusef had invested a load of their money and quadrupled it overnight, and that is when he suggested doing it again but on a much grander scale.

Sooty was up for it to, however Lee didn't fancy ten years inside and I was there when he actually told him no. He was impressive. He was always impressive, but that was Lee for you. When he said something he always meant it.

Lib had clocked onto Sooty the second time she'd come down. I could say it was a whirlwind romance but that is not what it was at all. They just sort of grew on each other – and one thing led to another, however the fact that shared a few common interests must have helped such as politics, smoking and sex. Oh yeh – and her parent's family were loaded and Sooty loved money.

They were always on about setting up some film company, however I loved my life how it was and the thrill of seeing all the DVD's being made and of course the money and people coming and going was really exciting. Sooty's idea was to go in the porn industry; however, Lee's was not, and after having a go at a few different things, they eventually settled on a sports media company, though they were always arguing the toss as Lee never took on any of Sooty's ideas.

"I give him an idea, we discuss it and then we do his idea," he used to say. "It's like working with fucking Brian Clough."

Lee was brilliant and I used to watch him in awe as he'd put some movie together on some high-end and totally pirated Adobe software and in one instance I watched him rip a porn movie to shreds and reconstruct it with some other bits of film and then make hundreds of copies – and all within an hour.

"What are you doing?" was my obvious question.

It turned out that Sooty's mum and dad were having problems with a near neighbour and Sooty had been secretly filming the exterior of the said near neighbours house – the man washing his car – the wife going out to the dustbin – and the interior – filming them watching television and cooking in the kitchen etcetera. What Lee had just produced made it look like there was some orgy going on in their house on a daily basis. It took Lee around 54 minutes to make that family's life a living hell as all the DVD's got distributed around the village and watching them both laugh their heads off about it while we ate a Chinese takeaway was something else. Our life back then was so uncomplicated and so brilliant – I never ever wanted it to end.

M phoned me when they landed in New York and firstly asked how I was coping, secondly about the kids and then about Sammy. I told her to just enjoy herself, and I knew she would.

Me, Lee, Sooty and Lib had flown out to New York on the run up to one Christmas and got booked into a Howard Johnson's Hotel on the same street as the Empire State Building. It sounded a lot better than it was as it was a total bloody rat hole. Sooty and Lib hit the nearest bar while I nagged to see the real Father Christmas in Macey's where Lee bought me my engagement ring and which I still wear to this day. It's not like Emily's ring as hers is quite big, but it's certainly as nice. I phoned my mother to tell her we were engaged and she refused to speak to me even though she carried on having the conversation for another twenty minutes. I remember us walking up to see the Christmas Tree in the Rockefeller Centre and Lee arguing with a Manchester United fan and threatening to put his lights out – not that he did however – over the small fact that Arsenal had just been beaten 2-0 by them at Old Trafford.

I wondered if Lee thought of us in New York, as I was doing now?

We used to have a McDonald's breakfast which he loved and I didn't. Well, I pretend I don't now, but I bloody did back then. "Can I have your Sausage McMuffin if you don't want it?" he'd asked.

He nagged worse than me for that sausage and just to piss him off I ate it really slowly.

"You didn't really want it," he'd said.

I didn't – but he certainly wasn't having it.

We used to go to a Sbarro fast food restaurant across the road from Madison Square Garden where we saw Scrooge and where I would watch him as he talked about all these big plans he had while spilling his meat balls everywhere. "Jesus, I'm as bad as you at handling them," he winked.

"Shurrup and eat your food," I told him, and I spent the next half hour wondering if I was actually that bad!

I always thought about stuff like that, and even more so with him and M.

They seemed as happy as we were back then, and then I think were we really that happy and is there something that I am missing that just makes it look like that? Your head can drive you crazy at times!

Emily never really mentioned sex, which is a good job really, as that would most definitely piss me off. I see how she dresses and how she puts on her make-up and it drives me green with envy. She has one of those faces that looks as good without make-up as it does with it and the fact she still looks about twenty does I have to say, still do my head in especially when I know it is her that cuddles up to him at night and not me.

When we were living in Muswell Hill I had to be constantly applying my make-up, so much so I was sure my face was getting bigger. "Do you still think I look pretty?" was the most insecure question one could ask, but believe me I asked it – about a million times.

"Sat on my face – definitely, but sat on the bog – definitely not," he'd say.

I made a point of turning that house into a nice home, even though the million-plus DVD's were still part of it. M did the same with the house on Frederick Street, which is a bit of a sore point. Lee was earning a lot of money at the time and we needed some form of trusts setting up. My idea was to leave him with one hundred pounds in his pocket and hide the rest as I knew he'd struggle a bit more to cop off with some 'bit of skirt' if I did. He just went out and put nearly a quarter of a million pounds into a house, mortgaged the rest and chucked some tenants in it. I screamed and shouted like hell at him but he just looked at me with a blank expression whilst taking it, before hitting me with a one liner. "It'll be worth twice as much in a couple of years' time."

The house over the road was recently sold for just over £3 million and it's nothing compared theirs since M has been there. And I'm supposed to be the more prudent one?

I nagged him like hell after I'd seen a house on Church Hill in Southgate that I liked. The house in Muswell Hill was big, but it was also rented. He gave me exactly what I wanted. That is a line that should be framed. He always gave me what I wanted, and I'm sure M would tell you the same, but she appreciates it – as for me? I messed up.

"When are you going to marry me?" was another question I hit him with.

I pushed him into doing a lot of things that I shouldn't have. We had a truly brilliant life and I was continually testing him, and pushing him into doing this, that and the other.

I showed my mother and father the house on Church Hill, which when my dad saw the price he baulked at. "I can maybe give you about ten thousand pounds towards it, Jin," he said.

"I came to show it you dad," I told him, "Not ask for a hand-out,"

Lee just paid for the house with cash and I told my mother as much.

Moving to Southgate was a mistake – he worked off Euston Road and was never in, which was something else I nagged him for. That and the wedding, which turned out to be an event and a half.

Sooty had dragged their stag party around Soho, slipped Lee a Mickey Finn and put him on the overnight sleeper to Inverness which culminated into fits of laughter at the actual wedding as we were a groom light. He jumped off at Berwick-on-Tweed and hitched as far as Doncaster where he jumped on a train to King's Cross. He was an hour late and looked like he'd been dragged through a hedge backwards, but I married him all the same – I had to – as I wasn't letting anyone else have him.

We were supposed to fly out to Barbados for our honeymoon; however, we overslept and missed the flight and that being the case we jumped on the next available British Airways flight and went to Helsinki, where I have to say that neither my bikini nor his daft shorts ever had an airing. But as for fun – it was bloody brilliant, and we went everywhere and did everything. I had him and he was all mine, but I lost him and now he is all M's.

M however, did something that gave me a bit of him back.

"Mum, my dad's new girlfriend is ace," my son had told me.

This was also confirmed by my daughter. "She is mum – she's really nice."

At the time I just wanted to poison her and hide her body under Hampstead Heath, however after I had met her and talked to her a few times my feelings changed. I still wanted her secretly poisoned and living out the rest of eternity in a shallow grave, but that was more to do with the fact that she was like some stinking Barbie doll than anything else. However she immediately took an interest in both my children and always asked my permission before she did whatever she did with them, one of which was to teach my daughter and both Sooty and Lib's how to play both the violin and piano. Before M had arrived on the scene in the dramatic circumstances that she did, Harmony's idea of playing the violin was to batter her brother with it, but within three months she was playing it very well and much better than Sooty and Lib's two, which was the only thing that she could usurp them with. It's the same with Jamie – he came home one Sunday night and wanted to get a telescope just like the one at the "Royal Robs oblong lavatory or summat" so he could see Pluto.

"Robs oblong lavatory?" I'd asked him.

"Yeh – M drove us to near to where she used to live to see the planets," he had said.

"You mean The Royal Observatory." I corrected him.

"Yeh – if you like," he'd said.

She had generated his interest in a lot of things, be it planets, dinosaurs or the sharks in the London Aquarium. She also invited me into their home, which I firstly found very strange as the green monster reared its ugly head, and I found myself crying myself to sleep.

Lee with M was not too dissimilar to me and Lee when we were living together in Muswell Hill. Back then I was laid back – well, very laid back really – as I was having to service Lee at least twice a day as he was always coiled like a bloody spring. Not like now. Now I seem to get irritable with the smallest thing and I find myself fantasising about being Emily, not as much as twice a day, but at least once a week – and I always hate myself for it afterwards, not that it ever stops me.

After Lee's company got bought out he threw some money at some dilapidated warehouse close to the North Circular and M mentioned it one night when we were going to keep fit or 'Bums and Tums' as she called it. "I'm concerned that it's a lot of money and that Libby told me that he squanders it," she said.

"There's a lot of throwing stones and glass houses over there at the minute," I told her. "Lee might act stupid, but he's certainly not stupid."

It was then I told her a bit about the property that she was living in, mine in Clerkenwell and about the two insurances my ex-husband who was now her husband had set up for Harmony and Jamie.

"He set up one for Sammy as well," she said.

"Well there you go," I told her.

"It's for a really lot of money," she said.

"It sounds a similar one to the one he's got my two."

She smiled but that was as much as she said on the subject, therefore I kicked it back up.

"What's he on about doing with it?" I asked. "The warehouse?"

"He's mentioned studios," she replied. "But he can't make football or sports programmes for another three years."

That got us both thinking.

"It has to be Arsenal-related," I said.

It did. Almost everything he did was draped in red and white, including both me and M who were at the time sat in her Range Rover both wearing Arsenal garb and strangely we both noticed each other's attire at the same time.

"Weird," we said – and both at the same time.

Post-New York, M picked Sammy up from our house and we had a chat for a good half-hour and both my kids were extremely pleased to see her, especially as she came bearing gifts. Sammy had been a pleasure from start to finish and even Paul had enjoyed his company. "I thought he was supposed to cry all the time?" he had said.

"It's just Lee and M winding us up," I'd told him.

"No he does – all the time," said Harmony. "Granny Sil' says that he takes after M as she was right miserable when she was a baby?"

"Really?" I'd asked.

"See you can sleep easy now you know you've found a flaw," said Paul.

I pulled M up on this during our half-hour chat and it was confirmed. "Yeh, I've got rubbish genes," she smiled. "My gran says it's from my dad's side as according to my granddad all their side are perfect."

That made me smile.

"So how did it go in New York?" I asked.

"Too quick, but Lee was great on Telly," she replied.

"He was on TV?" I asked, semi-aghast.

"Yeh – they love him over there," she said.

That was a strange one, as although he liked producing stuff for TV he was never ever in anything he did. "I like my privacy too much," he would say.

"NBC and Fox Sports both offered him a lot of money," she said.

I was going to ask how much, but that was a question for another day. "So where is he now?" I asked.

"When I left him he was outside arguing with someone who's took his parking space," she said both shaking her head and smiling. "There's a new couple over the road and they've both got big four-by-fours and they keep pinching his spot – He's threatened to have a couple of skips dropped off outside their house if they don't stop doing it – not that I believe him, however."

"I bloody do," I told her.

Chapter 6

The Warehouse

The purchase of the Warehouse went like a dream and it kept me busy, and I did my best to involve my kids – I bought my lad a hard hat and a plastic tool set so he could run around the place whilst asking his Granddad Mike a load of questions; however, after her first visit, my daughter preferred to stay at home with Emily and either bath and dress up the ferrets, practice on the piano, do some baking or just play with Sammy who was still as miserable as sin but now strong enough to try and escape from his chair.

Mike loved it down here, as did Lucy who was down almost every weekend. Never had I ever seen a young girl as happy as she was – bright as a button with always a million questions to ask. And she loved both her niece and nephews.

I was a bit reluctant at first, but I'd sorted her a rail card for First Class travel between Lime Street and Euston and told her to respect the fact that we trusted her in getting from A to B – well, I hadn't as such – their Emily had. I just told her I'd hate it if anything happened to her and that she had to be careful. Therefore on a Friday evening she would get on the train at Lime Street armed to the teeth with teen magazines, iPod and such, and Emily or myself would meet her on the concourse. It worked well until one day she had to switch trains at Birmingham New Street and we both ended up having kittens. Saying that, we both underestimated her and she did make her way over to the other train unhindered.

"What's a matter with you both?" she twanged in her sweet Scouse accent. "I am thirteen."

Not only did Lucy manage to get from A to B unhindered she had also mastered the Tube – which was something that she loved. She used to sit studying the Tube map for hours and then go on maps.google.co.uk to check out what was around each station.

"Can we go down Oxford Street and Chinatown?" was one of her many requests. And she loved sushi, but more so the sushi bars with those long stainless steel conveyors that carried the dishes around the bar of the restaurant. For a teenage girl she had everything down here, and she made the most of it. I have never seen anyone grow up so fast and I have to say that she idolised her older sister.

Her brother, Stuart was the envy of his mates. Ten months ago he had been on a road to nowhere – a road to ruin if you believed his granddad, but I'd shown some interest and he'd been given his chance and had taken it. That's not to say he never needed the odd kick up the arse from either Mike, Bill or indeed Tigger over at BBC Radio Merseyside, who in between was always asking me what my plans were and did I have anything in the pipeline that could include him?

"He's a nice lad," he told me. "He's very interested in everything that's going on around him."

They all meant everything to me, not at least Sil' and Mike, who suddenly had a spark to re-ignite their lives, and that was purely down to the fact that Mike was now a man in demand – especially up on The Wirral.

He had brought a few good lads down to work on The Warehouse – they initially stayed in a B&B not far from the job and he made sure that they grafted like hell – in fact they never ever stopped, and when word got back around the north-western circuit that Mike was converting an old warehouse in north London into some TV studios, his profile went through the roof. Everybody either wanted him to do work for them, or wanted to work for him.

However, having a ready-made studios and offices were no good if you couldn't utilise them and this is where I needed to really start work, and that being the case, I took stock of the overall situation.

I wanted to do what I had done before – produce sports documentaries and such, and I'd been working on a few things, one of which was Arsenal's 1958/59 season, and the similarities it had with their 1972/73 season. In both seasons they had led the league and looked odds on favourites to get to Wembley, however mismanagement, bad transfers and injuries took their toll and they ended up losing form in the league and getting knocked out of the cup by second division opposition. What was also similar is that both these Arsenal teams strayed away from their normal approach and utilised a different style. The 1958/59 side had Ron Greenwood as its coach and assistant manager, and he changed tactics telling the *Daily Express*, "Arsenal were all about having a tight defence and playing the long ball out to fast-raiding wingers to catch the opposition on the hop."

Greenwood went on to criticise the formula as being hopelessly obsolete, stating the fact that blood and guts without finesse gets you nowhere, and he had encouraged his Arsenal players to produce a more flexible, mobile style of play – fast-moving one-touch football, not too dissimilar to what Bertie Mee and Steve Burtenshaw had trialled 14 years later.

They were lauded in both seasons for their innovation, but after suffering a couple of heavy defeats they ended up reverting to type. They also had influential players suffer injuries as well as disciplinary issues within the club.

The 1958/59 season saw Arsenal have serious injuries to possibly the best goalkeeper in the world outside Lev Yashin in Jack Kelsey, as well as predatory Scottish international forward David Herd, whilst the 1972/73 side had injuries to Bob Wilson, Frank McLintock and most notably, their new £200,000 signing that was Jeff Blockley, the latter who was systematically blamed internally for the league defeats against

Sheffield United, Coventry City and the cup defeat up at Hillsborough against Sunderland.

The 1958/59 side had both the stylish yet outspoken Scottish international Tommy Docherty and ex-Leyton Orient forward Len Julians in trouble with football's governing authorities, and during the 1972/73 season the clubs enigmatic albeit outspoken extrovert that was Charlie George was in the papers nearly every week, firstly being described as a pay rebel, then playing hell that he wasn't getting picked for the side.

What was more interesting was that both these teams went into free-fall straight afterwards, with different managers being needed to change the club's direction.

The legal side of the deal we had signed, however made making football documentaries a total no-go area, but something was to happen which I didn't expect and it happened one Saturday whilst I was over at The Emirates with young Stuart who I'd treat to see a football match versus Hull City – a team who I was beginning to have a soft spot for, as my two favourite ever Arsenal moment's happened against them – the day me and their M went up to the KFC with the kids to see Arsenal destroy them and then whilst we were in Marrakesh Arsenal had beaten them 3-2 to win the F.A Cup. On another note – Jon Sammels of Arsenal had hit the *lost goal* at the old Boothferry Park in Hull during a 3-0 rout of Austria, and it was my then-girlfriend who had managed to get me the footage. As I said, I had something of a soft spot for Hull.

This day however, was different in that after we had battered them in the first twenty minutes they somehow managed to get back into the game and whilst sitting in the club level seats over in the west stand, I had a tap on the shoulder and was asked to "button it" by some guy in a suit. I had to admit – I had been going on a bit; however I turned around to see ITV's head of sport.

The first thing I did was to lean over to him and offer to shake his hand and apologise for how my then-firm had let him down by selling out after getting a contract.

"I'm not making excuses — but I knew very little about it until after my wife had had the baby," I told him.

"I thought you had gone over to New York," he said.

That was strange, I thought. *How did he know that?*

"I met with NBC and Fox," I told him. "But I couldn't leave my family."

"They offered you a deal?" he asked.

I nodded. "Yeh — They were very nice people."

We met up at half-time where I got grilled a bit more before he asked my thoughts on the shower of shite performance my team was knocking out.

"I'd go for a draw — two-all," I said. "Probably with some last-ditch equaliser, I reckon."

My luck was in and although we played rubbish, I had again predicted the outcome.

"Why don't you come in and talk to us?" he asked me after the game.

I couldn't believe it and I duly thanked him for the offer.

ITV had been really pissed off with us selling the company and nobody knew this more than me, and when their head of sport phoned me to set up an informal lunch meeting, I thought it may well be just to give me another bollocking.

Emily listened to what I had to say, never opinionised and just gave me a kiss.

"Just be yourself," she said. "That should be more than enough."

We met at the Café Royal on Regent Street, which was anything but informal and on seeing ITV's head of sport sat with its development director and the director general and another suit, I knew it was serious.

The director general immediately issued his bollocking towards me and it was then I played on what I had learned from Libby. And Jeanette. And Emily. And that was just tell the truth.

"I didn't want to sell out," I told him. "Sooty and the other two partners did – I had no choice."

It was then that I handed them a brown envelope. "These are the actual minutes of the meeting," I said.

The truth that was the minutes of the meeting proved that I wasn't lying. Unfortunately it also told them that I couldn't create a similar company for three years.

"That was the bit I didn't like," I said. "That and fucking you over that is."

It was then that they sounded me out about NBC and Fox Sports – not so much the offers they made me, but more on what they wanted from someone like me.

I explained that they had invited me over as some guest pundit for the Arsenal versus Manchester City clash.

"How did it go?" asked the director general.

"Arsenal? They threw it away at the end like they always fucking do," I quipped.

"No – how did you do?" he asked.

"Sound," I replied. "Ninety percent of pundits know absolutely nothing about the game anyway – even those who have played it – It's even worse over in the States."

As soon as I said that they were hooked.

"Tell me the pundits you rate?" asked the head of sport.

"What, really?" I asked.

They all looked at me.

"Roy Keane is okay – I'd make him shave off that stupid beard though as it makes him look like a suicide bomber – Gary Neville is sound and talks a bit of sense – but if you want a bit of honest football punditry – get Joey Barton on a show. Him and Keane would be dynamite."

"What about Jamie Carragher?" asked the director general.

"I like Carragher – more the man than anything else – but he's got a really strong Liverpool accent, and that's bad for

TV – I cringe at hearing my voice, so Christ knows how he feels after watching himself."

There was quite a bit of laughter.

"So how much did Fox Sports offer you?" asked the director general.

"Two point one," I said, "but the tax on that over there is horrendous – and then there's having to find a place in New York – as I said – my family comes first."

"What about NBC?"

"A bit less," I told them. "But it was a three-year deal with a better job title."

They sat back and looked at each other.

They made no secret that they needed innovative ideas, but me not being able to make sports programmes restricted things. Well, I thought they did.

"So you could work for us directly, though?" asked the head of sport.

'Well I suppose I could," I said, "But I'll be honest with you, I'm just in the process of setting up some studios off Bounds Green Road."

"I wasn't aware there were any studios up there?" stated the director general.

"There aren't," I replied. "I'm converting a warehouse into around hundred-thousand square feet of studio and office space – It's looking okay – You want to come and see it."

The meeting lasted for near-on two hours and was, if I am being honest, quite nice – however, I knew ITV weren't NBC nor Fox.

I got back in to find Emily trying to succumb our whining lump of DNA with some of Cow & Gate.

"It was a damn sight quieter when he was up your jumper M," I said.

"He's not the happiest lad around, is he?" she replied.

"He's got Arsenal DNA in him, that's for sure – I can't believe that you were this miserable," I said as I tasted the food she was trying to ram in his chops, before spitting it straight back out. "Good god M, that's rank – no wonder he's pissed off."

"The only time he's happy is either when he's with Jeanette or he's eating those chocolate puddings."

"He's just scared of getting a bollocking off Jeanette," I said. "Just give him a pudding."

"I can't keep giving him puddings – he'll end up weighing a ton," she said.

"I'd prefer him looking like Augustus Gloop than screaming all the time."

We ended up doing a bit of a wine and food tasting thing with him, which was interesting in that he spat everything out that was good for him – and then let us know exactly how shit it tasted by screaming; and wolfed everything down that was bad for him – and let us know just how great it tasted by screaming. There was a common denominator in there somewhere which concluded that we had indeed brought another Michael Owen into the world.

In the end I phoned up Jeanette to see if she fancied fetching the kids over and as soon as they got over here I slung her the screaming machine, who immediately shut his trap and started coy-coying and goo-gooing.

"He's such a lovely little lad," she said.

"Really?" I replied. "I'll take your word for it."

I then got a phone call I wasn't expecting – it was ITV's director general, therefore I took it in the other room and listened to what he had to say. He did hand me out another bollocking, although the crowd that had taken us over weren't doing that bad a job, it was just that in the back of his mind, we had used his company to generate the sale of our company.

I got back into the kitchen and after the nineteenth time of him asking, I told my lad that he could bring the ferrets into the room but under no circumstances should he take them anywhere else – therefore the first thing he did was take them up to the bathroom!

"Dad this shampoo won't come out!" he shouted down some ten minutes later.

It wouldn't – It was baby oil, which M had been using by the bucketful all through her pregnancy to counteract the potential problem of stretch marks – which, rather strangely had worked.

"What have you used that stuff for – the ferrets are as slippery as heck now."

That made him giggle, and even more so when I tried juggling around with them and dropped them both head-first into the bath.

I managed to get them downstairs without dropping them, and did quite rightly state that although they were a bit greasy, we could put a nice centre parting through their hair – something which both Giroud and Arteta truly enjoyed. They looked like a pair of crooners from the 'Manhattan Transfer' jazz-swing combo who sang Chanson D'Amour – rat ta tat ta ta.

After Jeanette had left, Emily noticed that I had something on my mind.

"Are you okay, love?" she asked.

I was. I'd had an offer I couldn't refuse. ITV had numerically matched the American's offer, however I failed to let them know that it was dollars that the Americans had offered me and not pounds.

"Two point one million a year," I told her. "But as a big favour I have to give them three normal programmes throughout the week and probably work most weekends."

After she'd nearly dropped through the floor she told me that she was dead-glad she'd married me and that it certainly wasn't the money that was keeping us together.

We sat on the settee and were immediately joined by my two kids.

"We should do something nice to celebrate," said Emily.

And we did – we ended up driving through Camden Town and up to a Frankie & Benny's on Finchley Road where it took ages to get served. There was a plus point, however – the company was great, and even Sammy appreciated a bit of 'Music to watch the girls go by' – so much so he did a bit of goo-gooing and coy coying, before having a massive shit, which had his brother and sister and the family sat next to us nearly heaving, as it stunk.

"He saves it up for when we take him out in public," I told the couple next to us. "He likes showing us up."

I took him to the baby changing room along with a fresh nappy and a shovel and vowed to leave him at home and lock him in a cupboard the next time we went out.

"Did I used to poo that much?" my lad asked.

"Not even Sooty's sister does that much – and she weighs three ton," I told him.

After our meal I called in at Clerkenwell and dropped off the kids, only to find that Jeanette's parents were there.

"Oh hello, Kate ...... Michael," I said, sort of acknowledging them.

"You're looking well," said her mother.

"Yeh – you too," I said. "I hope you're both well?"

She nodded, but that was as far as the conversation went.

"Have they been okay?" asked Jeanette with regards to the kids.

"They're always okay," I replied, whilst rubbing my lad's head.

"Is M outside?" she asked. "She's not met my parents, yet."

Mmm – that was a tricky one, I thought.

"Does she want to come in?" she asked looking through the door and waving over at her.

However before I could sort of nip it in the bud, Emily was climbing out of the Mean Machine along with the shitting machine. This was something that I definitely wasn't looking forward to.

"Mum, this is Emily or M – Lee's wife," said Jeanette smiling. "And you've met little Sammy."

Her mum – Kate was never my biggest fan, nor was her husband if I am being honest, however it wasn't as bad as I thought, and they were really nice with Emily, and even more so with the baby – who not once whined, grizzled or frigging groaned – even when Kate picked him up and gave him a cuddle.

"Aw, isn't he lovely?" she said.

Wow. I was impressed. If I'd have done that he would have screamed the place down.

"How's he been sleeping, Emily?" asked her mother.

"He sleeps okay – Dead miserable through the day though, but that's only when he's with us," she smiled. "He loves your Jeanette – His eyes light up when he sees her."

"He's so cute," said Kate showing him my ex-father-in-law, who showed about as much emotion as he ever showed me.

We stayed there around half an hour, which had me on tenterhooks more or less the whole time, but in all honesty it wasn't all that bad. It wasn't that good either, but certainly not bad all the same.

"You were great in there," I said to Emily as she climbed behind the wheel of her car.

"They seem really nice people," she smiled.

"I'll take your word for it," I replied.

We got in the house and I rang Emily's dad who was still over at The Warehouse with a few of his lads I and let him know that I'd be having some dignitaries coming over from ITV at lunchtime to survey his work.

"ITV?" he asked. "I thought they'd given you the cold shoulder, lad?"

"They topped both NBC and Fox Sports' offer," I told him. "They want a guided tour, some ideas putting forward, and if what I give them is acceptable, for me to go in with my lawyers to sign a contract that I can't wriggle my way out of."

I was going to get Eddie on the blower next until I found out that he was on site with Mike and had been tasked with mixing plaster.

"He's down here with me," said Mike. "Do you want him?"

It turned out that as they were trying to push for a quick completion, Eddie had offered a hand, which I thought was a really nice gesture.

I stayed up until late and managed to print out some rangy ideas and cobbled them together to look semi-professional – well, sort of, and next morning I shot over to the work site where I met Mike and Eddie, the latter of who was up a ladder.

ITV's director general and development director arrived at The Warehouse around lunchtime just as I was on the phone to some high-end digital camera supply firm, trying to get them to throw me a deal for a load of gear.

I shook hands and exchanged a few pleasantries as I showed them around what to them must have looked like a bomb site; however, the director general was more than intrigued.

"So all you've ever done is produce sports documentaries and the terms of your company's buy-out prohibits you from doing it for three years, yet here you are investing what I assume is your own money to convert a huge warehouse into studios and offices?" said the director general.

I nodded.

"Why didn't you just go and get a job like your partner did?"

"That's not me," I replied.

"To do something this size and with your own money means that you must have a lot of faith in your own ability," he said.

"Me and Sooty worked well together, but we wanted different things. Producing any TV programme is relatively straightforward, be it sports of general programming – It's the content and how you deliver it that is key."

He listened as I spoke, whilst at the same time showing them around. It was then he mentioned what I had first put forward to the head of sport while we were on with our 'Sammy project'.

"What — The results service?" I asked shrugging my shoulders.

He nodded. "Would it work?"

"If you set it up right, what you could achieve is endless," I said.

I had said this before. It was a case of cutting new blood and possibly creating the talent of the future.

"And you would never go with ex-pros?" he said.

"Never," I replied. "I know hundreds of people better-equipped to talk about football than any ex-footballer."

I told him that I had jotted some ideas down at short notice, but I hadn't been aware sports programming would be a part of the deal. It was, however. They wanted me to run a weekend football channel as part of the deal they were going to offer me. However, it was here that what they asked got slightly misconstrued — by me that is, as I was under the illusion that the 'deal' was a job lot-lump sum type thing.

"Could you do it?" he asked.

"Of course I could," I replied. "Just as long as I have some form of time scale to work to."

There was a hitch however — he demanded that we shoot the weekend channel from ITV's studios and not ours — and use their infrastructure, manpower and equipment — and up in Manchester.

"Is that a problem?" he asked.

"Not really," I replied, although I knew straightaway it was.

He never took my draft that I had taken six hours to put together, nor did he ask about what I had in mind for the programmes — however, that would come later when I was dragged over hot coals to promise to deliver what would be more work than I had ever handled in my life.

I looked over at Mike, who I knew had been half-watching me talk to the suits.

"Change of plan," I said.

Chapter 7

Hamilton Square

Amidst 'Herbert the Great' or 'not so great', continually grizzling and kids coming in and out of the house for music lessons, sometimes in two's or three's, I managed to draft together ideas for the weekend football channel. Without sounding conceited, I knew that the money ITV would be investing in me would be reaped back in full as the work I would be doing was more than I had ever taken on in my life. That aside – any football documentaries I made – would be theirs – including marketing, copyrights, future sales, etc. The lock stock and two smoking barrels. ITV were nobody's fool. On that score, and if they played it right they could get their money back within months, whilst through the week my company LMJ would make programmes to fill the football channel as well as knocking out the three normal programmes they wanted – using our soon-to-be completed studios with its own infrastructure. The deal I was soon to sign for looked very good, but ITV knew what both Fox Sports and NBC knew – me signing with them meant that they would own all my ideas including the two I had been working on – The Parallel's: The Throwing away of the Doubles and The 1964 Football Betting Scandal, both of which, if they were put together professionally could easily earn them half a million net profit with DVD sales. I was that excited about that part of the deal that I hoped they would forget about me having to do the normal programmes. That, however, was never going to happen.

However, I'm jumping the gun a bit here and first things first was that I needed a general manager and that is when I called Sooty to ask if he fancied it. Amidst a few pleasantries, asking about Libby and his two brats and some gossip about things down at Nubeon Entertainment, he gave me a resounding no, and that was when I did no more and poached Abi Tyson from the firm that had bought us out.

"Would you like to manage a weekend sports channel for ITV?" was my first question. Well, it wasn't really, it was how was she getting on with the new firm and were Ginge and Fred still causing bother?

"They sacked Ginge and Freddy will always be Freddy," she said.

"They sacked Ginge?" I asked.

"Yeh, he's working with his brother-in-law doing some houses up over in Brentford."

Ginge was always an accident waiting to happen and if he was given enough rope he always had the tendency to be one of those who could hang himself. Young people need both a mentor and nurturing, especially people such as Ginge. When I left, he was obviously left to his own devices and pissed someone or someones off.

I therefore sounded Abi out and she was definitely up for it but as with all staff – she gave me the hundred-thousand dollar question.

"You can be either on the books with my production company – LMJ full-time, which means that you'll also be my slave for some other stuff I'm doing through the week or you can go self-employed via ITV," I told her.

"Sweet," she said. And she immediately handed in her notice and I gave her the title of Assistant Producer, which she loved.

I then made a point of phoning Jeanette to get Stevie Kell's number. Whilst I was with Jeanette I had been close to both him and his wife, however his missus had decided that as I had been the twat in all this, I was deemed not good enough for a friendship to continue so she took sides and chucked her lot in with Jeanette. I wonder how that was going? I also made a point of calling Les Crang and Oliver Norgrove – two Arsenal nuts, who were academically ahead of anything that sat in front of a camera on Sky Sports Saturday – both of who had letters after their names and had quite good day-jobs if I'm honest. Les worked at the University of London as some content advisor or something whilst Ollie was a freelance journalist currently employed by some London-based rag.

"We are good to go," I told Les. "A brand new ITV channel for the football junkie."

He didn't seem that impressed. I then rang Oliver and told him more or less the same, and I got more or less the same response. What was it with everyone? This was big. I then checked my watch to see that it was 2:10am in the morning and then I understood why. I had been sat at the breakfast bar in the kitchen since around 4:00pm drafting up ideas. My head was a shed.

I went to bed but I couldn't sleep. Firstly because my mind was racing but later on as Sammy was in the middle of us and booting the covers up in the air.

"Oi – stop it," I told him.

By the expression on his face I assumed that he had told me to bollocks.

I then told him that I'd sling him in with the ferrets if he didn't alter his expression. He didn't – he still looked at me as though he was going to rip off my head and use my neck as a vase.

"What's your problem?" I asked him. "You've got a great life, but you treat everybody like shite."

He said very little and still looked at me with some disdain.

"I suppose it'll be better when you can talk," I told him. "I think?"

Then Emily turned around and smiled over at me. "Who are you talking to?"

63

"Herbert," I said. "He keeps booting the covers up in the air."

"Well at least he's not crying," she smiled. "That's a plus."

"Yeh – I suppose so," I replied.

Then the strangest thing happened – he burst out laughing and just wouldn't stop and then recommenced booting up the covers in the air. I have no idea why, it was if some curse had been lifted.

"Wow – what was all that about?" asked Emily.

I hadn't a clue – but at least after a few months of misery, it was some improvement.

The next thing I knew it was morning and I had Les Crang banging on the front door. I think what I'd told him a few hours earlier had sunken in and Emily had to open the door before he kicked it off its hinges.

"All I know is that it's a new TV station which runs from early Saturday morning to midnight Sunday," I told him. "And I've got to fill it."

"It sounds awesome," he said, as Emily passed him a coffee.

"The downside is that it's going to get broadcast from ITV's Manchester studios – They won't let us do it from London."

He spent nearly an hour at the house before I had to forcibly evict him.

"It sounds an awful lot of work for you," Emily said afterwards.

"Over two million a year gives us freedom to do whatever we want," I told her. "Just think of the amount of shoes you could buy."

"I thought of that as soon as you mentioned it," she laughed.

"I bet you did," I replied.

"I love being married to you," she added.

"I know you do."

I did, as she told me numerous times throughout the day, every day.

I shot over to the work site where my architect mate from Block 16 gave me the thumbs up to the work that had been slightly altered.

"Are you sure this is what you want?" he asked.

Well, I thought so, I thought.

I'd had a re-think of The Warehouse and I decided to leave it open plan downstairs as opposed to cutting it up for individual studios – as we could use temporary works studios if need be – there was a method in my madness, and that would soon come to light when I got back home to see Emily standing at the door of our house holding our kid in her arms and talking to one of the neighbours. It was hardly one of those Kodak moments as she made Sammy wave to his dad and, that being the case, his face resembled a badger's arse as he watched me climbing out of the car.

"Say hello to your dad," she told him.

There was more chance of him telling me to 'Go drop dead' looking at the expression on his chops.

"Come inside," I said. "I've got something to ask you."

Exactly three minutes later, screams of elation rebounded off the walls of the house – Put it this way, she was dead happy.

"That's an absolutely brilliant idea," she told me.

"Yeh, I thought it might be," I winked.

"I won't have to stop my music classes, though would I?"

"I wouldn't have thought so – just don't take on any extra students until I know where I am on all this."

'The ITV sessions', 'Inside True Britain' and 'Thursday Night Live at the Warehouse' were what I had proposed to ITV in regards to the three programmes which were to be produced on the budget they had given me to work to – and which I had assumed was zero, and I laid the bare bones of them out on the table in front of me.

ITV had hated Inside True Britain but quite liked the other two. I think they wanted entertainment value rather than a factual programme.

"Stick with me on it – You haven't seen the content yet," I had told them. "I'll make it compelling viewing."

I never went into great detail but they trusted me. I have said it a few times before – I must have had one of those faces.

Emily hosting the Thursday Night Live at the Warehouse and The ITV Sessions shows was what all the bouncing off the walls was about.

"Do yer think I could do it okay?" she twanged rather excitedly.

"Of course I do," I replied.

"Really?" she smiled. "Do you think I could?"

"Definitely," I winked.

I got a really big love for that, so much so – even Horrible Herbert had to cover his eyes.

She then asked – albeit very excitedly, what I had in mind – which literally blew her mind, however something else hit home.

"You mentioned earlier that you'll be based up in Manchester on a weekend," she said looking concerned. "That means I'll see even less of you."

"Do you know I love you?" I asked.

"Yeh – I know yer do," she replied giving me one of her Scouse twangs, which was followed by one of her Colgate smiles.

"And you know why I never went to New York?"

She nodded. "Yeh – because you didn't want to split the family up."

"Always remember that," I said. "Always."

I got another love.

"I love you so much," she said.

"I know you do and I love you too."

Now this is where I was to earn the biggest brownie points ever – and you have to take into consideration everything that I had been offered and more to the point what I had turned down, that had preceded this moment, and as such I made Emily sit down as I picked Sammy up out of his chair, sat him on my knee and rammed the dummy in his chops. I then told her that ITV 7 would be the new station which I would be running.

"And you're right," I added. "It will mean me staying up in the northwest on a weekend."

"We can stay at my mam's," she interceded, looking slightly concerned. "All of us – There's no need for us not to be together."

"Yeh, I know," I replied. "But I have the kids and there's no way we can put on your mum each weekend."

She looked at me – still concerned, but still beautiful. "But my mam won't mind," she reiterated.

"Do you know Hamilton Square?" I asked.

"What, in Birkenhead?" she asked.

I nodded.

"I've just got my lawyers and accountant to put an offer in for a house up there."

"What – We are moving from London?" she asked.

"Don't be daft," I said smiling. "I'm hoping it could be our weekend house. That's if you're okay with it."

"So we'll have two houses?" she asked.

I nodded.

"Wow," was all she could say.

"It's a really big property M – You'll love it," I told her before passing her a brochure out of my briefcase that I'd had printed off.

It was a really big property – much bigger than ours – a Grade 1 listed building that had been used as offices.

She looked at it and then broke down in tears, so much so Herbert spit out his pipe and set off grizzling.

"Don't you start," I told him. "I'll probably have your Gran to contend with in ten minutes."

She gave me a great hug before looking up at me and wiping her eyes.

"You've done all this for us?" she said. "I can't believe it."

"Well, believe it," I said.

She looked at the printouts again and again and then around the house that she had help turn into a home and back up at me.

"Can you remember when you said that we would be okay when I was first pregnant?" she asked me.

I nodded. "Yeh – sort of."

"I didn't really believe you and I certainly never ever envisaged any of this, yer know," she said, both smiling and shaking her head.

"Yeh – but remember this, M – When have you never not been there for me or not backed me up? When have you ever bitched at me, opinionised about my life or shown that you've been pissed off with me? And when have you ever not been nice with my kids?" I said. "Emily – you're just a great wife."

I totally surprised myself saying that, but it was true.

"I'm just so happy," she said.

"It's just a pity Herbert here doesn't feel the same," I said.

She laughed before asking if it would be okay to tell her mum about it all.

"Aren't you wanting to have a look around it before you start telling everyone?" I asked.

All I got was a beaming smile in response, which was swiftly followed by her telling her mum and gran, which then had Mike ringing me up from some temporary digs off Palace Road that he and his lads were staying in around twenty minutes later – and whilst I was still talking to an elated Sil' on Emily's phone.

"All I know, Mike is that it needs the basement ripping out and a big kitchen putting in, some electrics, plastering, bathrooms and a couple of boilers installing," I told him. "I'll get the architect on it."

And then came another one hundred thousand dollar question.

"Yeh – Mike, it goes without saying that you can have the work," I said smiling to myself, and the next thing I knew him and Sil' were talking to each other through mine and their Emily's phones.

I looked over at my wife – Asking her to marry me aside, this was the happiest I had ever seen her.

Chapter 8

The Jeanette Show

ITV had been advertising its planned new station ITV 7 as soon as I had been in to sign off on the contract with my new lawyers. A 100% football channel running from 6:00am on a Saturday morning through to 11:59pm Sunday night.

They had also been advertising the proposed Thursday Night Live at the Warehouse programme, but strangely not the Inside True Britain nor The ITV Sessions, both of which I had already started doing my groundwork on. Now here was a story.

Eddie had been currently wired to Mike's hip helping my father-in-law and his mates undertake the completion of The Warehouse. They got on really well together, and it was planned that once the sale of the house at Hamilton Square had gone through then he would be up on site helping Mike.

I, on the other hand, needed Eddie for this Inside True Britain programme. I knew what I was doing. I had loads of ideas but I needed a voice to do the narration. I also needed someone with journalistic qualities to write up the guts of each programme, and more to the point – I was very concerned about economics – my economics, however ITV nipped that in the bud straight away.

"He's too old," I got told by ITV's development director.

"How do you mean he's too fucking old?"

"You need a young face to put your stories over," he told me. "If you're struggling we have several faces we can put you in touch with."

"Listen – he's an accredited journalist – This isn't some Jackanory programme I'm on about putting out," I told him.

It was no good, however – It was what it was. ITV called the shots, but the last thing I wanted was one of their tap dancing wannabes.

I mentioned it to Eddie, who completely understood and as always, I mentioned this setback when I got home.

"If I start using TV people it's going to cost us a fortune," I said.

"Ask Jeanette to do it," Emily told me.

"Jeanette works in Sainsbury's," I said. "She's never done anything like this before."

"Nor have I," she replied.

"Yeh – but you've spoke in public and had to give presentations," I replied. "You are confident."

"And so is Jeanette," she said. "Go ask her."

I pondered whilst I ate some concoction of grilled chicken and greens – Spinach, rocket and watercress – I think.

"Anyway, when is your gran coming down?" I asked. "At least you bake when she's here."

"Go ask Jeanette," she said giving me a nudge, a smile and a kiss – and all in that order.

"And you wouldn't mind?" I asked.

"No, would I heck," she twanged.

After my tea I rang my ex-wife and asked if I could see her.

"It's important," I said, which was followed by her regular twenty questions – Were me and M okay? Is Sammy okay? Have I done anything wrong? You know – that kind of thing.

I drove over to Clerkenwell where my lad was dead-pleased to see me. Well, he was until he found out I'd not brought him anything.

"Where's your sister?" I asked.

"Rehearsing or summat," he said.

"Rehearsing or something," I corrected him.

71

He was starting to sound like Sooty.

"I've come to talk to your mum," I told him – "But you can come back to the house with me if you want. Some DVD's arrived today – Those Laurel and Hardy ones you like."

That cheered him up. Well a bit, anyway.

"Can we call in at the KFC or McDonalds?" he asked.

"You're not supposed to say that in front of your mum," I told him.

He wasn't. Jeanette always bollocked me for taking him there, and I immediately saw a change of expression on her chops when he'd mentioned it. That was soon to change, however.

"I need a bit of help," I said, looking over at her.

Jeanette was always very matter of fact and sat across from me with her legs crossed – possibly expecting the worst.

"I need a nice face and I would like you to present one of the programmes I'll be putting out," I said.

Jeanette was rarely emotional when it came to me, however I copped a smile like no other after that.

"Really?" she asked.

"I've not made my mind up on a title – as ITV hate it – but it's sort of an Inside Britain kind of thing," I said. "It'll be right up your street."

She was still smiling.

"And I want you and Emily to take it in turns to introduce an idea I have to promote young bands – The ITV sessions."

She was ecstatic.

"Why me?" she asked.

"Because I love you and you deserve it."

A great smile came beaming over at me.

"And I need someone I can trust."

She was still smiling.

"And I know you'll work for nothing," I winked.

"Bollocks, Lee," she said.

That was more like 'my Jeanette'.

£2500 per show was what I'd factored in and I told her so.

"Two thousand five-hundred pounds?" she said, smiling. "I can't believe it."

"Yeh – so will you do it?"

"Of course I'll do it, you bloody idiot," she said.

And then I copped a hug off her.

Mmm, this felt strange, I thought, especially as it lasted quite a while.

"You'll need to talk it over with Paul," I said.

"Why?"

"Because he might not like it," I explained.

"Why?"

"Well, because he might not," I said.

I got another "Why?" but I refused to be drawn into placating her with another answer otherwise I would have probably been there all night, therefore I didn't.

On driving back over to King's Cross a thought occurred to me, and I recalled what Jeanette had first said after I'd told her that I'd turned down the offers from NBC and Fox.

When I turned them down she had broken down crying, which initially made me think that she had wanted me to go. However, all I had done is shown her just how much I loved both her and the kids.

"I'm so glad you're not going," she said. "You've definitely done the right thing."

It had been a massive decision and Emily's dad had also thanked me for doing it, which put a right lump in my throat as he rarely showed his emotions.

"Thanks for doing that, son – I know it must have been hard," he had told me.

That coming from him was worth ten times what NBC or Fox could have ever offered me.

This is why you look after the things you have got. I didn't know it back then but I do now and I felt a real happiness knowing that I'd just given Jeanette something to aim for. On another note she did ask me if it would affect her maintenance.

Emily was always pleased to see the kids, and my lad clung on to her every word, especially when it came to music – however, here is the thing. He had the concentration span of a frigging gnat when it came to most things and Emily had offered to teach him piano – but because he couldn't knock out Mozart's twenty-third piano concerto in 'A major' after half an hour of bashing at the ivories he decided to knock being a musician in the head.

"What's up?" I had asked him.
"It's dead boring," he had told me after kicking up his X box and shooting a few monsters on screen.

"Your sister plays," I had told him.
"Yeh – but she drives me around the twist with it."
He did have a point. She drove me around the twist with it too.

However, Emily listened to all types of music and could recite just about any song from any era. However something strange happened. My lad had heard her singing along to a song one day while she was cooking – on Radio 2 I think – and a few days later he started whistling – and trying to sing a chorus, with 'trying' being the optimum adjective.

"Der da, der der der da der da – Honey, der, der der der da........" he sang.

"What are you singing?" I had asked him.
"A song on the radio that M was singing to."
This took both me and Emily aback somewhat and as she sat on the sofa she called him over. "Which one was it, love?"

He shrugged his shoulders.
"Sing it to me again," she had asked. "It sounds really lovely."

And he did.
"I think that's 'Sugar Sugar' that you're singing," she said.
He shrugged his shoulders again.
"Do you like it?" she had asked him.

"Yeh," he replied.

Emily did no more than put him on a stool at the breakfast bar and get it up on YouTube and not only did he totally recognise the song – the YouTube footage was a cartoon – He was hooked and wouldn't shut up. She even showed him how to do the dance, which was all a bit gay if you asked me, but I had to hand it to her she had got him off the X box and straight into music.

The amount of DVD's and CD's she cut him after that was unbelievable, so much so that he started carrying them around in his little Adidas satchel and never went anywhere without them.

This was all very nice until Emily mentioned 'The Monkees', and that blew his mind.

"They were a pop group who used to have a TV programme when your Granny Sil' and Granddad Mike were younger," she explained. "They were really funny."

"The Monkees – Were they real monkeys?" he had asked.

"No, they were four young lads – one of them was from Manchester – near where Granddad Mike and Granny Sil' live and where your dad will be working."

And then she got them up on screen. And suddenly he became their No. 1 fan – Emily had to tell him anything and everything about them, and for a few weeks every conversation became Monkee-related.

I didn't mind the first three-thousand times, but after that it got a bit repetitive – and even Jeanette had said that he'd become a little obsessed.

He may have, but it brought him and Emily very close and once the finishing touches had been done down at the Warehouse, he was down there with me, M and misery guts and forever jumping on one of the stages and pretending to be one of his idols.

The ITV Sessions was a play on a BBC Radio programme from the 1980's where bands recorded live in a studio; however, what I had was an angle. My idea was to use this programme to not only project the stars of the future – but to help part-man up the Thursday Night Live at The Warehouse programme which Emily was going to host. I'd immediately put several adverts in the music press and the indie bar where me and Emily frequented stating that I needed bands – No rappers, boy bands or girl bands – If you're not musicians then piss off. I wanted to put it but I didn't – I sort of put it. Please send me a CD with photograph and a detailed summary not exceeding 1000 words, with the carrot being the fact that I would give each act that were successful studio time to cut their best six tracks and get them on video – and if they appeared on the 16-week ITV Sessions run, LMJ would pay them a fee of £1,000. If they made it to Live at The Warehouse, we would pay them £2,000, which was one hell of a carrot because what I had in mind for that programme was fairly impressive. The ITV Sessions programme would be for the music nut and not the cheap and fast-track route to celebrity-stardom. As stated, I needed this to part-man up the Thursday Night Live programme, but I also needed the latter to drag in the former. The Thursday night programme, however had one hell of an angle as a lot of the audience would be celebrities and their partners – this was to be a beautiful place for beautiful people, which when ITV found out where I was coming from they again tried to block me.

"This will be no cheap ticket for ratings," I told them. "It will be unique."

"It sounds a bit like a take on TGI Friday," said one of the suits.

"It will be nothing like it," I replied. "There's no ginger-haired, four-eyed fucking motor-mouth – nor will there be any stand-out performers as everyone who will be seen there will be the star."

"I don't get it," said the suit. "Who will you get and more to the point, how will you get them?"

That however, was my problem.

We started receiving applications for The ITV Sessions programme almost immediately, and after Abi had worked her notice she was put in total charge of The Warehouse, and immediately poached Faranha who was very pleased to be with me again. I still missed Sooty being around, however I had started seeing a little bit more of him again, more so after we had christened Sammy and which by the time we had been recording bands I was seeing him every day. It was a brilliant feeling as we had known each other since being kids; however, the christening had put things into perspective a little bit.

Neither me nor Emily were of a religious background, although I made no secret that I loved Christmas, and Christmas Carols especially – maybe they subconsciously reminded me of my dad – I don't know? Bill and Edie were however, and Edie had asked if we would have him christened.

We had no problem with it so we did, and Jeanette and Paul were put forward as godparents, which Jeanette was particularly taken aback at – in a nice way that is. However both Sooty and Libby were not.

"Come on Libby," Jeanette had said. "Since they've had Sammy you've both been nowhere near and have been wallowing in your own self-pity – Everything he had, you took off him, and at the worst possible time."

Jeanette had batted my corner. She was Libby's best friend and confidant and the only one capable of giving it her how it was.

"He has a lot of people who depend on him – you just thought about yourselves and making sure you were all okay."

"He did very well out of it," Libby had said.

"And so did both of you," Jeanette had replied. "Can't you see? That man thinks the world of you both and for weeks he didn't know what he had done wrong."

I wasn't privy to that conversation, however Jeanette had told Emily who had dropped it out to me as she felt that it was something that I needed to know. Jeanette was right, it was exactly how it was.

After the christening we all went back to ours and had a bit of a party, which was quite nice and it was here where Sooty had apologised to me.

"We were in a mess," he had said. "Libby didn't want to say anything as it was her who was always bollocking you and telling you where you were going wrong."

"It's okay," I had told him.

"No it isn't," he had said. "We were wrong."

There was another thing which happened at the party afterwards in that Jeanette's mum turned up at the house to pick up my two kids to take them over to their friends birthday party. I had known about the birthday party for weeks and it certainly wasn't a problem; however, Jeanette's mum nearly made it one by saying something out of turn about me – and in the earshot of Emily's mum.

"I'm sorry but I'm certainly not having you saying that," Sil' had said. "That's my son you're talking about."

"He's your son-in-law," Kate had replied.

"I regard him as my son – and there is no way on earth that I am having anything bad said about that lad – Not today nor any other day."

There was nothing aggressive or sinister about it, just a bit matter-of-fact.

I didn't get to know about it until a few days later when I was upstairs trying to drown the screaming machine after his mum had nipped out to her 'Bums and Tums'. Well, by the noise he was making that is what he obviously thought I was doing.

"Dad, can we put the ferrets in with him?" my lad had asked. "Maybe that'll cheer him up."

"Maybe," I had said. "But we can't have him both screaming and stinking of ferrets. The midwife at the clinic already thinks we are slipping anti-freeze in his milk."

"Why is he so unhappy, Dad?" my lad had asked. "It's great living here."

"I don't think he realises that just yet. Sometimes you don't realise things until you get older – When you grow up you see things a lot better."

"Do you see things better, Dad?" he had asked.

"I think so," I'd replied.

"Grandma Kate told mum that you will never grow up and Granny Sil' heard her and went mad," he had said.

"When did your Grandma see Granny Sil'?"

"When they picked us up to take us to that Birthday party – At Sammy's christening party."

Kate was never my biggest fan. The problem was that Jeanette told her far too much, and to an extent still does. Kate was pissed with me – not just for what I did on Jeanette – it was more to do with the fact that I hadn't gone on some downward spiral and resorted to drink and drugs before losing everything. She would have liked that immensely as she could have told me what a huge, huge mistake I had made. The fact that I managed to hold on to what I had had really pissed her off – however possibly unbeknown to her, it was their Jeanette and to an extent Libby that kept me afloat for weeks after I had been slung out. Jeanette, by talking to me at length and Libby, making sure I didn't spend everything I had. Another thing that narked her is that Jeanette still heavily relied on me.

"Why don't you just cut him off," Kate had said. "He's always been no bloody good."

I know she had said that as I was there when she said it, although for some reason I never ever answered her back. It was strange that as I never did.

While lying in bed that night Emily told me how much her mum and dad thought of me – and how they couldn't wait for us to move up to the house in Hamilton Square.

"We're not moving there, mam," she had said. "It'll just be our weekend house."

"I know love, but I still can't wait," she had said. "I'm really excited for you."

Her dad walked around Birkenhead like he was ten feet tall and was always on about us, something that I was regularly told by both Stuart and Lucy.

"Our dad thinks you're great," Lucy had said. "He was around at Hamilton Square taking photos of that big house with my gran and granddad."

"Jamie told me about your mum bollocking his grandma earlier," I told Emily.

"I didn't want to mention it," she replied.

"Why?"

"Because I don't want your feelings hurt," she replied. "I never want you hurt."

I knew I more than deserved to have my backside kicked as I'd been a total git with Jeanette and I told her so.

"That was you then and not now," Emily said. "Look how my mam and dad love you."

"And I love them," I said.

"Dad was dead proud of you when you turned the job in America down and when you said that you didn't want to split the family up," she said. "Mam said he was really choked up. He really does think a lot about you, yer know. He went crackers when he heard what Jeanette's mum had said."

How I was with young Stuart had a major bearing on how I was perceived – not just by Mike but by Mike's father-in-law, Bill. And Stuart was another part of my ever growing fan club that was extremely glad I never went state-side.

He was always wanting to come down here, but his responsibility was to himself, and his college course and part-time job were a huge part of that said responsibility.

"Work hard and learn and I guarantee that you will have everything," I had told him.

Mike knew I wasn't piss-balling, especially when I mentioned the other weekend about the lads Christmas present.

"You've done enough for him already," Mike had argued; however, when I laid it out on the table to both him and Sil' they understood exactly where I was coming from.

"I met him in April and he was nothing like the lad he is now," I had told them. "He looks smart, he's polite and he's knuckled-down and worked hard to get his grades and now he's doing a college course with a part-time job – and believe me – I am calling up and checking in on him every week and he's doing well."

The last bit was obviously news to my in-laws.

"I have no other family and the lad deserves a bit of trust," I said. "Please let us do it for him."

It was mine and his sister's idea to buy him a new moped.

His dad was under the impression that it was going to be some form of crappy second-hand Piaggio; however, I'd already nipped to the motorcycle shop on Pentonville Road and ordered him a brand spanking new Yamaha TZR 50 sports moped, and if I'm being honest I was truly excited for him.

"You're like a big kid," Emily said, nudging me after I'd done the deed.

I knew he'd got a provisional driving licence because all he wanted to do when he was seventeen was pass his test and buy a Maserati. He used to trawl through Auto Trader drooling over the 3200's or, in one instance a Merak with a semi-affordable price tag of £8,000.

"What do you reckon, our Lee?" he'd asked me over the phone with reference to the internet link he had sent me.

"It looks shit-hot, Stu," I told him. "You'd be the coolest kid in Liverpool with that."

The lad – just like both his sisters and parents – was awesome, and in my mind, getting him a moped was nothing – but to him, I knew it would be everything.

Chapter 9

Jeanette's Tales – Take 4

It was about 5:15pm on the 3rd of November when Lee called on me and asked me to present a TV programme.

"Why?" was all I could say.

He told me he loved me and that I deserved it and it was then I shared a moment with him and we held each other. I wanted to kiss him but I didn't. I really, really wanted to kiss him. It wasn't down to the fact that I felt emotionally close to Emily – which I did, it was the fact that I couldn't handle rejection and the thought of him turning me down – and with Emily in the background that was always a possibility. I thought about it for ages afterwards as I had with the missed opportunity on the landing.

He had offered me £30,000 for twelve weeks work, which when you factor in the time it takes to shoot one programme it is a hell of a lot shorter than one week, so basically it was that amount for around 25-35 days' work. How do I know that? I had known him for over 11 years!

I rang my mother to tell her but she wasn't talking to me for the bollocking I had given her for talking out of turn about Lee. She can say what she wants about him or any other person in this house or hers, however doing it in his house was way out of line. I got dad on the phone and told him my news and he seemed really pleased for me. "Maybe you'll get back together?" he said before adding, "That would be nice."

That wasn't what I had in my mind, but I have to say I didn't mind the sound of it and on hearing my dad say that my mother was immediately on the phone to find out exactly what was happening. "He's using you again," she snapped. "Don't fall for it, Jeanette."

I mentioned the money and that kept her quiet – well, for a bit anyway.

My mother had my life planned out for me – University where I would eventually get my Phd in Biochemistry and I would settle down close to home with some boring professional type like a doctor, heart surgeon or lawyer and where I would eventually give her a brace of ugly grandchildren. In comparison, Lee looked like he had the life of some rock star and was a million miles an hour, and that being the case a million miles from what my mother had in mind for me. I managed to drag him up to meet my parents one weekend and my mother immediately gave him the thumbscrew treatment and wanted to know everything from his family background to his bio-genetic code. He was extremely honest with her and told her about his mum, who he rarely saw, his dad's mum who had already seen me barge into the bedroom and nearly drag her out of bed – not forgetting the unforgettable memory of her walking in on us while he was battering hell of me under the duvet – and his wicked aunt from Rotherham, who he told her he was planning to murder. Yeh, he really said that!

His dad had died young – as had his granddad, and Lee was one of those people who always thought he was next in line and as that was the case, he lived life how he did. As for me – I thought he was bloody great and when we laid in that crappy bed he had in Muswell Hill, which incidentally drove me potty as I knew there had been around two hundred women there before me, he told me that he couldn't wait to have kids and after I had bollocked him for not telling me this earlier, I wasted no time in flushing my contraceptive pills. However and as it does, it never happened straight away and every month I used to get as depressed as hell.

"Are you sure we are doing it right?" I'd ask him.

"I fucking think so," he'd laugh.

I was a right foot-stamping bitch.

It was my intention to phone Libby but I had M on the phone who was as excited as I was and we spent the next hour talking firstly about TV and then a variety of other subjects, one of which was that they had bought a property up on The Wirral.

"What? You're moving?" I asked.

"No – we need somewhere to stay on weekend as ITV are making Lee shoot that weekend football channel in Manchester," Emily replied.

I thought she was on about some crappy old flat or house and nearly dropped through the floor when I googled the thing. I looked around at my surroundings and at the four bedroom terraced I lived in and which my ex-husband paid for. I should have been content but I wasn't. Emily was getting a mansion on The Wirral as their second home and all I had was a hand-out in Clerkenwell.

"What's the matter with you?" Libby asked when I eventually phoned her.

"Every time he gives me something, M gets it as well – but just bigger and better," I told her, before apologising for being a moody cow.

"You want to be in my shoes," she said.

No thanks, I thought.

I had known Sooty quite a long time before Lib did, and although he was a great friend and fun to be around – he was sex mad – especially after a drink, and on a couple of occasions when we were in Muswell Hill I'd had to beat him off. I never told Lee, but I certainly told Sooty.

Lee told me after he'd landed the job with Nubeon that it would only be a matter of time before the shit hit the fan. "He'll be like a kid in a sweet shop," he said. "I'll give it two months."

Nobody knew Sooty like Lee – they were inseparable.

"Tim's doing my frigging box in," Libby told me. "This job he's got is messing with his head."

"Why, what's up?" I asked.

"It's good money but he's spending a lot of time down there," she said, before asking the question of how much was I going to get for presenting a show.

I told her and there was a short silence.

"So how much are ITV actually paying him?" she inquired.

Ever since I knew them both, Lib and Sooty were always 'about the money'.

Me and Lee used to blow money on going out, clothes and cars, but they didn't – and with Lib getting some job in some financiers after she's left uni' they used to hoard the bloody stuff.

"I'm not sure," I told her. "He sort of has two jobs with them – one on a three-year contract and the other through his own company."

She couldn't get her head around it, but to be honest nor could I.

"I know it must be a lot of money," I added, "As he turned down both NBC and Fox Sports and according to M, one of them offered him two point one million."

You could have heard a pin drop at the other end of the phone.

As I said, Sooty and Lib were all about the money and I knew Libby's next point of call would be to sound out M as she always told the truth, which was something no-one could accuse her husband of doing!

Within an hour Lib was on my doorstep. She had phoned M and like M always did, answered her questions. It turned out that her husband's ex-business partner – who I personally thought they had both shafted – had looked at all the options available and had dropped on the deal of deals.

"Fucking two point one million a year," Lib said aghast.

I nodded. I knew it must have been a lot. "He's a talented guy," I said. "Just think what he'll make from the three TV shows."

Her mind was ticking like a bomb. Libby thought that it was Sooty that was holding the business together. It wasn't. Me and Libby had been holding Lee together while Sooty was just holding Lee back. I certainly thought it, but I never said it.

"What do you get out of all this?" Libby asked.

"Nothing," I said. "He looks after me and the kids and if I need anything he's always there."

He was. The boiler broke – he had a new one put in. I wanted a new kitchen – he had one put in. If I asked, I always got. And he told me he loved me every day. From the outside it might look that it was a strange and complex relationship – but it wasn't really. He had two families, and not Lee as such but M, helped bring us all closer together. Whereas M was all for happiness, Lib was all out for control.

When Lee and Sooty set up, both myself and Lib had a stake in the company. I let them get on with it, but she wanted involvement. It sounds like I don't like her, but that is certainly not the case. She was from Derby and I was from Buxton and we bumped into each other at university and got on like a house on fire, so much so we moved out of our dorm's and rented a house in Edgbaston along with three other girls. She was okay with me but she was a right bossy cow with the others and she was always being subbed by her parents, so much so she always had new clothes, car and everything, yet she always made sure we coughed up on time for the rent. I had a part-time job in Sainsbury's – strange one that! – but I was always pot-less and in one instance Lib had subbed me a few hundred pounds, on which she had added ten percent – really! I went down to Lee's on a wing and a prayer one Friday night hoping that the fuel in the car wouldn't run out only to get to an empty house. He was always out all hours but he left me the key under the dustbin.

He rolled in at around two o'clock in the morning and I was never as happy to see him.

"I thought she was your friend?" he had said before just shrugging his shoulders and giving me the contents of his wallet. He was like that – just very generous.

A couple of weeks later him and Yusef had been doing some work in Birmingham and he knocked all the house up around 'half-one' in the morning, him shouting through the letterbox. "Open the door Jeanette – I'm freezing my bollocks off out here."

You just had to love him.

There were five of us living in the house, and on the other four – including Lib – all seeing Lee and Yusef, you ought to have seen them trying to doll themselves up – it was dead funny.

"What are you doing up here?" I'd asked.

"Don't ask," he'd told me.

I never did, I was just glad he was there and I tried my best at feeding them, but there was never any food in the house. We all watched on in awe as they sat at the table eating a concoction of toast and soup. As I said, they were like a pair of rock stars.

"So who are your friends?" he smiled.

As I sat on his knee I introduced them, including Libby who he'd sort of seen before, but who he told me he couldn't remember. I felt like a princess. He always made me feel like that and M sort of told me the same.

M had had a really bad pregnancy which wasn't helped by her lunatic ex-husband, and not only did she have to contend with Lee's idiosyncrasies she had me and my two in the background, and I have to say I did my utmost best at being a total cow.

"I'm sorry for saying this," M had told me. "But I really do love him."

I knew she did. She looked at him in the exact same way that I had looked at him.

"I'm just not sure whether I could ever keep his interest – He's all over the place."

I had felt the same, however one thing I did know was that Lee liked his dippy females who were heavily reliant on him. He had made sure I went through six months of university with extra money in my pocket – He told me that it was a loan that I could pay back with sex, but if that was the case then Libby's ten percent was utter bloody peanuts at the side of the interest rate he must have been charging me – not that I ever minded however. M needed him, but she needed him to show her that he wanted her. As I was in 'conniving bitch-mode', I just wanted shut of her and told her that if he really loved her he would go after her if she left. Knowing that Lee had nil-constitution when it came to women trying to manipulate him I surmised that I'd never see her again after she left to go up to her parents. I nearly died when I found out that he'd gone after her and I was as miserable as sin. The thing is that it was Libby of all people who had advised him to go!

Just before I dropped out of university altogether I had sensed that he was just a bit busier than I wanted and my nightly phone calls – I'll not go into details, but dirty sex played a part – in fact thinking of it, dirty sex played quite a big part – were becoming very short and sweet. I had imagined him in every conceivable position in what I had termed as 'our house' in Muswell Hill with every conceivable and available female and believe me, wherever he was there was always women coming on to him so much so it drove me crazy. I had spent the odd week at the house and just about every weekend but I couldn't focus on classes and I knew my grades were nowhere near good enough and I phoned him and asked if I could come down and live with him.

"Yeh – if you want," he said.

It was the best decision I had ever made in my life – but I messed it all up.

A few days later I had M on the phone, Lee had flipped his lid over Arsenal. I say I hated Arsenal, but it doesn't stop me from watching the results come in on a Saturday and the sense of satisfaction I get from knowing that Lee and both our kids are happy when they win. To be an Arsenal fan you have to be a bit special, I mean which team goes 3-0 up and ends up drawing 3-3, and against some rubbish European side. Probably the same team that goes 4-0 up against Newcastle United and ends up drawing 4-4!

"I thought Anderlecht were good?" M whispered over the phone.

"I don't think they are, M," I replied.

"Didn't that Sammy score the winning goal against them in that European final?" she asked.

"Yeh – but back then they were supposedly a good team," I said.

I couldn't believe I was discussing bloody football with my ex-husband's new wife.

I used to go to football matches quite a lot, but not so much after we were married. Lee's first point of call was always to the Arsenal Supporters Club on the corner of St. Thomas's Road where an Alfred Hitchcock lookalike was always standing outside in a black suit complete with bowler hat and cigar. I think he was some sort of steward. All the people in there were like one big family and for a time I was a part of it, although after I had Harmony, I stopped going altogether. It's a shame as they were all such lovely people. I have been to a few European away matches. I went to Milan where they beat Inter 5-1, but my best memory was when Lee asked if I fancied Madrid. I assumed we'd go Club Class on British Airways, but I found out that some Arsenal lads had chartered some old jet that was flying out of Gatwick. "Will it even get us there?" I asked on seeing it. The thing even had wallpaper on its interior.

I had just been caught on with Harmony and the ride was as uncomfortable as hell – but the company was good. It always was – and the Arsenal lads, when it comes to women being in their company were absolutely great and none more so than Stevie Kell who had took Jane away with him. Lee had booked us into some three-star rat hole just off some main street and after we unpacked we had hit the nearest Tapas bar and by the time we got to the Bernabau we were wrecked, but Lee soon sobered up when the match started.

"We're going to win this," he told Stevie. And you know what? They did.

Thierry Henry ran through the lot of them and stuck the ball in the corner of the net and everyone went crackers. It was bloody magic. Us four and another couple– I forget their name – and Alan Herd and Lee Johnson, the latter who was nicknamed the Strawman and who possessed the filthiest mouth ever as every sentence he spoke contained the C-word – hit the nearest bar, which we thought was a sports bar as it was called 'Chelsea'. However, here is where we would be wrong as it happened to be some strip bar-cum-knocking shop. On getting in there Lee ordered a load of champagne – or some sparkling wine that was wrongly described as champagne – and him and the lads ended up doing the 'Agadoo' on stage while this performer on stage was trying to shag this woman – we couldn't stop laughing and in the end the bouncers tried to throw us out. I say tried as Stevie rammed one of their heads through a plate glass window and as for The Strawman – well, that was a bloody classic! While the others were resisting being ejected from the bar he was doing some strange Kung Fu moves to one of the bouncers. Have you ever seen the Beatles' film 'Help!' where Leo McKern and his Indian cult break into their house and try to sacrifice Ringo and Ringo does all these cha – cha – cha – cha – karate moves before getting red paint chucked all over him? Well that was The Strawman before he got slung over a table.

A fight started out on the street and thankfully Gaz Lawrence and a few of his mates saw us and they ended up kicking hell out of the bouncers. As for Lee, Stevie and The Strawman – they were by now bollock naked in a fountain over the road. A couple of police tried to get them out but they weren't having it.

"Lee, come out," I told him.

In the end the police woman threatened to Taser him, which quietened him down a bit, so much so he asked if she fancied coming back for a threesome, providing she took her boots off.

"I can't believe you said that!" I told him. Well, I could really as he was a right dirty git, but he was dead good fun to be around.

We overslept and missed the flight home. Somehow I had ended up in bed with Jane, and Stevie had locked Lee in the shower, thrown up and fallen asleep.

"What have you locked him in the bathroom for?" I had asked him.

"I had to do," Stevie had said, "he was out of control."

Lee was a total lightweight when it came to drinking and one sniff of the barman's apron was enough for him to flip his lid. We had some breakfast, booked another night and went shopping and then on a bender around Madrid.

Next day Lee came into the hotel foyer smiling and saying he'd got us some transport – He had hired a car.

"What have you got that for?" I'd asked him.

"We'll drive back."

We all jumped in and drove up through Bordeaux towards Paris and then Calais and Lee and Stevie never stopped talking about football all the time. It was lovely and one of the nicest times I'd had, but it didn't end there. Lee parked up outside the Eastenders Duty Free warehouse ordered a taxi –filled it with booze and then he set fire to the hire car.

We were all speechless in the taxi as it made its way over to the port but Lee was laughing like some schoolboy. Not only had he blown around five hundred quid in the sex bar, paid for a hotel room and a hire car plus petrol all the way from Spain – he had paid for it with Sooty's American Express card.

"I can't wait to see his face when he cops the bill for that lot!" he laughed.

Paul's idea of happiness was getting five pence a litre off his petrol at Tesco's – Lee was on a completely different planet when it came to having fun.

Chapter 10

University Challenge

The Warehouse was a massive white shell when the decorators had finished and I tasked Emily and Jeanette with furnishing it as in all honesty a million other things needed my attention.

"Why ask me?" asked Jeanette.

"Do you want to do it or not?" I asked.

"I don't mind," she said. "I just don't know why you're asking me."

"Well, seeing as you'll be working here maybe you might want a say in what it looks like."

That got her head ticking.

"And choose yourself an office," I said.

"What – I get my own office?"

Yeh – she got her own office – she was always in mine – as was Emily.

I had prepared for all these programmes, so it was no big issue as such although the seat nearly went out of my pants when ITV brought the scheduling forward. And I mean really forward. The Sessions on late Saturday and Sunday night – starting 8th November, the relabelled Inside True Britain on Wednesday night and Live at The Warehouse on Thursday night starting 12th and 13th of November respectively, with the latter having to actually be done on a Thursday night.

I sat in what we had dubbed The Boardroom – It wasn't as such – it was just a big area with glass desks and computer points for Apple Macs – that me, Abi, Eddie (who was working for me two days a week) and Les could brainstorm, however once ITV 7 kicked off Les would be involved solely in that side of the business.

Jeanette had had an input into our previous business when it kicked off, but not so much so after that. She also had a two percent stake which our accountant at the time conned her into parting with after we had split up – for £20,000 – and who made himself over £270,000 when that said business was sold, which was one of the reasons I refused to use the fat fucker again unless he did the right thing, which of course he didn't. I'd begged her not to sell her two points, but she'd already done it – the irony was that Sooty had already offered her £15,000 for them, which when I found out I went ape shit and accused him of trying to rip her off.

"What do you care?" he had replied. "You've been ripping her off ever since your Harmony was born."

I didn't like what he said, but he had a point.

Jeanette had had some post-natal depression after my daughter was born and instead of helping her through it I got hooked up with a certain Katrin Yefremov who was a third-year student over in London studying English Literature whilst working as some hotel receptionist. She was decent-looking and once she knew I was interested wanted me to leave Jeanette. Once Jeanette knew about her she went through the roof and threw me out and, me being me I tried blaming her for my extramarital affair, which was very, very wrong. Looking back it, I still can't believe what a bastard I was. She got the hump with me for a few weeks after I'd been let back in and it sort of got swept under the carpet; however, Katrin pleaded with me to give her a chance and I must say she did her level best to keep the relationship going, that was until I did her flatmate and the flatmate told her. Jesus, that was nasty! Jeanette's Greek background had nothing to come when compared to some unhinged Cossack brandishing some bread knife in her mitts, and how I got out of there with my bollocks still intact still remains a mystery.

As regards the TV rescheduling, I knew what I wanted and that was to get the bands recorded for the ITV Sessions, but the short time-frame ITV had given me created a minor panic, and my writing up football documentaries was put on the backburner for a few days. I had already drafted a few ideas up for the rebranded Inside True Britain show that Jeanette would present, one of which Eddie had already given me some heavy copy and which I'd re-written and which when he read it nearly gave him a coronary. "You're making it look like it was murder," he said.

"No – the viewer is thinking that it's murder," I replied. "We have said nothing about it – it's what we term as compelling viewing."

I loved Eddie, he was a great guy – so much so I took him on my next mission as my editor in chief.

I'd got Les to get me in at the University of London to sound out some media students to see if they fancied their hand at writing me up some copy.

"You're going to use students?" asked ITV's rather aghast director of programming.

"Certainly – We all have to start somewhere."

I certainly meant that, but at the same time I also knew that I would get my copy written for literally nothing, therefore keeping a bit of a cap on my outgoings.

London's Birbeck and Goldsmith University had hundreds of media students and when they read all the notices that Les had fly-posted around the place I had the lecture halls at both colleges packed to the rafters.

I ran with the same lines at both and told them firstly who I was and secondly want I wanted – which was mainly a load of 'Bright Young Things' that wanted to slave for me for pennies.

"I did more or less exactly what you are doing now although I never got the break that I am giving you," I told them. "You are the future and if you are hardworking, show a bit of nous and if I see some talent shining through – the opportunities for you are endless."

I wanted teams of writers to produce me some copy for thirteen programmes and I told them so.

The Programmes:
1) *An All Exhuming Love* – Fred and Rose West
2) *The Bible John Murders*
3) *Auf Weidersehen, Pet* – The True Story
4) *The Black Eyed Child* – The story of the Ghost of Cannock Chase
5) *Milly* – The story behind the killer of Milly Dowling
6) *DC5* – The story behind The Tottenham Sound
7) *The story behind Cover-Up* – The Jeremy Thorpe Affair
8) *Paint it Black* – Who is Robert Black?
9) *Whatever Happened to the Likely Lads?* - The True Story
10) *Through the Eye of a killer* – Dale Cregan
11) *The Rape of Nanking*
12) *The Piper at the Gates of Dawn* – The untold story of Syd Barrett
13) *The Baby-Faced Assassin* – The story behind the murderer, Jamie Bain?
14) *Faces of the 1960's*

"Eddie Mardell here with me is my point man and editor in chief," I said. "He has already done one of these programmes – impress him, then I get to know about it. If you're interested I want you to team up in three's, fours or even five's and see what you can offer me."

"Which one has he done?" asked a student.

"I can't tell you that," I said. "I don't want to limit your scope."

"Yeh – but then we'll be working for no end product if we end up writing up the one he's done," said another.

"No you won't – You are out to impress me – If it's better than Eddie's, I'll use it," I said.

"What, really?" another asked.

"I want brilliance. I'm always open to ideas and I'm not so deluded that I don't believe there is no one out there who is better than me. I want you to show me what you can do."

I said a lot more and when one of the professors or whatever thanked me for my time the hall stood up to applaud me – both at Birbeck and at Goldsmiths.

I drove home that night deeply touched – especially by what the Professor, Tutor or whatever had said. "It's really good of you to take an interest at the ground floor," he had told me.

"I'll try my best to make it work for them," I said, before realising that I had said something similar to Emily after our Sammy had been born.

I'd had various so-called teams tap me up during my talk with the Professor, one of which was a three-girl team who Emily would most certainly have got the hump with as they certainly weren't backwards in coming forwards, one of who immediately asked if I was married.

"I am – You'll meet both of my wives if you give me some good copy," I replied.

"I'd definitely give you some copy," one of them grinned.

I suddenly envisaged Les Crang being in the job of all jobs when this lot arrived on site. Les lived in Bow and was in a relationship that had run its course and that being the case outside of work he was banging everything in sight. He tried it with Faranha at one stage but I pulled him to one side and had a word. "Work is for work," I told him. "I don't go in for office relationships as everything gets fucked up."

I'd taken Faranha home a couple of times but I knew it was a bum idea – I blamed her family for not wanting outsiders in, but that really wasn't the case. In business you need a rigid organisational structure and a boss banging a receptionist not only creates toxic gossip it makes the said receptionist think she's at director level when she's not. The boss dumps the receptionist and it makes it ten times worse. That is why I loved Abi – Totally beautiful and totally uncomplicated.

"Do you actually fancy me or are you winding me up?" she once asked me.

"I totally fancy you but I love you too much to lose what we have," I'd replied.

"You mean you respect me?" she'd asked.

"I wouldn't go that far," I had winked.

"Bollocks, Lee," she'd replied.

Abi appeared to have the job of all jobs and when I'd told her what she would be earning she nearly wet herself. "Can you actually afford to pay me that?" she'd asked.

"If we can make all this work what we can achieve together is endless," I'd told her.

In the meantime I'd been sourcing top-notch talent through Stevie Kell, who his wife had since let talk to me after Jeanette had had a word with her – we needed twenty roving football reporters along with some presenters and immediately I got pointed the way of some marketing executive who ran a popular Arsenal blog. "Do you know him?" Stevie asked.

"Not personally – but I've read some of his comments," I said.

"And?"

"He's a bit up his own arse to be truthful," I told him.

A lot of the owners of these football blogs are. They suddenly become both pedantic and self-important because they have a hundred or so dick heads – half of who are either glory boys or foreigners passing comment through their websites. I preferred the old school Arsenal supporter – The Gaz Lawrences, Tony Fishers, Martin Whittles and Stevie Kells of this world. They think before they speak and what they say is always worth listening to. Les Crang is the same.

We'd made a short list and had a few in for a screen test, which was very funny, as half of them wanted to talk a load posher than they actually were. I hated the sound of my voice being played back to me – not quite as much as Jeanette's, as it was generally bollocking me, so I could truly understand them wanting to alter them.

We also screen tested Emily and Jeanette and I thought they were both brilliant, but then again I did ask Abi her thoughts as I didn't want to appear to be giving favour to someone who didn't deserve it.

"They're really good," she replied.

I totally enjoyed giving Jeanette her screen test and had her doing all sorts of stupid things, which must have been very reminiscent of Alfred Hitchcock with Tippi Hedren.

"Tell me again why I have to crawl on my knees?" she had said.

I couldn't keep a straight face and informed her that from now on that she would have to call me "Boss".

"You can stuff the stinking job up your arse if I have to do that," she snapped.

I was going to tell her that Emily didn't mind but I thought better of it so I winked at her and just asked her to repeat her last line.

"You can stuff the stinking job up your arse if I have to do that," she said before adding, "Boss."

"That's perfect, Jeanette," I said. "Really good."

She managed a really nice smile which Abi definitely noticed.

"No office relationships," I said. "Not unless I can watch anyway!"

I got in that night to what seemed like a billion emails and Herbert squawking and grizzling as his mum had just finished feeding him. It turned out that in his humble opinion there hadn't been enough milk in his bottle.

"Has he been like that all day?" I asked.

"What are yer on about," she twanged, whilst giving me a kiss. "He's been like it since birth."

That made me chuckle.

"Can you remember what I said to you straight after you'd had him," I asked.

"Yeh – you asked if the nurse had put a couple of extra stitches in for you," she smiled.

"Did I say that?"

"Yeh, yer did," she said whilst playfully prodding me.

Mmm, I forgot about that, I thought.

"You also said that you'd do what it takes to make everything great – and it is. I certainly never expected all this."

I smiled at her last comment. I was becoming untouchable, but unfortunately at that moment in time I had a knock at the door and looked through the window to cop sight of Libby with her two brats.

"Piss off, we don't want any pegs," I told her.

On her getting in the house she did a bit of grizzling at me – not as much as Herbert who was by now screaming the place down.

"What's up with Sammy?" asked Libby.

"He was alright until he saw you," I lied. "Anyway, what do you want? Our laundry's not due to be collected until Friday."

"Funny ha ha," she quipped.

I kicked the TV and Xbox up for Sooty's two kids and dug them out some chocolate from one of the drawers that Emily thought I didn't know about.

"They can't eat them," said Libby.

"When they come here there are rules," I said, whilst winking over at the two kids. "The first rule is that chocolate is absolutely compulsory and the second one is that all mums except Emily are daft and should be totally ignored."

"What about Auntie Jeanette?" asked Mia. "She's a mum and you don't ignore her."

"Auntie Jeanette's a bit more ferocious than your mum," I told them. "She makes sure no-one ignores her."

"No she isn't – Auntie Jeanette is nice," said Zooey.

"Yes, she is love," said Emily, who passed Libby a cup of coffee.

It turned out that Libby wanted me to offer Sooty a job.

"I offered him one and he turned it down," I told her.

She didn't know that and I could have kicked myself for letting that particular cat out of the bag. I could be a total gob shite at times and a further twenty questions ensued, one of which involved how much money had I offered him?

"I didn't," I told her. "The conversation never went that far."

"Would it have been more than he's getting now?" she asked.

"It would have probably been a similar amount," I said.

She then hit me with something that hurt in that if I was being paid in excess of a couple of million why was her husband only worth five percent of that?

"ITV offered me the deal and I took it," I told her. "I work for ITV and they pay me."

"What about LMJ?" she asked.

I couldn't believe what I was hearing.

"What about LMJ?" I asked.

"Well, you'll be earning money from that as well?" she asked.

"Quite possibly," I told her.

"Jeanette says you've offered her thirty grand for around thirty hours work so you must be earning a lot of money from it," she said. "And if Jeanette will be earning that, what about M?"

"What about Emily?" I asked.

"I'm not earning anything," Emily said. "Lee asked me if I wanted to do it. Money never came into it, Lib."

"I'm sorry Libby," I told her. "I love you a lot but I'm not having this conversation."

It was the first time I had ever put her in her place. They had sold the business from under my nose and I'd had to look to create something from scratch knowing full well that I would possibly never be able to work in TV again. I had been extremely lucky; however, what was strange was that neither Emily nor Jeanette thought that was the case.

I let Sooty know that his dragon wife had been pissing in my ears and he apologised before telling me that she was a bit more than pissed at him recently as she had picked up on a few text messages between him and one of the actresses he had supposedly been humping down at Nubeon. It was a nice conversation which started with me asking him if he had the codes and password for the billion terabyte Dropbox file that we had backed up all our files from our previous business and concluded with the fact that he would let me have a few of his girls for the launch of Live at The Warehouse.

I needed the former to piece together the Parallel's – Arsenal's throwing away of the Doubles documentary as I knew there were a lot of 1972/73's matches on it. I also knew there were a few matches from 1958/59, one of which was a cup replay at Bramall Lane, whilst the need of the latter was quite obvious.

"What are you on with," Sooty asked me.

"A take on Arsenal's throwing away of the Doubles," I said.

"They've thrown away loads of Doubles," he replied. "And Trebles."

He was right; however, these two seasons I was looking had never really be spoken about outside your average Arsenal historian.

"Did you know Malcolm Allison was being tipped for the Spurs job just before they appointed Bill Nicholson manager?" I asked.

"I wonder how much that would have changed history?" Sooty had replied. "Tottenham ran everyone ragged for the next three or four seasons and according to Jimmy Greaves should have won far more than they actually did."

We then got into a conversation about the 1958/59 season which started with Allison, who played over 200 games at centre-half with West Ham United and whose career was ended prematurely by a bout of tuberculosis after he fell ill after a game against Sheffield United and who had to have a lung removed. He never played again but got involved on the coaching side and was integral in the establishment of the academy at the club, helping nurture the likes of Bobby Moore, Geoff Hurst and Martin Peters, who would later help the club lift both the 1964 FA Cup and 1965 European Cup Winners Cup and form the basis of England's 1966 World Cup success, which Sooty and myself despised talking about, although a mate of mine didn't as he was a life-long Hammer and was claret and blue through and through. I had bumped into Brian Allan whilst we were piecing together the Sammy documentary and he suggested that I should do a documentary on football violence – not so much the darker side as that has been bled dry, but more from a humorous angle, but that was another tale for another day.

"Ron Greenwood was Arsenal's assistant manager," I told Sooty. "He left to take over from Ted Fenton and inherited all the academy that he and Allison had helped set up."

It was true. West Ham United won the Division Two title in the season prior, a division that they had struggled to get out of for 26 years, and the next season they went to Highbury in late March to help further derail Arsenal's title challenge with a 2-1 win, with the *Daily Express* calling Arsenal's showing as 'shameful', and where John Dick had unleashed a 35-yard drive off a post after 14 minutes whilst half the Arsenal players were still stood around arguing the toss with the referee, who they felt had wrongly given a throw-in to West Ham. Not much changes eh? I remember Nigel Winterburn doing something similar in a F.A Cup game versus Leeds United in 1993. The 52,452 crowd were on their feet soon after when Arsenal's Scottish international and recent £18,000 purchase from League Champions Wolves – the fast and two-footed Jackie Henderson equalised after 37 minutes. Henderson had been doubtful for the match due to injury but could only watch on as John Dick restored West Ham's lead after 47 minutes by sending a looping ball over reserve goalkeeper Jim Standen, who had to go off after 80 minutes due to him sustaining a deep head wound.

The West Ham defeat would form part of Arsenal's late season capitulation, which saw them take just three points from a possible 14 after what had been a brilliant 3-2 win against fellow title chasing Manchester United on 28th February, 1959, and which had seen them sitting proudly at the summit of the Division One.

The 1972/73 season was highly comparable with the 1958/59 season as Arsenal had gone to Anfield in February 1973, where they outplayed the would-be League Champions, winning 2-0 in front of just under 50,000 to go top of the league, before they capitulated, and threw away the chance of doing a second double in three years.

They had beaten Leicester in the following game courtesy of an own goal after just six minutes from cultured Scottish centre-half Malcolm Manley and dumped a tidy Carlisle side out of the Fifth Round of the F.A Cup before going on a lousy run of 14 games with only six wins.

The win against Leicester was fortunate in that not only had Manley had turned a harmless cross by John Radford past his goalkeeper Peter Shilton, seconds from the end of the game a Bob Wilson mistake let in the barracuda-like predator that was Frank Worthington to put over a cross for John Farrington to head into an empty net; however, the winger couldn't connect and Arsenal were out of jail. A couple of 1-0 defeats followed, one of which was against Don Howe's bottom of the table and soon to be relegated West Bromwich Albion along with another – this time at home to the previous seasons League Champions Derby County, a team who had pummelled Arsenal 5-0 early on in the season at the Baseball Ground, and after which Bertie Mee had dispensed with his total football theory and reverted to type. However, what is rarely said is that

Arsenal should have been out of sight early on as Charlie George had failed to convert two fairly straightforward chances before the first of a series of Bob Wilson gaffes after 21 minutes let Derby in. The keeper and defence's dismal showing had Derby 4-0 up by 42 minutes, in which Roy MacFarland had also had a goal ruled out as the referee had called back Hinton as he was deemed to have taken a free kick too quickly. After 47 minutes the rout was completed when Kevin Hector played for a free kick and Alan Hinton sent over a cross, which Roger Davies duly headed home. Derby County were a classy side; however, their manager – the enigma that was Brian Clough – had bemoaned their poor away form prior to the match on 31st March 1973, which had involved only two wins, but in front of over 45,000 they came to Highbury and turned Arsenal over, as their captain and leader Frank McLintock over-hit a free kick with less than two minutes on the clock, which saw a Roger Davies – Kevin Hector - Steve Powell sortie cut through the defence, with the latter scoring easily from 12 yards. McLintock put his hand up to the mistake and to compound his misery, ended up being carried off after 40 minutes with a torn hamstring.

After the Liverpool game in February, Mee had heaped praise on his £220,000 acquisition Alan Ball by telling Harry Miller of the *Daily Mirror*, "He has given us many more dimensions to our play – There is possibly some truth in the suggestions that two years ago we were a little predictable in the way we played to the strength of our two front strikers – Ray Kennedy and John Radford, all the time, whereas teams now worry about us in midfield."

Neither Sunderland nor Leeds United worried about Arsenal's midfield however, as they suffered two more embarrassing defeats, one a 2-1 F.A Cup Semi Final defeat against Sunderland who were a mid-table Second Division side, along with a 6-1 mauling at the hands of Don Revie's Leeds United. What was strange was that they ended the season only three points behind Liverpool and four points in front of third place Leeds, who themselves suffered a shock in in the F.A Cup Final against the men from Roker Park, despite putting on a lot better performance against them than Arsenal had.

At the end of the 1972/73 season Mee made what is considered by many to have been his biggest mistake and sold Frank McLintock to Queens Park Rangers. Frank had been a leader of men, but as Manchester United fan and journalist Frank McGhee had said in the *Daily Mirror* after the fortunate 1-0 win at home against Leicester City, there had been mutterings in the dressing room and corridors of Highbury that the club should dispense with his services and, as he put it, "Let the old warhorse frolic in green pastures thick with pound notes from a transfer."

He did, and he went on to help an exciting QPR under the guidance of the brilliant Dave Sexton go close to winning League Championship some three years later. Warhorse indeed!

During their suicidal run-in to the 1958/59 season, Arsenal had also suffered a 6-1 reverse, this time at the hands of Stan Cullis' machine that was Wolves, and a club who would end up winning the league at a canter and who should have really done the first Double of the century a year later in 1960 after conceding ground on the last day of the season in what was one of the tightest league campaigns in history, and where Arsenal were a mere five points from relegation. Wolves were sitting at the top of Division One waiting for Manchester City – boasting one of the greatest strikers of the era in Denis Law – and a player who Arsenal had been looking to sign throughout the 1958/59 season, of doing them a favour by holding Burnley. However, it was not to be, and in front of a crowd of 65,981 a Jimmy McIlroy inspired Burnley produced a display that won them the match 2-1. Left winger Brian Pilkington managed to race to the byline to see his cross deflected into the net by the legendary Bert Trautmann after only four minutes and

Trevor Meredith hit the winner on 31 minutes to help secure Burnley their first League Championship since 1921.

Football and its history – how can anyone not love it?

I got off the phone from Sooty to see the wife snuggled up on the sofa half-watching TV. "My granddad says you've got to do a documentary on Liverpool," she smiled.

"I'd love to do a documentary on Liverpool," I told her.

Chapter 11

Jeanette's Tales – Take 5

I had been at work since 7:00am and I was due a screen test up at the warehouse at 4:30pm and on getting up there I felt a right scruff. Abigail was all dolled up to the nines along with some other woman Lee had had in his office and who I never got introduced to, but who Faranha had told me was being sounded out for the job of an accounts manager of sorts. I had obviously been there before, but not while there were this many people buzzing around the place and on Lee seeing me he gave me a hug and a peck on the cheek and from there on in I was treated like royalty. I'd seen Lee at work before, but I'd never seen this Lee at work before, as this Lee was certainly a lot different to the one I'd known.

"I need to put on some make-up," I told him.

"No, you don't," he told me. "You look great as you are."

And he said that in front of everyone.

I got took into a partitioned section of the huge downstairs gallery which had a dark red leather settee that I had picked, along with an Autocue and camera and I immediately knew that M had been there earlier as there were a pair of her shoes in the corner, which I must say were distracting me a bit. Well they weren't, they were distracting me quite a lot.

"Is M still here?" I asked.

Lee nodded and then went behind the camera.

"Where is she?" I asked.

I was paranoid about doing this anyway, without her being here to watch me cock it up.

"I've got you in focus, Jeanette and you look great," he said. "Now can you read from the Autocue."

I'd done this before when they'd had their first lot of offices off Euston Road and when they had bought this second-hand machine from auction. This wasn't second-hand – this was brand new – as was the big camera that I was looking into.

"Hello there, I'm Jeanette Janes," I said, reading from the Autocue. "I am five foot three, brunette, with all my own teeth and I'm available most nights for casual sex."

Everyone started laughing.

"Keep reading it Jeanette," said Abigail. "It's Lee messing around."

"I am being screen-tested for a TV series originally titled Inside True Britain. I was asked to do it by my brilliant ex-husband who is that brilliant that …."

I broke off and told them that there was no way on earth that I was saying the next bit.

Lee was in stitches but told me that how you handle yourself in front of the camera is key and me being myself whilst reading it would blow everyone away – And he actually said that.

"It's a serious business," he explained. "No matter what is on the Autocue – you read it."

I did the rest to laughing and I rode it through but not before he had his big laugh and had me on my hands and knees wiggling my bloody arse. The thing is that he knew exactly what he was doing. You might think he was just having a laugh – which he was to some extent – but he was also recording it for posterity if you like, as if any of these shows made it – the screen tests and out-takes or whatever would make really great viewing. He never ever threw anything away, and when we were living in Southgate the amount of film footage he hoarded drove me batty. We'd had the house done out from top to bottom, but you couldn't see half the furniture for all the DVDs and hardware scattered about the place. We'd have dinner with a few other couples and I'd be tripping over the bloody things. Saying that, when I found out he was knocking off some wife of an executive at ITV I took half of it outside and burned it. For as lovely as he could be, he certainly knew how to hurt me; however, I suppose past is past and it is better leaving it there. Not that I ever do, mind you!

On the home front Paul had asked me to marry him. I'd been married once and in my mind once is more than enough for anyone, but after what was around the eleventh time of him asking I told him I'd think about it. I did – I neither wanted marriage nor any man living with me again. Mine and Paul's relationship was solely girlfriend and boyfriend in that he went home on a night, and that way I had total control of my life. I mentioned his asking me to M, secretly hoping that she would tell Lee, but she didn't. You said anything to M and generally that was as far as it went. Between us we were forming a great friendship and I could easily see why Lee fell in love with her, so much so I detested the fact that I liked her so much, and that pair of shoes that were in the room during the screen-test had driven me potty, as I thought she'd purposely put them there as some form of statement or test. She hadn't – she just made it look like she had. It was as though she was playing with my mind and all I wanted to do as I sat on the red settee after the screen-test talking to Abigail was to try the bloody things on. Was I going mad?

Lee had a thing about great legs and feet and when I first started courting him I just thanked God for having a great-looking mother and dad.

"You've got fucking great legs, Jeanette," he'd tell me. Generally when they were wrapped around his neck, but also on the odd time while we were out, and I made full use of this by what I wore and how I acted – especially when he pissed me off.

On M moving in with him I got really depressed as she was exactly what I knew he liked and on our friendship prospering I found myself looking her up and down and meticulously watching her every movement. When she comes to the house, the first thing she does is take off her shoes and stand on tippy-toes to give me a kiss as though I were some giant which to this day still pisses me off. Not quite as much as her complaining two nights on the trot the other week that she had ballooned out to a 22-inch waist since she'd had Sammy.

"Why, what were you before?" I'd asked.

"Twenty-one," she'd replied.

Bitch, I thought.

And when she sits down she is always smiling and gesticulating but her legs and feet are flawless and I find myself continually looking at them so much so I rag Paul like hell when he comes around. The thing that really rattled me, though was the fact that she had smaller feet than me. Mine were small at a size four, but could I hell get my feet into those shoes over at the Warehouse. Yeh, I did try them on!

"What size are you, M?" I asked her.

"Three – three and a half," she'd replied.

That made me dead depressed. Even when I poisoned her and got Lee back I still wouldn't be able to have any of her shoes!

Sainsbury's were delighted that one of their staff was to be on TV, and Paul – bless him – did a great job in letting the head office know and sorted out me having time off; however, when I next got to The Warehouse there were people everywhere.

"Who are all these?" I asked Abigail.

"Writers for your show," she said.

My show. I loved those words. And when Lee came over to me and introduced me I felt like dying in his arms as I was his princess again. "I told you she was beautiful, didn't I?" he told them.

He said that in front of everyone, including some men who were about to be screen-tested for the ITV 7 sports channel, one of whom I was going to get to know a bit more than the others as Lee sacked him on the spot and had Basher from security throw him out, and when I say throw him out, I mean it.

What was to happen is that ITV 7 would have around twenty reporters at various matches, like they do on the BBC and Sky; however, whereas they had journalists, pundits or whatever, ITV 7 would not. I would say it was economics and keeping costs to a minimum, but according to Lee it was more to do with the fact that he despised ex-footballer's as pundits and a lot of journalist's who he often labelled as "Self-important".

Dave Morris or 'Moggy' rather, was one of these so-called reporters who had monikers or nicknames as opposed to their real names – I think it was more to do with relating to the grass roots audience than anything else. Moggy was extremely crude and fancied himself as a bit of a ladies' man and what was going to happen had me in a bit of shock. There were two sets of ladies' toilets on the ground floor and one on the landing for the office staff which were really, really well kitted out, and as good as any I had ever seen and which had mirrors everywhere. Lee always knew what women wanted and that being the case he made sure we got it. Moggy, however did not. He'd winked at me a few times and I'd reciprocated the gesture with a smile, however what was to come next I wasn't expecting and as I was washing my hands he came into the ladies and asked me something I'd rather not repeat before trying to lift up my skirt. I threatened to tell Lee and he called me a "stuck-up tart" whilst at the same time calling my bluff. I didn't tell Lee; I told M who immediately told Lee who went absolutely ballistic.

"You think I've never fucking sacked anyone before," he snapped as he rammed his finger in his face. "You're out, kid – Fuck off."

The security guards came up for him and Lee told Basher, "When I say throw him out, I mean it."

They did – and Me, M and Abigail watched the said CCTV footage quite a few times.

Lee then had some form of 'gather round' for the male members of ITV 7 and told them straight. "These two women are two of the people I love most in the world – please remember that – Fucking meeting over."

Me and M might have felt like princesses, but in The Warehouse Lee was bloody God.

I told Paul about it a couple of days later and he was really pissed off. Not so much with the guy doing the touching up, but of the power that Lee had and how he'd executed it.

Me and M were invited to do the ITV Sessions programme and we used one of the four stages – Stage 3 for the recordings as according to Lee and some lady he had poached from some London-based media company as studio director, who was the sister of Billy Merle – some Arsenal supporting stock car racer-cum-power lifter who Lee knew quite well, claimed it had better parabolics. Abigail was in total charge of everything that went on in The Warehouse – everything, that is apart from me and M.

"Lee says to leave you to your own devices on this," she said. "But I'm here if you want me."

Abigail was lovely, and we both immediately asked for her input, which I'm sure Lee would have known anyway.

I liked listening to music, but not the sort of rubbish that I was having to listen to that was being sent in; however, M did and some form of pattern was taking shape in that the music that we were settling on had its own unique style. When it came to music, M was on a completely different planet. She not only had some computer-like memory when it came to music, she could play loads of instruments and had a really lovely voice and one night after a sessions shot, she got on this piano-cum-synthesiser thing that one of the bands had left behind and after playing a few chords of what was The Lightning Seeds 'Sugar Coated Iceberg' – Abigail set the camera rolling and we started 'bopping' to the music, which was absolutely fantastic. Recorded for posterity or just a piss-take? Whatever it was, I totally loved doing it and when Abi asked M to play something that she knew – Wow – that was it. We started singing and dancing to Rudimental's 'Feel the Love' – and to Autocue. I felt like I was back in uni' again and it had me crying for ages when I got home. I was involved in Lee's life again – and get this – I was having fun.

As for Lee – where was he? At home, babysitting all three kids.

When we had our two he was out all hours and all I did when he got in was rag him about it. I'm not so stupid to think that he was totally at fault – he was that he couldn't keep his dick in his trousers, but I must have been a total bitch to live with at times. They were producing a film on the Winter Olympics in Canada one particular time and although it was sport – it wasn't football, and that being the case, Lee was a bit out of his depth and had to really research it and as such had been totally engrossed in it, which had me thinking he was engrossed in something else – which I now know he was not. Why? After he came clean with me on our break-up I asked him if he had been unfaithful at that particular time he told me no, and that he had been really struggling as skiing and ice skating were hardly something he knew much about. "It was just really hard, Jeanette," he had told me. "Sometimes I have to do work that I'm neither familiar with nor that I like. It's my job."

I remember restricting sex for two weeks during that time which was something that I did quite regularly and which was possibly another reason he sought it elsewhere. You have to understand, in Lee's profession there are women everywhere and the money he was earning, which I know is completely blown out of the water in comparison to what he is earning now, was a hell of a lot, and that being the case – a David Beckham lookalike – which he pretends he hates –

and in that environment would never ever struggle for attention.

After the first ITV Sessions went out it got viewers but I don't think it got as many as ITV would have liked; however, what was noted was that the tabloids had picked up on it and the *Daily Mirror* had run a two-page spread on it with both me and M mentioned in an article which was titled 'Changing the face of music – The new north London Sound'.

M was on the phone to me straightaway as her mum had alerted her to it and we were like two ecstatic teenagers screaming down the phone to each other.

The article was extremely complimentary and the next time I drove up to The Warehouse there were reporters and people everywhere, which Lee wasn't that happy with as he liked his privacy. However, he wasn't that stupid to know that the press didn't have its use and he invited them in to show them around and had both me and M making them coffee, which the men from the press must have thought was absolutely brilliant.

Two ITV sessions had gone out on air and next up was My Show and my mother rang me to tell me how proud she was. It was another thing that I cried my eyes out at, as she had never ever told me that before. Lee and a couple of students had re-written Eddie's take on Jeremy Thorpe, and the camera work on the show was unique in that it created some time-warp reminiscent of the era and which was something that was going to be a huge feature of The Warehouse. Most of it was shot in the studio with the exception of some locational shots. My job was easy – just read the Autocue – Lee and the team had done the rest. Three hours' work in front of the camera and I was a star and my mother was proud. I was happy with that, but not as much as Sainsbury's when they found out the extra traffic my newfound status was creating at their Chelsea Bridge store – suddenly they had my face everywhere.

However, what was to come next blew everything away. M's show was next up and it was live, and she told me that she was having kittens thinking about it. Fear is a strange thing, and it can knock you sick – or for six even, and on the build-up to the show she had asked me to be there with her and that meant M's mum coming down and babysitting all three kids as Lee needed to be at The Warehouse.

We knew from the big cars that were arriving and which were being picked up on CCTV over in Lee's office that we'd claimed as our own that it would be something special. There were footballers and their wives or girlfriends everywhere, and that being the case the press were on it big style. M was a bag of nerves and at one time I was sure she was going to pull out. As for Lee – he never broke sweat and just told her – Don't worry I'm right behind you and I know you'll blow them all away by just being you.

That hurt me a bit, as I thought he was showing her just a little bit too much affection in front of me.

Lee had had a make-up artist do my make-up for My Show, however M didn't and I watched her while she put on her own make-up which was a thousand times better than what I'd had applied. On the Sessions programme she looked like Mrs Everyday M – here she looked like some sixties model – and when she walked out into the huge gallery and in front of the camera I nearly died. Me on My show was utter pants in comparison and as everyone clapped her, any fear she may have had was gone. She was brilliant and I hated it. My new best friend was my ex-husband's wife and she was better than me and I was that upset I told him, "How can I compete with that?"

"You don't have to compete," he told me. "You're the mother of my kids and in my eyes you're fantastic."

"Yeh but she's more fantasticer," I said.

"Don't make things complicated Jeannete," he said. "I love you and I think you're fantastic. Please leave it at that."

The weekend's papers were on all three shows; however, the Live at The Warehouse had the bigger presence as Lee had worked a flanker in manning up the floor of the gallery. However, this was only the start.

Chapter 12

Good Morning Britain

I was summoned for a meeting with a few suits at ITV as regards Live at The Warehouse.

The programme had gone out live for its first airing and it was awesome. I'd had Sooty send over some of his Nubeon girls, and he didn't disappoint – he sent me twenty-one of them – all top-totty and the only one who outshone them was Emily.

"I can't wear that," she had said. "My mam and gran will be watching."

For as outgoing as Emily was, and she was, she always dressed – not conservative as such, more eloquent than anything, and the last thing she could ever be construed as was someone who dressed slutty.

"Wear it and I guarantee the ratings will go through the roof," I said. "Trust me."

"It's far too short," she said.

"No it isn't," I replied.

"I hate my legs."

"I fucking don't," I quipped.

She walked on to the set in the first show in a really short black-and-white sixties-type mini dress and she looked amazing. Jean Shrimpton had nothing to come. I was dead proud of her.

"Hello there, I'm Emily Janes live at The Warehouse – first up over on stage one – The Brian Jonestown Massacre with 'Hide and Seek'."

ITV had advertised it well and it kicked off with a few million viewers, however one week later after Joe Public got wind of the fact that there was a load of Premier League football players and their wives or girlfriends along with TV people as part of the audience those viewing figures doubled.

We had an eight-man camera crew hired in from ITV. I needed them just to keep track of Emily – she was everywhere. Talking with the bands, talking with the audience and dancing with everyone and everybody. It was as if she had done it all her life. It just came natural and the camera loved her.

Half way into its second airing some master-stroke occurred – totally unintentional – whereby Emily took her shoes off – and apologised to the viewers. "Sorry, me shoes are killing me," she twanged.

"Did she mean to do that?" asked one of ITV's suits.

"No, she does it all the time," I said.

Truth be known it was one of the TV moments of the decade and she spent the rest of the programme presenting it in stockinged feet. She never did find those shoes, either?

As for the programme, there was nothing wrong as regards its production or content. However, ITV wanted its host to spread herself out a bit more and help attract viewers for a few of their other programmes, especially as *The Sun* newspaper had run some daft online poll on the UK's sexiest women and my new wife had topped the frigging thing.

I explained that we were fairly private people and that being the case I told them that I'd rather pass on it.

"Have a word with her," said one of the suits.

Our Inside True Britain programme had kicked off, but ITV had severely re-branded it with the first documentary pre-penned by Eddie and presented by Jeanette – 'The story behind the Cover-Up – The Jeremy Thorpe Affair'.

It was a bit hard-hitting and if I'm honest there were a few complaints flying around, especially as we made it look a bit like the car crash in which his wife died smarted of foul play. It wasn't, but the way the story that got put over made you sort of think that.

Whereas Emily's programme was fun and vibrant Jeanette's was not, but that's not to say that my ex didn't enjoy it – she did. Live at The Warehouse took three and a half hours to film, whereas Jeanette's show could take a couple of days – especially as some of it was shot on location.

I had a bit more pressure forced on me by the suits and it was then I said that Emily would do it – which I knew she would have anyway.

"Of course I'll do it," she said.

"I think you like all this attention," I told her.

"I definitely do," she replied.

I explained it was only a spot on Good Morning Britain with questions about The Warehouse, clothes, holidays etc.; however, what was going to happen I certainly never foresaw. Well I would have if I'd thought about it a bit, but I got side-tracked as at the time she was in the studios I was having yet another meeting with the head of sports and a few other suits as regards ITV 7.

Halfway through the meeting ITV's director general came in with a great shit-eating grin on his kisser and explained that my new wife had just told three point two million viewers exactly who she was – well, more who I was, really.

"Emily Janes – The readers from *The Sun* newspaper voted the UK's sexiest woman," stated the presenter. "How does someone react to that?"

I didn't know much about it as I didn't read the papers – Sky Sports, Sky News and whatever was hanging around in Tony the Barber's was about my whack, however it was quite a big topic of conversation behind my back.

"It was really nice," Emily had said, rather underplaying it as I knew she had been absolutely ecstatic at all the attention and trying to get her head through the door along with her ego had been a task in itself.

The presenter then went on to ask her about the Thursday Night Live at The Warehouse programme she had been hosting and how she had become involved in it. It was then when I had been mentioned, which was bad enough; however, when the presenter asked her about the Jeanette Janes – who had been presenting the rebranded Inside True Britain programme and part-presenting the ITV Sessions music programme at the weekend along with her, did the shit truly hit the fan.

"So, are you related to Jeanette?" asked the presenter.

"No she's my husband's ex-wife," said Emily, in an air of innocence. "Although she is godparent to our baby."

"And your husband? This is the man behind the new ITV Seven sports channel and all three of these programmes?" asked the presenter.

Emily smiled. "He's the most wonderful man in the world," she said. "And the most beautiful."

"What the hell did you go and say that for?" I asked on seeing her.

"Well they asked me," she said sort of matter-of-fact before giving me a Scouse twang. "I aren't lying to them."

From then on, my life would become an absolute hell.

Every lousy paper and magazine wanted to interview me – or us rather, and take lots of photos. ITV however, thought it was great.

"This is not what I'm about, M," I said. "I don't want the bullshit of all this."

She just didn't understand it.

"Yeh, but yer great," she twanged.

I managed to sit her down, but she was on coiled springs, so much so she was making Mr. Zebedee look like Dylan the frigging rabbit.

"I know it's exciting for you," I said. "But we are real people."

The fact that 'I'm a Celebrity' and 'Big Brother' had tried sounding her out had literally blown her mind.

"They are demeaning, love," I said. "They are piss-take programmes for washed-up TV stars and wannabes – And you are neither."

I managed to talk her around but as soon as the media got wind of the offers and Emily had told them of why she didn't want to go down that route the thing snowballed and suddenly she was the most talked-about woman in the UK. The No. 1 woman – The ultimate girl next door. I couldn't believe it. I'd created a monster. Still it was a rather good-looking one who kept telling me she loved me loads – so I couldn't really fault that.

All I had asked her to do on set was look cute and sexy, introduce a few bands and talk to the crowd – and now this.

I got in from work one day to some reporter and photographer from *OK magazine* with Emily done up like a kipper and chatting away over a few coffees. I thought I'd walked into the wrong house!

"Oh hello love," she said before introducing me to the two people.

"Your wife's lovely," said the reporter.

"Yeh – I know – that's why I married her," I said.

And then they wanted photographs of me with Emily.

"Please ….." asked Emily, whilst giving me a peck.

I argued my case, but she was very persuasive and suddenly she was making me take off my tie and ruffling up my hair – oh yeh – and we had to have misery guts as part of the portfolio who wasted no time in advertising his sheer discontent for us.

"Her mum says he's just like M was when she was a kid," I said. "Dead miserable."

"It's true," added Emily. "My mam said that I was horrible and that she was thinking about having me adopted."

The photographer was laughing his head off, thinking that she was joking or something.

"Do you see your parents much?" asked the reporter.

"I talk to them every day," she replied.

"They are really nice people," I added.

"And they love Lee so much," Emily said, whilst smiling over at me.

It was then that my wife had some strange urge to give them a bit of backgrounding.

"I wish you'd stop being so frigging honest," I told her afterwards.

OK magazine was published and there we were. Five glossy pages of bullshit with Mrs Gorgeous and Mr. Dickhead along with baby Sammy who looked like a more sinister version of one of the ugly Lollipop Guild munchkins out of the Wizard of Oz.

"Doesn't he look cute?" said Emily on seeing Sammy.

"Are you looking at a different photo to me?" I asked.

"Don't be awful," she said. "He looks lovely."

"He certainly won't get kidnapped, that's for sure."

Within minutes it was all over Birkenhead and we had her mum on the phone – Some reporter from the *Liverpool Echo* had called around asking a few questions and wanted to interview her and Mike – but not before the kids Granny Sil' showed him both our wedding and Sammy's christening photographs and had told them anything and everything about us.

I couldn't make it up. I didn't even live in Liverpool but they were calling me one of their own, which was something that was made very clear when we all jumped in M's Mean Machine and drove up to Birkenhead early Saturday morning to pick up the keys for Hamilton Square.

Sil' had mentioned us buying a house to the reporter and the bloke was there waiting for us as we pulled up outside their house. The reporter was a really nice kid and like most Scousers he talked very fast, and from what I could make out he was extremely interested in ITV 7. He did probe me on another subject as well.

"What do you reckon has gone wrong at Liverpool?" he asked me.

"Luis Suarez leaving," I told him.

"Yeah but we were hardly a one-man team," he said.

"If Arsenal would have had Suarez they would have won the league," I said. "That's how good he is."

"Dad, why do people keep on wanting to talk to you and M?" asked my lad, as he tugged at my jacket.

"It's because of the stuff we are doing on TV," I replied.

"Why, are you famous?" he asked, which was something that quite tickled his Granny Sil'.

"No son, we are just normal people," I told him.

"Mrs Peters said you must be loaded," he said. "And that you and M must be creaming it."

"Who – the Mrs Peters who's your teacher?"

He gave me a nod.

"Maybe Mrs Peters ought to keep her opinions to herself," I said. "She shouldn't really be saying things like that."

"Jeanette said that she's a right nosy so and so," whispered Emily.

"She sounds it," I said.

We got inside and I spoke to the reporter at length; however, Sil' was on tenterhooks and wanted to go and see inside the house over at Hamilton Square. I could certainly see where Emily got her Zap from.

"Go take your mum round to the house, M," I said.

"What – without you?" she asked.

She was always making sure that everything was okay with me before she did either x, y or z – which was strange because as soon as a camera was thrust in front of her all she wanted to do was spew out loads of x, y's and z's along with other stuff that definitely wasn't okay with me. It was a weird one that.

"Go take your mum round," I nodded.

Sil' had grown up around The Wirral and Hamilton Square was The Wirral's version of Belgrave Square. And this wasn't our main house – It was a weekend house and I knew that she wanted everyone she knew to see it, as to her family and friends we had suddenly become more real than ever.

Emily wasted no time at all in scooting her mum and kids around to the house – minus misery guts – as he wanted feeding, and Mike ended up doing the honours.

The house was brilliant and my kids wasted no time in choosing their bedrooms – the two on the very top floor; however, there was a bit of an argument as they both wanted the bedroom with a view of the River Mersey and the Liver Building.

"Dad, where will Giroud and Arteta sleep?" asked my daughter.

"What, the real ones or the ferrets?" I asked.

"The ferrets, silly," she said.

Mmm. I'd not thought about that. This was a house that definitely didn't have any room or garden area for a pair of carnivorous rodents.

"We can build them a ferret hutch at ours or your Granddad Bill's," exclaimed Mike. "They're part of the family as well, so you can't go leaving them in London!"

That surprised me a bit as Mike was scared to death of them.

"Our Stuart and Luce will make sure they are looked after," he added.

Mmm. Now that bit didn't surprise me. I loved the way Mike delegated jobs – he had been the same on The Warehouse conversion. He was all 'You do this, you do that and you can do the other while I get on with this'. He never screamed and shouted and he always listened to anything worth listening to.

"Will you build it, Granddad?" asked my lad.

"We can both do it," he said.

That put a bit of a lump in my throat when he said that and for the life of me I had no idea why.

"Can it have an upstairs?" asked my lad.

"It can have a few upstairs," replied Mike. "Just like this house."

Later than night, whilst we were on *our* settee in the front room Emily mentioned that her dad had never been as happy and proud, which was something that was backed up by Sil' in between arguing the toss with young Lucy regarding who was going to feed the remarkably placid goo-gooing and coy-coying and not-so-horrible Herbert.

"He's really coming on," said Sil'.

"It's all those chocolate puddings Lee keeps secretly feeding him," said Emily.

"I don't feed him that many," I argued.

"I bought him seven or eight on Monday and they were all gone on Thursday."

"It's probably you who's eating them," I said. "You make me eat salads and stuff and I found about a dozen Marathon wrappers rammed in the tray on the driver's side door of the Range Rover this morning."

"Shurrup you," she twanged.

"What's a Marathon?" asked Lucy.

"A Snicker bar," I winked. "She treats that car like a skip."

Since we'd had Sammy it was a case of him in with Mike and Sil', me and M on the sofa, my kids – who were currently M.I.A over at Bill and Edie's – in with Luce, with Stu the only one who wasn't put out.

"Where is Stuart?" I was just about to ask, however the front door opened and in he walked with some young girl. I glanced at their Emily who returned it with a shrug of her shoulders.

"It's his friend, Paige," whispered Lucy.

I looked over at Stuart and gave him a shrug and I got a very red and embarrassed face looking back over at me. "Come on Stu," I said. "Introduce the girl to us."

"It's Paige," he mumbled. "She wanted to meet our M."

"Hello love," Emily smiled. "I'm M and this is my husband Lee."

"Our Lee is running that new football channel for ITV," said Stuart who was certainly more interested in being my PR manager than his sisters. "He produces that programme my sister is in."

"I saw you in OK magazine," said Paige looking at Emily. "Everyone thinks you're great."

A huge smile lit up Emily's face.

She loved the attention. It was only the other day that we were shopping in Asda over in Southgate that we ended up with a small entourage following her around the store. I thought I'd got a tear in the arse of my trousers but it turned out they were just interested in what toothpaste and hair conditioner she used – and then she spent around twenty minutes incessantly nattering to them while I had to contend with Rosemary's Baby who had decided that now would be a good time to have a shit.

I loved Sunday mornings at Mike and Sil's as there was always a proper breakfast and it was one which we always ate together – either some fry up or poached eggs on toast. I picked up the salt shaker and Emily made sure she gave me a nudge and took it off me. "I like salt," I told her.

"It's bad for you," she'd say.

"M, stop bullying the lad," her mum would always say.

I loved the way the mum and daughter bounced off each other.

"She was a pretty thing," I told Stuart, as regards the friend he had brought over the night before.

Their Lucy sniggered whilst Stuart just went bright red – again.

"Dad, will I have a girlfriend like our Stuart when I get big?" asked my lad.

"I would think so," I said.

"I think I'll have loads of girlfriends like you," he added, whilst tearing away at his bacon.

That got me one hell of a grin from my wife and a look of some disdain from my father-in-law.

"Why, how many girlfriends has your dad got?" winked Emily.

"Just you and mum," he replied, still chomping at his bacon. "Oh and my Granny Sil'."

"I didn't know I was your dad's girlfriend," said my mother-in-law.

"He kisses you and he always tells us how much he loves you," said my lad. "Doesn't he, M?"

"Aw that's so nice," said Emily giving him a cuddle.

Sil' might have added to that if she hadn't had a great lump in her throat.

Having the house in Birkenhead was going to be a big, big thing and I was duly informed exactly that by my wife whilst I was looking over the plans with Mike of "Wouldn't it be wonderful to spend Christmas up here?"

I couldn't think of a better place, but in my experience it was always better to walk before you can run.

"If my dad can do a massive warehouse conversion in a few weeks – he'll easily be able to do our house," she added.

She did have a point and I gave her a wink.

"I just love our life so much," she smiled.

Her dad then glanced me a smile that I could have framed.

Her life was only going to get better as I found out, when Faranha told me a couple of days later that there was some guy on the phone wanting my wife.

"Tell me that again," I said.

"He mentioned underwear," said Faranha.

It turned out to be an interesting conversation. My first thought was that he was some frigging idiot, but on speaking at length with him he was anything but.

"I'll mention it to her and I'll get back to you," I told the guy.

Not only had I been working on my Arsenal documentary, I had been drafting up part of this complex Sheffield Wednesday documentary, whilst Abi had been talking at length and at volume with one of the teams writing up a documentary – The Black Eyed Child – The Ghost of

Cannock Chase as part of the rebranded Inside True Britain series.

"What's the matter?" I asked.

"They don't like the subject matter," said Abi. "They reckon it's bullshit."

The writing team was made up of three female students from Birbeck and a male student from Goldsmiths. This particular subject along with the documentary – The Piper at the Gates of Dawn – The untold story of Syd Barrett, were the two which no-one really wanted.

I had just scrawled down a few subjects and let them get on with it, which to some could I suppose, sound pretty amateurish, but that is how I worked. I listened to the team on what they had to say and they had a point, however I couldn't appear to look weak and nor could I look to undermine Abi.

"When you get tasked with a job," I told them, "You do it as best as you can. I've made hundreds of programmes I thought were of a poor subject matter, but I did them – and look where I am now."

They never said a great deal.

"We often have to do things we don't like doing," I added. "Just do your best."

Young people can come across as angry and bolshy and these were no different.

I worked through lunch and nipped over to the Coffee Shop where I met up with Emily who was yacking with some old dear in the street, with misery guts sat in his buggy glancing around for something to complain about.

"Who was she?" I asked.

"She lives next door but one to that young couple on the street who keep on parking their cars outside our house," she replied. "She says that they are always arguing."

"Like you do with me?" I lied.

"What have we got to argue about?" she smiled as she tried to ram the buggy through the door of the coffee shop, which set Herbert off grizzling until he copped sight of Fosis, and then he strangely started coy-coying and smiling.

"I reckon we should both grow a moustache," said Emily.

"I'll definitely argue with you if you do," I said as I ordered an espresso for me and a latte for M.

"Does baby want anything?" asked Fosis.

"Apart from a personality transplant, I can't think of anything offhand," I told him.

We sat down and it was then I mentioned the phone call to Emily and asked if she minded taking her clothes off.

"What, in here?" she smiled.

"You're just being daft now," I told her.

I then went on to explain that Gossard would like her to model for them.

"You'll get loads of free underwear and fifty grand a year," I told her.

"We've got plenty of money," she said. "Anyway, I'm too old to model."

"You're only thirty-two," I said. "Well, that's what you told me anyway."

"Yeh – and that's too old," she said.

"You don't look old," I said.

She gave me a smile, but it wasn't something she felt easy about doing and told me so.

"He said he could get you in with Wonderbra as well," I informed her.

"I hate my body," she lied.

"I frigging don't," I said.

That put a smile on her face, and she duly booked me in for an appointment at 7:01pm. "Rule number one and rule number one," she smiled. "As soon as I get shut of my six o'clock class."

Well, that was something to look forward to, I thought.

"What should I tell 'The Man from Del-Monte' then?" I asked.

"And it's fifty-thousand pounds?" she replied.

"Loads of free underwear as well," I said, trying to further flog her the concept.

"Let me think about it," she smiled.

I certainly didn't need to try and think about it – It was continually on my mind until 7:01pm when I knew the pervert photographer would sling his model on the couch for a bit of rape and pillage, with hopefully more of the former than the latter, however the fact that Dick Turpin was running around the house with a mask and a pistol when I got in, I had to say put a bit of a dampener on those proceedings.

"Who is he?" I asked on watching the young masked reprobate telling his imaginary friend to 'Stand and Deliver' in some eastern European accent before shooting him to death.

"It's the son of that young couple across the road."

"Yeh – so, what's he doing here?" I asked.

"The child minder brought him home – his parents aren't in yet and she asked if he could stay here."

I thought nothing of it, and I let him play with the ferrets for a bit while I had some tea and did a bit of work. Exactly two hours later we knew something wasn't right and I went across the street and banged on their door for a bit and got no answer. The strange thing was that both their cars were parked up – one of which was outside our house – again.

"I don't like this M," I said. "Something's not right."

I rang a few numbers to see if anyone really knew these people and drew a blank. It was then I phoned the police and within half an hour I got a female bobby and her male counterpart at my door.

"The kid's fine here," I said. "I'm just concerned as to the whereabouts of his parents."

The two coppers had a look around the house across and copped a nosy through the letterbox and did a bit of shoulder shrugging. I left them to it, but the kid – Andrej they called him – was looking a bit worn-out so I brought him a quilt down and let him sleep on the sofa.

At around half past twelve there was a big police presence on the street – what I'd initially thought was just a neighbour doing a neighbourly thing in watching over a child until his mother and father got in, was anything but. Sometimes in life things are never that straightforward.

"Do you know them?" asked a detective.

"Not really," I said. "I've bollocked him once or twice for parking in my spot but apart from that, we've never spoke."

Emily was in a similar mind-set and told them so.

It transpired that there were two unnamed bodies in the property – one murdered, the other a suicide, or that's how tomorrows *London Evening Standard* would report it. As for the lad – young Dick Turpin – he was taken from us and we never saw him again.

Chapter 13

Mr Liverpool

"I don't like her, her, her nor her," said Emily.

"Why?" I asked.

"Because they're all good-looking," she said.

"You're not jealous are you?"

"Yeh – definitely," she replied. "I don't want you dumping me for any of them."

There was no way on earth that I was having any ugly women on ITV 7, and I told her so.

"Why can't me and Jeanette do it?" she asked.

"Because it will be hard work and cover a subject that neither of you particularly like."

"I like football," she argued.

"No, you don't," I said. "You moaned like heck when Arsenal were playing Anderlecht."

"No I did not – I moaned because you woke Sammy up shouting at the TV when the other team scored."

Mmm. That game was a bit intense, I thought.

"It took me ages to get him back off to sleep because they kept on scoring," she added.

"Okay – point taken," I said trying to end that particular subject.

"It's weird how the team just collapsed like it did," she said. "They threw away a three goal lead and undid all of Sanchez's brilliant work in what has become a familiar story of their season. Alexis is on another level yet Arsenal's defending was suicidal."

"That's not you saying that," I said.

"Yeh it is," she lied.

"No it's not," I said as I made a grab for her and pulled her over to the couch and gave her an Indian Burn. "Tell me that you're fibbing."

"Not fibbing," she lied whilst trying to struggle to get away from me and bullshit me further with a bit of 'robot speak'. "I know loads about Arsenal. I listen to what you say and you're brilliant."

"Rubbish – I've never said anything like that."

"No it was just my totally astute observation," she smiled whilst adding a further bucket of bullshit to her summation. "They can complain that Anthony Vanden Borre's first goal for Anderlecht was miles offside but that still does not fully excuse the way they threw it away in the end."

"That's definitely not you saying that," I said.

"It is," she lied.

It took me two more Indian Burns and the promise of a night out including a curry across from King's Cross station before she finally admitted that she was parrot-quoting John Cross of the *Daily Mirror*.

"I do love you, yer know," she said.

I knew she did and I picked up Sammy out of his chair who seemed fairly excited at seeing his mum cop a few twists to her wrists and said to him, "Isn't mum sneaky and underhanded?"

"Don't say that to him – he'll believe you," said Emily.

"You're dead right – he will," I said. "I tell him all the bad stuff about you when you're not here."

I did. He was always mesmerised. Especially about the bit her being a more miserable baby than he was and about his Granny Sil' secretly leaving her outside shops hoping someone would take her.

Looking at her now, she possessed the appearance of someone who butter wouldn't melt in her mouth with her lovely blonde hair and those big blue eyes.

She watched me as I did a bit on my Parallels documentary – Arsenal's failed 1958/59 and 1972/73 seasons, in between making me some tea and calling up her mum and gran, the latter of who wanted to know what I wanted for Christmas.

"All the family together on Christmas day," I winked.

"Wasn't that such a sweet thing to say," Emily told her gran after repeating what I'd said.

There was a few Yes's and No's floating about during the conversation, which due to their vagueness I had no idea as regards them being any particular answer to any particular question.

Bill and Edie tended to do their own thing, and I admired them for that, but I knew that both Sil' and Emily would love it if we all had Christmas together – especially dinner, but that was their shout and certainly not mine.

There was another feature of this Christmas, which would soon become apparent. Last year Jeanette and I were – estranged – if that is the correct word – and there was a huge resentment which bordered on hate towards me. I would be the first to admit that it was totally justified and that being the case I had a crap Christmas, as the two things most precious to me were kept from me. Things were that bad. Meeting Emily had been the turning point and she worked hard not just to keep me together, but to keep my family together, whilst unbeknown to me at the time – I had done a similar job with hers. Jeanette was wary of Emily at first, but not now. Emily loved Jeanette, not just as a friend but as a family member. There were a few unwritten rules that had to be adhered – one of which was that we had to keep the so-called history lessons away from the table, therefore mine and Jeanette's past life was a no-go area. We did have some great times together – but regardless of this, that and the other – It had to be kept in the past.

Jeanette played her hand a few times. I don't know whether it was just to rattle me or piss off Emily. Me having to run about after her if there was something wrong with either the house or kids and having to pay her huge amounts of child support, were a few things that a lesser woman could have baulked and kicked off at; however, Emily didn't and over a period of time these became less and less.

M asking Jeanette to be Sammy's godparent was a master-stroke in itself, not just the asking bit, but how and why it was asked.

"I want him to grow up with his brother and sister," she had said.

To Sammy, Jeanette was now Auntie Jeanette, and that being the case a few barriers came down and Jeanette watched over Sammy as Emily did with mine and her kids. Not a day went by when there wasn't a phone call or text between the two. And they were regularly on Skype, Face time or whatever through their laptops and talking at length – not that I was ever privy to sensitive parts of their conversation, as that was another unwritten rule.

Emily had sold me the concept of the Christmas of all Christmases and it was us that were going to have it. It was a good few weeks away but I couldn't wait. Even my lad was carrying around an Argos catalogue in his bag of tricks which he scrupulously studied well into the evening whilst cross-legged on the sofa.

"Dad can I have a train set?" he'd ask.

"Write it down and put it on your list to Father Christmas," I'd tell him.

"What about a Scalextric?"

"Write it down and put it on your list to Father Christmas."

"What about a bike?"

"Write it down and put it on your list to Father Christmas."

"What about a drum kit?"

"Certainly not," I told him.

Jeanette had told me that she and Paul were buying him a bike, and as that was the case – could I not buy him one or give him a present that would in any way usurp it?

"Sure, I'll do whatever you want," I'd said.

That was always an award-winning answer, but she knew that I'd renege on it as I spoiled them both rotten.

Whatever was around the corner, I was looking forward to it. Life was great; however, for Jeanette, something was going to hit her and it was something totally unexpected.

A three-man team from London University Goldsmiths had been liaising with Eddie on a two-part documentary for the Inside True Britain series – An All Exhuming Love – Fred and Rose West and the content was highly graphic, so much so it had rattled her.

"I can't do it Lee," she had said.

"Yeh you can," I had told her.

"It's absolutely horrible," she had said.

I knew exactly how horrible it was as we had nipped into the ITN Archives and got some fantastic footage and had spoken with reporters and authors that had covered the case and some of is content could cause you to vomit.

"Do you trust me?" I had asked her.

"What?" she had replied.

"Do you trust me?"

"Seeing as though you were shagging around behind my back with over twenty different women during the time we were married – no – not really," she had said.

"I'll rephrase that," I had told her. "Would you think I would do anything to hurt you?"

"Again – Seeing as though you were shagging around behind my back with over twenty different women during the time we were married – Yeh."

"Well, trust me this time then," I said. "I think if this programme is done properly it will pick up an award and it'll be you up there collecting it."

The fact that the script had been written the way it had was a bit ground-breaking in that ITV would be getting plenty of complaints – especially as we tried to put over a reason or some reasoning behind what had happened and not just paint them as a pair of sick and sadistic paedo's.

"It's really well-written," I had told her. "Trust me."

On watching it all Emily could say was "Wow" before getting straight on the phone to Jeanette. "You were brilliant Jin," she had said. "That's got to be up there with the best."

That wasn't an understatement. Me and Abi had worked on the editing and me asking or demanding rather, for Jeanette to wear a red dress whilst walking down the dismally-lit Cromwell Street in Bristol, a scene which we had shot in monochrome but had colourised the dress looked nothing short of brilliant. The series never got the rave reviews through the mainstream tabloids like Emily did with Live at the Warehouse but all the same it didn't go unnoticed and after turning Good Morning Britain down on three occasions she finally gave them an okay. ITV advertised the programme heavily with its main guest being Jeanette Janes – the TV presenter who never gives interviews.

She went on the show around 8:00am looking very Audrey Hepburn and listened and only spoke when spoken to – firstly it was polite chit-chat about the show and then bang! It was about her relationship with Emily and of course her relationship with me.

"M – You couldn't meet a nicer person," she said. "And you have to see her baby – he is such beautiful little boy."

"Is that our kid she's on about or do you have another one?" I asked, whilst chomping away at my toast.

"Shurrup you," twanged Emily whilst glued to the TV set.

"We talk most days," continued Jeanette. "Especially on a weekend when the children stay over."

"Now I'm going to ask a question about your former relationship with her husband and producer of your programme, Lee Janes," said the presenter. "How do you get on?"

"Emily is the one that makes it all work," she said.

I could see my wife's eyes welling up as she watched on.

"Lee is all over the place and an extremely talented individual," she said.

I quite liked that bit, I thought. *I could always do 'talented individual'.*

"I don't think ITV realise who they've got."

Wow, I thought.

"When we were together, I couldn't keep his interest," she added.

Well she could have if she wouldn't have nagged and bitched so much, I thought.

"I can be a bit of a bossy cow and I know at times I must have been hell to live with."

See?

"M is the exact opposite – I suppose that's why it works with them," she shrugged.

"So do you get on with your ex-husband?" asked the presenter.

Jeanette nodded a "Yes", however the presenter invited more dialogue by not following it up.

"If I'm honest it broke my heart when he remarried," she said. "And then he broke my heart and Emily's when he turned down what was a huge opportunity in New York because he didn't want to split the family up. I think M would tell you the same."

"So he's a good father?" asked the presenter.

"He's as daft as a brush with the kids," she said. "But I think that comes from his relationship with his mother; however, that's for him to tell you, and certainly not me."

"So you get on with him?" probed the presenter.

"Yeh – he's a good friend," she said, before adding a barbed comment. "Now, that is."

There was quite a bit of laughing between them before more polite chit-chat ensued.

"She definitely has to have told her something before she went on set," I said.

I got in work to a stack of hate mail, which had been redirected to us from ITV – as regards The Fred West Show, which according to Abi was how the fucking thing was being dubbed in *The Sun.*

"Nobody actually takes notice of anything that's written in it," I said.

"They actually state that it was a brilliantly executed documentary," added Abi.

"I take it back then," I said.

"What's the matter with you, anyway?" Abi asked.

I then told her about my ex-wife being on The Michael Parkinson Show for bored housewives and the unemployed – or unemployable, rather.

"She was on Good Morning Britain?" asked Abi. "She never said anything."

A grunt was all I could muster up.

"I can't believe how popular you are," exclaimed Abi. "You're in the news every day."

Tell me about it, I thought.

"ITV are on the phone," shouted Faranha. "Which room do you want to take it in?"

"The pink room," I said.

"We don't have any pink room," she replied.

"He means his office," grinned Abi.

I did – It was where Emily and Jeanette hung out and drunk pots of coffee and where the walls were covered with drawings done by my kids and the draws of my desk were full of nappies, sudocream and Cow and Gate puddings and the like, along with a bottle warmer and sterilising kit which furnished the top of it. I was just surprised there was any room for a laptop.

It appeared ITV were well impressed with what we were doing even though I could sense that there was a touch of laughter at the other end of the phone with "What's the matter?" being my obvious question. It appeared that the director general was finding it highly amusing that my private life was being aired over the station and was being discussed by everyone and everybody – that and the fact that he knew that I hated it.

"Well you're going to love this," said the suit at the other end of the phone. "They want you to be a pundit for the Wolfsburg versus Everton game."

"A pundit?"

"Yeh – You've done it before," he said.

"When?"

"For NBC," he said.

Mmm. I was hoping that they would have forgotten about that, I thought.

"Which studio is that being done in?" I asked.

"It's not – They want you over in Wolfsburg."

I might have heard of Wolfsburg – but I certainly didn't know where it was.

"You fly into Hannover," Emily told me later on in the coffee shop, whilst wrestling with the screaming machine – who wanted his bottle even though he'd drunk the thing bone dry.

"You can't have it," she told him as she prized it out of his mitts. "It's all gone."

He wasn't having any and he kicked off like a good 'un – that was until Fosis graced us with his presence and passed us two drinks. Then he shut up.

"I find it strange that every time he cops him," I said with reference to Fosis, "that he stops whining."

"It is a bit weird," admitted Emily.

Unfortunately as soon as Fosis went back to the counter he started grizzling again. That was until his mum whipped open some blueberry flavoured porridge.

"That sounds nice M," I said.

"It might sound nice – It certainly doesn't taste nice," she replied.

Herbert seemed to like it though, and he scoffed the lot. And then threw it up as he'd eaten it too fast.

"So, do you fancy coming?"

"Where?" she asked.

"Wolfsburg."

"Yeh, sure," she smiled.

However there was a problem – The game was a Europa League match – which meant a Thursday night – and a clash with her Live at The Warehouse show.

"This Warehouse show is starting to get on my tits," I said. "All our life has to revolve around it."

"Let Jeanette do The Warehouse for the night and I'll do one of her programmes," said Emily.

She made things sound so simple – even though it would possibly mean a million more questions about my relationship with my ex-wife.

"Will you have a word with her?" I said.

"Sure," she said, whilst slinging Herbert over to me.

Jeanette was apparently ecstatic at the chance to 'be Emily'; however, Abi wasn't so sure.

"She's not as bubbly and vibrant as M," she said.

That was true. Nobody was as bubbly and vibrant as Emily.

"She'll probably make everyone sit down and be quiet," Les added.

"Come on," I argued. "She isn't as bad as that."

"Yeh – she is," said Les. "She bollocked me for not sitting up straight and for slurping at my coffee."

"That is annoying, though," said Abi.

I totally agreed with her – Yes it was.

"So which of Jeanette's programmes are up next?" I asked.

"The Piper at the Gates of Dawn – The untold story of Syd Barrett," said Abi. "The one that no-one wanted."

"It's well-written though," said Les.

"What, you've read it?" I asked.

Les nodded. "And with your missus doing it, I reckon it will go down really well."

I trusted Les immensely when it came to copy and content. I wouldn't trust him behind the wheel of my car – or with my wallet – or with my wife come to that, but I trusted him on copy. He was a great writer and researcher.

When I got home I let her know the subject matter and I got one hell of a scream and a hug.

"My dad will love it," she said.

And she phoned him, and while she did my phone rang.

"How did you get this number?" I asked.

I listened to what the caller had to say amidst Emily bouncing around and talking to her dad and then her mum and then her dad again.

"Keep your dad on the phone M," I said, as I acknowledged the caller. "Tell him I've got Bill Kenwright on the phone – Do your dad and granddad want to fly out to Germany with him to watch Everton?"

"Who's Bill Kenwright?" inquired my wife.

"Just ask him, M?"

I heard her ask her dad and then saw her smile over at me and her eyes well up. "Yes please, he says."

I thanked Bill for his phone call and looked over at my wife still talking on the phone – mostly about her doing a programme on Pink Floyd – her dad's favourite band – and the man who penned the song that she herself was named after.

My phone was red hot some ten minutes later – firstly from her dad and then her granddad, the latter of who was extremely honoured as Bill Kenwright was the chairman of Everton F.C and Mr. Liverpool himself.

"All I know is that he asked me to ask you," I said. "He'll have you picked up and flown out with him."

"So you didn't ask him?" asked Bill.

"I've never spoken to him before," I replied.

"Then how does he know us?"

I truly didn't know, however the gossip that went on in and around ITV's sewing circle may have had some bearing on it.

I dumped Herbert off with Jeanette early the very next day and began piecing together the documentary; however, before we could introduce Emily into it, we had to wait for her and Faranha to get in – along with ten bags of shopping.

And then we had to wait another hour for her to put some 'slap' on.

"Okay, I'm ready," she said.

"Wow," said Abi. "You look great."

She did.

"I wanted to look Miss Sixties," she said.

"You look like Felicity Shagwell," said Abi.

"Who?" I asked.

"Heather Graham played her in Austin Powers," she replied.

I would have to check that one out when I got home, I thought.

I let them get on with it whilst I sought out some footage of the bloke the documentary was about – and I was surprised at how much there was and I knew then and there just how good this would be.

I took a call off Jeanette who explained that Sammy was being as 'good as gold' and did I mind if she took him up to her mums?

They can keep him if they like, I thought.

"Sure," I said.

It was strange how much her mum despised me yet she seemed to always be asking about me and M and wanting to see misery guts. I was going to ask Jeanette about this, but I thought otherwise, although I did quite often skirt around the subject.

"Mum says 'Hi'," Jeanette would tell me.

"Really?" I would reply.

"She loves Sammy – she says he looks just like you."

"Then why does she love him, then? She hates my guts."

Credit where credit is due, Jeanette never actually said that she did or that she didn't – but what narked me was the way he always goo-gooed and coy-coyed whenever he saw her yet when he saw me and M it was though he were being handed back to Fred and Rose West and he screamed the place down.

"Maybe we just look really ugly to him," Emily once said.

"I'd have to be as ugly as Peter Beardsley if his screaming is anything to go by," I'd replied.

"Who does he think I look like then?" she had asked.

"Roy Shiner," I'd said.

"Who's he?" Emily asked.

"Some really scary-looking ex-Sheffield Wednesday player from the fifties – Stick a sledgehammer in his mitts and he'd look extremely intimidating,"

"Really?"

"He had a really massive chin," I'd said.

"What – like that Jimmy Hill?"

"Bigger," I'd confirmed.

"Wow that is scary," she had said.

I checked in on Felicity Shagwell reading the auto-cue and yacking into the camera and on her seeing me she waved and told me how much she was enjoying it and then took a bollocking off Abi as it had to go for a re-shoot.

"Ooops. Sorry, Abi," she said.

Seeing as Jeanette had had Sammy all day I was saddled with my two plus Sooty and Libby's two brats for the evening – and totally noticed all their overnight bags and baggage.

"We're going out for a meal," Jeanette said. "I volunteered for you to have Zooey and Mia."

"Well, I'm glad that's sorted then," I replied.

There was nothing like a house full of kids to kick off a quiet night in, especially as having the kids over meant having the ferrets in the house – and a ginger cat.

"Where the heck did that come from?" I asked, as I rescued it from being savaged by Giroud and Arteta.

"We found it," said Zooey.

"Really? Where?"

"It was in the backyard," she replied, whilst at the same time nodding her head – albeit rather unconvincingly.

This seemed a rather tall tale as I'd certainly not seen it before and it was only after Emily's investigative approach did we get to the bottom of it.

"Where did you really get it from?" asked M. "We'll not be cross."

Mmm. She might not be cross, but I would. She'd lifted the cat from the back yard alright – the back yard of some house down Holland Park and had it in her satchel and now we were lumbered with it.

"What's it called?" I asked, as it meowed to be fed even more as Emily gave it my Mortadella ham that I'd been saving to have with a glass of Chardonnay during supposed quiet night in.

"Billy Bremner," said Zooey.

"That's interesting," I replied as I lifted it up by the tail and totally noticed that it was minus a set of balls and meowed falsetto. "Are you sure it's not a girl cat?"

"Dad can we have a cat?" asked my lad.

"Definitely not," I said.

"We could call it Sanchez," he added.

Mmm. That was a thought, I thought; however, I wasn't that behind the door that I'd let myself get soft-soaped by my soon-to-be six year-old.

"That's a good name," I admitted.

"So can we have a cat?" he asked.

"Definitely not," I said.

"Can we have a dog, then?" he asked. "We can call that Sanchez."

"I wish you'd stop requesting pets," I said, suddenly noticing that Sammy's baby chair was minus a baby. "And where's Hissing Sid?"

"Harmony and Mia have kidnapped him," Emily smiled.

They had – again. I walked into my daughter's bedroom with my lad hard on my heels and still requesting pets, to find that he'd been dressed up like Widow Twanky. The thing was – he loved it.

"He's going to end up growing up like Frank Maloney," I told her as I picked him up and took off a daft wedding hat and frock she'd just put him on.

"Who's Frank Maloney, dad?" asked my lad.

145

"He's a man with a bald head that looks a bit like Gary Speed's mum and who likes dressing up like your Granny Sil'," I said.

"Like mum's Uncle Melvin?" he asked.

"A bit, but not quite," I replied. "Your Uncle Melvin liked dressing up even when he had hair."

"Dad's going to buy us a dog," stated my lad.

"No – dad definitely isn't," I said as I rescued Misery Guts from his hell – not that he appreciated it as I was sure he told me to "Get stuffed" a couple of times. Well, if he didn't, the expression on his chops certainly gave the impression he had.

Emily knocked us all up some tea – including frigging Billy Bremner – who was now wolfing down a tin of red salmon.

"If you keep on feeding it like that, we'll never get shut of the thing," I said before looking over at Sooty's brats. "Anyway, I thought Billy Bremner was your dad's nutter dog's name?"

"No, that's Speedy Reaney," said Zooey. "Mum went crackers when he killed John Hawley and Ray Hankin."

"John Hawley and Ray Hankin?" smiled Emily.

"They were the canaries that Terry Neill was duped into buying," I said. "Probably the worst pairing since Peters and Lee."

"What – Martin Peters and Francis Lee?" Emily asked.

"No, them who sung 'Welcome Home, come on in and shut the door'."

"Oh *the* Peters and Lee," she smiled. "Did you know someone threw a brick threw his car window and blinded him?"

"Jesus – they must have been bad," I said whilst at the same time getting handed my customary salad and lump of chicken, whilst the kids ripped into cherry pie and ice cream.

"Where did that little lot come from?" I asked.

She was very evasive in answering the question as I hadn't seen any cherry pie in the fridge, and believe me I had looked. She was getting to be more deflective than Sooty. In fact I thought I would ruin the latter's night therefore I dropped him a text to let him know that their cat was at our house.

"We haven't got a cat," he messaged back.

"You have now," I told him. "A girl cat called Billy Bremner."

"I told her to leave the frigging thing alone," he messaged back.

"Where are U anyway?" I text.

"Berners Tavern – Having Halibut," he replied.

I looked outside and noticed it was pissing down – therefore I secretly rang up the restaurant and told them that I was from the crime section of *London Evening Standard* and asked them if they knew that there was a certain Mr. Sutton who was dining there as part of a foursome who were ripping off city centre restaurants with false credit cards and just to be on the safe side I had pre- reported both his HSBC Mastercard and American Express card as being stolen. I was initially going to call in a bomb scare however the last time I did that there was an explosion about three streets away at more or less the same time and I ended up having to sling my phone in the river.

"I don't suppose by any chance you've phoned the restaurant up?" a rather irate Sooty asked exactly fourteen minutes later. "I'm piss wet through trying to flag a taxi down because the owner as kicked us out."

"No," I lied. "How was the meal?"

"I never got to eat the thing – We just got asked to leave before they phoned the police."

I deflected the interrogation by mentioning the cat twice and telling him that his kids had eaten my cherry pie that M's gran had packed me up at the weekend. "Oh yeh and your Zooey's got nits."

That last bit had Libby straight on the phone.

"Don't worry Lib – Emily's just shaving her head as we speak," I lied.

Jeanette had reassured them that I was in fact only kidding but did secretly text me to ask if I'd cancelled Sooty's credit cards.

"Would I do a thing like that?" I text back.

"Most definitely x," she replied, further adding two smiley faces.

I managed to get them all tucked up in bed by nine and then had to tell them a load of stories for another hour before I managed to get downstairs to find Emily curled up on the settee stroking the pussy. Don't get too excited – It was the stray one that I ended up slinging out.

"Aw it's raining," said Emily.

"It's only been here two minutes and it's eaten my ham, a two and half quid tin of salmon, a bowl of ice cream and it's now having its chin rubbed by Felicity Shagwell," I said. "I think it's had a decent return."

"I love having all the children around, don't you?" she smiled.

I did. I enjoyed it a lot and I told her so.

Chapter 14

Measuring the love

Jeanette dropped both kids off at the house amid wailing coming from their younger brother who Emily, by the look of it, was trying to force-feed.

"Wouldn't it just be easier to feed him with a catapult?" I asked.

"I'm sure that would impress him," she laughed.

"Dad, how big are you?" asked my lad as he emptied his bag of tricks all over floor before finding out a ruler. "I told Mrs Peters you were about two hundred and fifty and she said that you wasn't – I told her that she doesn't even know you and then she shouted at me and called me stupid."

"Back track a bit," I said taking Sammy off Emily and firing him in his baby seat, whilst he continually tried to boot me before going rigid at the thought of being restrained. "The Mrs Peters, who's your teacher?"

He nodded before telling me that she smells a bit.

"What – nice-smelling like M and your mum or rank like your mum's Uncle Melvin."

That got his brain ticking a bit.

"I told her you were two hundred and fifty and she said I was being stupid," he reiterated.

"Two hundred and fifty?" I asked.

"Yeh," he replied.

"Well two hundred and fifty inches would make me about ….."

"Nearly twenty-one feet tall," said Emily.

"No, I'm definitely not that tall," I said. "That's like a giant."

"No, centimetres or summat," he said.

"Summat?" I corrected him. "It's something, not summat – Uncle Sooty may say summat, but we say something."

"Even two hundred and fifty centimetres makes you just over eight feet tall," explained Emily. "You're still definitely not that tall."

"So even though she stinks like your Uncle Melvin and called you stupid – she was right about me not being two hundred and fifty whatever it was."

"She might have meant millimetres," said my daughter.

"I doubt that," smiled Emily. "That'd make your dad less than one foot tall. That's smaller than a dwarf."

"Please don't mention dwarves, M," I said.

"Sorry love," she chuckled.

"We have to measure everyone in our house and write it down," stated my son. "And the TV and some other stuff."

"What other stuff?" I asked.

He shrugged his shoulders.

"Well, M is about five foot and I'm six foot," I said. "I think?"

"No we have to measure with the ruler," said my son.

"We'll be here all night measuring with that thing," I told him, and I therefore went and sought out a tape measure and had Emily up against the wall – to be measured that is.

"Five foot one and a bit," I said.

"We have to do it in centimetres," he said.

"Okay then – M is one hundred and fifty eight centimetres high – Get it written down," I said before pretending to bollock Emily. "And you, stop standing on your tiptoes – you've just grown two inches."

Emily took hold of the tape and measured me at 6'05.

"One hundred and eighty four and a half," she smiled.

"How big is the telly?" asked my lad as he scrawled it into his book.

"The one in here is about seventy-two – the new one in the kitchen about forty-eight and yours upstairs are thirty-six."

"What, centimetres?" inquired my lad.

"No, inches."

"Mrs Peters wants us to do it in centimetres," he exclaimed.

"She sounds a right bossy old cow this Mrs Peters – I'm sick of her already."

Emily suggested having both Giroud and Arteta get their measurements.

"What, for a suit?" I asked.

"Don't be daft," she twanged.

We spent a good hour measuring things – including the pair of foot-long rodents – one of who decided to get stuck beneath the washing machine, which pleased Sammy a bit as he started laughing – possibly because my other two did after I got my arm stuck.

"Dad, can we go to Marrakesh again?" asked my daughter.

"Ask M – she's in charge of booking holidays – maybe she fancies somewhere else?"

Emily smiled at the idea and it was suggested that we get all the photographs out – and that's what happened. There was something about looking back at photos that sometimes put a lump in my throat – possibly that's to do with the fact that I never took enough photographs when my two kids were younger. Emily had a camera and made sure that there was at least one billion photos to look back on. With me it was the odd snapshot on my phone – laziness, one could suppose.

"We should take more photographs," I said, as I looked on at the pictures of my kids and our Lucy dive bombing into the pool and at the smiles that had continually lit up their faces.

"There's one of you here, M," said my daughter.

"My god I was fat, wasn't I?" she said – sort of fishing for me to state otherwise.

"Yeh – massive," I replied. "But still dead good-looking."

That got me a bit of a wink and a smile.

Emily and my daughter went out around seven o'clock to meet the train from Lime Street station as Lucy was coming down, whilst me, my lad and the little bundle of misery sat on the sofa and watched some old Pink Panther cartoons on DVD.

The girls came in around forty minutes later armed to the teeth with half a dozen Pizza's with my lad remonstrating that his must not in any way shape or form have any mushrooms on it and more to the point – had M brought him any chocolate because he was literally withering away to nothing?

Friday nights were always great. Well, they were since Emily had been living here. I think she tried to recreate a bit of her childhood and she liked it when we were all together at the end of the working week vegging-out, eating take-out and watching TV.

Before I met her, Friday to me was like any other day of the week, but not now. Fridays were great and so would Christmas be – or so I was told by Emily. As a kid she had loved it, but in the years whilst she had been previously married she had missed out on it – or so she had told me.

"He didn't like me being near my family, and they didn't like him," she had said one night while she was sat cross-legged on the bed talking to me. "I should have known it was all wrong."

She went on to explain about the Christmases that had been spoilt and opportunities that had been missed.

"I've not had a proper, proper Christmas since I was sixteen," she had said.

"Well, things change," I'd told her. "You're in total charge of this one – so if you bollocks it up it's all your fault."

That made her laugh and she told me how much she loved me, but that was nothing new. As I've already said I got told it every day and on numerous occasions throughout the day. Sometimes I caught her in thought – quiet moments when she was pondering, so much so it was a case of snapping her out of it. Although she had a gregarious and loving nature, was both bubbly and dead good fun to be around, there was a lot that I knew that she wasn't telling me. She was great at keeping gossip from me, which meant that she only told me what she thought I needed know.

"I just love being with you," I was always told.

Her mum was the same with me and she always told everybody and everyone how much her daughter loved me and how great everything was, and it wasn't until early the next day when I got a text message from Jeanette that I realised that the woman I adored was carrying a lot of extra weight on those tiny shoulders.

"Can I see u? X" it read.

"Sure – Coffee shop ok? X" I replied.

"Plz – worried – 20mins ok?"

I text through an affirmative and put on my overcoat and told Emily that I was just nipping out.

"It's not like you to go out without a shower," she smiled, as she buttered the kids some pikelets. "Is everything okay?"

"Sure," I said.

Fosis, decked out in a white shirt unbuttoned to the naval, appeared very pleased to see me as I entered his premises and he furnished me with an espresso, whilst at the same time offering me a bacon sandwich.

"I could definitely do one of those," I said.

Jeanette followed me in and came straight over to the table.

"So what's the matter?" I asked, whilst at the same time summoning Fosis to bring her over a coffee.

"I'm worried about M," she said.

I gave a shrug of my shoulders to ask, "Why?"

"Her ex-husband has been talking to some freelance' who says he does copy for *The Sun*, the *Evening Standard* and the *Metro*."

"What about it?" I asked.

"He's been haranguing her over her mobile and has even been to your house," she explained.

"Who – the ex-husband or the reporter?" I asked.

"The reporter, you twit," she replied.

"She's not said anything."

"M wouldn't want to saddle you with this, Lee – You know she wouldn't, but she's really upset about it."

Emily's profile had gone through the roof since she had been on TV and the offers she had received from magazines and such had been unbelievable; however, that was just sassy feminine bullshit stuff – this I was going to find out, was downright dirty and spiteful.

"Her husband's given him photos and everything," Jeanette said. "I spent Thursday afternoon with her and she was really upset."

"Photos – what kind of photos?"

"I'm not sure," she replied.

"Anyway, what can he say that I don't already know?" I asked.

"She just doesn't want to ruin everything she has with you," said Jeanette. "She really does love you, you know."

I nodded and thanked her for the heads-up.

"So does this joker have a name?" I asked.

He did – and she gave me his name, phone number, address, the make and colour of his car along the registration plate which was nailed to its bumper.

"He's on Linkedin as well," she said.

"Jesus – what are you – some undercover cop?" I asked, looking at the scrawl on the piece of paper.

"Please don't tell M I told you," she said. "We talk a lot and I would hate to think that she couldn't trust me."

Jeanette had slung a right fucking monkey on my back and as I walked home I went through the various permeations – ignore it, tell him to back off or even pay him off – or better still ask Andreas and Turkish George to arrange for him to be part of the concrete sections on the proposed Hammersmith Fly-under.

I certainly had loads of options, however they were all rubbish.

"Are you okay, love?" asked a concerned Emily after I got back in.

"Sure," I lied.

She looked at me and knew there and then that there was something untoward.

"Come and sit with me," I said.

And she did – sitting at the side of me on the sofa and looking very concerned.

"You do know I love you?" I asked.

I got a nod, but I could see her bottom lip was wobbling a bit.

"And you know that part when we got married when the guy who married us sort of said 'For better or worse' and all that?"

I got a nod.

"Well, I really did mean it," I said.

"I'm so, so sorry, Lee," she said, before breaking down crying, which didn't go unnoticed by all the kids – including their Lucy.

"What's up with our M?" she asked.

"Nothing that can't be sorted," I said, whilst giving her a hug.

I asked Lucy to keep an eye on Sammy who she was currently being fed with some lousy apple concoction, whilst I went upstairs with her big sister.

"He's being really, really horrible," she said as regards the reporter. "He won't leave me alone."

Her ex-husband hated me like no other. I wasn't that stupid to know that the hate he possessed for me wasn't undeserved. I had not only taken his wife from him – I had helped break up everything he had worked for and as part of both mine and his ex-wife's actions he was now living in some rented flat near Maze Hill Tube station. Emily, on the other hand was being well-provided for and anything that she wanted was there if she wanted it. She sat on the toilet seat as I took a shower and she told me a few things – some of which she had told me before and some which she had not. It was hardly stuff that would drive a man insane but to an insecure or jealous guy the facts as part of the conversation would have possibly been very hard to handle, and to be honest they didn't sit with me all that well either, but it was what it was.

"And this is all true?" I asked as I dried myself off.

She nodded and then put her head down. "I'm so, so sorry."

She told me a bit more as I got dressed and I left the house whilst at the same time telling her not to worry. If I was being honest I didn't have a clue what to do – I just made it look like I did. I sought Sooty out down at the offices of Nubeon Entertainment who I wished I hadn't – but that was another story for another day and I found myself back in the coffee shop.

It was the journalists' intention to offer the story to *The Sun* for a huge fee as I knew from knowing part of its content, that it would create a huge interest to its readers. I didn't assume that – he actually met me in the coffee shop and told me this to my face.

"And you know this is my wife you are talking about?" I told him.

The guy was a right leeching bastard and there was nothing I could say that would change his mind; however, he certainly wasn't averse to hearing what Emily had to say about it.

"There is no fucking way that I am subjecting my wife to the likes of you," I told him. "And you attempt to contact her again and you will wish you hadn't."

That put him on his back foot a bit and more so when I called one of the briefs who worked for the corporate law firm that had handled the selling of the business and the purchase of The Warehouse and Hamilton Square – all of which surprisingly went like a dream.

The lawyer told me that it was out of his remit of works but he had a friend – a barrister – who was a member of his circle of friends who, according to him "was very well up on this kind of thing".

I immediately rang the number he gave me and explained to the barrister at the other end of the phone who I was before I furnished him with the edited highlights of the shit sandwich that we were about to be served – coupled with the fact that he had been hassling my wife of course.

Whilst I was in conversation the reporter rarely broke his stance and just sipped at his cup of tea.

"Is this person actually there with you?" asked the barrister.

"Yeh, sat right across from me," I replied.

"Well, put him on the phone."

Within seconds I heard the voice on the phone direct a tirade of complex legal language at him which quoted both notes and subsections of law along with powerful threats of counteraction not just through the High Court in the Royal Courts of Justice over in The Strand but by a certain high ranking policeman he knew within the Metropolitan Police, who would make sure that no newspaper would ever touch him again.

"You move to hurt these people and I will make it my life's ambition to end your folly," I heard him say. "And I assure you that it will be I myself that will drive the stake through your heart."

The reporter looked absolutely petrified as the barrister asked to be passed back to me.

"Now just be calm and give his details to me slowly over the phone," the barrister said to me. "I will ask you what you will assume are a lot of silly questions but I guarantee that it will rattle him – especially if you don't panic."

The guy was awesome.

He made me tell him the reporter's name and went back and forth on its spelling and he even asked me to confirm his date of birth along with the make and model of his car – and by the time all these details had been supposedly taken down, the barrister asked me to ask him – should the police contact him through the offices of the newspaper that supposedly employed him or at his home address in Ilford? – which the barrister must have found out himself while I was talking to him – and he even had me have the reporter confirm this to him including its postcode.

It was a blur. I had bullshitted my way through thousands of meetings but this guy was shit-hot.

"Now just keep seated, look him in his face and tell him to fuck off and I'll do the rest," said the barrister.

I did – and get this – he left. I couldn't believe it.

The barrister phoned me back ten minutes later and assured me that he would put some form of Interlocutory injunction in place and have some burly legal agent banging him up at the crack of dawn Monday morning to make sure he was aware of the writ as well as getting the police to serve him with a verbal restraining order and an indication that we will sue.

"It's basically a show of power," he said. "It should be enough."

I asked him what I owed him and he told me a £1,500 cash payment should cover it and that his daughter would be most grateful if I could post out four tickets for her to get into The Warehouse one night.

I couldn't thank him enough and I informed him that the money plus the tickets would be delivered forthwith.

On getting home and telling Emily about the meeting, the phone call, the forthcoming injunction and the restraining order, I received the hug of all hugs and it took me quite a bit for her to de-cling herself from around me.

It had taken up a Saturday morning and part of the afternoon, but there was no way I wanted any of my family hurt and when I told her this I had more emotion thrust on me.

"We are really good for each other, aren't we?" she said wiping her eyes.

"Well I certainly think so," I said.

That evening, as the rain battered down, Emily watched on as both Lucy and my daughter bathed face ache in the massive bath, whilst my lad and I sat downstairs in the room watching Sky Sports as the results came in.

"Are you going to work for Sky, dad?" asked my lad.

"No, ITV."

"Is that what mum and M goes on?"

"Yes," I told him.

"Does Uncle Sooty work for ITV?" he asked.

"No, Uncle Sooty makes films."

There was a short silence whilst some pondering from my lad took place, so much so I could hear the cogs in his head turning.

"Auntie Lib told mum that her and Uncle Sooty have been arguing a lot," he said.

"All grown-ups argue," I told him.

"Do you and M argue?"

"No – M is a bit special."

"What, like mum's Uncle Melvin?"

"Certainly not – Your mum's Uncle Melvin just likes wearing women's clothes."

"Do you and mum argue?" he asked.

"No – your mum talks and I just have to listen – a bit like it is with you and your sister," I smiled. "Nobody ever argues with your mum."

Emily brought Sammy downstairs and let my daughter feed him. He looked fairly pleasant until he threw up all over his new pyjamas and then he went ape shit as the bottle had to be taken away from him as his mum cleaned him up.

"Did I cry like that?" asked my lad.

"No, Granny Sil' says that he takes after M," I said. "She told me she used to leave her outside shops in her pram hoping that somebody would steal her – but they kept on bringing her back."

"That's not true at all," smiled Emily. "Your dad's kidding."

"See – M never argues or moans," I said to my lad. "It's why we all love her so much."

"Auntie Libby said Uncle Sooty was a dirty old 'prevert' and that he has been showing Auntie Libby up," stated my lad in a quite matter-of-fact kind of way.

"I've never heard of anyone being called a 'prevert', before," I laughed. "Have you M?"

"Not offhand," she smiled, as she gave misery guts back to my daughter who subsequently rammed the bottle into his chops.

Lucy picked up on this and immediately put it right. "I think he means pervert," she said.

"What's one of them?" asked my lad.

"It's a bit like a 'prevert' but it's spelt properly," I told him.

It was a pretty good answer as he shut up for half an hour – perhaps so he could try and work it out, but before he did Emily cracked open a box of Celebrations from out of the cupboard and he forgot all about it, however Emily hadn't and passed a few whispered comments over to me, that had come courtesy of Jeanette.

"I thought you never disclosed conversations between you and Jeanette?" I said.

"You've been really special today," she said, "So, you deserve it."

"Does that mean that you are special like M, dad – or special like mum's Uncle Melvin?" asked my son.

"Definitely not like your mum's Uncle Melvin," I replied. That night we watched a couple of films before I put my kids to bed, and then Lucy retired holding a DVD of The Texas Chainsaw Massacre at the request of her big sister, who subsequently gave me a huge hug and seeing as we were on our own she asked, "Did I fancy being a bit of 'prevert'?"

I could always do being a 'prevert', and I certainly wasted no time in telling her so, especially if she was going to play the helpless 'vrigin'.

"I can definitely do one of those," she smiled.

Chapter 15

Jeanette's Tales – Take 6

I'd never seen M upset before but she was. She had also never seen me upset, but that was soon to change; however, I'll not get ahead of myself, but one thing you need to know was that the 20th of November was never my favourite day, therefore I'll immediately apologise for the way I may come over.

My life had been one big blur from the first night the Sessions programme had actually kicked off. I had started working up at The Warehouse on Monday's and Tuesdays and, strangely the odd weekend when Lee and M had the kids. My show was strange in that it was shot in bits and pieces as opposed to all at once, and if I'm honest at first it was a bit hard to get my head around. Abigail certainly appeared to know what she was doing, though! As for me I seemed to be doing nothing but thinking about the goings on up there and every time I managed the drive up there I noticed that things were continually changing. Suddenly the place was buzzing with other people and Les Crang and the ITV 7 team were not only working apart from the rest of us but working really long hours and had suddenly been supplemented by some bird on a bike.

"Who the hell's she?" I asked Faranha.

"Kirsty Burns – She's going to be one of the presenters for some of the shows that form a bulk of the football channel," she said.

That surprised me as she dressed a bit dikey and wore jackboots and glasses and I knew that anything that didn't actually resemble a woman would never ever really be taken serious by my ex-husband.

"Abigail told me that she had been severely screen-tested and that Lee saw something truly good in her," said Faranha.

"What – really?" I asked.

As a bit of shit-stirring exercise I was going to let M know via text that we had some competition, however I didn't. In fact, there was getting to be a lot more bloody competition as not only had he now employed some hard-faced accounts manager who looked like Rosamund Pike that he'd given the title of finance director, he had two girls working from a small office at the end of the corridor handling the LMJ website and PR and I hated them as soon as I saw them, as they both had dresses up their backsides, with the blonde haired one in particular wearing one with literally no back in it.

"How old are they?" I asked.

I was told that Sasha was 27 and Georgia was 18 and therefore I was a bit narked, more so with the fact Lee was over with the ITV 7 crowd working on the editing of this massive documentary they were doing on Sheffield Wednesday's and hadn't even acknowledged me when I'd got in. He should have done really as this day played a big part in both our make-up; however, he didn't. He had then gone over to his office with the Rosamund Pike lookalike and the door was shut behind them. It was driving me bats and all these new girls were doing my head in, and none more than the new receptionist he'd just set on as Faranha had now been promoted to the role of PA to the assistant producer, which was of course Abigail and was swanning around in a short dress and a pair of heels. I made it my life's mission to be here more, and to find out about each and every one of them, but the strangest thing was that M was totally unfazed by it all. I just didn't get her at times. Her lack of envy when it came to potential competition from other women – or girls rather – was unbelievable. Me? I was chewing flipping glass.

It took exactly three hours and six minutes for my ex-husband to finally acknowledge me as he brought me over a coffee and asked me to follow him into what I was to become to know as 'Annie's office'. "This is our new finance director, Annie Dixon who will be doing the billings, chasing the payments and of course handling all the wages," he said as he pulled me a chair.

Mmm. I definitely didn't like the look of her, I thought before she reluctantly held out her hand for me to shake it.

Lee then carefully explained how the company worked, telling me that there had been an initial misunderstanding with ITV, but which had now been sorted, and which gave him what he termed as "Far, far more flexibility".

ITV 7 was a completely separate entity whereby they billed ITV on a solely manpower-plus basis, and LMJ billed ITV weekly for the three shows, that both M and myself presented.

I'd had always wondered how it worked and although me and M spoke regularly, I never really got around to asking the question, and what I wasn't to know until that moment was just how much money they were actually making.

"What?" I asked aghast.

It was a lot. No it was a hell of a lot, and after getting over the initial shock he gave me another one in that an American cable channel wanted to run with My Show, and it could be that there was a marketing angle whereby thousands of DVD's would be produced.

"I'm taking on some marketing executives to push it," he said, "And we need to tie you to a contract."

"Why?" was my obvious question.

"It will be better for you and better for us," he said.

 "Is M getting a contract?" I inquired.

He nodded.

Then I definitely want one then, I thought.

He then asked me to sign a few pieces of paper and passed me a cheque – for £50,000 and informed me that I would now be paid accordingly for both the Sessions and My Show – £5,000 and £5,000 respectively – and per week. I had gone into The Warehouse a right miserable cow and had come out of an office at lunchtime in a blur.

"Before you leave to pick up the kids," Lee had said, "Come and talk to me."

He remembered; however, in the haze that was to come I forgot that he'd said that. I shouldn't have really but my head was a blur as I got taken down to a temporary works studio within the downstairs gallery to read Autocue and then came back to a load of missed phone calls and a text from M.

I rang her and it was then she had mentioned that she was being hassled by someone who she had initially surmised was partly to do with her husband. I had never seen her husband – not even a photograph, so all I could go by was from the description of him by M.

"He was a big bully," she had told me one afternoon over at my house just before she and Lee had married. "I wanted out as soon as I got in but I'd burned my bridges with my mam and dad and that being the case I was his possession – a prisoner – as everything I had certainly wasn't in London – he had made me pack in a job that I loved and had to work freelance for some company over the internet – which meant me working from home – basically so he could see what I was doing. His firm getting a contract in Germany and meeting Lee changed everything."

I certainly didn't want to know the last bit but I had it told me anyway.

Since I'd known M she'd had a few problems, which were all ex-husband related and certainly not Lee related and the latter did what he considered was the best to sort it, a lot of which I didn't really know the intricate details of, although believe me when I say it – I probed!

I'm ashamed to say that I didn't see Lee before I left The Warehouse and that my newfound wealth also took

165

precedence over M as I did a bit of banking and picked up the kids before the reality of the situation hit home. I was being a totally selfish bitch, with my initial thought as I drove over the North Circular being what comes around goes around. She had Lee, so why can't he have the bollocks that goes with her?

"Can we go see M and our Sammy?" Harmony asked, on me picking her up from school.

That was when it hit home. Both my kids absolutely adored her.

When I'd been accosted in the ladies restroom up at The Warehouse, M was the first person I'd turned to and she had known exactly what to do. She was in trouble and I was her first port of call. Her husband was both my children's father and he had just given me more money than I had ever earned in my life and prior to that, his new wife had invited me further into their life by letting me be baby Sammy's auntie. I drove home from school ashamed with myself. My head was all over the place. I know the date was at the back of my mind but why were my feelings so bitter towards her as when she saw me, hers were anything but? We always got on fine and were the best of friends, so what the bloody hell was up with me? M had done nothing wrong.

I pulled up behind her car and the front door to their house was immediately opened as she gave both my kids a cuddle as they ran up to her – certainly never showing any self-pity.

"Did you get your contract?" she smiled.

I nodded a "Yes" and she gave me an excited hug and appeared really pleased for me.

We spoke about the Sessions programme and My Show whilst the kids ran upstairs, but not hers. She was a person who always thought about the other person first. She always did, and I felt an utter bitch on not asking her as regards her problem. She was with Lee and Lee loved her. He loved me, but not like he loved her. He loved her like he once loved me, and today it hurt more than any other day.

When I had first moved in with him we had flown out to Bangladesh from Heathrow on a whim, and a whim was exactly what it was. Yusef never ever backed down to anyone – apart from his mother and father that is, and he had been summoned over to be part of an arranged marriage five days earlier. I had put my posh frock and stilettos on and packed loads of nice clothes thinking that it would be a great experience. Lee treated me back then like just like he treats M now and was always great fun to be around. I was as upset as hell when they had gone to Marrakesh but when we had boarded the plane to Bangladesh nine or so years earlier I was a completely different person. I was elated and Lee telling me he loved me back then was a million times better than when he told it me now. Telling me back then could be supplemented with kisses and cuddles and certainly not just pecks on the cheek. Telling me back then could involve a lot of things that it doesn't now. M got that kind of love – I did not. Now I had Paul and Paul wasn't Lee.

Who goes to Bangladesh for four days? Who packs their best clothes including four-inch heels to be driven out in the middle of the jungle and have everyone looking at them like Clem? We did – I did.

"I feel a bit overdressed," I'd told him, and that was only whilst he was arguing the toss with the security guard about him allegedly flouting the laws of Islam by us drinking a white wine in the airport in Qatar. "What are you on about you pillock? I've just bought it from here," he had said.

Me? I was threatened with immediate deportation if I dared to sip another drop or indeed cross my legs again.

I clung onto his every word and when I linked him I felt really special – like M does now.

Everyone was looking at us as we boarded onto another flight onto Dakar and on our arrival you had never seen anything like it. There were around forty people waiting for us with Yusef and his brothers making sure that we were treated like royalty. I always felt like that when I was with Lee. M must feel like that now, but I certainly don't.

I looked over at Mrs 33-21-33 smiling over at me. Today I hated that smile as much as I hated the fact that she drove around in that big black Range Rover wearing those five hundred pound sunglasses that she always wears with her beautiful baby in the back. She was always pleased to see me, but today it pissed me off. The strange thing was that I really, really liked her.

"I've been a bitch with you, M and I'm sorry," I told her.

"Why?" she asked shrugging her shoulders.

"I should have been here for you and I wasn't," I said.

"Yeh, but you're here now," she replied.

I was, but that was mainly to do with both my kids demands topped up by my guilt.

What she preceded to tell me wasn't nice but underneath the surface I loved it. Today I loved it. The little blonde-haired Barbie doll that had posed in *OK magazine* with my Lee and who'd been voted the UK's No 1 sexiest woman by the press was now being hounded by one of them.

Tough shit, I thought.

"I don't want to hurt Lee," she told me.

Again – Tough shit, I thought.

When she had arrived on the scene, she came with only the clothes that she had on her back, a couple of carrier bags of stuff and a four year-old car. She may have looked like Betty bloody Cooper out of those *Archie* comics with the blonde 'bob' hair, but she didn't now. On moving in with Lee, she'd changed. She'd let her hair grow longer, had around twenty wardrobes full of clothes and had started dressing – well, not too dissimilar to me really, which was another thing that really pissed me off.

However the emotion she showed me this particular day reminded me of when she spoke to me around the time of New York. "You and the children are my ace card," she had said. "I'm really banking on you, Jeanette."

Yeh right. She never wanted to go and live in New York with Lee. I would have. I would have lived with Lee in New York, but I never got asked. I never got asked anything like that as it was always me who had to do the asking. I wanted Southgate – he gave it me. I wanted Clerkenwell – he gave it me. I wanted marriage – he gave it me. I wanted babies – he gave them me. However, what was never touched upon is that we also had another baby when we were in Muswell Hill but it died after fourteen days. If you want to see real hurt, well it's not some hack from the press digging up meaningless things from the past. When your love is all-consuming and you've been given something so precious just to have it taken away, that is real hurt. Maybe if he had survived, things would have been different between us, however he didn't. And watching the smallest coffin ever being laid to rest with part of you inside it was the worst feeling ever, as was watching the man who I loved so much and who was larger than life itself, break down crying only to be consoled by his dad's mum as his own couldn't be bothered to come. That was utterly heart-breaking.

Visiting Bangladesh was quite something else; however, it came at a cost. I had caught malaria and our first child died because of it. And whilst M sat there both clueless and shoeless I apologised again and came clean and told her how I was feeling. I was just glad the kids were upstairs in their bedrooms as we both cried ours eyes out.

"I didn't know that," she said.

"I think about it every day, M," I cried. "But especially today."

It was true. I resented the fact that he seemed to get over it and move on but I felt guilty. It was me who didn't take the tablets as they made me feel ill, so it was me who caught malaria. I hated the fact that I felt he blamed me, not as though he ever did.

"I drove him away M and I look at you and you just seem to know exactly what to do," I told her.

"That's not true," she said shaking her head. "We make mistakes when we are younger and I was no different and just recently they seem to be catching up with me."

"He loves you so much," I told her.

"And I love him," she replied. "And I also love you and the children."

I thought I couldn't cry anymore but I did. We both did.

I thought I'd turned a corner by getting it off my chest, but I hadn't. I had swept lots of things under the carpet but this wasn't one of them. Today coupled with M having both Sammy and Lee had brought it all back more than ever and it had all been boiling up inside of me from the minute I awoke.

I had presented a documentary that I didn't particularly like doing and it was Lee who had sat me down and given me the confidence to do it, and it was that good that I'd just been heavily rewarded. Lee didn't steal, he gave, and in my mind I had just been horrible to his wife. She couldn't see it as it was in my head – but it was there all the same. I make myself sound like a moody, insecure bitch, I know, but every now and again it really, really hurts.

I managed to pull myself around and do the right thing and I let Lee know what was happening as I knew just how much he loved her. As for me, straight after telling him that Saturday morning, I drove up Dartmouth Park Hill to Highgate cemetery to lay down some flowers.

The gravestone was exactly how I remembered it. 'Our baby. Lee Michael Janes born 6th November 2004, died aged 14 days. Dearly missed by his Mummy and Daddy.'

The irony was that there was already some fresh flowers there and I know that it wasn't my mother and dad who had been as they were in France, therefore I assumed it was M as it certainly wasn't Lee. "Your mum and dad always think about you and both really miss you," the accompanying card read.

LMJ? Lee had no middle name, however our baby had my dad's. Lee hadn't forgotten – he might pretend he forgets but he doesn't. Lee never forgets.

Chapter 16

The Curse of The Owls

All last week had been strange as had yesterday, and today was only going to get even stranger. Yesterday I'd had to interview some fleet-footed make-up artist called Chris Windley who was more interested in what my suit and shirt covered than the actual job he had applied for only to come home to be questioned over something that happened years ago and for a second time in a week – which if I was being brutally honest, was something I didn't like talking about, however Emily being Emily told me that I should talk about it.

"M – I love you but it was a long time ago," I said as she sat on the floor trying her best to look concerned. "I try to put it behind me."

Jeanette had told her about something that we had shared and then lost, and it wasn't something that I wanted to look back on. I wasn't someone that needed psychotherapy, I just filed things in my head under 'Things that I didn't want to talk about' and it had served me well thus far.

"You told me about your dad," she said.

"With my dad it was different," I said. "At least my dad had had a thirty-year shot at life."

Emily was loving and caring, and she wouldn't rest until she'd had me confirm the story, so much so she got that upset, it upset me. I'd say it upset Sammy, but what else was new. He had been boo-hooing like some ghost under a bedsheet from the moment he had realised that daybreak was only three hours away.

"If he wakes up any earlier he'll be getting up before he goes to bed," I told his mum.

On the ITV 7 side we were running with a few things, one of which was this Sheffield Wednesday documentary that had initially started out as The 1964 Betting Scandal but which had blossomed into what was a massive six-part documentary. It was looking extremely good; however, the downside of the documentary was that Sheffield Wednesday were no Arsenal, and that being the case the available film footage was a lot less. In fact it was a lot, lot less.

"Why don't we do a documentary on Wilf Copping?" Les had once asked. "He seems an interesting player."

"No problem," I'd told him, "that is if you can tell me how we can do it and how we can put him over."

Although there is some surviving film of thirties football it is certainly not the quality that would captivate a TV audience outside the die-hard Arsenal supporter, and even then it would be a struggle.

I mean, who wants some 100-year old bloke talking about his memories against some photographic backdrop of Charles Charlie Charles along with some rubbish clips and jolly good old commentary from British Pathé . I'd once packed up a few biographies for a holiday with Jeanette a few years ago, one of which was Eddie Hapgood's. As good a player as he may have been in his time – and I'm sure he was, he must have been the most boring man on the planet to pen that. I slung it after thirty pages.

"It's why we concentrate on the nineteen-fifties upwards," I told him.

As part of this six-part Sheffield Wednesday documentary we had come across several fantastic players which were part of the team during what has been described by supporters of the club as one of the greatest periods in their history.

They were a bit of a yoyo club throughout the 1950's but on winning the second division title in 1958/59 – one of my

Parallel seasons, they came 5th, 2nd and 6th for three seasons before coming 8th and a lowly 17th but going all the way to the 1966 FA Cup final after playing all their games away from Hillsborough and going 2-0 up in the final against their former manager's team – Harry Catterick's Everton, who, as history will tell you ended up turning the match around and winning 3-2. Watch for the next Everton – Sheffield Wednesday connection!

What is rarely stated is that if the team hadn't drawn as many matches in the 1960/61 season they could have very well stopped Tottenham Hotspur from completing the first modern-day Double.

There was also another player that interested me – Tony Coleman, the ex-Manchester City player that was shown the door after helping them win the League title and FA Cup in 1967/68 and 1969, respectively and who joined the soon-to-be relegated Sheffield Wednesday the following season, which was the start of the South Yorkshire club free-falling towards the bottom of the old Third Division. Coleman also played with Doncaster Rovers – a team who he helped win the Fourth Division on goal average in 1965/66, and who had the notoriety of being one of the few players to actually punch a referee. This was during a 3-0 home defeat on 6th May, 1966 against Notts County – the team Rovers pipped to the Fourth Division title.

During this game his side were frustrated by a number of questionable decisions awarded against them by Stockport-referee Jack Pickles, with a number of them serving to frustrate the home side's talented left-sided midfielder. Coleman had fallen victim to a number of cynical fouls that continually went unchecked by the referee and his frustration was beginning to grow as each moment ticked by. His mood was clearly not helped by his side's performance, as with a quarter of an hour to go Rovers were three goals down and it was at this point that Notts County winger Tony Flower 'went straight through' Coleman which again went unpunished by Pickles, and which proved the straw that broke the camel's back. Coleman stood up, the ball long since having gone, and booted the visiting midfielder in the midriff and left him lying poleaxed on the turf. Pickles immediately gave Coleman his marching orders; however, after setting off walking to the dressing room, he stopped and turned around and walked back to Pickles and did no more than smack him in the mouth, with players from both sides needing to separate the two. Coleman eventually left the field – strangely receiving the backing of his chairman. There was an inquiry and it was accepted that the referee had actually swore at Coleman as he left the pitch and this prompted his about turn and as a result, football's governing bodies adopted a lenient approach to his punishment, handing him only a six-week ban.

Whilst I was researching information for the Arsenal 'Parallels' programme I dropped on an interesting piece – also about a referee getting punched, however this incident was much more bizarre. On 1st October, 1958 York City played an away game against a Crewe Alexandra side, which included Mansfield-born left winger Alan Daley, who possessed a nickname that I was rather strangely going to get more familiar with over the next few weeks. 'Digger' Daley was the first man to be sent off under the F.A's new Code of Conduct, for questioning a decision by the official in charge who during the game had been haunted by a phantom whistler amongst the 8,350 crowd at Gresty Road, who to the amusement of them had been continually holding up play. Not only did he upset the home support by sending off Daley he also stopped play and sent a policeman into the crowd to confiscate the child's whistle. After the game, which York ended up winning 4-2, he was attacked and punched by a fan as he left the field under police escort. That referee? None other than Jack Pickles!

Daley joined Coventry City one month later and helped them to promotion from the Fourth Division, whilst Pickles was in an out of the news throughout the era, with incidents such as a contentious sending's off, dubious penalties awarded and even more dubious goals getting disallowed and on more than one occasion he had to have a police escort off the field of play. There's not been much done as regards documentaries on referees – especially from the era Pickles officiated in, but the more I read up on him the more curious I became.

If you ever want to see a clip of him – just pull YouTube up and you will see him during the toss-up of the Leicester City versus Wolverhampton Wanderers F.A Cup Quarter Final in 1960.

From a personal point of view he was born in Bradford in 1924, started refereeing around 1949 and rather strangely was employed in a pickle factory and moved out to Stockport around 1958/59, however it was from a football point of view that interested me, and immediately I dropped on to something. The Tony Coleman incident aside – Pickles was instrumental in a Spurs defeat in the same season at the hands of Nottingham Forest on 6th November, 1965. He was also booed off the field by the away support in a match at the City Ground on 15th February, 1957 – in the self-same fixture. You could state that booing a ref isn't that unheard of; however, if you look at the reasons surrounding it you start to understand why. He was booed off the field in a match between Birmingham City and Nottingham Forest on 30th August, 1961, as well as being manhandled by Birmingham City players in the same fixture on 17th October, 1959, and by Swansea Town players in a match against Notts County on 12th September, 1957. There was another game between Notts County and Port Vale on 2nd September, 1954, which Pickles was blasted after he had stopped play to request a new white ball – and only minutes from time with Port Vale 1-0 up. The dilly-dallying led to a stoppage which on the restart resulted in an equalising goal by County's Ray Chatham.

Reading between the lines a common denominator was forming – one could suggest that the man in black had a similar coloured character as over the years, both Notts

County and Nottingham Forest had quite a few strange decisions go their way.

The Notts County versus Swansea Town game at Meadow Lane saw Tommy Lawton's side on the end of a 4-2 hammering by the visiting Welsh side – even though the Swansea players thought he had done his damnedest to help County by awarding an extremely dubious penalty – so much so he had seven of them manhandling and pushing him, one of whom was Arsenal-bound Mel Charles – who ended up bagging a brace of goals.

The penalty incident happened on 68 minutes when Notts County's outside right Gordon Wills weaved down the left and Swansea centre half Dudley Peake was wrongly judged to have obstructed him. When order was restored Wills calmly put the penalty into the back of the net.

In the 1957 game which saw Nottingham Forest at home to Spurs in front of over 32,000, the London side were leading 2-1, then after 65 minutes Pickles blew for a penalty. Forest's Johnny Quigley was fairly tackled by Maurice Norman, the latter who came away with the ball. There was hell on, but fortunately Spurs' goalkeeper Ted Ditchburn saved the resulting penalty from Tommy Wilson, however fingers were being pointed at both Quigley for diving and Pickles for not recognising the fact.

On 19th October, 1959 the *Daily Express* ran a story post the Birmingham City - Nottingham Forest game in which referee Pickles had accused Birmingham outside right Harry Hooper of gamesmanship after the match, whilst Hooper accused referee Pickles of forcing him to move when he was injured. Hooper went down after 75 minutes, clutching his right thigh and Pickles ran up to him, questioned him, and refused to have a trainer on.

The Birmingham's players holding on to a 2-0 lead jostled Mr. Pickles angrily as they tried to hold Hooper on the ground as Pickles tried to force him to his feet in what was described as "an astonishing tug of war".

Harry Langton wrote, "The Birmingham Inside left Jim Barrett dashed up to Mr. Pickles and pushed him. Two more Birmingham players grabbed Barrett – who himself suffered a serious leg injury on the same ground when he was a Forest player, and pulled him away. Eventually Mr. Pickles ran away to restart play with £18.000 Hooper still stretched out on the turf. Mr. Pickles told me afterwards: 'It was gamesmanship. He could move his leg but he wouldn't get up. So I tried to assist him. Finally I told him to get off'."

In the 1965 game between Forest and Spurs Alan Williams of the *Daily Express* wrote, "Give credit to Forest in regards to taking their ninth minute goal, but I thought Spurs should have been awarded a free-kick. This was only one of a stream of baffling decisions by referee Jack Pickles which nearly all seemed to be against Spurs."

Minutes from time however, a looping cross by Cyril Knowles was headed home by Alan Gilzean; however, the referee disallowed it."

The Yorkshireman also had some history with Port Vale as well. During a game on 9th November, 1962 where the 50,000 capacity, albeit in this instance a near-empty Vale Park, played host to Barnsley on a cold Friday night, and where 8,798 watched on as Jack Pickles firstly took the name of Vale's left winger Colin Grainger and then sent off Stan Steele on 75 minutes after a rash challenge on Barnsley's Bob Nicol. Things became that heated on the terraces that the police had to escort him off the pitch, as they did on Boxing Day – the same day that Jimmy Greaves bagged a hat-trick for Tottenham Hotspur in a 5-0 hammering of Ipswich and on the same day as Brian Clough got injured and had his prolific football career cut short. In this instance and with the scores level at 1-1 Pickles had abandoned a game Between Mansfield Town and Bradford City after 36 minutes.

On 28th January, 1956 Pickles refereed a marathon F.A Cup Fourth Round tie between Burnley and Chelsea which ended in a 1-1 draw, and due to his rather gutless display in allowing a free-for-all in the penalty area in the second minute, all hell broke loose. He had given Burnley a free kick which got lumped into the Chelsea goalmouth and it was here where Chelsea's centre half Stan Wicks ended up taking a vicious kick in the head which was so brutal he lost consciousness to see any of the melee that followed. Norman Dixon of the *Daily Express* stated, "There followed a mauling scrum, which was more fitting to Twickenham than Turf Moor. It was disgusting – that's my verdict on this torrid Cup tie. Fouls – were littered all over the place as tension and tempers rose. Players were kicked, tripped, knocked over every few minutes. Players with fists raised had to be pulled apart by colleagues and it was remarkable that the twenty-two men survived to walk off the field at the end. What was even more remarkable, however, was the fact that the referee allowed them all to stay on."

The match ended in a one-all draw and back then, the referee stayed with the cup tie, meaning that Pickles would officiate the replay – or in this instance, replays.

On the same day Highbury had witnessed disgusting scenes, where Aston Villa's Welsh international goalkeeper had to have police protection as he was being pelted with objects from the 43,000 crowd after he had stamped on Derek Tapscott during Arsenal's 4-1 win.

Still, with the Burnley-Chelsea match – after three replays of 1-1, 2-2 and 0-0 the match was still tied and it ended up going to Highbury to be decided. However, the F.A issued a new ruling that in future – for second and third replays in all Cup matches the referee would be changed, which saw Pickles removed from the tie, with the F.A strangely stating that none of the clubs had complained about Pickles – even though he had been hammered again in the press after Burnley's diminutive outside-left Brian Pilkington nodded an equaliser in the 1-1 replay at Stamford Bridge – even though every one of the 26,000 crowd assumed he was offside – including me as I had raided the ITN archive for the match and took it home to work on it and had Emily sitting on my shoulder like Captain Flint watching me try to colourise it with the aid of some new plug-in's I'd bought from the United States.

"Yer red's not very good Lee," she twanged.

"Red?"

She nodded, "It's Arsenal isn't it?"

"No – love, Burnley," I winked.

"Oops," she smiled.

I then pointed at the screen. "That there is Jimmy Adamson – The F.A wanted him to manage England before Alf Ramsey, but he turned them down."

"Was he good?" she asked.

"In his era he was – very."

She then perched on a stool at the side of me. "So what are you doing?"

"Colourising it," I told her.

"I know that," she smiled. "I mean what is it for?"

"I'm interested in the referee," I told her.

"Is that the referee that you were talking to my granddad about last week?"

"It is love, yeh."

"The one that sent Dave Hickson off?"

"You remember that?" I smiled.

"Yeh – course I do – He was from The Wirral."

He was. Dave Hickson was born in Salford and was raised in Ellesmere Port and had played for all three Merseyside clubs – Everton, Liverpool – and Tranmere Rovers at the back end of his career. Although certainly not as prolific, he was likened to Derek Dooley of Sheffield Wednesday. In his heyday he had a slight resemblance to that of a blonde-haired Olivier Giroud. He was fearless, aerially dominant and possessed an explosive shot. It is said that he was quiet off the pitch but quite the animal on it – and in his words he would die for the shirt, and it was at Goodison Park where he became a hero – not at least during the run up to the F.A Cup Semi-Final of 1953.

The defining moment that kicked off his legendary status came in Fifth Round of the competition against Manchester United. Nearly 78,000 crammed into Goodison Park on the 14th February, 1953 – the exact same day when Derek Dooley broke his leg at Deepdale – to witness exactly the man who Dave Hickson was. With the Toffee's languishing in 13th place in Division Two and United just three points behind First Division leaders West Bromwich Albion, the game hung at 1-1 when just before halftime Hickson courageously dove to head a ball amongst a crowd of United players and got kicked in the head, emerging from the ruckus with a huge gaping cut above his right eyebrow. Hickson was lead off down the tunnel, with the crowd fully expecting Everton to play the game out with 10 men; however, he emerged from the tunnel in the second half, to be greeted by a huge ovation from the crowd, with the wound stitched up and within minutes he had hit what would be the winning goal. However, Hickson wasn't done – he then headed against an upright and opened the wound again ignoring pleas from both the referee and his captain to leave the field of play. At the final whistle, with blood streaming from his head, he left the field to an ovation probably never bettered at Goodison Park. Hickson also hit the winning goal in the Quarter Final against Aston Villa, with an explosive shot from the edge of the box and bagged one in the Semi-Final against Bolton Wanderers, where they fought back from 4-0 down to score three goals only to lose 4-3. In that game Everton missed a penalty and Hickson sustained another nasty head injury that forced him off the field of play for the last quarter of an hour. Bolton however, would go on to play in the F.A Cup Final against Blackpool and be on the receiving end of the same score line; a game that is possibly regarded as the most memorable of the era.

It was with Liverpool however, under the manager Bill Shankly that Hickson felt the wrath of Jack Pickles, when in February 1960 he had to go to a disciplinary hearing along with the then-Chairman of the Professional Footballers' Association, Jimmy Hill.

"Dave Hickson, Liverpool's controversial centre forward, was still in suspense last night about the verdict of an F.A disciplinary committee he faced yesterday," said Derek Wallis of the *Daily Mirror* adding that Derby County manager Harry Storer had denied allegations that his players had baited Hickson who he had cautioned. Coupled with Pickles sending him off against Sheffield United for violent conduct, he was charged by the F.A but eventually cleared with Ken Jones of the *Daily Mirror* reporting after the 95-minute hearing, "Controversial Liverpool centre forward, has been given a break by the Football Association. Hickson, sent off against Sheffield United in January for the third time in his turbulent career, was notified, yesterday, that he had been cleared of the accusation of violent conduct. Now I say it is time for some of his fellow professionals to lay off. Liverpool manager Bill Shankly may have been indiscreet when he named clubs whose players, he claimed, had provoked Hickson but the fact remains that the Merseyside tearaway has been the victim of whispering tactics, which have been used to upset him in some matches. For too long he has been taking the rap when referees should have been reprimanding other players."

"He was the childhood hero of Bill Kenwright," I told Emily. "He nearly went to Torino of Italy."

"Is that where that Denis Law who Arsenal were after, went?"

"It is love, yeh, I nodded. "When Arsenal wanted Law he was just a kid with Huddersfield."

Emily sat and listened as I waffled on whilst at the same time trying to associate grey levels in the ball-ache that was the colourisation process.

"I'm thinking of having a committed colourisation-arm within the company," I told her. "I reckon once I get used to doing it we'll be able to colourise every bit of decent monochrome footage from the ITN Archives and British Pathé ."

"I'll definitely never see you if yer do that," she twanged.

"Course you will – I'll train someone up for it and once we're up and running we can do contract work to make it financially viable."

"I can't believe how clever you are," she smiled.

"If I was that clever I'd devise you something that looked like a washing machine, but which could do the ironing."

"That'd be dead clever," she said. "I promise I'll do it tomorrow."

"You said that yesterday – I don't know why you just don't get someone in to do it."

I got back to doing the Chelsea-Burnley game whilst mentioning that during the 1972/73 Parallel season, Arsenal were looking at buying Burnley's left winger Leighton James.

"Was he good?" she asked.

"Yeh, very. I've no idea why they didn't buy him – perhaps it was because Burnley had sold Dave Thomas to Queens Park Rangers."

"Do you enjoy doing all this work?" she asked.

"Once we're up and running, it'll all run itself – I hope!"

"I hope so as well," she said. "I wanted to watch 'The Girl with the Dragon Tattoo' tonight."

"Well, put it on," I told her.

"Yeh, but it's rubbish watching it without you," she sulked. "We should have a new rule which says that we have to x amount of cuddle time on the sofa per day."

"We had a cuddle on the sofa yesterday," I winked.

"No, we did not," she smiled. "That was definitely not a cuddle."

"What was it then?"

"Definitely not a cuddle," she laughed.

I gave M the heads up for what would become her rule number eleven and saved my work. Chelsea ended up eventually beating Burnley 2-0 with goals from Jimmy Lewis and Ron Tindall; however, just over three weeks later

Burnley would get some form of revenge in a league fixture and battered Chelsea 5-0.

While Emily was on her hands and knees trying to insert the DVD, I thought back to the Tony Coleman incident and Jack Pickles being jostled. There have been similar instances in recent times, and one that springs to mind is that of Paulo Di Canio in a match in 1998 for Sheffield Wednesday versus Arsenal. Di Canio did indeed both manhandle and shove referee Paul Alcock, but certainly never ever punched him, although Alcock certainly acted like he had. Alcock staggered to the ground in scenes reminiscent of Ali versus Richard Dunn in 1976. Although the player was totally out of order – and he was – the referee had made one hell of a meal out of it, so much so, Di Canio was dragged over hot coals, fined £10,000 and handed an 11-game ban, and that being the case, his club – the total innocent party – suffered big time.

We did eventually get on the sofa to watch M's film, and to be honest it was as good as a film as I'd ever watched.

"Don't you think she's a bit like Kirsty Burns?" asked Emily in regards to the Lisbeth Salander character.

Maybe, but I totally preferred Rooney Mara with blonde hair, I thought.

"Why – because she rides a bike or how she dresses?" I asked.

"Yeh, both of them," she pondered, "But more in how clever she is and the chemistry between her character and that of Daniel Craig's."

"What you think I'm Mikael Blomkvist and she's the Lisbeth bird?"

"No – I'm just saying," she replied, before mumbling a "That's all."

"I prefer clever blondes," I winked. "And I hate tattoos on women."

She quite liked that.

"Spoilt rich kid in real life," I said in regards to Rooney Mara. "Her family are big into football."

"Yeh?" inquired Emily.

"Her mum's family founded the Pittsburgh Steelers, whilst her dad's family did the same with the New York Giants," I told her.

"Yeh but that's not proper football like we like is it?" she smiled.

"Most definitely not," I told her.

It wasn't – I liked American football as much as their other national sport – Rounders.

"The Americans make sure they are the best at it, so they play sports that no other country play," I said.

"Yeh – but they play our football as well," she said. "My granddad say's Gerrard's going to America."

"It's a final payday for him and a putting bums on seats thing for the club," I said. "If Gerrard was still – say twenty-seven – he'd not be going to The States as it would ruin his career. In football, a player's general aim is to play against the best – that's unless the player is just greedy and wants to play in America for the money, or even worse – in Qatar."

We went to bed but I had her sitting on the bed incessantly yacking and asking a million questions, a lot of which were strangely football-related and some which were not.

"Let me think about it, M," I replied to *one* that was certainly not.

The next day in work I was still being drawn by this Jack Pickles character and mentioned him to Abi, along with the fact that I'd like a colourisation suite made in one of the empty offices.

"Yeh, but it's time consuming, Lee," she said. "And financially it doesn't make any sense."

"I turned around nine minutes of F.A Cup football in next to no time last night," I replied.

"What do you mean by 'next to no time'?"

"About five hours," I replied.

She just looked at me as though she was going to tell me off.

184

"We could get a couple of media graduates in to do it and do some sub-contract work," I said. "Just as long as the original monochrome footage is okay, it's not that hard to do."

"So, how long have you been pratting around with it to get to this level of brilliance?" she winked.

"August," I lied before coming clean. "Well, I started dabbling around with it in July."

"No you didn't, I once caught you trying to colourise the fight between Ali and Henry Cooper at the old firm – You made a right pig's ear of it."

"It's mastering the grey levels – and these new plug-ins I downloaded from The States are shit-hot," I explained.

"We are already snowed under with work, Lee," she said. "It's getting as there aren't enough hours in the day."

"Placate me on this, Abi," I said. "If we can run with this – ITV Seven could be more brilliant than we ever dreamed."

She just looked at me whilst in thought. "So how many uni' grad's to run it?" she asked. "And remember you will have to show them how it all works."

That was indeed the downside.

"Get me three," I said.

"Male or female?" she asked.

"Female – as they generally do as I ask," I winked. "Just don't mention that when you're advertising it."

She just shook her head before going over to Annie's office.

Still with Jack Pickles on my mind I went back into the guts of the Arsenal Parallel's programme to come across a piece from early February 1959 – about a batch of Arsenal players being suspended for 14 days as part of the F.A's new Code of Conduct which was put into force in late September, 1958, and during a season which Arsenal were beginning to earn quite a few plaudits.

George Swindin had been in the Arsenal side that won the rather fascinating League Championship in 1937/38 – a season in which Preston North End could have achieved a second Double if it wasn't for the fact that Arsenal had beaten them 3-1 up at Deepdale on 23rd April, 1938 and which only 16 points separated the champions from the bottom of the league club. Another strange thing was that the League Champions of the previous season, Manchester City were relegated – and after scoring 88 goals – the most in the division.

Swindin was also Arsenal's post-war goalkeeper and was in the team that had picked up two league championship medals in 1948/49 and 1952/53, a F.A Cup winner's medal in 1950 and had played in the 1952 FA Cup Final where the 10-men of Arsenal were beaten by Newcastle United. He was ousted as the clubs No. 1 by Jack Kelsey – the goalkeeper who would be held in as greater esteem as the likes of Lev Yashin – the Dynamo Moscow and Russian international goalkeeper with the huge frame and sultry good looks, who during his career saved a remarkable 151 penalties and had 270 clean sheets to his name.

Swindin was reputed to be a very hard man and had set out his managerial career at non-league Peterborough United, but had returned to Arsenal when Jack Crayston had resigned after a dismal 1957/58 season – which had seen Arsenal get dumped out of the F.A Cup 3-1 by Northampton Town at their three-sided County Ground.

What should be noted was that George Swindin wasn't the first name the Arsenal board went for. Sir Bracewell Smith had offered the £3,000 a year job to ex-Arsenal captain Joe Mercer in late May, 1958 when he was still manager of Sheffield United, and although he was confidently expected at Highbury, thousands of Sheffield United supporters sent in letters begging him to stay with the club. But here is where the story of fickle fans comes into play, and by the 23rd December, 1958, Mercer had had a change of heart with Bob Pennington of the *Daily Express* writing, "Scores of letters, telegrams, and petitions from factories and clubs influenced him to stay, but the support given to Mercer personally has not been continued at the turnstiles this season."

Sheffield United had just been beaten 1-0 at home by Derby County and were sitting 13th in Division Two when he decided enough was enough and duly applied for the vacant Aston Villa job.

Pennington added, "Why should he say 'No' to Arsenal, where there is a tremendous bond of sentiment, and 'Yes' to Villa, whose playing resources are decidedly inferior?

Mercer explained to Bill Holden of the *Daily Mirror*: "Money had nothing to do with it. It is just that the prospects at Villa Park appeal to me. I know there's a tough fight ahead, but I like the idea of a challenge. At Villa I will have the facilities to expand. They do not exist at Bramall Lane, through circumstances beyond United's control as the gates have been very disappointing this season. And that's no help to a manager wanting to buy players. But I still think United are booked for promotion."

Bob Pennington added comment, "I think history has an excellent chance of repeating itself as far as Arsenal and Aston Villa are concerned. Arsenal, after failing to get Mercer, have found success with George Swindin, who has proved an incomparable leader."

The Aston Villa job was something of a poisoned chalice, as Villa were a struggling side at the foot of Division One with only 16 points when he joined. They were inevitably relegated on the last day of the season after getting a credible 1-1 draw against a title chasing West Bromwich Albion at The Hawthornes and in front of a crowd of 48,170. A glanced header by Villa's Gerry Hitchens seemed to have made the Birmingham club safe, but just two minutes from time a 20-yard drive from Ronnie Allen sent them down as fellow strugglers Manchester City turned a one goal deficit into a 3-1 win at home against Leicester City. It was strange that it would be Manchester City who survived to send his club down, as it would be at Maine Road where he would become highly revered as one of their greatest ever managers; however, what is even stranger about events on the night of the 29th April, 1959, was that Mercer had left the ground thinking his team were safe to make his way as one of the 750 attendees to witness a celebration of an England player over at the civic hall in Wolverhampton, and that he didn't know his club had gone down until half an hour after the end. That player? Soon to be Arsenal manager Billy Wright.

Mercer, however was free to push forward with his plans at Villa and within two seasons his young side had been champions of Division Two and League Cup winners. However, if fickle fans are one thing – Ruthless and heartless boards of directors are quite another. His team were dubbed "Mercer's Minors" and had demonstrated a very entertaining style of play. However, by 1964 Mercer had suffered a stroke and while he lay at home ill the Villa board decided to terminate his contract.

History will tell you that after failing to get Mercer, Arsenal made an approach for Manchester United's chief coach, caretaker manager and Matt Busby's right hand man at Manchester United, Jimmy Murphy.

Murphy told the Daily Express on 24th November, 1958, "It is true that four leading clubs had approached me recently, including Arsenal. Did any of the clubs who have approached me have a chance? I will be frank. I reached my decisions with no prompting from anyone else. In most cases it was easy to say no but I will say quite frankly that I gave much thought to the Arsenal job, after all, they were to pre-war football what United have been to the post-war era. Arsenal are a great club. Anyone would be proud to be associated with them."

One of the other four clubs that were after him would be Mercer's new club, who had just sacked manager Eric Houghton.

Arsenal therefore appointed the rather debonair Swindin – born in the mining village of Campsall, north of Doncaster – the same village as Graham Rix – and he made his presence immediately known. Whilst Arsenal undertook a pre-season tour of Germany, Holland and Switzerland, the club's new manager was able to run the rule over his squad and on 23rd August, 1958 prior to the opening game of the 1958/59 season up at Deepdale, Arsenal paid £20,000 for Preston North End's 30-year old vociferous right half Tommy Docherty and two days later after the 2-1 defeat which Docherty sat out, *The Daily Mirror* ran with the story of Arsenal's 'Shop for success', with journalist Bill Holden stating that Hibernian's 18-year old Liverpool-born sensation Joe Baker would be next in through the door, which at the time was the equivalent of Arsenal going for Charlie Nicholas.

Hibernian's Chairman Harry Swan told reporters – albeit with a hint of exaggeration that he would rather burn down the clubs grandstand than see Baker sold. The irony was that Hibernian did sell its prized asset and he did eventually go to Arsenal, but this would not be the time. Hibernian had eventually baulked at Baker's wage demands for £17 per week a couple of years later and shipped him out to Torino where he was involved in a near fatal car crash, before Arsenal eventually signed him. However the fact was, that Arsenal were looking for players to spearhead their attack, with Celtic's diminutive Scottish international Bobby Collins certainly interesting them, with Everton already offering his club £24,000 for him.

Swindin told the *Daily Express*, "We have asked Celtic to name their price for Collins and are still waiting to hear from them – I will never take part in any auction. Whatever the player, whatever his reputation, you don't break principles."

However, come the Mel Charles and Denis Law sagas, Swindin would soon abandon that train of thought. The game of football was changing, and changing fast.

The man at the other end of Swindin's phone call to Celtic was none other than the great Jimmy McGrory – the ex-Celtic centre-forward who plundered a remarkable 469 goals in 448 games before the war and who at one time was subject of a £10,000 transfer to Arsenal in August 1927, who himself called it off after a series of meetings in London with Arsenal manager Herbert Chapman and chairman Sir Samuel Hill-Wood, with legend having it that the man himself had said, "McGrory of Arsenal just never sounded as good as McGrory of Celtic."

Although Tommy Docherty tried to persuade Collins to join Arsenal, history will tell you that he never did. The player would sign for Everton – a team he was destined to join as a 17-year old, but a move that the Scottish F.A blocked, and go on to be integral to the history of the machine that would become Leeds United, and who, regardless of his age would be voted Player of the Year, some years later in 1965.

Four games into the season – Saturday 6th September, 1958, whilst Arsenal travelled to Goodison Park and turned over a rather pitiful Everton 6-1, representatives from the club were at Brisbane Road to watch Leyton Orient destroy Barnsley 5-1.

The *Daily Express* claimed that they were there to run the rule over the club's Welsh international inside right Phil Woosnam, who was also a schoolteacher – teaching physics in east London and who played the game as an amateur and who during the game versus Barnsley showed exactly why he was being watched, as he plundered three goals plus an assist.

Whether or not Arsenal dithered is a valid talking point, however what was said when West Ham United eventually pipped Aston Villa for his signature after parting with a £30,000 fee for the 24-year-old, was that The Hammers had made a play for him in summer and although Orient had refused, they had given The Hammers the first option on him should they want to sell. Arsenal on the other hand eventually plundered Orient for the clubs centre-forward Len Julians who scored the other two goals that day.

Faranha brought me over a coffee and relayed the fact that I had to give the heads up to a job advert that was due to be emailed over to the *London Evening Standard*. "You also need to sign off on some new Apple Mac hardware for this colourisation suite you're on about," she said.

"That was fast," I replied as I signed the order.

"I don't think Abi is too keen," she said.

"And why's that?" I smiled.

"Because she thinks she'll end up having to do it."

That made me chuckle.

"Oh yeh – and ITV have been on wanting to know if you've sorted your flights and accommodation for the Wolfsburg versus Everton match."

"I thought they were doing it?" I asked.

"It doesn't sound like it," she said.

I therefore got Emily on the phone who was trying to placate Baby Face Finlayson with a tin of Heinz.

"What, beans?" I asked.

"Don't be daft," she replied. "He's having Organic Peas followed by Peaches."

"Jesus Christ – he gets treat worse than I do."

"Shurrup you," she twanged before adding a bit of a white lie. "Anyway, what do you want – my boyfriend's due round in a bit?"

"ITV have not sorted the Wolfsburg trip – Can you do it?"

"Possibly – if we are really, really sure that they haven't and we are not booking another set of flights and accommodation."

"I thought you weren't going to mention that again," I said, sensing a hint of sarcasm in her voice.

That was sort of a sore point. When I was invited over to The States I'd sorted the flights – well I hadn't really – M had – and then we found out that NBC had already done it. It took some mucking about, but it eventually got sorted. I told American Airlines a white lie. Well more black lie really. As Mike hadn't really fell off a ladder and broke five vertebrae!

"I can't believe you said that," Emily had gasped. "What if it really happens?"

"If you're that worried, tell him to stay away from ladders for a few years," I'd replied.

The thing was – Emily had actually told her mum what I'd said.

"Anyway, how has Herbert been?" I asked.

"The DPD man woke him up around lunchtime."

"That sounds ominous," I said.

"He wasn't right happy about it," she said. "I had to take him out in the buggy to appease him."

"Where did you go?"

"King's Cross station to see the trains and then up Pentonville Road to 'Grimaldi Park – I've just got back in."

"Did he drop back off?" I asked.

"You must be joking – I saw Mrs Sosk though – she was waiting for her niece coming down from Grantham."

"Did she show you her bunions?"

"No, I saw them last week."

"Yeh – me too," I said. "I nearly threw up."

"Anyway what are yer up to?" she asked. "That black and white football match you were secretly colouring in at two o'clock this morning."

"No, I finished that – It doesn't look bad either."

"Yer going to have to slow down, Lee," she said, albeit rather concerned. "You must have only had a couple of hours sleep last night."

She was right. My head was continually buzzing and when I eventually got off the phone – I say eventually as once you get M on the thing you can never get her off it. She puts it down to the fact that she misses me, however I put it down to the fact that she just likes talking! I sought some solace in my 'Parallel's' programme, but immediately got interrupted by Faranha.

"What's up now?"

"A guy on a motorbike has just dropped this envelope off at reception," she said whilst slinging me the package. "It feels like there are keys inside."

"Yeh it's so I can lock the door of my office from the inside so as not to be disturbed by you," I lied.

"They are all watching that football match you colourised," she said. "It's dead good."

"And?"

"Abi told Les that you'll probably want to colourise all that Sheffield Wednesday programme."

Abi was right. That was exactly what I had in mind.

Back to the 'Parallel's' – The story surrounding Len Julians' transfer to Arsenal was quite bizarre and illustrated the stranger side to George Swindin's transfer dealings. Signing Docherty and Jackie Henderson made complete sense as they were exceptional players; however, Julian's signing smarted of just signing someone for the sake of it.

George Harley of the *Daily Mirror* wrote, "Arsenal and Leyton Orient, two clubs on the slide figured in the most unexpected transfer deal of the season and just before the Christmas matches. Arsenal signed Len Julians, the Orient centre forward. Orient received, in exchange, right back Stan Charlton, reserve centre forward Tony Biggs and £3,000. Charlton is the Londoner who went to Arsenal from Orient with Vic Groves in a £30,000 deal three years ago."

There was a story within that story that not many people know – in that Arsenal's Tony Biggs knew absolutely nothing about the transfer to the struggling Division Two club as officials from the club weren't able to contact him as he was out shopping on Christmas Eve, with Harley stating that if Biggs declined to leave Arsenal – Orient would receive a further £5,000. As for Stan Charlton – it was strange he would go to Orient when Division One basement boys Portsmouth had bid for him in mid-November 1958.

History will tell you that never happened and that Biggs – who was a prolific goal scorer in the reserves, and who had scored a headed goal for a much depleted Arsenal side after three minutes in a 1-1 draw with Wolves on 18th October, 1958, a game in which Gerry Ward also rattled the woodwork with a 30-yard drive – did go to Orient. History will also tell you that although Len Julians' career with Arsenal started off with a bang – it was very brief.

Harley further commented, "Julians, who has had a lean season with Orient, scored in the first five minutes for Arsenal – but Arsenal, so recently the League leaders, suffered their fourth defeat in five games."

Julians' debut was on Boxing Day 1958 at Kenilworth Road where Arsenal were beaten 6-3 by would be F.A Cup finalists, Luton Town. As has been said, the Christmas fixtures always threw up some strange results, and the very next day a soft Jimmy Bloomfield goal exacted some form of revenge to give Arsenal a 1-0 win over The Hatters, even though Ken Jones of the *Daily Mirror* stated that Luton had enough chances to win the game and was it not for a great display by Arsenal's centre-half Bill Dodgin, the result could have been a lot different.

The 1958/59 season and the 1972/73 had not only a lot of strange similarities as regards Arsenal, but the 1958/59 season had an affect with what happened in 1972/73 at other clubs – take Luton for instance.

Arsenal's chief torturer during the Christmas period was Luton winger Billy Bingham and inside-left and Scottish international Allan Brown, with other notable players that day being their captain, Syd Owen and their Irish international inside left, George Cummins. Two of these would have an impact on the 1972/73 season and Leeds United in particular.

In November 1958 Don Revie was transferred from Sunderland to Leeds for £14,000 in somewhat acrimonious circumstances as even back then Revie was 'all about the money', as it was thought he would go to Derby County. In the same month George Cummins was being lined up for a £20,000 move to Middlesbrough as their prolific striker Brian Clough was continually banging on in the press each week about how unhappy he was with the lack of service he was getting. Unfortunately for Clough, his playing career would sadly end exactly four years after Billy Bingham and Allan Brown hit two goals apiece in Luton's 6-3 rout over Arsenal. As for the Cummins transfer, that never happened.

At the end of the Leeds United's 1972/73 season – that being their acrimonious European Cup Winners Cup Final defeat in Athens against AC Milan – Revie was to leave Leeds for Everton; however, something happened in that it never did, and while the Everton board were supposedly out in Greece to meet Revie, they appointed the-then manager of the Greek national side who was none other than Billy Bingham. In 'other news', Clough's Derby County did the Double over Arsenal to help derail their title challenge and would a couple of years later himself take control of the Damned United. As for Syd Owen – he was a loser at Wembley as he was in 1959, but this time as the coach of Leeds United, and that being the case he was also in Athens to see not only Leeds get robbed of the European Cup Winners Cup but also see his ex-team mate be appointed manager of Everton, instead of Revie.

Yeh, but what of Allan Brown, you may ask?

Allan 'Bomber' Brown had previously played for Blackpool in a match on the 28th of February, 1953, where he broke his leg after scoring the winning goal with just two minutes to go of an F.A Cup Quarter Final in front of 69,158 – and against the would-be League Champions, Arsenal at Highbury, to stop them winning the first Double of the century. Strangely, he would also score the winning goal in the F.A Quarter Final in the 1958/59 season – against his former club Blackpool – a game in which Syd Owen would earn much praise on his way to becoming the 1959 F.W.A Player of the Year.

You can't beat football and its history!

I had a couple of surprises that Wednesday night, one from Emily and one for Emily if that makes any sense. I got in the house to a wife who was dressed to kill. Obviously

Gossard had been doing their level best to entice her to model for them as there was a lot of Oo Lah Lah about what she was wearing. She also had her hair up and had thick make-up applied along with a set of handcuffs dangling from her right wrist, which only meant only one thing. Well, I think it did.

"My boyfwend has stood me up and I've no-one to pway with," she said in her very much put on spoilt bitch accent.

I must admit, that this was one of my favourites from her vast catalogue of acts, one of which was a French maid who actually spoke French and which I must say was absolutely brilliant.

"Where's face ache?" I asked whilst grabbing myself a Perrier water from the fridge and then at her seductively clip-clopping across the wooden floor towards me in some shoes that I had never seen before.

"I had to sell the baby so I could buy these shoes," she lied. "Pwease don't be cwoss with me?"

"I'm not," I replied gulping from the bottle. "You did sound."

"So?" she asked as she slithered up to me.

"Do you fancy doing something that will get you really out of breath?" I winked.

She nodded at me whilst pouting. Like I said – I totally loved her when she was in spoilt-bitch mode.

"Well, see how quick you can run upstairs," I grinned. "Your mum and dad have just followed me onto the street,"

"What?" she replied sort of semi-aghast.

I nodded. "Your dad's going to price up a bit of work tomorrow morning and he's going to take all the stuff up to Birkenhead that you've been buying for Hamilton Square."

Credit where it was due; she was a damn sight quicker across the floorboards going back upstairs than she had been coming across them.

"Our M not in?" asked Mike, as he came through the door. "I've been trying to phone her for the last half hour."

Within two minutes she was back downstairs and wearing a dressing gown.

"You look nice love," said her mum whilst taking off her coat. "Are you going out?"

"Definitely," I said.

"Are we?" Emily asked, whilst at the same time looking at me a bit dumbfounded.

"Yeh," I told her, and I made her just put a dress on over the Oo Lah Lah combo and had her fidgeting like hell all the way up Pentonville Road and on to White Lion Street.

"Dead uncomfortable these are," she said.

I knew exactly how uncomfortable they were as she struggled to get out of the car, as the elastic on whatever she was wearing underneath was obviously twanging more than her accent. "What's this place?" she asked whilst trying to fight some losing battle with her dress, underwear and seatbelt —and all in that order.

I'd been offered – if offered was the right word, the chance to buy a small factory for cash by our corporate law firm as one of the firms they were representing was going out of business and the new accountant I had set on – who everyone in the office appeared to give a wide berth to – had said that I had to start spending some money.

"I wouldn't fucking cross her," Les had whispered. "She'd whip a knife across your throat before look at you."

A few of ITV 7's male reporters had said the same. "She says she gets on with men better than women," Andy Marden had told me. "I only asked her to check that my tax code was right and she told to go crawl into my pit and die, therefore I'm assuming she's got some frigging hit list drawn up for your Foxy Fab Four."

Emily never mentioned her outside, saying that she looked like the nutter wife of Ben Affleck who faked her own murder in a creepy film that the director of NBC sent me over after its US release. Jeanette thought the same after M had lent it her, and referred to her as Rosamund Pike, which sort of caught on in the office after the said DVD had passed around a few people, one of whom was Les.

"Jesus Lee," he said. "That's her."

I must admit, I was that curious I had to watch it again, and he was dead right, but that's a story I'll get to later. As for Emily she got out of the car and looked at the factory. "What do you want it for?" she asked.

I didn't answer her straight away and as we went in I switched on the lights and it appeared a bit run down and was both damp and cold.

"Can you remember when you mentioned property when you were told how much your settlement would be after the divorce?" I asked.

I got a nod.

"And I told you that paying off the mortgage was a rubbish idea," I added.

I got another nod.

"Well it was then, but it's not now," I said. "While things are good I'm paying off the house on Frederick Street and I'm buying this," I said, adding the fact that the upstairs could be possibly converted into a three bedroomed apartment for her mum and dad to stay in when they were down – or even their Stuart once he got working for me full time; whilst the downstairs could be split into a studio for her to give her music lessons, and possibly a recording studio as we were being hassled by both ITV and a lot of the artists to push them further, with the head of entertainment continually telling me that we were missing out on a great opportunity.

"I don't mind filming them," I'd told him, "but I've got millions of other things to do that's more important and certainly more profitable than setting up some crappy record label."

"One of the bands you've had on has had over six hundred thousand hits on YouTube in the last two weeks," he said. "That's big business."

"Really?"

He nodded.

It sounded interesting, but well out of my line of work; however, he had urged me to have a 7:00am breakfast meeting with him about it the very next day. However, that was tomorrow and this was now.

"It sounds great," Emily smiled. "Does mam and dad know?"

"No," I told her.

She stood in thought before asking me, "Did I tell you my boyfriend stood me up?"

"Then he must be an idiot," I told her.

"No he's not," she said. "He's lovely."

And I got a kiss. No, that's a lie I got a bit more than a kiss, so much so the room heated up pretty sharply and by the time we got back to Frederick Street my suit definitely needed a visit to the dry-cleaners. It was that bad, I looked like I'd been mugged.

"Where the heck of you two been?" asked her mum on us entering the house.

I think the fact that the back of my jacket and trousers were covered in dust and Emily's knees and hands were dirty told its own story, but we got asked the question anyway!

After a bath – in which she insisted on having with me – even though she was having a two-way conversation with her mum through the door as she did, we sat down to some supper while Emily and her mum continued their dialogue. As I've said, I'd never known anyone talk like her before – apart from her mum that is, and I even saw Mike shaking his head once or twice.

Herbert woke me up at 4:25am, and after fifteen minutes of hoping that his Granny Sil' would come down from the top floor and go to his rescue, I ended up having to get up.

"Stay in bed and go back to sleep," I told Emily as I nudged her, knowing full-well that she was already awake.

"I am asleep," she lied.

"No you're not – you heard him before I did – You're just dead lazy."

"I need me beauty sleep 'cos I'm on telly tonight," she twanged.

"No you're not – I'm cancelling your show for lying to me," I lied.

"Then I'll sue for breach of contract," she lied. "And I'll restrict sex."

"You restrict sex and I'll sue," I told her.

"Well, in that case I'll not do that if you see to Herbert."

Mmm. She was getting dead crafty, I thought.

The upshot was that I had to go across to misery guts' bedroom and crane him out of the cot as he had a very full nappy. "How come you always shit through the night?" I asked him. "No-one else does – I'm going to have to start lacing your bottles with Imodium."

Once downstairs I kicked up the kettle and removed the bag of shite from around his waist and stuck him under the tap, which must have impressed him as he peed over the drainer.

"Do you actually do these things on purpose?" I asked him as his mum came into the kitchen and cutchy-cooed and kissed him, which did no more than set him off screaming.

"I wish you'd stop doing that," I told her.

"I was only giving him a kiss," she winked.

"Well don't – You know he hates it," I lied.

"It's rubbish having a son that hates you," she sulked.

"Well at least he doesn't pee on you," I told her as I juggled with both baby and his bottle.

"I love him though, don't you?" she smiled.

"Yeh – when he's asleep he's okay," I said before further describing the pound of cabbage that I'd had to extract from his arse.

"Was it green again?" she asked.

"Mmm. Not so much a mint green but a dark rural green – maybe it would be a nice colour for the kitchen in Hamilton Square."

"Yuk," was all I got back.

"You want to stop feeding him those tins of Organic Peas."

I'd left the house before Mike and Sil' had got up but had told Emily to tell her dad that I'd be in the Coffee Shop with a couple suits from ITV from 7:00am onwards who over a bacon, egg and mushroom sandwich explained the record label set up. "Didn't you say you've got a mate working for Radio Merseyside who's mentoring your son?"

"Which one, the baby or the soon to be six-year old?" I asked before putting them right that it was indeed my brother-in-law.

There was another angle that interested them in that they thought it could be an extremely good idea as it could make a factory renovation documentary-cum-Simon Cowell type programme.

"Fuck me – how many jobs do you want to give me?" I asked.

"Come on Lee," said one of the suits. "This could be amazing."

I left the coffee shop in a daze and just as Mike was on his way in. "Are you alright lad?" he asked.

"I'm fine," I lied. "Did you sleep alright?"

He did and he told me so as I drove him over to the disused factory over in White Lion Street, where I gave him a quick guided tour before my architect mate from Bock 16 arrived.

"Three-bed apartment on the top floor, recording studio on the second and music studio on the bottom," I said, and as Emily hadn't yet spilled the beans to her mum during her million miles an hour conversation the night before that covered anything and everything Mike raised the question.

"Apartment?" he asked.

"For you and Sil' when you come down," I said. "It may also come in handy if Stuart keeps up the good work."

He was speechless and even more when I mentioned that he might be on TV doing the actual renovation. "I don't know what they are planning Mike – all I know is that they are taking some massive interest in me – I don't know whether it's the fact that they actually like me or that they just want to see me crash and burn."

I was also sick to death that my privacy had been taken away and that we were in the papers nearly every day, which, unknown to me at the time was only going to get worse.

I got into the office and got stuck into the Sheffield Wednesday documentary, in particular the part where they had been robbed of an appearance in the 1960 FA Cup Final after Alan Finney had a legitimate goal ruled out for offside.

"Didn't Dooley play for them then?" Kirsty had asked.

"Nah – That was a few years earlier," I said.

The story that surrounded the man that was Derek Dooley was barely believable. At 6'2 and weighing in at 13½st, he had already scored 16 goals for Wednesday in his first season in the First Division. However, his short albeit prolific footballing career came to an abrupt end in a league match against Preston North End at Deepdale on the 14th of February, 1953 – the year when Arsenal won the league title on goal average to the self-same Preston side.

Wednesday had recently been dumped out the F.A Cup losing 2-1 at home by its eventual winners Blackpool – who, has I've already stated knocked out Arsenal by beating them 2-1 in the Quarter Finals – and were currently sitting in mid-table and on a five-game losing streak, which would soon become six after they travelled to the table-topping Lancashire club.

Dooley was pursuing a long pass from future England midfielder Albert Quixall – a player George Swindin made tentative enquiries about before Manchester United got out the cheque book, knowing that the advancing goalkeeper was more than likely to get there first and in the event, the goalkeeper collided into him just as he made contact with the ball, breaking the centre-forward's leg in two places, which after three days in hospital he had to have amputated as gangrene had set in.

George Thompson was that goalkeeper, and was three years Dooley's senior. He had been born and raised in Maltby, a mining village few miles up the A631 from Dooley's Sheffield birthplace of Pitsmoor.

Dooley himself, appeared like some Dan Dare-cum-Roy of the Rovers character out of some teenage boy's comic book. He was the flame-haired centre-forward with the size 12 boots and nicknamed by the press as the kid with the cannonball kick who possessed a rather unorthodox playing style that at the time attracted huge controversy.

According to the former football journalist for the *Sunday Times* and *Corriere Dello Sport* Brian Glanville, his style didn't appeal to everyone, and he was frequently booed when Wednesday played away from home with his bulky frame, huge feet, ungainly movement, abrasive approach to the game and his perpetual harassing of goalkeepers, making him quite a contentious figure.

Glanville added that were he playing today, he would never be able to inflict such punishment on goalkeepers as they went for high balls, but that was all part of the tactics that won games back then. Back then harassing the goalkeeper by barging into him or shoulder-charging him was permitted and as such it would be so easy to take a keeper out and get the opposition down to 10 men, minus the goalkeeper – which was exactly what Sheffield United had done with Arsenal's Jack Kelsey in the F.A Cup Fifth Round Replay in 1958/59.

As regards Dooley, there was never any malice about him, any more than there would be recriminations or self-pity.

According to freelance football journalist Ivan Ponting who wrote for the *Independent*, when Dooley was initially offered senior opportunities – one in the Second Division in 1949/50 and another in the top flight a season later – he performed rather disappointingly. Though he was quick, bullishly strong and utterly fearless when fighting for the ball, he appeared cumbersome and poorly balanced when a degree of finesse was required.

However the picture changed dramatically in October 1951 when, his team languishing dangerously low in the Second Division table, the then-secretary manager Eric Taylor called him up to face local rivals Barnsley at Hillsborough. The raw 21-year-old responded with a double strike which set him off on a phenomenal goal rampage which carried the Owls to the Division Two title. After a mere dozen appearances he had registered 24 times, including five in the annihilation of Notts County and four against Everton, and by the season's end his tally was an exceptional 46 goals in 30 games.

Fans who had previously denigrated his clumsiness now hailed the savagery of his right-foot finishing, his fearsome aerial prowess and a willingness to strike from any angle which yielded several seemingly impossible goals. Though arguments continued to rage about the perceived rashness of the young warrior whose aggression risked injury where more polished performers would hold back, his chasing of apparently lost causes was applauded.

Still, there were doubts about how the 'comic-strip hero' would fare among the élite, and when he was goalless as Wednesday struggled through their opening Division One fixtures of his life changing 1952/53 season, the 'I told you so' brigade was out in force. However Eric Taylor remained loyal, alleging a vendetta against his prodigy by opponents, rival fans and even referees, and soon his faith was justified as Dooley's touch returned with a vengeance, with 16 goals against the cream of the League's defences between September and February. However, just as talk of an international call-up became increasingly insistent, disaster struck during his clubs 1-0 defeat against Preston North End on that fateful Valentine's Day.

"They had another player who lost his leg," I told Kirsty. "Dougie McMillan."

"I've never heard of him," she said.

"You won't have – He had his career ruined after a crash on the A1. The team bus was coming back from a one-all draw at Highbury on Boxing Day, 1961."

"That's some bad luck they've had," Les added.

"And then there's the betting scandal where Swan, Kay and Bronco Layne got banned for life," I said.

Les then stated the word "Cursed" and it was then we came up with 'The Curse of The Owls'. I liked that. I liked that a lot.

I got in that evening to find my daughter at the breakfast bar, which was strangely covered with a white sheet whilst she was painting some plastic football orange as Emily juggled about with a pair of smaller balls. That sounds a lot better than it actually was as they certainly weren't mine.

"So where does this one go, love?" smiled Emily.

"Right at the end, M," said my lad before he turned his attention to me. "Hello Dad."

"Hello, love," added Emily.

"Hello dad," further added my daughter.

"What are you all up to?" I inquired.

"We are making the solar system," said my lad pointing to the ping pong ball – That one is Pluto."

"Oh yeah," I said.

"And I'm making the Sun," explained my daughter.

"Tell your dad which is your favourite planet," Emily asked my lad.

"Saturn – It has rings around it," he said. "M said that the rings are ice, rocks and dust and that it has winds of over one thousand miles an hour, which is loads."

"Oh yeah," I replied.

"M says that we can paint a wall in my bedroom dark blue and we can make some stars out of tin foil," explained my daughter.

"That should knock a few thousand quid off the house price," I said.

"Shurrup you," twanged my wife. "It'll look great."

I'll take your word for it, I thought.

Jeanette had been catching up with her hours at work and as that was the case, I was seeing more of the kids. The downside was that Jeanette wasn't, and I mentioned it after I'd dropped them off, only to get grilled about the fact that my lad was full of paint.

"It'll wash out," I said.

She eventually apologised for being a bitch and I left. She was getting particularly good at these conversations and I told her so.

Chapter 17

Foxy Fab Four

ITV 7, like most things on TV had to be viewer-friendly. You can't have any TV show presented by a bald bloke with a big nose or some bleach-blonde Trollope with black teeth no matter how beautifully-spoken or how knowledgeable they are and that's what I told the suits at ITV when they saw the photo portfolio of my Foxy Fab Four.

"Wow," said ITV's head of sport. "How does Emily feel about them?"

Emily had pondered a bit on seeing them, but she knew I loved her and that was that.

Kirsty Burns was first in through the door at The Warehouse. She reminded me of Emily but she was nothing like Emily, if that makes any sense. Like Emily, Kirsty was non-stop and extremely humorous, but more a laddish humour than anything, and her presence in front of the camera was awesome. She may have looked like a dead ringer for Debbie Harry but was definitely Dirty Harry when it came to verbal as she was a right fucking potty mouth.

"For god's sake you can't talk like that on camera," I told her.

In her appearance she was slightly shorter than Jeanette but taller than Emily but she dressed like neither, which for me was her only downfall – however, that was only superficial and could be easily addressed.

In the office she was bubbly and very quick to learn, and she knew her football, which at times pissed Oliver Norgrove off as in his head he thought he was brilliant.

It was thought that a girl called Lucy was going to join us, but I pulled the plug on her joining at the very last minute. She was an extremely pretty woman and whose profession was that of an actress, which totally showed when she whizzed through the screen tests. She also dressed really well and whereas Kirsty had that laddish charm, Lucy did not and was very feminine in her mannerism. She knew enough about football; however, to me she was more concerned with the bullshit of her acting career, which I found out when after the second interview she'd picked up four tickets for the Live at The Warehouse show, which I didn't mind in itself, however what I didn't like was how she came over when I had watched the complete footage of the show. I say complete, as although it is live, it goes on air an hour and a half later than it starts and in reality it is two hours long but edited down to one hour if you understand all that. It would be much easier to film the show on a Wednesday and put it out Thursday, but then it wouldn't be live, but I'm digressing. Emily was talking to a West Ham United player and his girlfriend when Lucy hit the camera with her three mates and I immediately knew that employing her on something as high profile as ITV 7 would be a bad move and we ended up wiping the interview. I'll not say what happened but it was unprofessional bordering on embarrassing.

"Are you sure you really want her, Lee?" asked Abi.

She didn't need to ask me that and I phoned her the very next day and told her she was out which left a hole in my plans and totally out of the blue Kirsty dragged a rabbit out of the bag.

That said day it had been absolutely hounding it down by the time I pulled on to Frederick Street and I got in to see Emily baking whilst yacking to her mum on the phone, with face ache sat in his baby seat and strangely not crying.

"You're all wet," she said grinning.

"Yeh – I had to park halfway down the street – again," I replied as I took off my very wet jacket. "It's bouncing a foot off the floor out there."

"My mam is asking how you are," she smiled.

I was just about to continue the conversation when there was a knock at the door. I looked out of the rain-splashed window and into the grey street before I opened it, and was greeted by the sight of a woman with two young boys, who were absolutely drenched to the skin.

"Hello," she said. "Are you Mr. Janes?"

I nodded.

"I'm sorry about coming to your house, but my car broke down and I missed you in the coffee shop."

"Come in," I said.

"I'm really, really sorry," she continued.

"So you must be Kim Stowe?" I asked.

She nodded.

Emily rang off from her mum, wiped down her hands and went over to them and dried off the kids with a towel.

"Yer'll both catch cold," she twanged.

"So where's your car now?" I asked.

"On Clerkenwell Road," she said. "I managed to push it into a side street."

"What and you've walked all the way up here?" Emily asked.

"We went to the coffee shop first but the man who owns it said that you'd just left – I got your address out of the phone book – to be honest I thought you'd have been ex-directory."

"We don't use the phone," said Emily. "We just have the line for the internet."

"Too true – I was sick of some call centre from India ringing in the middle of the night and waking him up," I explained whilst pointing to Sammy.

"He's so cute," said Kim.

"Is he?" I replied. "This is a good day. As soon as he realises that we are enjoying his company he'll start whining again."

"Does he cry?" asked Kim.

"Only while he's awake," smiled Emily, as she passed Kim a towel. "While he's asleep – he's great."

"Anyway," I said, changing the subject and looking at the two drowned rats. "Who are these two 'Likely Lads'?"

"Danny and Billy," proudly answered Kim. "Danny's six – and Billy's three."

Emily offered them a temporary change of clothing – two of my lads Arsenal kits – a third kit, which was a bit snug for the eldest and a home kit that was exactly the opposite on the youngest.

I had called Kim on the recommendation of my rather ballsy Debbie Harry lookalike.

"She's really nice," Kirsty had explained. "She's just split up from her husband."

"Why did they split up?" I had asked.

"How the hell do I know," she had replied. "I don't know her that well."

It transpired that she like Kirsty was another Arsenal nut, but not just that, she had an aura about her. Whereas Kirsty wasn't backward at coming forward with her opinions and let anyone and everyone know her feelings – I was to find out that Kim was the exact opposite – but hard as nails with it. Something which was made quite obvious by the fact that her vehicle had broken down and that she had dragged her kids a long way in the pouring rain to make her presence known. I quite liked that.

"I'd love to come and work for you," she explained. "My parents said that they'll help with the children."

"That's nice," I replied.

She then told me that her parents – Jean and Frank – lived near Woodford Green tube station so getting to King's Cross wouldn't be a problem.

I then informed her that I didn't work in King's Cross –
and that it was a torturous westbound journey around the
North Circular to Bounds Green Road during the week and
then a weekend up in Manchester or at some football
ground.

"You can have Mondays off if you want," I told her.

"I thought it was just a weekend TV channel," she said,
whilst she sipped at her latte which had been made by Emily,
courtesy of one of the wedding presents given to us by Sooty
and Lib.

I shook my head and smiled to myself. "You'll be part of
a twenty-strong team that will help put programmes together
and help broadcast them," I told her. "It will be really hard
work."

"Can I ask you a question?" she asked.

"Certainly."

"Why me?"

"Why not?" I said.

"I have no experience whatsoever in media."

"I have – so don't worry – you'll be with me," I told her.
"I'll look after you."

"He will," smiled Emily, backing me up.

Whilst I showed her some of the stuff I'd recently done
on Arsenal's 'Parallels' on my laptop – I noticed that she
kept on looking at Emily through the corner of her eye
and as time went on she did it more and more until she
finally twigged and plucked up the courage to ask the
question. "Are you Emily Janes from the Live at the
Warehouse TV show?"

Emily nodded. "Lee produces it."

"ITV forced my arm," I told her. "They told me I owed
them."

"I'd never been in media either," said Emily, whilst
checking her baking in the oven.

"Do you like it?" Kim asked her.

"Don't get her started on that," I said. "It's been a full-
time job getting her back down to reality."

"I love it," smiled Emily.

She wasn't understating it either.

Both Kim's children seemed to like my kids' X-box and big TV – the eldest especially, although the youngest did complain about the fact that his brother kept on shooting him.

Kim and her two kids had a couple of hours with us while I got the AA to sort out her car – the rain had apparently caused some electrical fault and it had cut out. Well, that's what the AA man told me during our 45-minute conversation – me wet-through and freezing my bollocks off, and him under an umbrella, half of that time covering the fact of how brilliant he was with auto electrics, a traffic contraflow up on the North Circular and why Arsenal will never ever win the League under Arsène Wenger.

I'd got back in to a screaming kid and his mum threatening to drown him. Well, she wasn't really, she was bathing him – him screaming blue murder just sort of made it look like that.

"He generally likes a bath," she said.

"When was that?" I asked. "He has a face like a busted cushion when I sling him in – In fact it never alters that much outside of him having a bath."

"He's been good today – bless him."

"I'll take your word for it," I replied.

I'd had nine hundred and sixty applicants for the ITV 7 job. Either it was my outstanding persona that they craved, or me offering them between up to a couple of grand a week to watch and talk football. Les Crang had told me that it was the former, but I certainly didn't believe him – especially when his alter ego announced it to his one billion followers on Twitter that he'd landed a job in football on some mega salary.

The other two successful applicants who waltzed through the screen test and two interviews were Sinead McKenneny and Karen Beckley, who like Lucy were 100% female. Sinead was hardly a shrinking violet and had sent in portfolio of photographs, which I spent a week carrying them around in my briefcase before I could show them Sooty – that was when I finally managed to pin him down to have a coffee at Fosis' place.

"She sent me these," I'd said as I passed him them.

"Well if she doesn't get a job with you she can definitely have one with me," he'd replied.

Fosis had more or less said the same in between trying to wrestle them off Sooty and show Turkish George, the latter of whom said that the girlfriend he'd had in Liverpool was far, far better looking. Fosis told him that that he was talking bollocks and that he'd known him twenty years and never seen him with a woman. Well he had really, as he regularly took his mother to the doctors in the clapped out old Honda he drove around in.

Sinead was glamorous looking on the photographs, but more so in real life. It is strange as when you see people either on screen or in photos and then in real life as they tend to look smaller. Emily and Jeanette were always being pulled up on it.

Karen was a more voluptuous version of French actress Lola Reve and ITV's head of sport was absolutely smitten by her.

"She's definitely a woman you could leave your wife for," he told me.

I told him his wife would probably say that she was a woman that she could definitely leave him for and credit where it's due, he did admit it, before he spent the next fifteen minutes thinking about it.

On seeing Sinead and Karen, Kirsty noted the common denominator and had said, "They are both Arsenal supporters and they look like models."

"Yeh, and?" I replied.

"Nothing – I'm just saying."

Kirsty was right. The media business is not only a bit cliquey, it's also more than a bit shallow. On one of my first meetings with ITV I had to stand my ground as I was being offered over thirty potential pundits and god knows how many potential reporters to help me man up the job. I tried to explain that I didn't want any star-struck tap dancing journo and one of the first names that was dragged out of the hat was that of sports broadcaster Ian Abrahams who, in my mind, was exactly that.

"You got to be joking," I told the suits. "We need to attract viewers, not scare them off."

"He's no different to Adrian Chiles," said one of the suits.

"Yeh – and he's another one I wouldn't have," I said.

It was true. I found them both to be up their own arses and I made that fact quite known highlighting the fact that they both looked as appealing as Labour MP Gordon Brown, but it was nothing to what Kirsty had said, and it was like a red rag to a bull when Chiles was mentioned.

"I detest the man – He should be hiding under a bridge somewhere scaring small children," she snapped. "It looks like someone has set his face on fire then tried to put it out with a fork."

Les and Oliver on the other hand not only knew their football inside-out, upside-down and back to front, they were extremely viewer friendly and never ever took themselves that seriously.

"I've got two lads who will blow them all away," I had explained to the suits. "I don't need the so-called pundits, I need knowledgeable football people who present a nice face and who have an aura about them – and from the terraces, not the playing field."

Karen had no media background and after watching her in front of the camera I couldn't believe it and even more so when she told me that she was a driving instructor. All the four girls that would get on set all had varied backgrounds and as with Kim and Kirsty she had separated from her husband. I never asked why but she told me anyway and "Really?" was all I could say.

Kirsty had also been extremely forthcoming, even though I never asked.

"I got married at twenty-one and divorced at twenty-three and I'm now proudly single and someone would have to be extremely awesome to change that," she told me. "So, how are you fixed?"

She was my wild card!

I had been all over the place the morning when I first actually met Sinead, and rather than drive through the north London traffic up to Bounds Green Road I met her in the coffee shop to sound her out and as half the shop's customers had already drooled over her portfolio all the shop went quiet as she walked into the place. I never thought a jaw could drop until I saw Fosis hit the counter – and which was followed by a dull thud. No – it wasn't the sound his jaw dropping, he had fallen over a crate of Keo. Nevertheless he was a dribbling, gibbering wreck when she ordered a cappuccino and was at all sixes and sevens when she asked him if he would put some cream in it. I knew there and then, that if she spoke on set as good as she looked, we'd be onto a winner.

I had read her CV and it wasn't anything out of the ordinary, which was something I liked. Anyone can bullshit on a CV but hers was anything but. The one thing she was, was honest. She was some account executive in an insurance agents and she loved Arsenal.

"Are you Lee?" she asked as she came over.

"You're Irish," I replied, shaking her hand.

"That's not a problem, is it?" she asked.

"Certainly not," I replied.

She sat upright across from me and crossed her legs and answered every question I threw at her with a great answer, so much so I thought she'd hacked into my laptop the night before.

I explained that it was a six days a week job and that it would be really demanding.

She nodded a confirmation.

215

"I'm only asking as I see you've got a husband and young daughter," I said.

"And?"

"And that it will probably be a strain on your relationship," I added.

"I assure you that it won't," she replied giving me a look and a smile that made me feel that I needed to take a cold shower.

The meeting lasted less than an hour and when I gave her the heads-up she was ecstatic. I don't know if that was because of the job or because of the salary that came with it as her smile was explosive when I mentioned the latter.

Thankfully she had left before Emily wheeled in Sammy who was in a somewhat joyous mood before he copped me looking at him and then he gave me a gaze as though I'd just taken a dump in his cot.

"How did your meeting go?" she asked.

"Dead right," I replied. "She looked awesome."

"Really?"

I nodded my second confirmation of the day.

"So, should I be worried?" she asked.

"Nothing compares to you," I winked.

It was then I could see that she had concerns about me being surrounded by north London's equivalent to Force Fox-Four.

"Please don't hurt me Lee," she said.

That bit shocked me a bit.

"Come on M," I said. "This is not you – you know I love you."

"I'm sorry, love," she said shaking her head. "It must be my hormones – And Herbert doesn't help."

"How's he been?" I asked, obviously knowing the answer to my question before it was answered.

"Horrible," she replied. "I'm thinking about letting my mam have him for the week."

"Sound – Do you need any money for a box and some stamps?"

That cheered her up.

So ITV 7 was manned-up and it was then that we decided on who would do what, and this is where all the fun started as Les wanted to do everything and in the end I made the call. This is where ITV would put me in my place – but not until post-Wolfsburg, however something was going to happen that night which put work on the back-burner as on answering a knock at the door I was met by Libby plus her brats.

"The dustbins are round the back," I told her, "But close the lids when you're done."

"Can I come in?" she asked, not taking on my comment, which I thought strange.

"Course you can come in," I replied, immediately noticing that something wasn't right. "Are you okay?"

That was it, she started crying which was supplemented by, "I've left the bastard."

"Who, Sooty?" I asked.

"Well, who else would I leave?" she snarled.

Trying my hardest not to look dumb, I gave a shrug of my shoulders, which possibly concluded that I was indeed exactly that.

"He's knocking off one of the girls at work," she further snarled. "I don't suppose you know anything about it, do you?"

Well, I sort of did – seeing as I had walked in on him wearing just a pair of Spiderman Y fronts allegedly screen testing two Rumanian birds wearing nothing but a smile, but there was no way I was going to get involved in any conversation about it.

"She's eighteen you know."

Mmm, they sort of looked around that age, I thought.

I was going to ask her what she expected of him working at a place like he did. But again – I thought better of it, however Emily being Emily didn't and it was the first thing she said.

"He's never done anything like this before," Libby said.

I definitely didn't like the way this conversation was heading and I felt like making myself scarce, but not before Libby had a go at interrogating me.

"Well, he hasn't, has he?"

"Not that I know of," I lied.

There was no way on earth that I was going to be the Amazing Mr. fucking Truthful on this subject and before I could ask the question of what her intentions were, Emily beat me to the buzzer – and not just to the question – but to the answer as well.

"Are you wanting to stay over, Lib?"

"Please, M," she replied before looking over at me and grinding her teeth. "You don't mind, do you?"

Well I did, but there was no way I was going to tell her that and rather than fuel the flames by inviting confrontation, I let both her kids know they could kip at ours and took them upstairs.

"Is mum going to leave Dad," asked the eldest.

"Nah," I said. "Only your Dad would be stupid enough to have her."

"That's what mum said about Auntie M with you."

"Really?" I replied.

"Yeh – she told dad that he was a womanising tosser just like you."

"Thanks Zooey – I appreciate the heads-up on that one," I replied. "Is there anything else I should know before I stick my head back in the crocodile pit?"

"Just that Dad tried blaming you."

"How?" I asked.

"He said it was a pair of one of your girlfriend's pants she found in his car."

"Really?"

Both kids nodded.

"They were really nice pink ones," added Zooey.

"Really?"

"Mum found them under the front seat," she further added.

"What was she doing looking under the seat?" I asked, knowing that this was a valid question as I never looked under the car seats. Jeanette may have done on a couple of thousand occasions as part of her weekly reconnaissance back when we were married, but I certainly didn't. Maybe it was a woman thing.

"I don't know," she replied.

As both kids clambered into my daughter's double bed I switched on the TV for them.

"Mum doesn't let us watch TV in bed," said the youngest – Mia.

"Yeh – but me and Auntie M do," I said as I threw them some extra pillars. "You get treats when you come here."

I debated going back downstairs, but I decided against it and ran a bath – and got bathed – and then did some other stuff hoping that M would come to bed before I had to go back down. Unfortunately for me I was summoned for execution – around 11.00pm according to the clanging chimes of doom from my knocked-off watch and walked into the room where Libby duly opened her trap and set about me.

"If you were him would you have had an affair?" she candidly asked me.

"It's a daft question," I replied. "I'm not Sooty."

"I know you're not – but I'm still asking the question."

"Yeh – probably then," I said.

I could see from Emily's expression that this was a really bad answer.

"But if it makes you feel better," I went on to say, "if I were you I wouldn't have looked at Sooty twice – You might be a bit on the butch side, but you are decent looking – Especially when you put make-up on."

"Do you just say these things just to piss me off?" asked Libby.

"No," I innocently replied.

I didn't – it just sort of came out, but I could see from Emily's expression that this was a really bad thing to say.

219

"I think you look like Grace Slick," I said. "Back when she was good-looking – not now."

I thought that was a great line, but the expression of her face never altered – well, not much, anyway.

"She sung 'White Rabbit'," I innocently said. "She was with Jefferson Airplane – I can get her photo up on Google if you like."

"I know who she is," she replied.

"I found out he'd been texting her," Libby told Emily. "She told him that although they were apart they were still looking up at the same moon."

I couldn't hold it back and I laughed. I didn't mean to – It just came out.

"What's so funny about that?" snapped Libby.

"She might be looking up at a moon," I said, "But if she thinks Sooty's a catch, her moon must have the fucking Clangers living on it."

That even brought a grin to Emily's face and it was the first thing that was mentioned when we got in the bedroom.

"I can't believe you said that," she whispered as she sat on the bed.

"Libby's been bollocking me for years – she deserves a bit back."

"She found a pair of knickers in his car," she whispered.

"Yeh, pink ones," I replied. "They were probably Sooty's."

"What, really?" she asked.

I gave her a wink.

"You'd never have an affair on me would you?" she asked.

"Just so long as you never nag me, I won't."

"I'll definitely not nag you then."

"Good."

There was a silence. Well, for a few seconds anyway.

"How did you know they were pink knickers?" she inquired.

"Because according to their Zooey the git tried blaming me for some pink pants her mum had found under the car seat."

"Yeh, that's what Libby said," Emily confirmed. "By all accounts, they were really tiny ones."

"No chance of them being Libby's then," I winked.

"God, you're awful," she whispered.

I knew I wasn't that awful as seconds later I was asked to remove a similar-looking pair of white ones from my wife, who spent the next fifteen minutes telling me how she wanted to be held down in the back of a car and mercilessly raped by a balding man wearing pink knickers. I broke the momentum somewhat when I asked her to confirm who she actually wanted wearing the pink knickers as I assumed it to be the balding pervert who was raping her.

"No – me wearing the pink knickers," she said.

"Righto," I replied, and I continued doing what I was doing however the bloke in pink knickers was doing my head in and was totally breaking my concentration, so much so that I was complimented on my brilliant stamina that managed to help bring her off twice in as many minutes.

"Blame the bloke in the pink knickers," I said afterwards. "I had little or nothing to do with that one."

I got up the next day and had a jog around the block whilst managing to speak to Sooty on my mobile who was obviously back in his germ-free adolescent and young, free and single-mode and talking bollocks.

"She's awesome at sex," he told me. "And she says she loves me."

"Sooty, there's a reason for both – she's a fucking porn actress."

"No it's not like that," he replied. "She says she doesn't like it when she does it with other men and that she has to switch herself off."

"And this is that little blonde haired bird in that DVD you gave me who was jumping around on the scruffy old granddad bloke in that bedsit?"

There was a silence at the other end of the phone.

"Yeh – she looked like she didn't like it," I added.

He then told me that if he didn't try having a go at a relationship he would live the rest of his life not knowing. Not knowing what I hadn't a clue? He then brought me and Emily into the equation as a prime example of how having an extramarital affair or an affair on a partner can work.

"That's total bollocks," I told him. "You saw how my life was after Jeanette kicked me out."

"Yeh, it was great," he replied. "You were banging everything that moved."

"There was a downside to that."

"What? You seemed happy enough," he said.

"I lost seeing my kids grow up."

Trying to talk sense to him was like pissing in the wind, and to be honest this 'All new Sooty with added zest' was beginning to get on my nerves and I ended the conversation before getting in the house where I was greeted by two kids arguing who was having misery guts on their knee. Saying that, he was doing an awful lot of smiling at them.

"Have you seen him?" Emily grinned, as she passed me a coffee. "He's really happy this morning."

"Yeh – Do they want to take him with them?"

"Why do we have to go home?" asked Mia.

I shook my head. "No, not if your mum doesn't want to."

"We like staying here," she added.

I let Emily know that I'd tried having a conversation with Sooty, and that the upshot was that he was having the time of his life, and there was no way on earth that Libby figured in his future plans.

"He said that?" asked Emily.

"No," I replied. "I've just given you the edited highlights but sugar-coated them a bit."

"Crikey," was all she could say.

Libby came into the kitchen and poured herself a coffee and let us know that she had been on the phone half the night to Jeanette and that being the case it was hardly a conversation I wanted to partake in, however Emily did. "Marriages break down, but life goes on," she said. "It has to. True – it all seems a mess at the moment, but it can be sorted out. We are here for you, and Mia and Zooey can stay here as long as they want while you both sort it out."

Wow. She sounds just like Libby, I thought.

"I was really unhappy with my husband," she told her. "I wanted out, but he was horrible – Tim isn't – he's just a bit daft and he thinks that he's found something that he thinks he wants."

Shit – I definitely wouldn't have said that, I thought.

"Do you think it can be worked out?" Libby asked me.

"I told you last night, Lib. Me and Sooty are totally different people. We handle things differently."

"Yeh – but you had an affair," she said.

"What's that got to do with it?"

"Do you think you could have made it back up with Jeanette?" she asked.

"Libby – that's a really horrible question to ask while my wife is here," I said shaking my head. "Affairs are tacky and sordid – I was lucky in that I bumped into M when I did and I've never been happier since, but if you take into account the mess that preceded me meeting her, the percentage of an affair being a success is very low – The grass is rarely greener on the other side – You know that as you continually ragged me about it when Jeanette slung me out."

I dropped both her kids off at their school and promised them that I'd pick my two up later and that we'd all have a McDonalds or something as I could see that the oldest had their mum and dad on her mind.

Chapter 18

VFL Wolfsburg v Everton

Football is a truly brilliant sport, and you will find that some of the old school appreciate it more than most and one such person was the chairman of Everton F.C.

There was a story here that I didn't yet know about, but what I did know was that he had called both Mike and Bill and that a car would be picking them up to take them to Liverpool Airport to board an aeroplane chartered by the club.

Me and M, however had to make the 7:55am flight from Heathrow which was a ball ache because we had to do a bit of juggling with Sammy as under "No circumstance whatsoever" was anyone to look after him except his Granny Sil'.

"You palm him off with anyone else and I'll never speak to you again," she told us.

She may have told us that but I knew that it was a great stinking fib.

So while Mike and Bill were to get the V.I.P. treatment from door to door, we were tasked with slinging the little bundle of misery in the boot of the car and doing the 450 mile round trip up to Birkenhead.

Saying that, Emily did want to see the progress that was being made at Hamilton Square; however, Sammy hated the M6 as much as I did and told us as much.

"Think about all those treats and loves you'll get off Granny Sil'," his mum told him.

He wasn't having any of it and while I listened to 606/909 live in between Emily domineering or trying to domineer the radio he duly whinged and whined to his heart's content.

Nearly four hours of torture both outside the car with the traffic and inside with him grizzling concluded when we pulled up outside Emily's mum's around 6:00pm and after she had showered Herbert with kisses and furnished him with a big love, it was my turn.

"Was the traffic bad, love?" she asked.

"Horrendous," I replied.

"It'll not be long now – and you'll have that beautiful house to live in," she said.

I think Sil' was still under the impression that we were going to leave London and move up here permanently. It wasn't just me who thought that either – so did her youngest daughter.

"Your house is looking mint," said Lucy, as she tried to relieve her mum of Herbert who was strangely looking quite angelic since he'd got shut of us.

"Where's Stu?" I asked.

"He's over at the house with Mike," said Sil'. "He wants you up here more than anyone."

"I took some of my friends round to show them," Lucy told her big sister. "It's really massive M."

Emily made us all a coffee whilst Sil' fed Sammy.

"Aw he's so gorgeous," his gran said.

"Is he?" I replied on being passed my coffee.

"We can drink these and go round to the house," smiled Emily.

"Dale Fox's mam is dead jealous," whispered Lucy, before mimicking her mum and going all posh. "Mother told the Foxes that the family would quite possibly be dining at Hamilton Square on Christmas Day."

However, that was nothing compared to the fact that Bill Kenwright would be picking Mike and Bill up from straight outside her house – well, Bill and Edie's house really – and whisking them off to Germany to watch Everton.

"My granddad went into Liverpool and bought a brand new suit," said Lucy. "He's telling everybody – It's 'Mr. Kenwright this' and 'Mr. Kenwright that' down there."

"He's as proud as a peacock," added Sil'.

That fact was confirmed when the front door opened and in he walked. I loved Bill – no airs and graces – he said it how it was. According to Bill, that certain Mr. Kenwright and the chairman of Everton F.C had personally phoned him and they had been on the phone for over an hour and a half talking about football – mainly about the great Everton and Liverpool sides. Everton hadn't always lived in the shadow of Liverpool and what is sometimes forgotten, possibly due to it being sandwiched between the success of their alleged slicker city rivals, is what a fantastic side they were – both with Howard Kendall as a player, and then as a manager.

"I think he got wind of this thing we are doing on Sheffield Wednesday," I told Bill. "As Harry Catterick plays a big part in it."

Bill listened as I told him about what a fantastic manager he was – both with Sheffield Wednesday and then with Everton.

"The history books don't give him the credit that his endeavour deserved, as he was a truly remarkable man," I added. "He was a hundred percent Evertonian – A bit like Bill Kenwright, if you like."

"He says you remind him of him," smiled Bill.

I had no idea why that was. I didn't own a football club and it certainly wasn't a path I was going to go down as only a madman would want that kind of stress.

The Sammy documentary had created a massive interest in the football world, something that was highlighted before Arsenal's abysmal capitulation in the home match versus Anderlecht, when the 1970 Fairs Cup winning team were present and duly received their accolade over the loudspeaker system to a crowd of 60,000. That team would never have surrendered a three-goal lead. At the minute Arsenal lack a natural leader – and that is something that could be aimed at Arsène Wenger.

We drove around to Hamilton Square to see Mike multi-tasking – sort of doing electrics, whilst at the same time giving orders to his son who was barrowing rubble into a skip.

"You're both working late?" I said.

"Our Stuart wants you in by Christmas," smiled Mike. "He's been grafting here every night after college and work."

"How's Paige?" his big sister asked him.

"She thinks you're ace," he said.

"Jeanette is doing tomorrow night's show," Emily told him. "We swapped programmes – I've just done a documentary on Dad's favourite band. It should be on next week."

"She was a nightmare, Stu – loads worse than Eddie – she wouldn't read what was on the autocue."

"It's really hard – I prefer just talking," she said.

I had noticed that, and I duly informed her of the fact.

"Shurrup you," she twanged.

Emily walked around the house in awe both linking my arm whilst leaning into me. "It's magnificent isn't it?" she said.

"It is," I replied.

This was something that we were doing together. This wasn't my house that she had come to share with me – this was our house, and I gathered from her constant albeit dead enthusiastic nattering in my ear that she knew exactly what she was going to do with it. You just had to love her. "White – I'd like everything white," she said. "A red carpet for the staircase, solid wooden floors in every room and huge cream drapes."

I'd never been one for interior decorating – so long as I had Sky TV, a bed and a settee I was sound. Emily had been like a whirlwind from day one of her moving in and the house in King's Cross was totally unrecognisable. Well, apart from the ferrets racing around the floorboards on a weekend and the great mountain of ironing that you could stick a flag on top of, that is. I had a lot to thank her for, and one of the ways of thanking her was to give her something like this. And she was right – It was magnificent, but so was she.

We had some supper at Mike and Sil's, gave Sammy a kiss and a cuddle – not that he appreciated it however, and made the drive back down into London. Wolfsburg here we come!

I woke up at 4:10am to The Association playing 'Windy' on the downstairs radio and the percolator hissing and Emily in my new 1971 Arsenal shirt that she'd swiped off me as soon as it had arrived off Ebay and humming along to the music. As soon as I came into the kitchen I copped a kiss, a cup of coffee and Sky Sports was turned on and muted so I could read the headlines – and all in that order. Like I said – magnificent.

Emily had booked us on a British Airways flight and into some hotel on Braunschweiger Strasse which she had thoroughly vetted, insisting that it had to have a squeaky bed, thin walls, no headboard for her handcuffs and a broken shower. Well, if she didn't that's we got – or would be getting.

The drive into Heathrow was like Wacky Races and you needed to have eyes up your arse to negotiate the way into the place and that being the case I was dead glad I'd ordered a taxi.

"I couldn't do this every morning," I said, looking out of the window at the headlights of cars flying backwards and forwards.

"It is a bit mad, isn't it?" replied my wife.

We got to the terminal where Emily, even though she was wearing a cream dress and a sort of matching Muslim head scarf Hijab 'thingy', which incidentally she had quite a few of, was immediately spotted and that being the case I noticed lots of mobile phones coming out – some secretly and some not so secret, with one girl in particular taking a selfie with my wife as part of it.

"You're really tiny, aren't you?" said the girl.

"It's crap having a famous wife," I said.

"No – it's definitely not," she said, obviously loving all the attention.

She also loved flying Club Class and made no secret of it by stating that the 'Golden queue' was far better than having to stand with all the peasants. My lad's utter snobbery when it came to frequent flying and air miles had obviously rubbed off on her; however, what was to happen next I certainly wasn't expecting – nor was Emily.

"Your money from the house should be through soon," said a voice.

She turned around only to cop sight of her ex-husband – a certain Mark Smith. The man whose wife I stole and more to the point, the man who had tried to make her lose the child that she was then carrying – the child that would become our Sammy.

"Do yourself a favour pal – And fuck off," I said.

He just looked at me and sort of gathered his thoughts. "Just make sure she doesn't go and have an affair on you," he smirked.

"Sorry love," said Emily after we had got shut of the luggage.

"Why, it's not your fault," I said giving her a cuddle. I detested the man, not so much because I knew him, because I didn't. Apart from getting beaten up by him twice and him calling at my door to confirm he wouldn't stand in the way of his wife's divorce – I'd never seen him. However, Emily described him to me time and time again whilst looking in the crib at Sammy – and of his botched-up job of child destruction, whereby he had thrown her down a full flight of stairs. She also told me about how cruel and manipulative he could be.

"I was his toy – He got me out when he wanted me and put me back when he'd finished with me," she had said. "I couldn't do this and I couldn't do that – I was his possession. I couldn't even buy my own clothes."

"Yeh – but you're with me now," I had replied. In fact I always said it and I always got that beautiful smile back. "And look at how many pairs of shoes and how many clothes you've got now."

"Yeh – you're great," she'd say.

I loved that bit. I always loved that bit.

The deliveries from Modatoi and other online stores were fairly regular, so much so I did in one instance state that it may be easier if she just ordered everything at once – or go and live in a distribution centre or warehouse. The DPD man must have had a bad back, the amount of stuff he had to carry up the street and ram through our letterbox.

"What have you been up to today," I'd ask her.

"Just tidying my shoes and clearing out my wardrobe."

She had to be lying as you needed to nail all her wardrobes shut with the amount of clothes that were in them and don't even mention her billion pairs of shoes, which were always scattered about here, there and everywhere. I was always falling over them.

"Do you like these?" she'd say, giving me a bit of a pose in some new shoes that she'd bought.

"They're exactly like ones you've already got?" I'd reply.

"No they're not," she'd say. "These have got a smaller heel," or "These have got a bit of silver in them." And then it was a case of her diligently pointing out the difference to me – no matter how trivial. "Can you see?" she'd ask.

She had worked out – as had my kids – that any request she made would generally be met with a "Yes" – well most of the time anyway – as I certainly didn't want another pet to look after – or, in M's case another baby, as that is what I got asked three nights on the trot the other week. Not so much could she have one, but did I want one?

"Not if it's going to turn out like the last one I frigging don't," I'd said.

"Yeh, but you love children," she'd replied.

230

She was right, I did – I loved them a lot.

Seeing her husband had rattled her a bit, but we'd been together now nearly eleven months, around eight of which she had lived with me – and she knew that she would always be looked after, therefore her 'being rattled' didn't last that long and after a couple of coffees, a trawl around the Duty Free and a phone call to her mum she was buzzing again.

"Mam says she's recording the match tonight and that she can't wait to see you," she smiled.

Her mum was one of many other things in my life which I loved.

We touched down in Hannover and we flagged a cab and got shuttled what seemed like a hundred miles to the hotel where under no circumstances whatsoever could we leave until we had christened the bed as she had some fetishist attraction about doing the deed in different surroundings. That was a big mistake as we had half the landing out. The Germans definitely make more durable cars than they do beds as ours was in bits after M had finally found what she was looking for.

"What's up, don't you love me anymore?" I asked.

"The bed kept putting me off," she said.

I totally acknowledged the squeakiness of the thing, however the noise she was making sort of drowned most of it out.

It had been a similar scenario at her Auntie Joan and Uncle Bryan's Silver wedding anniversary, who lived just around the corner from her mum's and which was really a story for another day.

"You okay, M?" her auntie had asked on her getting out of the bathroom.

"Yeh sure," Emily had said whilst giving a shrug of her shoulders.

"You were making an awful lot of noise in there," her auntie had added.

Tell me about it. It was me who'd had to put my hand over her mouth whilst she was doing whatever she was doing whilst at the same time trying to demolish the toilet and break both femurs in my legs. It was that intense it took a good couple of minutes to get the feeling back in my arse.

In this instance however, and after nearly breaking my neck in the shower – as she insisted on getting in with me and pissing around with the soap – we went to the Volkswagen Arena, which was like a mini-Emirates and where I picked up my press badge. A few Everton fans were there, one of who immediately noticed my wife and within minutes she was standing posing for photographs with them. Some football supporters get a bad name, but these were as courteous as you could meet and her coming from Birkenhead was a really big thing to them.

"My husband's reporting on it for ITV," she told them. "It will be Lee who's running the new ITV Seven football channel in the New Year."

"Yeh – I've seen you in the Echo," said one. "You did that documentary for Sky on the World Cup and that one where you sourced all the old footage."

"Jon Sammels of Arsenal," I nodded.

"Yeh – The paper said something about you moving up to Liverpool," he said.

"We've bought a place, but it's just so we don't put on M's parents on a weekend," I said. "As ITV Seven will be broadcast out of Manchester."

"So how do you think we'll fair tonight?" asked another lad.

"Sit back and play it on the counter and you've got a great chance of winning," I replied. "That's if you don't concede in the first twenty minutes."

"Do you rate them – Wolfsburg?" asked another kid.

"Everton are well-equipped to do them – two-nil – both goals on the break," I said.

I was sticking my neck out, but I knew if they kept them out for the first twenty minutes, the Germans would run out of ideas.

"They were all really nice lads, weren't they?" said Emily, as we walked around the ground.

She was right – they were.

"If I didn't support Arsenal then I think I'd support Everton," she said.

I told her that there's always a reason why a person chooses a football club, and what she had just said was a valid one.

"You shouldn't support a club just because I support it – It should be your own decision," I said. "Everton are like your home town club as well."

"Yeh?" she smiled.

"And it'd really piss your granddad off."

She laughed at that.

"No, I couldn't start wearing an Everton shirt – not after wearing the Arsenal one," she said.

"A lot of players think like that," I said.

"What, because they like the red top with white sleeves?"

"Not exactly," I smiled.

I met up with an ITV camera crew around an hour later – and the director – if you like, wanted me to speak to a few Everton fans about the game which would be part of the Thursday night programme.

"M, do us a favour and go and get those lads over there that we've just been speaking to," I asked. "Tell them I want them on TV."

Emily didn't need asking twice and came back with an entourage of around two dozen of them.

The director gave me my cue and I hit the lads with a few questions, however they initially kept on interrupting each other.

"Listen lads," I told them. "This is a piece of piss – one at a time – Let each other speak – and here's the thing – think before you speak – that way we can put Everton over in a good light – as it's you who are currently flying the flag."

I got a few nods as well as a few smiles.

"I'm here outside the Volkswagen Arena in Wolfsburg with some of the fantastic travelling Everton support," I said looking at the first lad who I'd already spoken to earlier and I gave him the nod. "So for the Everton supporters back home, where have you travelled from this morning?"

"I've come with around four mates who are from the Edge Hill area of Liverpool and we flew out of John Lennon'," he said.

"There's around eight of us from around West Derby Road," said another. "We were all on the same flight."

"It would be a stupid question to ask if you are looking forward to the game, so I won't ask the obvious – who do you reckon could be the players to look out for from Wolfsburg?"

"Apart from Bendtner and Luis Gustavo, I'm not that up on them," the first guy said. "They've got that Kevin De Bruyne playing for them as well."

"There you go," I replied. "Three players you know plus two Croatian internationals – Olic and Ivan Perisic – neither who are that fantastic. You weather the home attack early on in the first period and that's all they've got to throw at you."

Another lad piped up, "Do you rate Perisic?"

I smiled at the question. "Not particularly – although he did score a nice goal against Arsenal when he was with Dortmund, but if I'm being honest it was one of those volleys that could have gone anywhere."

"What is he – a striker?" asked another lad.

"Not really, he's supposedly a winger but one of those Arsène Wenger-type wingers that can play either side of the main man as well as behind him – He's a big lad too, to be honest – but if he was *that* good Roberto Martinez or one of the other top-tier Premiership managers would have bought him – especially bearing in mind both his age and the fee he went to Wolfsburg for."

"How much did they buy him for?" asked the other Everton lad.

"I heard around eight million," I said, "but whether or not you can believe that or not, I don't know."

"Do you rate Martinez?" asked another lad.

"I do," I replied. "And the fact that the Everton board have let him throw over thirty million at Lukaku, means that, more importantly so does your club."

"Who's your team?" asked another.

"For my sins, Arsenal," I replied.

"What's happening there?" he asked.

I shook my head. "The system is built around Olivier Giroud being able to hold up the ball – he's been out injured so once they lose possession up top, the ball quickly ends up back in their half – too many players doing the same thing and wanting to show boat."

"Do you rate Welbeck?" one asked.

"Not particularly," I said.

"What about Sanchez?"

"He's a great player with a great work ethic – however, it's a team game and he needs to work on his link play and not to give the ball away so cheaply – it's nothing major – but he's another reason why Arsenal are currently prone to getting hit on the counter – that and the fact they don't have a cynical anchor man in midfield."

"You reckon Lukaku would have fitted in at Arsenal?" another lad asked.

"No – Wenger has a problem when it comes to handling ego's," I said.

"Why – you reckon he's got one?"

"For Mourinho to bring an ageing Drogba back to Chelsea instead of using Lukaku tells its own story," I said. "I'm not a fan of the man himself, but I am of his management. He obviously thought there was a problem."

The questions were coming fast and furious and whereas it was me supposedly asking them, it was them asking me – and this went on for over an hour, which by that time I had around two hundred Everton supporters around me.

"Will you start supporting Everton when you move to Birkenhead?" one of the lads asked.

"I think that once you start supporting a club, nothing can change it – that is, of course if you are serious about football and not one of these so-called Manchester United fans," I replied. "Your city's other club were a massive European super club when the majority of you were kids, yet you follow Everton – You have to be proud of the choice you made as it says everything about you."

Everything went quiet around me.

"You think I'm kidding?" I asked.

There was a bit of nodding and shrugging.

"I mean what I say – It takes a lot of guts to follow the club of your heart, when the club next to you are winning everything and are everyone's darling."

"Do you rate Liverpool?"

"Everyone's now found out that Liverpool are nothing without Luis Suarez," I said. "Rodgers was extremely fortunate to inherit him, as he was the sole reason they got where they got."

"What about Raheem Sterling?" one asked.

"He was a revelation in the Premiership last season, but for me personally I don't like players with no end product as in football it is always the end result that matters," I said.

"Keep it going," said the director, sort of giving me the 'thumbs up' that this was all good stuff.

"What this?" I asked.

"Just keep doing what you're doing," he said nodding.

I looked around and caught a glimpse of Emily smiling over at me, who I knew by now must have been bored to tears.

"Two minutes lads," I said, before summoning her over.

"I got you a coffee, but I didn't want to interrupt you," she said. "It may be a bit cold."

I gave her a cuddle and had a sip at my coffee, whilst the camera kept on rolling.

236

"So when does this new football channel kick off?" one of the Everton lads asked.

"Third of January at six o'clock in the morning," smiled Emily. "You watch and yer'll see that it'll be fantastic."

"She's my PR manager," I lied.

There were a few smiles after I'd said that along with one of them saying, "I wish she was mine," which had everyone laughing.

"You could do with leaving me a few of your numbers, as a lot of ITV Seven will be very grass roots," I told them. "I'm trying to steer away from your boring Shearer – Hanson – Savage type punditry and give the viewers a different and more honest and forthright angle of the game and M's right – It will be good as some of the ideas we have for it are fantastic."

"What footballers have you got?" asked another.

"None," I replied.

"None?" one asked.

I shook my head. "I've just had over an hour talking to around thirty or forty Everton supporters right here and not one of you has asked a stupid question nor made a stupid comment and there's been no tasty language nor bloopers and the camera has been continually rolling. When I said you should be proud – I meant it – most ex-professionals would have dropped some bollock at some point."

That got a few laughs.

I could have chatted to them all day, however what would happen next had them all in shock as Bill Kenwright, of all people, walked into the crowd and offered me his hand amidst him getting patted on the back along with a few "Hello Mr. Kenwright"'s.

"How are you, young man?" he said as I shook his hand.

"Fine," I replied before introducing my wife. "This is M – Mike's daughter and Bill's granddaughter."

Emily smiled and shook his hand whilst at the same time giving him a peck on the cheek.

"I've just been telling some of your lads that they have done their club proud," I told him, whilst the camera was still rolling.

"Really?" he beamed.

"Really," I confirmed.

"Your father-in-law tells me that you've bought a place in Birkenhead," he said, partly looking at me and then playing to the audience. "Does that mean we'll see you at Goodison Park?"

"I can't see why not," I replied.

"So how do you think we'll fare tonight?" he asked.

I told him what I had said before, that providing Everton didn't concede in the first twenty minutes the Germans would run out of ideas and could be picked off on the counter.

"Everton are well capable of winning this competition how they are playing at the moment," I said. "However, it depends on what form you are in when you get to the knockout stage as regards getting to Warsaw – but all the same I wouldn't write you off."

"You think that we can win it?" asked one of the lads.

"Put it this way – there's nobody in this competition you should be scared of," I said.

We managed to get a break from the camera and a now rather bullish chairman as I bought us both a coffee.

"You'll look great on camera," said Emily.

"It's not quite what I had in mind when I signed the contract," I told her. "I prefer being in the background."

"Nevertheless, wait until the public see yer," she twanged.

I was right – She was definitely my PR manager.

Within an hour or so, two faces we knew were pinpointed and an ever-so-proud dad and granddad came over to give their daughter and granddaughter a hug.

"Are you both enjoying yourselves?" I asked.

"Sil' says you've been on the telly already," said Mike. "The regional news."

I deflected the comment and gave a somewhat nonchalant nod of my head. "Bill Kenwright's knocking around here somewhere," I said.

However, over in Liverpool Sil' had been spot on and for some reason ITV's Granada Regional News were covering the support, which I learned was a lot to do with ITV trying to push their ITV 7 station – and me.

"You looked brilliant, love," said Sil'. "And ever so smart."

"I told yer, didn't I?" Emily twanged.

The match itself went more or less exactly how I envisaged, although I think the referee made a hash of the disallowed goal which Perisic put in the net and during the halftime break I said as much. Even Bendtner had a goal disallowed, but on seeing the replay, I think the referee got that one right.

The co-commentary was a piece of piss, but I hated all the hanging around, especially as I knew it must have been dead boring for Emily.

"You okay?" I asked.

"Course I am," she lied.

We went into the town centre and we had what turned out to be a cracking meal off the Schloss Fallersleben along with a couple of bottles of dead strong German wine, which had Emily slightly reverting back to her Scouse accent before I ended up piggy-backing her all the way back to the hotel.

"Are you drunk?" I asked.

"Most definitely," she replied.

She said she couldn't really remember the sex, but I certainly could. It wouldn't have made it into my top ten but I had to admire her effort and when I awoke next day it felt like Vinnie Jones had been groping my genitals.

"If you want another kid, you can't be manhandling me like that," I told her.

That immediately got her attention and a conversation ensued whereby I was sounded out about the possible planning of a new addition.

"Are you serious?" she smiled.

"Let me get the end of the season out of the way," I said. "I need to be sure that we are all okay financially."

"We are – we've got loads of money," she said.

It was then that I mentioned to her the worry I had, which was linked to the fact that my dad had died young and that this was always at the back of my mind. "I just need to know that you will all be okay," I said.

She just looked at me – a bit strangely, if I'm being honest.

"Please M – just bear with me on this."

"And then we can start trying?" she smiled.

"We've no need to try M," I told her. "Let's make sure the timing is okay and we'll just see what happens."

"Can I tell my mam?" she asked.

I smiled at her suggestion and gave her a nod and within a few minutes I was talking on the phone to Sil' who told me that she hoped we could give her a granddaughter.

"That would be nice," I replied. However my phone started ringing – it was Abi.

"How did it go last night?" I asked, as regards the Live at The Warehouse show.

"Totally brilliant TV," she replied. "But a bit scary at the end."

That took me aback and I listened as Abi relayed what had happened. "Just pick up *The Sun* or the *Daily Mirror*," she said.

"How's Jeanette?" was the first question I asked, however before I could get an answer I noticed that ITV were trying to contact me and were on call waiting. "Let me ring off Abi," I said and I answered the incoming call. It was their head of entertainment.

"Pure dynamite," he said. "The phones have been red-hot and all the tabloids have picked up on it."

As soon as we had got the viewing figures for Live at The Warehouse we had dispensed with the mainstream music and had gone more down the route of these new indie groups we were auditioning via our Sessions programme, three of which had been on last night's show along with a really high-end female singer with dead long blonde hair called 'Menna' who was from South Wales who I did like, but who Emily certainly did not.

"She just wants to shag you," Emily had told me, sort of giving me one of those looks as though I had just told her to go and do all the ironing.

As it transpired the three bands – C.G.G - The Cockney Green's, who were a five-man band from the Barnsbury Wood area of north London, Electric Ladyboy a four piece band from Muswell Hill and a four piece band called Seager who were fronted by a young girl called Jody Reeves who you could say sounded like a cross between Sonya Maden and Shirley Manson, but who looked like neither, and who if I'm being honest looked like a dead ringer for the actress Clémence Poésy. Emily thought she was incredibly talented. She also thought she was incredibly good looking, so much so she asked me my thoughts.

"Yeh, she seems good," I said, sort of underplaying it.

"She's carrying them that's for sure," Emily said. "The rest of the band are dead rubbish."

She was right. Jody Reeves may have fronted the band, but the guy pulling all the strings and allegedly making the decisions was the guy who the band themselves were named after, and none other than their rather self-important and extremely pedantic keyboard player. He could have never have been described as another Manfred Mann, as he was about as musically inclined as Linda McCartney.

I tried to have a word with Jody offset, however she was being continually policed by the said keyboard player. All I knew of this guy, was that he lived with his overbearing sister in a poky little house in Chandler's Ford and who according to Emily had had some restraining order put on him by Coleen Rooney. I must admit, that bit was pretty interesting. "What, Wayne Rooney's wife?" I asked.

"That's what that Jody told Jaime Hudson."

That had me immediately thinking that he had been hassling her by either sending her a billion love letters, continually phoning her mobile or at worst, flashing her.

"No, he was apparently hassling her husband," whispered M.

Sound, I thought. *He's definitely gone up in my estimation.*

However this is where I would be wrong. It took M the best part of an hour to explain it to me as it was that frigging unbelievable. There was to be a lot more surrounding this Jody Reeves-thing, however that was in the future and certainly not now.

Cue: Abi, and another problem for me.

I never thought on when me and Abi put the guts of the show together that there was some rivalry between the two London bands – and by rivalry – I mean football rivalry. Bar the drummer, the Cockney Green's were an Arsenal band who I'd had to advise them to abbreviate their name from Cockney Green Gooners to C.G.G., as it would have certainly affected their potential. They were quite fine with that and in all honesty they were a very impressive London Irish band that according to Emily sounded very stringy in a Rickenbacker type of way, whilst at the same time had a good thumping sound. Electric Ladyboy I was led to believe were a bit more sedate, but it was here is where I would be very, very wrong.

The Session's programme was recorded in a studio and this is all we saw, the upshot being that we had no idea how they would be in front of an audience. As it turned out, Electric Ladyboy's original rendition of their song 'Serial Offender' would be the song to finish the show, and as it turned out the show finished in a riot, not at least because they were from Muswell Hill and were a die-hard Tottenham band and the first thing the lead singer did on being introduced to sing out the show was tear off a false skin on their drum kit to reveal a cockerel on a ball to the sound of police sirens very much similar – and very possibly a rip off of The Sweet's No. 1 hit 'Blockbuster'. However that is certainly not where it ended and their song suddenly changed from 'Serial Offender' to 'Sex Offender' with lines in its composition heavily reworded – to 'He was a nailed on fucking ringer for an Arsenal left winger', which had the members from some of the Cockney Green's as well of a few Arsenal players in the audience barracking the lead singer who just soaked it up before hitting them with another reworded line that which resulted in a little bit more than a scuffle as the drummer kicked over a few pieces of his kit as the two guitarists smashed their instruments into their amps, but not once did the music or sirens stop as the end credits rolled.

When we actually got back to the UK and saw the footage we knew we were onto a winner. Electric Ladyboy had arrived on the scene.

Chapter 19

Jeanette's Tales – Take 7

ITV had run a bit of film on Lee over in Germany, which had M passing him a coffee whilst he cuddled her, whilst at the same time talking into the camera and it went viral with everyone picking up on it, including the *Daily Mirror* who'd had some photographer out there and whose photograph got published on the front page, along with the heading of 'The UK's most beautiful couple'.

Pages four and five had shown the carnage post Live at The Warehouse where a band finishing the show had smashed up their equipment on one of the stages and where security had had to come and separate two bands from fighting. In the self-same edition the sports pages carried the headlines 'Everton's Messiah' with a photograph of Lee talking to Bill Kenwright, whilst a few pages back there was a big splurge with the four beautiful faces of ITV 7's new Fox Force Four – The Three K's plus one – Kirsty, Kim, Karen and Sinead.

Lee had truly arrived.

There were also continual rumours in all the newspapers that he was sat on some multi-million portfolio and was earning a million pounds a week, something which I knew was untrue but certainly not that wide of the mark.

Every time I went up to The Warehouse the buzz I got was tremendous, and as soon as you arrived in the car park there were people and photographers everywhere, and one day I even had a reporter and photographer on my case as I pulled up. I didn't particularly like the attention and at times it was a bit alarming. As for Lee, he hated it, however he was never that stupid to know that this was part of media's double-edged sword. Everyone wanted to know about him – this high-flying sports-media mogul and David Beckham doppelgänger with the beautiful TV star wife on his arm. He didn't just look the part – he was the part. ITV knew what they had and they wanted him to catapult their brand into space and blow the competition out of the water.

I'm making it sound that ITV were using him. They weren't as such, as a lot of them were very nice people, but they knew what they had got. At the behest of ITV Lee had started doing press conferences on a Monday and Friday mornings and really buttering them up by getting the girls in the office serving coffees and biscuits – he hated it, but he did it. Lee going to Wolfsburg with M was nothing short of a master-stroke by ITV and they knew exactly what they had done by sending him. He thought he was going as a pundit, but he wasn't. He was made to mingle in with the crowd and ask them questions, and M being with him and showing everyone that she was the adoring wife had blown everyone's mind. I didn't hear it from Lee but from Abi. ITV had sounded him out about doing a lot of other work for them and I knew that there was something going down in the fact that LMJ's lawyers had just gone in and hammered YouTube as there was some breaches of copyright. He had said nothing to me outside of asking about me and the kids and telling me he loved me.

The girls over at ITV 7 were hard to get used to as they weren't like me and M, they looked like girls but they had the mentalities of men, but I suppose that was because of the job they were doing. Kirsty was dubbed the 'Pocket Rocket' due to the fact that she was always kicking off about something or other. To be honest, once I had got talking to her she was fairly okay, but I always felt I was being looked up and down. Kim was astute and pretty but didn't say a lot to me, whilst Karen was like some high-end model with big boobs who Les and Oliver had dubbed 'Lola'. Sinead? Wow, now she was something else. She both looked and sounded like one of the singers out of The Corrs but that was where the similarity ended, but I'll get on to that in a bit. All four girls stuck to each other like glue and never let anyone outside of ITV 7 in – me included.

One morning during a press conference we were minus Lee for a bit. Well we were minus Lee plus Faranha for a bit and it got me and all the others thinking, especially when they both came out of the room at the back of The Warehouse where rubbish and boxes of stuff were stored and she was brushing down her skirt – or what she termed as a skirt rather – and straightening herself up as though she'd just managed a quick 'how's your father'. As soon as I knew that my hackles were raised, however he was still in dialogue with her as he walked over to where the six or seven press men were sitting and apologised to them for being late, before he asked me if I wouldn't mind telling Faranha how I'd like it.

How I'd like what? I thought.

"What's he on about?" I asked her, as I sat in on the conference.

It turned out he wanted to make some form of professional press room so he could wheel the press men in through the back door rather than have them either sitting at our desks or mooching around the studios.

I looked over at Faranha still thinking that something had gone on, especially when she smiled back over at me with a rather false smile.

Libby had told me that she thought Lee had given her one, but when I pulled him up on it he said that was never the case; however, no woman goes anywhere with Lee without losing their pants which brings me back to Libby, who had recently been blaming my Lee for borrowing her Sooty's car to take some girl out.

"Why would he borrow an Audi estate to take a girl out when he's got a Maserati?" I argued.

"I found these," she said holding up some scanty pair of female underwear.

I say female underwear rather than woman's underwear as the said underwear in question was really small.

"How old is she, twelve?" I asked.

"Eighteen," she replied.

She knew that as she had hacked into all the messages on his phone.

Lee was always the one who messed around, although Sooty had certainly had his moments and even when he was with Libby he had been seeing a lot of call girls as Libby had the details of all his credit card transactions. Sooty had also made a play for me, which I told neither Libby nor Lee about – around ten weeks before I actually moved in with him and another time when I'd thrown Lee out. There was a time in between, but it was one of those where he was just drunk and talking rubbish.

The first time it happened I had got to Lee's house on a Friday night and let myself in with the key under the dustbin. Even though I wasn't domesticated I always made a point of trying to look it, and had generally cleaned up and had some tea ready for him. My mother had packed me some food and had written down how to actually make a dinner and I meticulously followed her each and every instruction. However, Sooty coming in to pick up six boxes of DVD's and trying to force sex on me certainly ruined the steak pie. I wasn't behind that door that he would get what he wanted but it certainly wasn't for the lack of him trying.

The time when I had chucked Lee out was worse as both kids were upstairs. I was going to just let him get on with it so as to get back at Lee but thought, *Why should I?* before managing to stop it dead.

He loved Libby and both Mia and Zooey; however, Libby was never his first choice. Lee said Nubeon would be their undoing and it was, and although Lee obviously knew what was going on down there he never told M, therefore I never got to know; however, and this is where the story gets interesting – Sinead of all people did.

As I worked only a few days at The Warehouse I was a bit of an outsider and as I've already said the ITV 7 lot stuck together. However, one morning whilst I was in the infamous ladies toilets, Sinead stopped off for a chat. To my knowledge Sooty never ever came to The Warehouse, my thought being that envy played its part even though Lee would have given him the shirt off his back. Therefore the fact that Sinead had casually mentioned both meeting him and seeing him, meant that she had met him outside of The Warehouse and possibly down at Nubeon. I was going to dig a bit further, however Chris the make-up man wanted me at that precise moment as a photographer wanted some stills. There was also some fashion designer guy waiting to talk to me at the same time about exclusively doing my wardrobe – 'Ms. Jeanette Jane's wardrobe supplied by Milan Baros, London' it would say on the end credits of each show I did.

"What, the ex-Liverpool player?" Lee had asked me, on him contacting me through The Warehouse switchboard.

"Don't be a pillock," I had snapped.

I mentioned to M what Sinead had said, although she certainly hadn't heard anything. M however, was the sort of person who just went in like some steamroller and asked the question anyway regardless of what it was. She also answered questions in the same vein which not only had Lee panicking at times, it often pissed me off.

"Your sex life," a girl from the *Alternative Press* magazine asked, "How is it?"

"Brilliant," she said. "I can be a bit demanding, but Lee certainly has no problems with that."

"Is it varied?"

"Good god, yeh," she laughed.

The bitch, I thought.

She drove Lee batty with her honesty.

M was like a dog with a bone and we were sat astounded as Sinead casually reeled off that she was having a bit of a fling with one of the male performers down there – and one of the actresses – and the cameraman – and a technician, but not Sooty. He was in love with an 18-year old Rumanian who had previously had a fling with the technician, who Sooty had got jealous about and just sacked. We were both sat gob-smacked, not so much with the lowdown on Sooty – but Sinead.

"I thought you were married?" M asked her.

"I am," she said.

None of us said anything to Lee nor anyone else but I'll tell you something, we were certainly now very aware of her so much so she started having a coffee with us and a chat at lunchtime and we even swapped mobile numbers, and I'll tell you something – if you wanted juicy gossip, this was your girl.

As for Sooty, it turned out that he had actually asked Sinead out for some ménage et trois but she'd told him that she couldn't do that on Lee, which made M take a couple of steps back and which definitely gave her the hump.

I liked Sinead.

Chapter 20

Annie, I'm not your daddy

Herbert had been screaming his lungs out since 5:00am which meant one of us had to get up and Emily, pretending to be asleep with the pillow over her head, obviously thought it was my turn.

"What's up with you?" I asked him on getting into his bedroom.

He just looked at me and gave me his standard Edward G. Robinson-type glare.

"Are you sure you are actually mine?" I asked him.

He never denied it and just kept on staring at me.

I picked him up and changed his arse – obviously the contents of his nappy had been pissing him off a bit.

"Does that feel better?" I asked him.

He didn't say it did and he didn't say it didn't, however, I assumed it did – even though he was still looking at me with that cold wincing glare of his.

"Come on," I told him. "We'll go down stairs and I'll get you some snap."

I walked down a couple of flights of stairs and into the kitchen where I kicked up all the lights and had him blinking.

"See – your mum's tidied everything up and your bottles are all cleaned for you," I told him.

He still wasn't that impressed even though I juggled him about a bit whilst making his breakfast.

"You can have, milk, milk or milk," I told him. "And maybe if you don't whinge and whine I'll heat up some chocolate pudding because I know you like them, even though your mum does say they will make you fat."

He still never said a deal although he did watch me as I meticulously loaded up his bottle with a few scoops of powder and boiling water.

"See – I'm not like your mum – I make it up fresh for you – She likes to make up loads of bottles beforehand – and heat them up. Dead lazy, your mum is."

He still didn't seem that impressed, even though he was watching my every movement.

"Your mum is laid in bed pretending to be asleep while I'm doing this," I told him. "As soon as you're old enough she says that she's going to send you to a blacking factory in Liverpool."

I had to admit – he didn't appear too overly concerned about his future either.

"I argued your case though," I told him.

He still didn't seem that bothered as I shook up his mixture and stuck it in a measuring jug full of cold water to cool.

"Two minutes and it will be done," I told him.

He just looked up at me and said nothing.

"Your mum told me that she would never ever breast feed you as it meant her getting out of bed," I said, whilst sort of educating him at the same time. "She told me that there was no way on earth that she was getting out of bed at all hours to feed you – she said that since the day you were born you've been a right pain – and she can't wait to stick you on that stagecoach and wave you off to Liverpool. She said that when we get shut of you we can have our nice life back."

"Who are you talking to?" came a voice from around the corner.

"See – it's your lazy mum who's come to see you," I told him. "But don't trust her because she wants to get rid of you."

"Don't be telling him that," she smiled. "He'll grow up hating me."

"He will," I said. "I've just been telling him about the blacking factory in Liverpool."

"What blacking factory?" she inquired.

"Don't deny it – You said that when he's five you're going to send him away to a blacking factory in Liverpool – a place where they send bad kids."

"Don't believe him, Sammy," she argued. "He's fibbing. Dad says that he's going to send you to a special school on the Isle of Dogs for maladjusted children – I don't want you to go – but he does."

"Don't believe her, Sammy," I told him. "Mum is mean and lazy – and remember it was me who changed your bum this morning – she was pretending to be asleep."

"No I wasn't," she argued.

"Yes you were – I saw you open one of your eyes."

"I do love you – yer know," she twanged.

"I know you do," I replied, as I tested his bottle.

"It takes ages doing it that way," she said. "I find it better to heat them up – not the other way round."

"Yeh, but then he ends up with belly ache," I told her.

She made us a coffee and passed me mine.

"I can't drink mine before he has his – He'll go berserk," I said.

"Do you think he's old enough to try and manipulate us?" she asked.

"Certainly," I replied. "You think it's bad now – wait until he's two."

I rammed the bottle in his chops and he tugged away at it like the proverbial teenager in the shopping precinct with a bottle of Bud'.

"Stop gulping it," I told him. "Drink it nice and you won't get colic."

Emily kicked up Sky Sports on TV for me and turned the volume down so I could read the headlines and then put on Radio 2 for her, whilst she made us some breakfast.

"Have you got much on today?" I asked her.

"I've got three coming in for piano and violin lessons between four o'clock and seven."

"Why don't you have them all at the same time – I don't know how you stand that racket."

"Don't be mean," she said. "You've got to learn sometime – And Sammy loves it when other children come round."

"That's not what he told me," I lied.

"Why, what did he say?"

"He said he hates all the noise they make and when he's old enough he's going to flog that big piano and blow all the money on chocolate puddings."

"He told me he's going to support Manchester United when he grows up," she argued. "And he's going to have pictures of Wayne Rooney on his wall."

"What – he told you that?"

She nodded an exaggerated 'Yes'.

I looked down at him gulping his breakfast. "You're a right mate you are," I told him. "You get me up at the crack of dawn and make me change you and feed you and then you do that to me?"

He didn't say a deal and just knocked back the contents of his bottle.

"I did tell you that everything will change once Arsenal get rid of Arsène Wenger," I said to him. "You can't go giving up on the club like that – I supported them when they were rubbish."

"I thought you said they were rubbish now?" smiled Emily.

"I never said that," I argued.

"Yes, you did, you fibber," she winked, as she snuggled up at the side of me and while the eggs were grumbling over in the poacher. "I do love our life."

I knew she did and there wasn't a day that went by when I wasn't told it.

I drove out to The Warehouse around eight o'clock and on getting to the reception area I noticed Faranha speaking at length with the postman, who was incidentally dropping off two sacks of post.

"We need some other people working here," she had said, after all three programmes went out on air. "It's like this every day – It's taking me half a day to separate the proper mail from the fan mail that both M and Jeanette are getting."

Fan mail was a sore point – and one that was rarely discussed. Emily had around a hundred letters a day – some from nice normal people and some from not-so-nice and not-so-normal people. Jeanette had a mini fan base too, however the programme she hosted didn't attract the frigging idiots that Emily's did.

In the end I got Abi to employ two really nice girls – Sasha and Georgia – two stonewall Goonerettes – who I had dubbed 'Pepsi and Shirley' to handle the so-called fan mail, separating it and letting both Emily and Jeanette have the more appropriate – with the girls either responding to or in some cases binning what was left.

Most of the time it was kids wanting signed photos as pin-ups or something to wank over – but sometimes it wasn't, and one of the girls came to my office and tentatively offered me one of these that wasn't.

"I'm sorry Lee, but I had to show you this," she said.

I had an open mind, but this was downright disgusting – some fucking idiot from some backwater town in the Midlands telling my wife what he would like to do to her didn't sit well with me at all. And it wasn't just one letter, either – it was a series of letters.

I may come across as some shallow and conceited prick at times, but my family are everything and trying to act normal when this was constantly at the back of my mind was near-on impossible. However, whilst my mind was on this, a letter sailed beneath the radar and Jeanette had had one passed on to her as part of a batch of forty-odd and it was me who was at the end of a panicked phone call. Some idiot had seen her on the rather riotous Live at The Warehouse show she had hosted and had been writing her lines from some Edgar Allan Poe novel, which in itself was more sad than anything else. However when he mentioned the fact that he fantasised about her menstruating and him being there to do whatever he wanted to do to her – well, it freaked her out.

"Should I be worried?" had been her first question and, "Do you think he knows where I live?" had been her second.

I sought some legal advice from my corporate lawyers; however, the fact that it wasn't threatening in any way, shape or form left me with little or no options. However, I couldn't let Jeanette know that nothing could be done, and I had them draft up a standard letter on their headed paper which would be hand delivered by a legal agent along with a policeman to any idiot that advertised their address, which strangely – they often did.

The two girls who I gave the title of PR executives – which was a really good move by me as when I did they thought I was great – also handled the thousand or so requests via both mail and our website for tickets for Live at The Warehouse. They may have handled them – but I made sure who they were handed out to. I would be the first to admit that this was an extremely shallow and non-pc thing to do – however, the last thing the public wanted to see was ugly men and women on set.

Tickets to the general public cost £150 a piece, which was relatively cheap; however each person was seriously vetted – and when I say seriously vetted I mean seriously vetted. A thousand of these tickets went out every week – and no-one could get a ticket unless they provided or uploaded a scanned copy of either their passport or their driving licence, and it was that I.D that needed to be presented at the door along with a named ticket. This would be a great idea to bring safe standing and terraces back at football grounds; however, I don't think that that will happen any time soon. There were also complimentary tickets that got sent out to the so-called 'in-crowd' – footballers plus their partners, actors, actresses and other showbiz types and I always made sure Sooty had a dozen or so of his Nubeon girls there to make up the numbers.

After four weeks on air we had around 14 million viewers and a waiting list of around thirty-thousand people, and wasted no time in advertising the fact.

This day was no different and on sifting through the mail Faranha passed me what she assumed was the mail I wanted to see – in particular, the mail that contained cheques.

As I have already said, when ITV initially sounded me out about their new football channel, they wanted three hours of TV off me as part of this 'sprat to catch the mackerel' scenario. I'd initially assumed that they had wanted these three hours doing for nothing as not only did they know that sports media was my baby – and that I wanted to get back into it, they also knew that due to the sale of our company I now had a bit of financial clout. They also knew I had ready-made studios, which added to their alleged *nil outlay* scenario. Therefore after I'd signed the contract for ITV 7 I was invited to attend a meeting with ITV's head of entertainment, some other suits and one of their top number-crunchers as regards the mainstream TV we were to knock out. In meetings such as this it is always better to listen to what they have to say and only speak when spoken to and I was immediately made aware of the fact that they only had so much in the kitty, and that they really would prefer to be billed on a cost-plus arrangement, similar to how ITV 7 would be structured. As I said – in these type of meetings it is always best to keep your mouth shut. In reality I could have produced all three programmes (four shows) with change out of £50,000, however I never, ever said that, and when the number-cruncher mentioned factoring in my wages, I became aware that I'd actually be able to earn money from these programmes.

"I know I'm being petty, but can we cap your wage at forty thousand pounds per show?" he had asked whilst dotting I's and crossing T's, him knowing that for the four shows – the equivalent of my four weeks wages, it would be a saving of over £1,500.

I loved the guy, he was trying to cap costs on everything from studio time to locations to wages, and the thing was – if they would have asked, I would have done the lot for nothing.

Afterwards, the head of entertainment apologised for the frugal nature of their bean counter and let me know that so long as we came in at under £250,000 per show we'd get them signed off and that is exactly what I did.

I remember Emily sat on the bed cross-legged whilst I relayed to her what had been said.

"So yer'll be earning a million pounds a week for this?" she whispered.

"What are you whispering for?" I whispered back.

"I don't know," she whispered.

It wasn't really as much as that, as when ITV saw how cheaply I could knock out the two Sessions programmes they had told me in no uncertain terms not to take the piss. The ITV people were great and knowing that ITV 7 would set us up for life, I agreed to shave £50,000 off.

Due to the money we would be handling we had needed an in-house accountant so I mentioned that fact to a girl who worked in corporate accounting for Big Deckers firm – Johanne Edgington.

"You fancy a job, Jo?" I'd asked her.

"I'd love to, but I'm tied into a three-year contract," she replied.

She did, however tip me the wink about an exceptional freelance accountant who had 'issues'; however, she didn't really go into the intricate details of what these frigging actual issues were. "She's really good," she went on to explain. "She worked in our Swansea office, but the traveling was too much for her as she suffers from fibromyalgia."

I mentioned this to Emily, who enlightened me a bit.

"It's sort of neurobiological," she told me. "They have a low threshold to pain."

"Not like you then?" I winked.

"Definitely not like me," she smiled, before telling me. "One of my aunties had it."

"Which auntie? You've got millions of them."

"Auntie Heather," she said. "It made her dead miserable, but my dad always put that down to my uncle Jimmy."

Annie Dixon was a single mum from Llangrannog on the west coast of Wales who, on first meeting her face to face, had scared me shitless as she just seemed to look through you and never ever smiled. There was no denying the fact that she knew her way around finance though!

"She looks like that psycho woman in that film with Ben Affleck we watched the other week," I had told Emily as I looked for it.

"You mean Rosamund Pike," she replied. "Jeanette borrowed it."

I tried to get it off Jeanette, however she had noticed the resemblance and lent it Les who had lent it Kirsty who had lent it Sinead who had lent it Oliver ... and so it went.

"So who's got the DVD now?" I'd asked.

"What DVD?" asked Annie, as she had suddenly appeared behind me.

"Nothing," I'd lied.

She did the banking, made sure cheques were signed and paid the bills – she was more organised than Emily and a much bigger bitch than Jeanette, therefore doing the job she did totally suited her.

After Mike and his mates had completed the warehouse conversion I then had them tart up Bondy's flat in Cockfosters and gave her the keys and told her it came free with the job. Unfortunately I had failed to tell the actual guy who owned the flat, and one night when he was moving in between continents, his intention was to grab a couple of nights in London. However, on her copping some big Asian coming through the front door while she was sat on the sofa in her nightie watching an episode of 'Mad Men' – she attacked him.

"It's me who owns the flat, you silly cow," he'd shouted whilst trying dodge a second and third blow from a carving knife.

I took an irate call from him. "Can you just tell this stupid cow who I am," he snarled down the phone. "She's just stabbed me with a bread knife."

I'd say she apologised but that would be a lie and by the time I had got up there they were partaking in some really intense dialogue – her with the bread knife still in her mitts.

"I reckon this is a hospital job," I'd told him after giving him my humble medical opinion.

"You don't fucking say?" he'd replied.

Annie was quite unfazed by it all. "Do you think Don Draper's wife looks like Freddie Mercury?" she asked, while still sat on the sofa holding the bread knife.

Mmm, she did a bit – especially when he was going through his pushing the hoover around in a skirt phase, whilst at the same time wanting to break free.

I got Bondy into the car and drove him to casualty where they stitched and bandaged him up before kicking him out.

"Anyway, what are you doing over here," I had asked him.

"A bit of a job for Sooty," he had told me.

"What bit of a job for Sooty?" I'd inquired.

It transpired that Sooty, like myself was sourcing young up-and-coming talent for the camera, but whereas mine was extensively from the Arsenal fan-base his was not, and was more Rumanian and Philippine if I were being honest.

"What – so you're human trafficking now?" I asked.

"Nah," he replied. "Just getting him girls."

"Yeh – human trafficking."

"Do you want one?" he had asked. "I've got one of those little ones who looks really cute."

"No thanks," I had replied.

I mentioned this to Emily when I finally got home and I have to admit she thought about it – well, for just under ten seconds anyway. That could have been due to the fact that she was indeed deliberating about it, or that it was just a shock question.

"What you'd have some young foreign girl living in?" she asked.

"Well, she'd be able to do all those jobs you hate like ironing and cleaning out the ferrets …."

It wasn't often she did it, but when she did I could certainly tell where Herbert got his miserable look from. Generally all I had to do was throw her in the room full of ironing or refuse her sex to cop this look, the latter of which had only ever happened about three times – Once when I'd pulled my back shifting the washer to retrieve a ferret – another time when I'd picked up some stomach bug after a meal down Brick Lane – and the other time on 'Black Sunday' after Arsenal threw away another lead in the last fifteen minutes at Swansea City.

"What, yer don't want to do it with me because Arsenal lost?" she twanged, whilst stood at the foot of the stairs arms-folded, her hair tied up and wearing only a pair of stockings and shoes, the latter of which had strangely been delivered that morning.

Mmm. A bit of Déjà vu there! I thought

I might have refused it but I certainly got it. Afterwards I told her that the new shoes were just like the ones she wore to go to my mum's funeral. She said they were similar but were indeed a more gun metal grey than black. She also asked me if I thought she looked like Margot Robbie's character in 'The Wolf of Wall Street' which we had watched the night before on DVD.

"No, you're about five inches shorter and much better looking," I told her.

She quite liked that, but as for Bondy's offer of a rather pretty and diminutive Philippine girl pandering around after me, that was a definite no-no, but I'll tell you something – the ironing got done straight after I'd mentioned it!

As for Bondy himself, he didn't hang around long after that.

The Warehouse had been a bare shell after its conversion and I asked Sooty to come and have a look at it, but he was more preoccupied in what he was doing than what I was looking at doing, but both Emily and Jeanette were amazed at how the architect had redesigned it and my ex put a lump in my throat when she told me how proud she was of me.

"She means it," Emily had said.

I knew that. Jeanette rarely said things that she didn't mean – and this was the case when we first started auditioning bands for the Sessions programme.

'Rubbish – crap – don't like him – what a dick – shit – rubbish – crap – You must be bloody joking.' were all statements that would affect someone or someone's life.

We had a recording studio in The Warehouse that was as good as the one we once owned on Euston Road even though we had to reorder the glass for it twice as the glaziers kept on cracking it whilst trying to install it and, on getting it finally completed we started recording bands.

"There's no need to put on a show," I told them. "Just knock the tracks out as best as you can."

"Yeh – but you're filming us, man," said a certain Ross Bain who was with a band called the Queen and Pistol.

"I know – but it is the music we are after," I explained.

I was sick of telling them that.

The thing was that with shows such as Sessions and other reality TV is that they are dead-cheap to produce – which is the sole reason why TV and media companies in particular love them.

Sessions was an ongoing thing and we recorded band upon band upon band.

So as not to have Emily backwards and forward to The Warehouse we just slung them up into cyberspace on

Dropbox and she watched and listened to them and gave me her verdict – as did Jeanette.

I got in one night and Emily was listening to some band from Glasgow who we'd had down a few weeks earlier– I forget their name, so they must have been good! She did however, say that they reminded her a bit of Lloyd Cole & the Commotions.

"Which bit?" I asked.

"Don't be horrible," she said, as she snuggled up to me on the couch whilst we watched them on her laptop.

I liked Lloyd Cole. Well, that's a lie – I liked Lloyd Cole when he was with The Commotions – as he went a bit weird after they'd split up, even though his 'No Blue Skies' was quite a lovely song.

This track Emily was engrossed in had a similar morbidity about it, but they were certainly no Lloyd Cole.

"Did you know he was from the same town as Jeanette?"

"Who?"

"Lloyd Cole."

I thought he was from Glasgow and I told her so.

"No, he's from Derbyshire," she said. "He went to Glasgow Uni' though."

"I thought that was that nosy doctor who you said went to Glasgow Uni?" I asked.

"Yeh – he did," she said. "So did Lloyd Cole."

There was another story here and not about Lloyd Cole.

Sammy was only a couple of months old when we changed doctors as the Pakistani one we had hated my guts and insinuated that we must have been horsewhipping him – Sammy, that is.

"No baby cries like that," he had said.

"Well, this one does," Emily had replied.

Him telling her that 'she can't be treating him right' rubbed me totally up the wrong way, so much so I showed him the door prior to me threatening to give him a kick up the arse.

My macho showing must have impressed my wife as I got treat to a special love that turned out to be a little bit more special than I was generally used to and which three days later had us both sat on the bed – her in a pair of stockings – again – and me in my boxers both scratching our heads and sniffing around like a pair of Bisto kids – however, there was nothing very "Ah Bisto" about this little lot.

"Jesus, M – I can't put my head in there," I told her.

"Does it smell bad?"

"Well, it doesn't smell good."

"Thank you very much," she said.

"No, you generally smell great," I informed her.

"But I don't now?"

"Not particularly," I said.

Since I gave our regular doctor the boot, we had registered with the one Sooty and Lib used who just happened to be one of Sooty's Sunday morning golfing buddies – and on booting Emily out of the door I plugged in a couple of Airwick fresheners, chucked a bit of Fabreze around the place and kept my fingers crossed that I would be soon be back 'whistling Dixie' in my favourite place ever.

"He was really nosy," said Emily on her return.

"Really?"

"Mmm – He asked if we engaged in the old rule number one," she said.

She was dead right – he did sound nosy, I thought.

"What did you tell him?"

"I told him not since last Tuesday and before that probably Saturday or Sunday."

"Jesus, you can't go telling him shit like that!" I gasped. "His wife is a mate of Jeanette and Libby."

"So?" she protested.

This honesty thing with Emily was a right pisser at times and I told her much.

"He can't make a proper diagnosis if I start lying, can he?" she said.

She had a point but I wasn't going to tell her that, but him discussing my sordid sex life with his pals over eighteen holes or to his witch of a wife made me feel rather uneasy.

"He's a doctor – he'll not say anything," she added.

"What else did he say?" I asked.

"He just wanted to know about our sex life," she said.

"What about it?"

"About rules number one and number one, and that while we are doing it, we should try not to engage in rules number three or four until you've had a bath," she said.

"So what did he say is up with you?" I asked.

"He says I've got Bacterial vaginosis."

"What's that?" I inquired.

"A stinky flue," she said.

I knew that already and that being the case I had to call her on it.

She then went into her handbag and she got a small toothpastey looking thing out and passed it me over. "It's a gel – He says to take it for seven days."

I gave it a bit of a squirt and it tasted like shit.

"Christ, M – that's horrible."

"It's for me, you great nit," she laughed. "And you're supposed to stick it up your thingy – not eat it!"

Back to the Sessions programme – we used to record it on a Sunday night and pass it over to ITV the next day; however, there was an initial jockey to be top dog between Emily and Jeanette – not that they ever told me or that they ever made it obvious, it was more to do with the fact that Emily knew more about music than Jeanette did and that Jeanette thought that Emily highlighted that fact just a teeny little bit more than she should have done.

On interviewing a band member Emily could casually ask why they had suddenly jumped from an A minor chord to a D and back again? or sit cross-legged on a stool intensely asking a rather unnerving question of "So, why use an A major dominant, then flip back to a B minor submediant?" or in another instance amid carefree aplomb, mention the fact that this particular band quite resembled The Teardrop Explodes – so much so that even Julian Cope would be intrigued.

Jeanette's dialogue however, was more to the point in 'Where do you come from?' and 'When are you going back?'

Emily's star was rising as soon as it hit the screens, although the viewing numbers it attracted made ITV think really about dumping it after three shows – and was it not for the fact that they were receiving hundreds of letters a day, I'm sure they would have. Ours was never something as tawdry, cheap and nasty as the X factor – this was real and earthy and very 'John Peel', and Emily was its star.

Chapter 21

The Terminator

Jeanette had been moaning like hell about how long it was taking to cut part of a documentary as part of the rebranded Inside True Britain series.

"So tell me – why have I got to go up to Edinburgh – again?" she asked. "M has never had to go further than Bounds Green Lane."

We'd had a team of three from Burbeck London University write us up what was a fantastic documentary on 'The baby-faced Assassin – Jamie Bain' – a guy who was currently serving a life sentence with a minimum tariff of 22 years after he gunned down a former boxer in some pub in the city back in 2006.

It was obviously not as high profile as Fred and Rose West, but it was a very complex story with a lot of stuff that had never been mentioned before – and the two girls and lad who had done it had done a remarkable job. It had been a great bit of journalism and I was extremely happy with the content. However, if Jeanette thought Edinburgh was a bit off the radar, I knew she'd go absolutely potty when she found out that she was currently being processed through the Chinese Embassy for a Visa. I must admit I couldn't keep a straight face as I spilled the beans – all ten tins of them.

"What, you're sending me to China?"

I nodded.

She never said a deal but I could hear her head ticking ready for her mouth to explode.

"Why China?"

"It's a bit hard doing a frigging documentary on the Rape of Nanking if the furthest you're wanting to go is Zones One and Two on the Tube," I said.

"So what about the kids?"

"What about them?" I asked.

"It's like you just keep sending me away so I'm never at home. I had four days in Edinburgh last week."

"I looked after the kids," I said.

"Yeh – and don't I bloody know it," she snapped.

There was a story here that sort of started Monday and concluded Wednesday with Jeanette supposedly having to go in for a bollocking from the headmaster at my kids' school. Well, he thought that would be the case but what transpired was that with Jeanette M.I.A up in Scotland, I would be summoned to take her place, and the strangest thing occurred.

The week had started with Jeanette dropping the kids off at daft o'clock on Monday morning as she had to go shoot some stuff on location north of the border and also needed to get into HMP Shotts in Lanarkshire between 2:00 and 4:00pm for an exclusive interview with the gangland murderer himself, which if I'm being honest I was more than a bit surprised at us getting. However, with us not getting it at that specific time for some reason or other that was out of our control – it meant her going back up the week after. That aside, Emily and Sammy dropped the kids off at school in the Mean Machine and I picked them up and drove them home – strangely via Buckingham Palace as my daughter was insistent on having her photograph taken outside the horrible place for some project they were doing at school, and believe me trying to get parked up at 4:35pm on a Monday evening in and around that area is a nightmare.

It was all nice and exciting when we got in as their Granny Sil' had come down on the midday train to help out a bit as she knew their mum was busy, and on them sitting at the breakfast bar Sil' dished them up bacon, sausage and scrambled eggs – so when I say exciting – I meant for me as well, as unlike Emily – Sil' always made sure I got the same treatment.

"Mrs Peters doesn't eat meat," said my lad. "Mrs Peters is a vegetable."

"Oh yeh?" I replied as I scoffed my tea.

"I think you mean vegetarian, love," smiled Emily.

My lad acknowledged her as he chomped at one of his sausages. Mrs Peters says that these come from a pig," he said.

"No they don't – They come from Asda," I said. "You know that as you were there when we bought them, as we had to buy them because you stuck your finger through the plastic."

That raised a few giggles.

"Mrs Peters said that meat is bad for you," he added.

"Your mum and M eat meat," I said. "And look at how beautiful they both are ...."

Both kids – and Emily if I'm being honest, appeared dead interested in where this was going.

".... Then look at the state of Mrs Peters."

"Lee – Shush – you can't say that," smirked Emily.

"Can – just did," I winked. "Mrs Peters isn't a vegetarian, she's a big ugly herbivore from Essex, who secretly eats spiders and woodlice."

"Is she, Dad?" asked my lad.

"Definitely – Like a Stegosaurus."

"Is that the dinosaur with the big plates on its back," he asked.

"Just like Mrs Peters," I nodded.

"Dad does Mrs Peters have plates on her back?" he asked.

"I would imagine so – you just can't see them because she wears all those horrible clothes."

"Mum and M don't wear horrible clothes," said my daughter.

"There you go," I said. "They aren't herbivores."

"If we aren't herbivores then what are we," asked Emily.

"You are definitely a carnivore," I replied. "Especially on a Friday night after a bottle of wine."

"Behave," she smiled.

"M's like one of those Veloceraptors," I said. "Now your mum – she is definitely a Tyrannosaurus Rex."

"Why can't I be a Tyrannosaurus Rex?" asked Emily.

"Your mouth's not big enough," I replied – before telling the kids that under no circumstance whatsoever should that sentence ever be repeated to their mum – Ever.

"But mum eats vegetables as well," said my daughter. "And so does M."

"Then I'm wrong," I said. "They aren't carnivores they are omnivores – because omnivores eat both."

"Dad – am I an omnivore?" asked my son.

"Yeh – definitely."

"What about our Sammy?" asked my daughter, as she looked over at Horrid Henry as he sat in his chair watching us all – and strangely smiling.

"I think he's definitely a carnivore," I said.

"Aw, stop being awful," said Emily nudging me.

"Wait until he grows teeth – Not even the ferrets will be safe," I said.

"I love it here," said my lad eating his tea. "Do you like being here as well, Gran'?"

"I do love – I love being here," Sil' replied.

"Yeh – it's not bad, is it?" smiled Emily, as she passed Sammy over to her mum and gave my kids a cuddle.

Tuesday was D-Day. I've no idea as regards the intricate details of exactly what happened – well, I didn't at that point in time, however I took a phone call from Jeanette which I wish I hadn't. I've no idea what she said exactly as I couldn't make it out due to the noise of her voice. Jeanette never swore much – but when she did it was reserved just for me, therefore I coped a bucketful of superlatives in between "I've had the school on the phone" and "What have you been saying?" and "I'm up in Scotland".

I knew she was in Scotland as it was me who sent her up there? As for school and what had I been saying? I thought nothing of it really.

I'd seen a few calls come onto my mobile, but as I never ever answered 0800, withheld nor private numbers there was no chance that anyone at the end of them would ever get my attention.

"Lee, I've got your children's school on the phone," shouted Faranha.

That however, got my attention.

"What's up?" I asked the idiot at the other end of the line.

There was a bit of conversation aimed at me but if I am honest it was dead-boring.

"We are aware that you and your wife are separated," *it* said.

"Too true – I'm in London and she's in Scotland," I told them, further adding that I was hoping that she would be in China next month.

"Do you speak to one another?" was the first question that *it* slung at me.

"She mainly does the talking, but yeh – we speak."

It then transpired that my lad had mentioned his teacher – a certain Mrs Peters not being human and that she was some prehistoric mammal with spinal plates beneath her blouse and that she regularly went to Essex to seek out the best insects.

"Is that it?" I said.

It then spoke down to me which I must admit pissed me off a bit. Well, not a bit – a lot really, and I really shouldn't have said what I said. Cue Jeanette and the bollocking.

Tuesday was always a busy day and Emily picked up the kids from school and was apparently in stitches whilst discussing the events with her mum.

"Dad – M was dead cool with Mrs Peters," said my daughter on me getting in from work.

My lad never said anything as he was engrossed in watching TV.

I would have asked my wife what happened, but as soon as she started telling the story she sort of broke down laughing, but I already knew it had something to do with something that I had said which I shouldn't have.

"Aw Lee," chuckled Emily. "You ought to have seen her."

"No thanks," I said.

Every time she tried to relay what had been said she creased up.

"I've had Jeanette on the phone," I said. "I have to go in and see the headmaster."

That just made her laugh all the more.

"Good, I'm glad that's all sorted then," I said.

"Don't worry – I'll come I and hold yer hand," twanged my wife, before creasing up again.

Cue: Wednesday 11:00am.

"I'm Ted Marsden," the headmaster said, before introducing my son's infamous teacher. "And this is Joanne Peters."

I knew who she was as I'd seen her before; however, we reciprocated the introductions and I shook his hand before we were invited to sit in two chairs at the other side of his oak desk – which I must say didn't go unnoticed by Emily who glanced me a look as if to say, "Please don't".

"Please sit down," said Mr. Marsden.

"We're okay," smiled Emily, as she stood against his window and looked out into the car park as I did what I was told and sat in what I assumed was some child's chair.

The headmaster gave me a summary of why we were here and that was the fact that my son had informed Mrs Peters what I had said of her in front of 25 pupils plus an assistant teacher – one Ms. Ulia Turishheva, in that 'My dad says that she can't be a vegetarian as she must be ramming summat down her throat other than salads to be the size she is'. It wasn't word for word but I did eventually correct him that it was 'Something and not summat'.

"I was wrong," I said coming clean and admitting the dirty deed. "I said something along those lines after my son had said that Mrs Peters had told him that she was a vegetarian and eating meat was bad, so I do apologise."

I thought that would be it, however it wasn't.

"Your son also mentioned something about her eating woodlice in Essex," he added.

Mmm. I wasn't expecting that, I thought.

"Yeh – I think I may have mentioned something like that as well," I said. "So I apologise for that as well."

Then came the bollocking in that I should be a more responsible father and that our lifestyle – including Jeanette's, wasn't the best environment for a child to grow up in etcetera, etcetera.

"Your son has a very low constitution and distracts the other children," added Mrs Peters.

"Yeh – and you called him stupid," I told her.

"No I did not," she replied.

"And you said to him that me and M were loaded – And that we must be creaming it."

"I never said anything of the sort as regards either you or his stepmother," she argued.

Then fucking boom!

"I'm not his stepmother, so don't make me sound like some cantankerous old witch with a poisonous apple from some Grimm's fairy tale," snapped Emily looking straight at her. "To little Jamie I am M – his friend – and I will tell you now you silly, odious woman – that this little lad you've just called this and that – is the most sweetest boy you could ever meet – and one thing he never ever does is lie."

"Now, now, Mrs Janes," said Mr. Marsden.

"Now, now nothing," said Emily. "This woman isn't fit to be a teacher."

"Well, I don't party on TV if that is what you mean," smirked Mrs Peters.

The head' tried breaking up the tit for tat cat-calling; however, Emily never broke her stance.

"Just for the record I am a fully-qualified music teacher who gained her BA Honours in both music and English literature," she said. "I am fluent in two other languages – French and Spanish – and not so fluent in German, but I can get by – I'm not at concerto level but I play piano to a grade seven – and just for the record I have eight GCSE's at A and B and have seven A Levels including maths, music, four languages and a science."

There was a short silence.

"I currently teach Lee's daughter, Harmony both violin and piano along with seven girls from Colliegate private school on a weekly basis," Emily said. "I can't take anymore pupils as I am busy with my family and the seven or eight hours I do a week at the studio because I was asked – I don't class it as a job – I do it because I was asked."

They were both speechless as was I, but Emily wasn't done.

"All children are brilliant in their own way – Harmony is as good as you will get for a seven-year old on violin – she's struggling on the piano, but that is because she is learning on a Steinway – and it's a bit big – but I supposed you didn't know that?" she said. "Little Jamie thinks the world of Lee and to him, his dad is the ultimate hero and yeh – Lee says things he perhaps shouldn't in front of him – but which parent doesn't – However, if you take time to ask him about either planets or dinosaurs he could tell you that Mercury is the closest planet to the sun or that Saturn is the one with the rings around it or that a Stegosaurus is the animal with the plates on its back or that the Archaeopteryx was the first bird with feathers – Why? Because we don't party as you call it – we take time to educate them and regularly take them to places such as the Natural History Museum or the London Dungeon. He's six years old – a six-year-old needs

273

stimulation – not being bitched at by someone he should be learning from."

Rooted to the spot, Mr Marsden listened on whilst his co-worker's head was both red as a beetroot and ready for exploding – well, that's what it looked like anyway.

"He also loves his music – not playing it, but learning about it – but I suppose that is another thing you don't know," said Emily. "Their mother Jeanette has done a fantastic job of bringing up these two wonderful children and I'm not having anyone try and demean them."

The head broke his loyalty and apologised on the spot; however, Mrs Peters did not.

"Look," I said. "I apologised – but I'm with M on the fact that my lad doesn't lie."

Which is something I'm definitely going to work on to rectify, I thought.

Emily still stood at the window with her glare directed at Mrs Peters.

"Please leave us, Joanne," said the headmaster, "And I'll sort this."

And she did, although it was in a bit of a huff as she slammed the door – or tried to rather, as it had one of those hydraulic hinge mechanisms on it and that being the case she nearly dragged her arm out of its socket.

He then went on to accept my apology and apologised on behalf of the school for Mrs Peters allegedly saying the things that she said, which she had said she hadn't, but which if she did, she certainly shouldn't have – if you get that.

It was interesting, I'll say that much. I'd never seen Emily in Terminator mode before and I was truly impressed.

"You were red-hot in there," I said as we walked back to the car.

"I did go a bit bonkers didn't I?" she said.

"Yeh – but you were dead cool."

"You look after us all," she said linking my arm and pushing herself up against me, whilst walking over the playground and trying to boot a stone at the same time. "It does rub off, yer know."

I liked that.

Later that evening M rang Jeanette and told her that everything had been sorted and that the headmaster had apologised. I never got any details fired my way only that Jeanette was fine.

Chapter 22

A Couple of Skeletons in the Closet

I got in from my morning jog to find Emily looking over some paperwork and Sammy in the high chair strangely gurgling.

"Is everything okay?" I asked.

"Not really," she replied, and she passed me what she had been reading. It was a print-out or hard copy rather, of the article about my wife that was originally going to appear in *The Sun*, or so I was told.

"I thought you said we had some court order stopping it," she said.

I nodded. "We have. This gets printed – he loses everything – It's that simple."

She shrugged her shoulders. "So why this?"

"He's telling me that he doesn't like being bullied," I said. "Therefore he's hitting me with this."

I looked at it. It was 100% tack written up by a person purported to be a journalist which was 100% pure embarrassment – for us – not him.

"I'm really sorry," she said.

I knew the story of Dale Fox and his half-brother Mark Smith – the man she married. However if I am being honest the story as regards the former was absolutely nothing like what I initially thought it was. I had however, never seen Emily on a beach wearing a bikini in another man's arms before, nor had I any real idea who Andrew Gardener was, even though he was with stood with Emily in another photograph with his finger on her lips telling her to "Shush". I had certainly heard Emily mention him, but I'd certainly never known or ever seen him. This made everything seem … well, more real.

"He was my first love," she had told me, so I wasn't behind the door on that, however I had never known that while she had been with her husband they had split up and that she'd had some brief encounter with him.

"So how long ago was this?" I asked.

"About two or three years ago," she said."

I must admit – that hurt.

I read the article from left to right, paragraph after paragraph. Both the reporter and her ex-husband knew exactly what they were doing.

"It says here that he was having sex with you right up until the day you left him and that he suspected nothing," I said reading the article.

"That's not entirely true," she said.

"Which bit? Him not suspecting you'd had a fling or the two of you still having sex?"

She said nothing as I handed it back to her and went for upstairs for a shower.

I knew our relationship had been founded on deceit and that we had both left our respective partners. But the so-called journalist had made it all look dirty, and none more so than my wife.

"He was known as 'Digger'," Emily had told me one night while we were in bed. "All the girls used to fancy him."

"Digger? What for?"

"His surname was Gardener – He came over to live in Wallasey from Dingle."

"Oh yeah?" I remember saying.

"He started calling for me and one night when my mam and dad were out – we sort of – yer know."

She always said 'Yer know' and never ever went into explicit detail – not to me anyway, however she had for her husband, which I found rather strange if I'm being honest.

I got into work and I couldn't get it out of my mind. Between the husband and the reporter they had done a great job in trying to mess with my head.

I could cope with Dale Fox and Mark Smith – but the fact that this fucking ghost of a man had been going back and forth in and out of her life was I have to say, driving me around the bend. He was there before and there in between. What's to say he couldn't be there again? In the print-out of the article he had stood there with Emily – my Emily, with his finger to her mouth whilst she was smiling. What was he actually doing? What did it mean? What was so funny at the time? Why was he telling her to "Shush"?

The day came and went with no phone call nor any text message from my wife. I always had a phone call – I always had some text or other, whether it be an "I love you" or another photograph sent of Sammy whining. And I always got a bunch of X's and smiley faces – Always.

I stayed at work late and got in to find Emily sat alone at the breakfast bar. The house felt cold and empty – like we'd had intruders or we had been burgled.

"Do you want something to eat?" she asked.

And that's when I told her how upset I was. I couldn't help it, but I was really upset and she didn't help matters much when she burst out crying.

"I wanted to call you all day," she said. "I really, really did."

I believed her. I wanted to call her all day.

"It's made me feel so dirty and horrible," she said. "And you are so nice – you certainly don't deserve this."

We had a cuddle and had a go at trying to change the subject, but it just kept on getting brought back up.

"Come on M – there's just me and you who know about it," I said.

"What about him?" she asked. "He knows about it."

Emily knocked us up a dry pan-fried chicken with a Ricotta, spinach, rocket and water cress salad while she talked, trying to fill in some of those gaps from her thirty-two years that she hadn't yet shared with me. Andrew Gardener had been a huge presence in her life, and had nipped in and out and taken a shit whenever and wherever he pleased.

"Dale knocked heck out him two or three times," she told me. "He hated him."

I wasn't that fond and I hadn't even met him, I thought.

"Mark found out I'd seen him when I'd been back up to see my parents – and that he had phoned me and we'd met up down here – that was bad," she said. "That's when I first left him."

She never went into specifics or logistics but all the same it was a bit of a kick in the guts, but not as much as he took from her ex-husband.

"Has he contacted you since we've been together?" was my obvious question.

She initially shook her head to say "No" and then back-tracked and nodded a "Yes".

Ouch, I thought. *That hurt.*

"When we had just got back from Marrakesh he text me asking to meet," she said.

"And?" I asked.

"I told him no," she said. "He was in London buying some paint."

"It's a fucking long way from Liverpool just to buy some paint?" I said.

"He owns some decorating shop," she said. "He buys it wholesale."

I couldn't make this shit up, I thought

"I'm sorry – I should have told you," she said. "I left Mark because he was horrible – I wanted a way out."

She may have done, but all the same she went back.

"I would have left for good, but he was married," she said.

"What – he chose his wife over you?" I gasped.

I got a nod.

"What does she look like?" I inquired knowing full-well that nothing could compare to the woman I was asking.

She shrugged her shoulders.

"What you don't know?" I asked.

"Tall and dark," she nodded.

I could do the dark bit, but I was never particularly fond of tall women, as tall women generally meant massive feet.

"Has she got big feet?" I asked.

Emily laughed, which brought a bit of levity to the situation. "I do love you, you know," she said.

"I know you do," I replied.

It was my experience that things such as this blow over. What's bad today is generally not so bad the next day and so on and so on and this really needed putting to bed.

"Well, tomorrow is a new day," I said.

"Thank-you," she smiled.

I came in from my jog the very next day to find the coffee on and Sky Sports playing – but no Emily, which was strange. It transpired that she was up in one of the bedrooms with Hissing Sid – and doing the ironing.

"I thought I'd get this lot out of the way," she said.

I was all for both my wardrobes being replenished with nice crisply ironed clothes, but as I knew this was her way of trying to offset me being pissed off, by her trying to please me by doing something that I wanted – but which she really hated, it didn't really sit with me that well.

"M – nothing has changed," I told her. "You are still the Emily I married."

She nodded me a nod but I could see her bottom lip wobbling.

"I just don't want to lose you," she said.

"And you won't," I replied.

"Promise?" she asked.

A promise is what she wanted and a promise is what I gave her – I did ask her if she'd finish the ironing though, which brought a smile.

I got in work to find Les taking notes of timings whilst watching some footage from the ITN archives and taking down notes. It was all part of the six-part series of The Curse of the Owls, and the piece he was watching was of the 1960/61 season.

"They were a good team," he said.

He was right – they were a good team.

Abi came in and told me that ITV's director general had called.

"Really?" I replied. "I wonder what he wants?"

"He just asked if you'd call him when you got in," she said.

I gave him a call and he wanted a favour although how he put it made it sort of look like he was doing me the favour. An indie company that was pencilled in to shoot a six-part fly-on-the-wall type documentary on both London Borough Council of Town Hamlets and the London Borough Council of Lewisham had gone under and there was six hours to fill and could we do anything to fill the void? There was a bit of a glitch in that there wasn't much of a budget for it, as it was hardly prime-time – 10:30pm – 11:30pm.

"How 'not much of a budget'?" I asked.

"One hundred grand per programme," he said. "Although I could get it to one hundred and twenty-five if you can come up with a good idea."

"And it's got to be a fly on the wall?" I asked.

"And it's got to be a fly on the wall," he replied.

The Warehouse was extraordinarily busy and we were totally swamped with work but that didn't stop the director general for summoning me in for a meeting at 5:00pm at their office in Waterloo with ideas and an itinerary.

"That's a bit short notice," noted Abi.

It was – It was also a bit extremely low budget and I told her as much and I spent all morning distracted from the football channel trying to put together ideas for some stinking fly on the wall documentary that no one would be interested in, until a thought occurred to me and it was then when I picked up the phone. "Set up a meeting at seven o'clock tonight," I said.

By one o'clock my head was a shed. I was working harder than I'd ever done, so much so I think it was taking toll on my eyes and I skived off to the coffee shop where I was met by my wife, offspring and two kids, neither of whom belonged to me.

"Now then, why aren't you two at school?" I asked the brats.

"Auntie M said we could have our music lesson, then go see you," said Zooey.

"That's nice," I said. "Go ask Fosis if he'll get you a Coca Cola or a beer and an Ouzo chaser."

"What, really?" smiled Zooey.

"No, I was kidding about the Cola."

Whilst the two kids demanded two beers and Ouzo chasers and got served pop, crisps and two big sticky buns, Emily informed me that things weren't that fantastic down in Holland Park, hence why she was watching over Bill and Ben.

"That's strange, I've just been speaking with Sooty," I said. "He's not said anything."

"Libby's with her solicitor," said Emily. "She's ready for filing for a divorce."

"That's not good," I said.

"I feel sorry for the children," she said, as we watched them walking back over to the table.

"We can go down Nubeon tonight and have a look if you want," I said.

"What, really?" she asked.

"Sure – but we can't take the kids."

"Shurrup," she twanged.

We had a natter and she cheered up – quite a lot actually – It was either the thought of going down and catching

282

Sooty doing something he shouldn't be doing or meeting this bird whose stage name was 'Jackie Blue' on the latest DVD he'd dropped in and who she'd watched get tied up by some fat old bloke and prodded and poked about with for half an hour before she got slung over the settee before finally doing the deed. It was one of those where you are wondering where the hell it was going and before it actually goes anywhere it ends. I couldn't figure it out, yet Emily thought it worthy of an Emmy.

"What – You thought that was good?" I'd asked.

"Yeh – not half," she had replied. "Do you fancy having an early night?"

"It's only half-eight?"

It was hardly an early night and I managed to get to sleep around 2:00am after being subjected to the art of tying knots with rope – she ought to have been a sailor – jamming, lashing, whipping, friction knots, open loops – I was amazed at how much she knew – she had to have been in the Brownies or something.

I managed over half an hour with Emily and the kids and informed her that ITV wanted some fly on the wall documentary and of the fact that my eyes were hurting.

"You might need to go to the opticians," she said taking a closer look at them.

I think she was right, even her giving me a peck on them both didn't do much.

She also told me that Ted Marsden had called and did we fancy a meal over his house?

"Who you, or me and you?" I asked.

"Shurrup," she twanged, knowing full well that he'd got a bit of a soft spot for my wife – especially after she'd given my kids' teacher a bollocking. "Both of us."

"That sounds ominous," I said shaking my head.

The meeting was changed at the last minute to ITV's office on Grays Inn Road and I managed to get there on time to be whisked by some P.A into a boardroom of sorts where I was introduced to the chief executive officer who candidly informed me that they were investing a lot of money in me.

I know that – that's why I broke my neck getting here on time, I thought.

By 5:30pm we had everyone in and some dialogue took place as regards the indie company that had gone under supposedly taking around £90,000 of their money and leaving six hours of TV space to fill.

"Lee, do you want to tell us of some of your ideas to fill it?" asked the director general.

I think they wanted me to stand up and do a presentation, however I didn't – I just asked them a question. "Are you looking at just filling space for filling space's sake or are you looking at something a bit compelling that will get everyone talking?" I asked.

"Definitely compelling," replied the chief executive looking over at me.

"I've got a couple of things," I told them. "The first covers human trafficking, which would be more expensive, whilst the second is on your doorstep and covers the adult entertainment industry with the latter involving a bit of the former and which I could do relatively cheap."

"How cheap," asked the director general.

"For one-twenty-five a programme, but I'd want it all paying up front," I said.

"That's three quarters of a million," said the chief executive.

"What about if we just wanted the space filling?" asked the director general.

"Then you'd struggle to knock out premium advertising space," I replied. "With what I have in mind they'll be fighting like hell to get their products shown."

"The Sky channels have done the adult entertainment industry," stated a suit. "In fact, they've bled the thing dry."

"What they've produced is shite," I said. "I'll blow a fucking hole in it and get everyone talking."

I got out of the meeting and rang up Annie Dixon who was strangely still creeping about the office.

"You need to contact ITV's finance department – They are raising an order for a new six-week documentary to be billed as a one-er," I said.

She didn't say a great deal, just about the fact that we could do with spending a bit. "If you don't spend something we are going to get hammered with tax," she said. "I'm serious."

Sooty and Libby had always busted my chops about not looking after my money properly and I knew from Jeanette that they had initially said that I'd do a Viv Nicholson and most likely fritter away the money that I'd made from the sale of the company. How wrong could they be? Having Emily in my life had turned everything around and when I got home, there she was – along with my ex-wife who was just taking Sammy over to Clerkenwell to stay the night, and who after the initial pleasantries, told me that I needed to sort an appointment at the opticians.

"Where are the kids?" I asked.

"With my mum," she replied, whilst looking into my eyes with me wondering what she was actually looking at.

I nodded a nod – kissed them both and they were gone.

As we drove over to Nubeon's offices and studios, Emily dropped something on me that I didn't know in that Jeanette's Paul had moved to his company's head office in Holborn.

"I thought he was a supermarket manager?" I asked, as I negotiated my way through the traffic.

"He is – like an area manager," she informed me, along with the fact that Jeanette wanted to buy the house.

"Which house?" I asked.

"The one she lives in," she replied.

"What – in Clerkenwell?"

"Why, which other one does she live in yer great nit?" Emily smiled.

That was news to me.

"Well, it'd be tight, but she could probably afford it," I said.

"She just wanted to know if you'd sell it them," she continued.

"Them?"

Emily nodded.

"What – is Paul on about moving in?" I asked.

Emily gave a slight nod as an acknowledgement but said very little else apart from, "It would be nearly three thousand pounds a month we'd save."

There was something here that didn't sit quite right and that my wife wasn't telling me.

"Do you know something I don't?" I asked.

"I know loads of stuff that you don't," she smiled.

"And you think I should?"

Emily nodded. "I do love, yeh."

I rang Jeanette, whilst stuck in traffic and got Paul.

I've never described Paul before apart from him being a Brentford supporter who is a bit quiet around me but who is both very good with Jeanette and my kids. If you ever watch an old episode of Monty Python in the sixties and you see Michael Palin – especially that milkman sketch, there was a lot of him about him – looks-wise that is. And as I've already said – he wasn't the biggest of guys.

"Hiya Paul – M's just told me about the house," I said. "What are you wanting to do?"

That took him a bit by surprise, but I always considered it being best to get to the point rather than skirting around the subject.

"Jeanette wants us to buy the house off you," he replied rather sheepishly.

"What about you?" I asked. "Is that what you want?"

He gave me a bit of an oh-so-quiet "Yeh" before Jeanette was handed the phone.

"Lee?" she asked.

"I've got it on hands-free and M's in the car with me," I informed her.

286

"Oh, right," she said.

"Hello Jeanette," said Emily.

"Hello M," came the reply.

I had to let her know that Emily was privy to the conversation as I wouldn't have liked Emily hearing how Jeanette sometimes spoke to me.

"Are you sure you want to buy it?" I asked.

"Yes," she replied. "But you'll need get it valued."

"I don't think there's any need for that," I said. "I'll see my lawyers and get them to get it signed over to you – just take over the mortgage."

"What?" she asked.

"I'll get it signed over to you," I said.

"Why?"

"How do you mean, why?" I asked.

"Why would you do that?"

"Why not?" I replied.

There was a bit of quiet at the other end of the line as Emily tried to pretend that she wasn't taking any notice of our conversation by looking out of the window.

"We'd prefer to buy it," she said.

I didn't know if this was for my benefit or Emily's, in that Jeanette didn't want to look like she was taking more hand-outs from me.

"If you want the house I will sign it over to you as by me doing that – it will save you both a shed load of money."

"Yeh, but you'll lose money on it," she said.

"No I won't – you and the kids will be in it – I'll lose nothing."

There was more silence at the other end of the phone as Emily glanced me a half-smile.

"Jeanette – if it's what you want – you can have it," I said.

There wasn't much dialogue after that and I rang off as we pulled up outside the offices where Sooty allegedly worked.

"That was a really nice thing to say," said Emily.

The offices and studios of Nubeon Entertainment Inc. were an assortment of different rooms in a building off Old Kent Road that were on par with the offices that Sooty and I first rented out on Chase Side near Southgate Tube station, which were absolutely nothing compared to those we had on Euston Road and that being the case they were certainly nothing compared to The Warehouse.

Just after Emily had dropped the bundle from up her jumper, we had vegged out one night and had watched 'The Sweeney' film starring Ray Winstone; it was then I mentioned to her that I'd like offices like the New Scotland Yard offices that the Flying Squad occupied. "Bright, clean and open-plan," I told her. "I want somewhere where people feel that they want to go into work."

Therefore after Mike and his lads had finished its conversion, I had a firm of decorators come in and after they had done, it took Emily and Jeanette next to no time to organise its furnishing. It was really nice, but what was nicer was that between them they had the exact photograph, both blown-up and segmented, of Sammy of Arsenal in that lost match in the snow against Sheffield Wednesday in 1967 and they had hung it on the wall in the foyer.

"Close yer eyes," Emily twanged on getting me into the office. I knew about the furniture and hardware, but not about the huge photograph. It was a very nice touch and I told her so.

"I could have got it colourised for you, but I know how much you like black and white," she smiled.

I did – I loved black and white.

There had been another story that I'd been told – by Frank McLintock of all people – "I scored a brilliant goal in that game – from thirty yards – and they called the thing off," he said. "I couldn't believe it – it was the best goal I'd ever scored."

Nubeon's offices were as depressing as hell and were it not for all the totty that frequented them I would assume that it was a pretty shitty place to work.

Sooty, as he always did, made a fuss of Emily and had some underling take her coat and offer her a drink whilst telling me that I was late.

"The traffic around Blackfriars Bridge was a nightmare," I told him.

I wasn't lying either. Some utility firm had been trying to fix a burst pipe and the traffic lights they were using had a mind of their own as the northbound traffic was flowing like a good 'un whilst trying to get south of the river was a one- and two-car at a time job.

"So what did you want the meeting for?" asked Sooty as he introduced me to his immediate boss who he had already informed me lived in some mansion out in Cheshunt, and two of his distributors, both of whom were by now drooling over my newly famous wife.

Emily had never ever seen me in a meeting before and she got the shock of her life when I started talking.

"I've just been asked by ITV to do a six-episode fly-on-the-wall series to kick off just after Christmas," I told them. "I've given them several options; however, the angle on the adult entertainment industry I've given them was something that intrigued them."

It hadn't really – I'd had to sell it like hell as they thought it would be dead tacky.

"What, you want to film here?" asked Sooty's boss.

"Not how it stands," I told him. "I'm wanting the firm who we'll be fly on the walling – to look really professional, and not some seedy fucking business run out of a shed in the backstreets of London that's sole aim is the exploitation of women."

"It's hardly that," explained Sooty. "This is a twenty-three million pound a year business."

"Maybe so," I said. "But how it stands now, if I bring the suits from ITV down here they'll turn around and demand we look at something else."

They all looked at me – including Emily.

"Sooty knows that by us doing a good, clean, interesting six-part documentary, Nubeon's profile will go through the roof."

I spoke at length about what I had proposed and it was then that I gave them what they perceived as a bit of the future. "I have four girls who will be presenting various aspects of the new ITV Seven football channel that goes live in the New Year – I initially thought that I could get them to work on it; however, ITV insisted on a face," and it was then I pointed to Emily.

"What, you want me to do it?" she asked.

This was a bit of a shock as she just thought that she was coming down for a snoop around the place.

"You never said anything," she smiled.

I hadn't. I liked surprises.

Nubeon most definitely wanted us to do the documentary, and Sooty's boss revelled in the fact that he'd be on mainstream TV with Britain's No. 1 girl doing the narrative and offered to show us both his wealth and success by inviting us out to Cheshunt at the weekend.

"It sounds very nice," I lied. "However, I have the kids at the weekend."

He then informed me that he was not some suntanned, bling-wearing deviant who had a bleach-blonde bint with an Essex accent at home. He might have looked like it, but he told me that it certainly wasn't the case.

"He has a really nice setup," Sooty said. "You, M and the kids would love it."

I'll take your word for it, I thought.

We had a bit of a guided tour before we drove home and Sooty thanked me profusely.

"Don't get too excited," I had told him, "I need to get the order first."

"He's a right pervert, him," Emily whispered.

"Sooty? Yeh I know."

"No, the owner," she said.

"If you make football documentaries it helps if you know a bit about football," I told her. "I suppose it's the same with sex."

She thanked me for being a great husband and I agreed.

"Do yer fancy watching that DVD again?" she winked.

"Not particularity – I'm not that good with knots."

"Shurrup," she twanged.

I got up early next morning, had my jog and a coffee and nipped over to Clerkenwell to pick up misery guts only to get back to King's Cross to a wife who had a rather unhappy expression on her chops.

"What's up? It can't be the ironing as you did it yesterday?"

"Who is Yasmin Cowley?"

Mmm. I didn't like the sound of that, I thought.

"Are you asking me because you don't know who she is, or have you googled her and know who she is, but just want me to tell you?"

"The second bit," she said.

Mmm. The second bit was definitely lots worse than the first bit, I thought.

It transpired that 'our friends' *The Sun* had run a two-page article on the woman I'd bedded down with straight after I'd been thrown out by Jeanette and my name had been mentioned. Well it was mentioned a few times actually.

"My mam's just phoned to tell me," she said.

"I didn't think your mum read *The Sun*," I innocently replied.

Just then my phone went. It was Jeanette.

"Can I call you back?" I asked her to which she replied, "Who the fucking hell is Yasmin Cowley?"

"Let me call you back," I said. However I was never going to get off that easy and I now had a screaming ex-wife pissing in my ears. "Please Jeanette – I really need to call you back."

It would also transpire that my ex-wife would be at my door within thirty minutes; however, before I could savour that interrogation I had had my current wife to deal with.

The Sun – bless them – had posted a huge photograph of Yasmin Cowley – topless on a beach in the East Indies, with a few other snapshots – one of which included me with her in some wine bar on St. Martin's Lane in the west end. She had been in the right place at the right time or the wrong place at the wrong time after I had been thrown out by my ex-wife.

"She's the woman that did that Christmas advert on TV for Bailey's Irish Cream isn't she," Emily asked. "The Bailey's kiss-thing."

It was true – she had. The paper – or *The Sun's* online edition rather had also stated that she was both an actress and model in Manhattan.

"Did you see her when we were over in New York?" Emily asked.

"No," I replied.

"She's pretty," noted my wife.

I certainly wasn't going to answer that.

"So, how long did you spend with her?" asked Emily.

"Six days," I said.

"Six days?" she shrugged. "It says here that she wanted to marry you?"

"It was the worst six days of my life,"

"I certainly don't believe that," Emily said whilst looking straight at me.

"And as regards marriage – that's certainly not true," I told her.

I would have been wrong to assume that Ms. Cowley had cottoned onto the fact that I was doing the job I was doing and that being the case wanted to raise her profile by sort of attaching herself to me as I had involved both my wife and my ex, who were currently presenters of what were very successful shows and by her mentioning a marriage to me, it may gee-up her career – not that it needed geeing up however as she was never out of work doing either commercials or modelling. She had even made the final three for the lead in 'The Good Lie', which was given to Reese Witherspoon. What was strange was that she had auditioned for 'Wild', which Reese Witherspoon also ended up starring in. How did I know that? Because whilst I knew her auditions were all she ever frigging talked about. However here is where I would be wrong. She had just landed the role of some senior intelligence operative gone bad in a 12-part crime series that would be going on air in the New Year and somehow and completely unbeknown to me at the time Live at The Warehouse had been mentioned and it had been said that the shows presenter was the wife of one Lee Janes who produced the show.

"It's probably her agent that's behind it all," was what I initially said.

I looked at Emily and I'd never seen her like this before. "Come on – for better or worse," I told her. "Remember what I said the other day when that guy was going to run the article on you and that Gardener bloke."

"Yeh – he owns some rubbish emulsion shop in Knotty Ash – he's not some good-looking actress with massive boobs who lives in New York," she said. "And he's not twenty-two either."

"It wasn't the whirlwind romance you're making it out to be," I told her.

It wasn't – it was just arguments and sex, although again – I thought it, but certainly never said it.

"Really," she snapped. "Just look at her – How can I compete with that?"

"What's there to compete with?" I asked giving her a cuddle – or trying to. "We're married – I married you, not her."

"It's dead embarrassing for me," she said.

"I know and I'm really sorry," I said. "This is what I meant by trying to keep our lives private."

However what I thought was me managing to smooth it over would soon turn out to be an epic encounter with the dark side as Jeanette turned up at the door in between me getting around half a dozen missed calls on my mobile.

"Why didn't I know of her?" asked a rather seething Jeanette as she entered the house. "It says you left me for her."

"You know that's not true," I said.

"She said you lived with her," added Jeanette.

"Not really," I replied. "I crashed at hers because I had nowhere to go."

"Did you sleep with her when you were with me?" asked Jeanette.

"Look – this is my house, with my wife in it – you can't go interrogating me in front of Emily – it's not fair on her."

"Answer her question, Lee," said Emily.

Mmm. I didn't like the sound of that! I thought, therefore I shook my head and told a great big dirty fib.

"Twenty-two," Jeanette added. "Twenty-two years old – that would make her twenty or twenty-one when you were seeing her."

Jeanette was always the great mathematician when it came to matters such as this, however I preferred to say nothing, which I immediately knew was a mistake as she began parrot-quoting *The Sun*. "It says that she begged you to divorce me and marry her," she said.

"And did I?" I replied.

"No – you divorced me and married Emily," she snapped. "Just look at her?"

What was it with women? Why the hell did they both want me to look at her?

"I've loved only two women in my life," I said. "And you're both here."

That stopped them in their tracks and it was then I invited them to sit down as I reeled off my six days of hell as the housemate of Yasmin Cowley. "She had a problem," I told them.

"She doesn't look like she's got any problem," insisted Jeanette, who even had an actual copy of the paper in her mitts.

"She was extremely manipulative, possessive and angry – and she nagged like hell," I said.

"You said that about me," said Jeanette. "In fact, you said it all the time."

I shook my head again. "This one was on a completely different level to you," I said. "This one made even you look like Doris Day."

Mmm. Maybe I shouldn't have said that, I thought, however it was quite true.

She had bipolar, she stabbed me with a pair of scissors and threatened to take an overdose if I left her and I told them both so. "It was bad," I said. "I got the paramedics to her just in time – she'd swallowed a full bottle of Paracetamol."

"What, just because you left her?" asked a bemused Jeanette.

I nodded.

"What is it with these women?" asked my ex-wife shrugging her shoulders. "Why all the drama of trying to hang on to you when you're leaving them or when you have dumped them?"

That took me aback a bit, and although I thought of a great answer to counteract that question, I kept my mouth shut, however and rather strangely, Emily didn't.

"Come on Jeanette, would you not want Lee in your life? Would you never want to see him or talk to him again?" she asked her. "I certainly wouldn't."

I sensed the grinding of teeth from Jeanette but Emily did have a point; however, that never stopped me having to find answers to another hundred questions from the floor and before I knew it I'd had another five missed calls on my phone.

"Look," I said. "I've got to get to work."

I left a wife and ex-wife mulling over my answers surrounding someone who had allegedly wanted to be my future wife, although as hard as I tried to think I couldn't remember any conversation that covered the subject.

I got into the office to see a smirking Les Crang. "She's fucking awesome, mate," he said. "You wanna get her signed up for ITV Seven."

"No thanks," I told him.

Chapter 23

Jeanette's Tales – Take 8

Lee had the power to control my emotions. He always did. Lee telling me he loved me always kept my interest and if I am being honest with myself, I was always setting him tests to see how much he really did love me. He had given me a contract at LMJ and paid me an obscene amount of money when he had no need to. He also paid me a massive amount of child support when he didn't need to as half the time the kids were at his and M was always rigging them out in nice clothes. I was living in a house worth a lot of money that he had paid for and he had offered it me with no strings attached. Why were there no strings? Being honest, I wanted strings. I wanted to sit with him and cuddle him, like M did. When they watched TV she cuddled him, she linked him and put her legs over him and was in total awe of the man that was once mine. I had not seen it much, as M never really rubbed the love she had for him in my face, but I'd seen it all the same. Where were these strings? Most men want a quid pro quo situation where they get you something and want something in return. Lee used to be like that – why wasn't he like that now? I loved the fact that if I'd wanted something and got it that he'd want something in return. When we were young there were always strings attached. I wanted strings. Strings would tell me that he really loved me. Whilst in Muswell Hill I couldn't wait for them and I'd wait in anticipation for Friday's when I knew that he would want this, that and the other – although at times I did have to remind him.

I'd got a credit card – not for much, but I kept on maxxing it out, and I loved telling Lee I was struggling to pay it.

"What you're just going to give it me like that?" I'd stomp.

He'd shrug his shoulders.

"You generally make me do things to earn it back," I'd tell him.

"Well, go hoover the landing," he'd say.

I'd stomp about even more as I was a right stroppy cow back then. In fact, if I'm honest I'm not much different now. "That's not what I meant," I'd tell him.

It was definitely not what I meant.

During the screen-testing for the Sessions and My Show it had given me flashbacks of how we were. He was really funny and made me do all kinds of silly things. The screen-test might have been in front of other people, but in my head and at the time there was just me and Lee.

"Go on your hands and knees," he told me.

I'd given him a right glare when he'd asked me that, but I did it. Abigail said it was to see how I responded to direction, but it wasn't really, Lee loved it when I did that, although back then and at times I had to demand it myself.

"I'm not bothered," he'd say.

"Yeh, you are," I'd tell him.

"No I'm not," he'd say.

It was fun – he was fun – life was fun, and I loved the 'strings attached' bit in our relationship, however now they were none, as I was now in complete control. I think.

He had just given me everything with no strings attached, and then boom, Yasmin Cowley had arrived on the scene and there were the said strings. I had raced around to his house to give him the bollocking of bollockings but he had turned the story around and told us that he loved us. I could have dropped to my knees there and then and done anything he wanted, however I didn't and neither did M. She was hurt.

She hadn't been in touch for a couple of days, which was strange in itself as generally we bumped into each other at The Warehouse where, between us we did our utmost to piss Lee off by commandeering his office and have everything strung about the place. M was ten times worse than I was, as she stock piled nappies and baby food there; me, all I had was 'Presents for dad' from the kids, so his office walls were full of drawings of dinosaurs, sharks, planets and such, although Harmony did draw a nice one with all of us together on a boat somewhere, which not only had me thinking but also M. "I wonder what she was thinking when she drew that?" M had said.

Lee didn't. He just stuck it up on his wall.

"Where's M?" I asked Lee on day three of me not seeing her.

"There's a Silver anniversary in Birkenhead, so she's been a bit all over the place," he replied.

He also mentioned Hamilton Square and that she was having to oversee some floor that was being put down.

"So she's not in London?" I inquired.

"No, but she'll be back for the show," he said.

I didn't think what I said – It just came out. "Why don't you come round and see the kids," I said. "I'll do you a meal."

"Okay," he replied, before going over to the ITV 7 team to have his Foxy Fab Four drool over him.

That Wednesday I did my best to get everything ready. I really, really tried, although Paul was a problem in that he wanted to come around – however that definitely wasn't happening.

6:00pm came and no dad. 6:30pm came and again no dad. 7:00pm came and again no dad.

"When's dad coming?" Jamie asked.

"I've no idea, love," I replied, but as I did his car pulled up outside.

He was always pleased to see the kids and he wasted no time in having one at either side of him being shown everything and anything. I watched them for a bit and I put some food on.

I could certainly cook a lot better than I cooked back then and did my utmost best at making something quick and simple that he liked. I also did my utmost best at trying to look the part but the fact that I'd spilt cheese sauce down my dress I had to say put a bit of a damper on the last bit.

New potatoes, cauliflower cheese, broccoli, corn on the cob and lamb steaks I knew were very different to the foods that M served him up and he ate every bit whilst talking at length with the kids. As for me – I just watched them, and it was beautiful, especially when he put Jamie on his knee and started a Q and A session about planets and Martians.

M phoned him, so I made myself scarce and went upstairs to run the bath for both kids, and came back down to do the dishes only to find him still on the phone to her whilst he was drying them as Harmony – who he'd stood on a chair, was washing them.

"I always wash the dishes at dad's house," she smiled.

This is dad's house, I thought.

Then Lee handed me his phone and I got M. "Hiya Jin," she said. "How are the children?"

I took the phone over to the table whereby suddenly a queue of two wanted to talk to her.

"Mum spilt cheese sauce down her dress," said my son, before asking if he could go to his Auntie Joan's party in Liverpool.

"Please," he said. "We'll be really good."

I took the phone off him and spoke at length with M. The anniversary party that was being planned was on a Friday night and she knew I liked them in bed by 9:00pm, and M being M always adhered to any requests regarding the kids. I also knew that both the bedrooms at theirs had TVs and as such, going to bed and actually sleeping were two completely different things, not that I ever pulled either of them up on it.

I got off the phone and handed it back before I administered bath time and made myself scarce for a bit. I was intending to change out of my dress, but I didn't. I don't know why but I didn't, and as I walked into the kitchen to see Lee tidying away I got a flashback of us – not in Muswell Hill, which was my greatest time ever with him, but in this house just after we'd moved in.

"How are your eyes?" I asked.

"I can still see you, so they're not that bad," he smiled.

I walked over to him and just gave him a cuddle.

"What's that for?" he asked.

I looked up at him and just wanted to kiss him, but I didn't, even though in my mind all's fair in love and war.

"I do love you, you know," I told him, before sticking the proverbial fishing rod out and pointing to the stain on my dress, "Even though I do look a mess."

"Can you remember the time when you set the chip pan on fire?" he asked.

"Yeh – you remember that?" I laughed.

He nodded. "And half the kitchen."

Whilst at Muswell Hill I'd tried my hand at homemade fish and chips and had battered the fish before I'd cut it and ended up chucking what was Moby Dick into a red hot chip pan with fat flying everywhere.

"We had some good times," I said.

"We did," he nodded.

"I've been thinking a lot about them of late," I admitted.

"You were always beautiful," he told me.

What an award-winning bloody line he had just thrown me; however, back then he'd follow it up and I'd be face down in a pillar or trying my best not to look at the lousy Artex on the ceiling as I had half my clothes removed. Now he did not. He meant exactly what he said as he did back then, but his actions that followed it were very different now. Why? Because he loved M. I can always try to look beautiful for him, but I can't stop him loving M nor her him. Even bloody Yasmin Cowley couldn't do that.

He went 'absent without leave' as he tucked up both kids and read them a story and managed to get downstairs before his retitled Inside True Britain started. He sat at the side of me as the introduction music played and there I was, doing some documentary on a Scottish gangster; however, to me that came secondary as in reality I was now snuggled up to the only man I'd ever loved, but who was now another man's husband.

I loved watching me on TV but I loved sitting next to Lee more, and as I snuggled I did what M did and tried to climb inside him by linking him and putting my head on his shoulder. I knew M would be watching the programme at the exact same moment, but she would be watching it with Mike, Sil', young Stuart and Lucy – Me? I had her husband.

For exactly one hour I had him close to me and not once did his hands or mind stray, even though I was fully available to him the whole 60 minutes. I might have had cheese sauce on my dress, but everything else was fine. I would say I was disappointed, but I wasn't really. I just loved him so much and as Lee often said, in life something is better than nothing. And the man I loved had given me more than something – He had given me everything, which was told to over two million viewers next day when a certain Ms. Cowley appeared on 'Good Morning Britain' to be interviewed by Susanna Reid about the series that she would be starring in come the New Year. However ITV must have given Susanna some form of remit as exactly two minutes thirty-four seconds into the interview a certain Lee Janes was brought up.

"He was the only man I ever loved, but at the time he was still very much in love with his wife," she said.

This beautiful actress-cum-model sat there with not one hair out of place, whilst I stood watching her in the staff room of the London Bridge store in my standard Sainsbury's assistant manager-stroke-lesbian attire and big badge, whilst she spoke about the wife of ITV's new golden boy and her not being able to compare with me.

"I saw her on last night's show," Ms. Cowley had added. "I can understand why he loved her as she's very intelligent and really very pretty."

I couldn't remember much else of the interview as I was crying my eyes out. Lee had indirectly just put me on a pedestal – Ms. Cowley looked brilliant; however, I was better.

Chapter 24

BBC

I hated Manchester United.

I had been at The Emirates in late November with Les Crang when Jack Wilshire ran through on goal and fluffed his lines early on whilst Danny Welbeck ponced around and show boated to his ex- team mates throughout the game supposedly showing Louis Van Gaal what a huge mistake he'd made in letting him go. Arsenal played well enough, but got caught on the counter on two occasions and bang! United scored.

"Fucking Déjà vu, this is Les," I said.

He agreed. It was.

How many times had we battered at the door only to concede possession and be caught on the counter attack? Arsenal would be Wolfsburg and United Everton, and Olivier Giroud returning from injury and rattling a great goal was the only bright spot of the game.

"Wenger needs to go," Les added, as we queued for the tube at Gillespie Road.

He was dead right – He did. However, we suddenly became embroiled in a conversation with a few others, some of who were very much pro-Wenger.

"Who the fuck do you think you are?" asked a guy in his early twenties.

"I know exactly who I am," I replied, before giving him the answer.

"Talking about football on telly is different to coaching," snapped the guy.

"Of course it is," I said. "But half the stadium know what the problem is and I'll tell you now that Arsène Wenger isn't part of the solution."

Suddenly we had around two dozen people talking to us about this, that and the other – or Dis, Dat and Da other if you speak to some Arsenal supporters – this one in particular.

"I'm sorry pal, I can't take you serious if you talk like that," I told him.

"You're slagging off Dat Man Welbz," he said.

"Anyone who calls himself 'Dat Man' must be a pillock, kid," I told him. "And yeh – Welbeck played shit."

"He was all over the place and back defending," he said.

"He was racing around like a headless chicken and chasing back to defend after he'd lost possession," I said. "He's a big improvement on Sanogo, but that doesn't tell you a deal – I reckon Akpom is no worse than Welbeck."

"He's better than Giroud," said the kid.

"Don't talk bollocks – Giroud's a team player," I said. "Giroud fits into the system Wenger has created – Welbeck doesn't."

Just then a guy with a TV camera picked us out and I had some reporter from the BBC in my face asking me to repeat what I'd just said, however I knew from my contract that I couldn't give anyone – especially the BBC – any free punditry without ITV's permission. Then again, I didn't like to show my ignorance so I obliged them.

"Here is Lee Janes, the producer of ITV's new football station, which goes live in the New Year," said the reporter. "What's your take on today's game, Lee?"

"There are a few problems – the players Wenger is running with don't suit the system – and Arsenal's defence was non-existent – including the goalkeeper – who I really didn't think was injured."

"You reckon he was feigning injury?" asked the reporter.

Shit – I knew I shouldn't have said that, I thought.

"Yeh I do," I said. "He knew he'd messed it up on the flight of the cross and then produced a bit of drama reminiscent of Bob Wilson – however, credit where credit is due, Wenger didn't hang around for a diagnosis – he just dragged him off."

"Arsenal have got a tricky Champions League game in midweek against a great Dortmund side," added the reporter. "How do you think the team will respond?"

"There's a couple of points," I said. "One of which is that Dortmund aren't that great side anymore – In fact they are dog average."

The reporter nodded.

"Wenger knows his system with Welbeck in it, is flawed, therefore he'll start Giroud or god forbid the French kid up top and he'll get a result – the thing is with Wenger is that although he fails – he never really fails that hard."

"So Arsenal will beat Dortmund?" he asked.

"Two-nil or two-one," I nodded, "which will please all these glory boys."

There was hell on after I'd said that.

BBC's camera's picked up the lot and around 9.00pm that night I had a visit from ITV's head of sport – along with his wife on the way home from a restaurant.

"You're going to get me a right bollocking for that," he winked, as regards the BBC coverage after the game, before adding, "You'll be on Match of the Day in a bit."

I nodded whilst I took his wife's coat and offered her a glass of wine. "It's my job to stress him out," I lied.

Emily hadn't met him before and on coming downstairs after tucking my kids in she politely said her "hello"s and gave them both a peck on the cheek.

"You're a lot smaller in real life," said Mrs ITV.

"Everyone says that," she smiled.

We watched Match of the Day and Arsenal's defence were as bad on TV as they were at The Emirates; however I felt as if I was being probed as regards certain aspects of my home life and his wife was asking one hell of a lot of questions that didn't really relate to anything that was either being said or what had been said.

Fast-forward to a couple of days after the Yasmin Cowley-thing I was summoned into a meeting and ITV told me in no uncertain terms that I could not work for the BBC nor any other company – neither as myself nor through LMJ Media. I was sure I could, although I never argued the toss. Another thing that had been happening was very strange too. Every meeting I had with the suits at ITV was now being videoed and I noticed a guy that I hadn't seen before present at each meeting and drawing as we spoke. This would be something that would become a very regular occurrence, so much so that after one meeting I was asked if Emily and I would consider posing for him over at The Warehouse as part of some ITV 7 paraphernalia they were on about knocking out – with my wife in an Arsenal shirt.

"What you want to draw us?" I asked.

"I do," said the artist. "It will look really good."

I'll take your word for it, I thought.

Emily had been a bit hit-and-miss as regards the Yasmin Cowley-thing and if I thought that things couldn't get any worse I'd be wrong, as ITV seemed to be revelling in my personal life and 'Good Morning Britain' were due to air their Friday morning's programme with Susanna Reid and Ben Shephard's main guest being the one and only Yasmin Cowley.

"Your ex-girlfriend is on TV this morning," said my wife, as I got in from my jog.

"Yeh – and that's why I'll be in work," I said, picking up my coffee and noticing a strange look on her chops as I did.

"You're not watching it, then?" she asked.

"You must be joking," I told her.

The previous night's Live at The Warehouse show had seen a more sombre Emily than normal, but seeing as she was generally a ball of energy, the toned-down Emily was still very camera friendly and even so, the show would have carried itself as the bands and the music had been exceptional. Emily did apologise for being downbeat however, and actually mentioned on air of "trying to deal with press men who keep on digging up skeletons".

I may have given 'Good Morning Britain' a wide berth, however Annie Dixon and the Fab Four plus Les and Oliver did not and I was scratching my head as I was suddenly a team light – they were in the editing suite not only watching it on ITV but also recording the frigging thing.

My phone was mad after the programme had finished with Jeanette the first to text me. "Sorry – I thought U were lying to me x," she said.

I didn't see the content of the programme therefore I couldn't comment, however Kirsty relayed every question asked and every answer that was answered. "It sounds like she really loved you," she said.

"And?" I replied.

I had tried to put the six days of hell to the back of my mind, however all the publicity surrounding her past relationship with me was attracting massive attention and ITV must have loved it as the tabloid media were on it big style hence the traffic on my phone and hence why I switched the thing off. I'd met her on some photo shoot for some sportswear – I can't recall what, but I am sure Sooty could as at the time he was besotted with her.

"What, you've got a date with her?" he had said.

I had, but it turned out to be more than a date, as on dropping her off I got dragged into her flat in Hammersmith and it was there I stayed for six days – mainly because I had been dossing in some hotel that I'd had to abscond from as the wife of the Tall Dwarf had been staking it out, therefore I didn't turn my nose up at the offer of some solace and a decent-looking girl. It all started off nicely after a 10-hour bedroom romp and breakfast, however after that she didn't want me to leave for work and by 11:00am I had had over twenty missed calls on my phone wanting me to go back for some lunch that involved another two hour romp. Although the sex was very frequent it was nothing out of the ordinary and certainly nothing compared to Emily – nor even Jeanette, come to that, and instead of putting her heart and soul into the deed, she reserved her energy for her insane jealousy – and if you thought by having me imprisoned in her flat that the said jealousy would be offset, you would be wrong. She hated the fact that I'd been married and even more so as regards the reasons why I had been kicked out, and even though she hated the thought of me being with someone else, she wanted to know every little detail about it, which when I elaborated on sent her off her rocker.

Day 2 had been like Day 1 but Day 3 was truly something else and after I had tried sneaking off to work I had an iron thrown at me. "What, you're leaving me, you bastard?" she snapped whilst trying to pull me back in the flat and tear off my suit. My words of "Look this isn't working," resulted in a big pair of scissors being thrust into my arm and loads of blood, the sight of which sent her into some shark-like frenzy. When I got into work Abi was really concerned so much so that she had initially offered me a bed at hers, which although it had been a nice gesture, I'm not sure that her partner would have liked it. The blood had made it look a lot worse than it was and I had nearly one hundred apologies text through from Yasmin who had told me that she'd not been taking her medication for what she had described as bi-polar.

Seeing as Sooty had been a bit pissed off with me for taking her home he never said a deal and just chucked me a couple of smirks; however, Abi advised me to give her a wide berth. I did go back to find her in a completely different mood and looking quite normal. She apoligised profusely, so much so she even got on her hands and knees, which I must say really turned me on, so much so we ended up in bed where I awoke to find her on top of me with a claw hammer in her mitts telling me that she felt like smashing my skull in. I wrestled it off her, which resulted in really angry sex, during which all she wanted to do was ask me about was how I had done it with my wife, so much so it drove her to the point of insanity. I had a deep wound in my arm and my back was ripped to shreds come Day 4, which had started surprisingly well until I got a text through from her suggesting that I was banging Abi, which when I told her that wasn't the case as sometimes x + y doesn't always equal z stating that Abi wasn't really interested in men, got sort of misconstrued.

She was as mad as a fucking hatter and on getting back to her flat I packed my bags, where she firstly wanted to rip my head off before wanting sex before re-wanting to re-remove my head. In the end she did neither and copped a full bottle of Paracetamol, which had me ringing 999 and requesting an ambulance.

Post-stomach pump she was monitored but left the hospital in a black cab to find me at her flat. Again she apologised but I told her it couldn't go on. Day 5 was much better, but not what I had in mind and on Day 6 I left her while she screamed profanities at me down the stairwell. Like I said, I wasn't lying when I said it was the worst six days of my life; however, what she had told Susanna Reid on Good Morning Britain resembled something or someone completely different, although she did kindly state that Jeanette had just kicked me out as that at the time I was being stalked by some wife of an executive from ITV, bless her.

Annie Dixon had loved the gossip as much as Kirsty, and both appeared highly interested in who I really was, behind the ripped-off Savile Row façade.

"I've never ever met anyone like him," she had told Ms Reid. "It was the most exciting week I'd ever had. He was brilliant to be around and everyone fancied him – but I wasn't for him."

"That's not entirely true," I told Annie and Kirsty.

She was also asked as regards Jeanette who she referred to as being intelligent and pretty and Emily, who she described as "looking like some gorgeous little doll".

Good Morning Britain's sole purpose one would have thought was to promote the series that Yasmin Cowley would be starring in, but they appeared to be wanting more background on me, especially when Ms. Reid asked her if she had anyone special in her life?

"Not since Lee," she smiled. "Lee made me feel nice. I like nice."

I certainly wasn't relishing seeing Emily after that.

I spoke to the kids over the phone as I left The Warehouse and told them that I'd pick them up tomorrow lunchtime.

"Why can't we go up to Auntie Joan's party?" was all my daughter could ask.

"It'll be really late by the time I get up there and then I have to sort out some stuff on the new house and drive back down to London," I replied.

"Well if we come, you won't have to drive down to London – we can stay with our Lucy at Granny Sil's."

My kids always had things worked out, which made me smile; however, the real reason I didn't want to take them up to Sil's cousins 25th anniversary is that I wanted things to blow over as regards the Yasmin-thing. I saw it as protecting them, although they both thought I was depriving them of being spoilt by their gran and granddad.

I had never ever experienced an empty house on a Friday evening as it was always mad – always – with the kids and M doing something or other. I went out into the garden to both handle and feed Giroud and Arteta; however M had cleaned them out and slung them a chicken.

I copped a shower and put on a suit and set off on the torturous journey up the M6 to Birkenhead, where in between I spoke to Stuart at length who relayed me all the gossip, which included the fact that Yasmin Cowley was loads better-looking than his sister.

"That's certainly not true, Stu," I told him.

"They've all been talking about you," he whispered.

"Is it bad?" I asked.

"No – our M's a bit upset and keeps mentioning getting a boob-job, that's all."

"How's your dad?"

"Well, impressed," he whispered.

"Really?"

I had also noticed from the texts that were going back and forth that Stuart would become an ardent boob-man. I also noticed that unless he had the privilege of juggling with a few pair before he was seventeen that he'd become an ardent sex-pest, therefore I gave him the heads-up on the fly-on-the-wall documentary.

"This is a bit special," I told him.

It was. The programme needed doing in-house, but as yet I had no-one to operate any of the twenty-odd cams that I'd bought.

"What are you wanting?" he asked.

"I need to sort it with your college first," I said, "But it will involve working down at Sooty's place for a couple of weeks."

"What – I'll be in London filming pornos?"

"Don't be fucking stupid," I told him. "We are doing some six-part fly on the wall documentary about the adult entertainment industry."

"Wow," was all I got back.

"Have you got a mate in that college who could hold a camera without shaking?" I asked.

He had – and I told him to email me down his details. Cue: Ginge.

Ideally I would have loved to have had Freddy Nerkland working back for me, however Freddy was never the most ambitious of people and he told me that he was okay where he was. Ginge, however had been working with his future brother-in-law on some rather iffy building work. I was led to believe it was construction, however he informed me it was quite the opposite and that they were ripping out radiators, boilers and electrics and scrapping it. It sounded all a bit illegal if I am being honest, but there you go!

"Are you enjoying it?" I asked.

"Well, I haven't got Sooty on my back," he laughed.

"You fancy working for me?" I asked.

Then came the hundred dollar question.

"Minimum wage – six-fifty an hour," I lied.

"Yeh – right," he laughed.

I offered him what he'd been earning in the previous job with us on Euston Road; however, I also told him that this set up wouldn't be as laid back as the last time he worked for me and that I was under a load of pressure therefore I wouldn't let him get away with what he had previously gotten away with.

"All I'm saying, Ginge is that you can't piss me about," I said. "Oh yeh – and it will be Abi who will be your boss."

"She got me the sack," he told me.

"No, she didn't mate – you messed up by opening your mouth and I wasn't there to help sweep up the mess."

He deliberated and then asked me what I wanted him to do and his first remit would be to train up Stu and his mate on the use of the new £25,000 a piece Sony Pro cameras that had just been delivered.

"It's not rocket science," I said. "I just want them filming this fly-on-the-wall documentary down at Sooty's place."

"What, Nubeon?" he asked, which was followed by a rather enthusiastic 'Could he do it?'

"No mate – Sooty wouldn't want you down there," I replied.

I eventually got stuck in a 12-mile tailback on the M6 and when I finally got to Mike and Sil's, the house, bar Lucy babysitting Sammy, was empty.

"How's he been, Luce?" I asked.

"Great," she said, adding the fact that her mum had been coming back over and checking in on him every hour.

"Where's our Stuart?" I asked.

"He went around to see one of his mates from college," she said. "He kept on mentioning working in London."

That made me smile.

"Our M hasn't shut up about that actress you were seeing," said a concerned Lucy. "She was on telly this morning and my mam recorded it for my dad – She was dead good-looking."

"She was dead unhinged as well," I added.

"What does that mean?" asked Lucy.

"A nutter," I replied, whilst looking at the clock which told me it was 9:15pm.

I rubbed her head and told her to have a look in my overnight bag as I'd lifted a load of PR and gizmo stuff for her from Sasha's office and I checked in on Sammy before I walked around the corner to her Auntie Joan's, where I immediately got accosted by loads of Emily's relatives, including one or two drunken uncles – Uncle Frank in particular – who was very interested in my exploits with the nutter actress. It was then I looked over at the other side of the room and there was my wife – standing arms-folded with a glass of wine in one of her hands, wearing a lovely cream dress with big brass buttons and nattering to both her mum and her Auntie Joy from Wallasey. She clocked me straight away and I copped a smile, but not before I had her mum come over to me. "You bad lad," she winked, as she pecked me on the lips. "Have you had anything to eat?"

"Nothing," I told her. "I've been busy all day."

She then loaded me up with some prawn Vol-au-vents and what looked like some tandoori king prawns and pork pie before whispering, "Go talk to your wife."

I looked at her looking over at me and then walked across the room to where she was standing and said, "Hello", whilst at the same time feeling that all the room was watching me, which they most certainly were.

"I would have been here earlier but the traffic was murder," I said.

She just looked up at me and smiled, but said nothing.

"I'm really, really sorry M," I said.

"Eat yer Vol-au-vents or my Auntie Elsie will be mad," she said, as she pampered me a bit by tidying up my hair.

"You look nice," I said.

"Have you had a good day?" she asked.

"Very," I nodded.

Then a song began playing and that is when Emily stole a Vol-au-vent form my plate and asked if I fancied a smooch to what was KC and the Sunshine Band's 'Please Don't Go', and although it was hardly a scene from 'Dirty Dancing', as we danced everyone watched on. I just loved her so much.

"I've been thinking about what you said," I whispered.

"What's that?" she asked.

"About a baby," I replied.

"What, really?" she asked sort of stopping in her tracks.

I nodded a reply, and then had to carry her, along with half a plate of Vol-au-vents throughout the rest of the song as she was wrapped around me, and on it stopping she immediately planted a kiss on my lips before seeking out her mum. "Mam, we're definitely going to try for another baby," she said.

It was the least I could do in light of the shit sandwich that had been served to her the other day.

"I want a granddaughter," said an adamant Sil'. "So don't let me down."

That made me smile, but not as much as being dragged upstairs and into the bathroom where I was raped – or it certainly felt like I was – as there was no way I was going back downstairs before the newer of the rules number one had been implemented, whilst at the same time managing to show me more stuff what Gossard had sent her and how much more manageable these were compared to the last lot.

Walking past the queue of relatives at the other side of the bathroom door was a bit embarrassing – for me that is, and not for Emily. I was knackered and could hardly walk, however I have mentioned this already.

We got back over to Mike and Sil's fairly late and this is where a new line of conversation had commenced as Mike was intrigued to know what I had in mind for his son – the trainee cameraman. As for Sil' – she just wanted to know about the baby.

"What would you call it?" Sil' inquired.

I shrugged my shoulders as my wife suddenly became draped around me and who insisted I should pick a name seeing as she had picked the last one.

"I like Emily," I told her, which immediately got her bottom lip wobbling.

"What, really?"

I nodded. I certainly wasn't lying.

"What about if it's a boy," asked her mum.

"It won't be," I replied. "You wanted a girl."

That set Sil' off crying and had Mike shaking his head.

"Emily Rose," said my wife rather excitedly. "I like Emily Rose."

My mum's name was Rose and Emily knew this.

"If you like – but we have to make it first."

Stuart came in all excited and that being the case we didn't get the full use of our couch until 2:00am and at 6:30am I had Herbert sat on my knee doing his rendition of the 'Screaming Ab-Dabs' while his Granny Sil' made him up his bottle.

"He plays yer both up, doesn't he?" she said on her return.

"You've noticed then?" I replied.

Emily may have partaken in the conversation, however she was under the quilt with the pillow over her head, which didn't go unnoticed by her mum.

"She's like this all the time," I lied.

"Don't believe him, mam," said the voice from under the pillow.

Stuart must have heard voices as within a couple of minutes he was in the room with us, dressed in his dressing gown and slippers.

"What's this?" I asked. "You've only been in television two minutes and you're dressing like Noël Coward."

"When can I come down with you?" he smiled.

"I'm all over the place at the moment," I told him. "And I need to clear it with your tutor at college."

"Are we stopping with you?" he asked.

"Who's we?" asked the voice from under the pillow.

"Me and Jonathan," he said.

That got her up. "Who's Jonathan?"

I then explained to him my idea, which was not only an idea to get him some work experience, but also get him a bit of life experience.

"What – so we aren't stopping with you?" he asked.

I then explained that I needed to see him be his own person. "I've got a mate of a mate of a mate who has a flat next to Wood Green tube station – it's one stop on The Tube from The Warehouse and it's a change at King's Cross and onto the Northern Line to get down to Sooty's place."

"Yeh – but I don't know The Tube," he said.

"I do," said a beaming Lucy at the door. "It's dead easy."

"There you go – if our Lucy can do it, so can you," I said as his sister came and sat beside me nearly squashing her big sister in the process. "Your mum and dad are currently doing everything for you – You need to show them – and me – that you can handle a bit of responsibility – and you're not on your own as me and your Emily are down there."

"So we get our own flat?" he asked.

"So you get your own flat," I said.

With that he was upstairs like a shot and on his mobile to his mate.

"Do you think that's wise?" asked his big sister, who was now sat up with the quilt draped around her.

"If he messes it up he loses everything," I said. "Don't worry – he will be told."

Lucy did the honours of feeding Herbert whilst his Granny Sil' put on some breakfast.

"Aw, he's so cute," said Lucy.

"Chuck him your M and you'll see how cute he's not," I said. "He'll scream the place down."

Chapter 25

Electric Ladyboy

Arsenal had recently won two back to back 1-0 games against West Bromwich Albion and Southampton and my mood I should say was buoyant until they bollocksed it up at all places – Stoke City and where the manager ended up getting some barbed comments and threats aimed his way at the city's train station. I'm all for putting my point over; however, it could have been done more civil. Perhaps the fact that he is that estranged from the obvious problem helped create the confrontation? I just don't know. Wenger has to be applauded for what he has achieved; however, football changes and sadly he doesn't. I thought he would have stepped down gracefully after the F.A Cup Final, but looking back on it – why would he? He has the best job in football on possibly one of the best salaries. George Swindin was on around £3,000 a year, which equates to around £25,500 in today's money. In sharp contrast Wenger's wages work out at somewhere around £7-8 million.

When Wenger came to Arsenal there was an immediate change of culture and there was a massive shake-up, with players leaving.

When Swindin took the reins he did the same and had a mass clear-out of players, with the supporters back then thinking exactly as they do now – replace the mediocre with class. It is not rocket science – it is how you improve a squad.

On taking over Swindin assessed his squad and immediately took a wrecking ball to it, selling Welsh international inside-forward Derek Tapscott to Cardiff, inside-forward Ray Swallow to Derby, and forwards Freddie Jones and Ron Clayton to Brighton and on 26th September, 1958 the *Daily Express'* Bob Pennington revealed that Arsenal had put seven more players on the transfer list, with it not only indicating that there was a major move for Mel Charles of Swansea on the cards, but the fact that he intended to break the bottleneck that had stifled the progress of young talent in Arsenal's reserve side. The not-so-magnificent seven were: 29-year-old centre-forward Cliff Holton, who would be the subject of a rather strange transfer tug of war; 24-year-old centre-half Jim Fotheringham, who had been the subject of a bid from Glasgow Rangers the season prior and was due to be selected for Scotland in their game against Wales on 18th October; 29-year-old outside-right Mike Tiddy who had been dogged with injury problems; along with reserve right back Don Bennett, who would join 'Digger' Daley up at Coventry City; 30-year-old goalkeeper Con Sullivan, who would never play first team football again; reserve wing half Peter Davies and inside forward Bobby Dixon.

What was strange is that if moves for these players had come off with immediate effect it would have left Arsenal with only one recognised centre-half – something which happened midway through the season due to injuries and which was something that also occurred in the 1972/73 season.

Heart of Midlothian eventually bought Fotheringham for £8,000 whilst Holton – who could also play centre half, was bought by Fourth Division Watford even though some top clubs were in for him including both Stoke City and Liverpool. What was strange about these two moves is that Holton – who once hit all four goals in a 4-1 mauling of Sheffield Wednesday at Hillsborough in March 1953 – looked like he was going to Reading before over 50 hours of negotiation between the Arsenal board and Watford chairman Jim Bonser thrashed out a deal in which Watford would pay them £10,000 on a half now – half later deal, with one of Holton's major points in the deal being that he could stay close to London, as outside of football he had an engineering job. As for the 6'4 Fotheringham – who it was thought would be the subject of a reignited interest from Glasgow Rangers and which was something that never materialised – was that he too would be linked with Fourth Division Watford come the March transfer deadline; however, this was more to do with Arsenal wanting The Hornets' 20-year old right back Vince McNeice – a player who they had been trailing since November – as part of the manager's new youth policy. Swindin told the *Daily Express'* Roger Malone on 14th October, 1958 – after watching Arsenal's reserves beat Tottenham 2-0, in that he had inherited a squad devoid of youth talent, with the only bright young things on show that night being John Read and Mike Everitt, neither of whom would go on to make the grade at Highbury, however the latter would certainly figure in one of the senior players' plans.

As regards McNeice, Watford chairman Bonsar told Roger Malone that he could not go to Arsenal in time for the transfer deadline as he was touring with the R.A.F team and if any deal was to be concluded it would be a straight cash job of £12,500.

As regards a possible part-exchange Bonser added, "We studied Arsenal reserve centre half Jim Fotheringham for the third time and we've decided he is not quite what we want."

Fotheringham's move to Hearts would come at the end of March 1959 and after the deadline, making him ineligible to play – something which rather strangely would never ever happen.

Fotheringham went north of the border without his wife. His grandson Andy explained, "He ended up staying with an aunt in Hamilton as the housing situation was a big problem for him during his time up there. My Gran stayed in Corby when he went to Edinburgh, but not because she didn't want to go. The club didn't supply players with houses and houses were harder to come by in Scotland. She went up to see a new build in Edinburgh but they wanted a fifty pound deposit and my grandad was on tour in Australia at the time and she didn't want to put the deposit down without him, therefore as they both had family in Corby they thought it best for her to stay here."

On the 12th August, 1959, just five months after he was transferred to Hearts, Northampton Town made a bid for him – Northampton's manager being none other than Dave Bowen – the Arsenal midfielder who had initially been dropped by Swindin but who had fought back to regain his place in the side and who would leave at the end of the 1958/59 season to become player manager with The Cobblers – and who, history would have it, would also pay Arsenal £4,000 for the services of the young Mike Everitt to help with the clubs meteoric rise from the Fourth to the First Division in just five seasons. Strangely a rejuvenated Cliff Holton would also join the club a couple of seasons later and be the subject of a £10,000 bid from Queens Park Rangers in December 1962!

As for Fotheringham his career at Northampton began rather shakily and he was even criticised by the *Daily Mirror* on his Fourth Division debut after his new clubs 1-1 draw away at Exeter on the 23rd August, 1959 with it saying that "Big Jim must improve".

A mistake by him on the 21st September paved the way to a 3-0 battering by Millwall, a match which he had to be carried off after he had been knocked unconscious, and which resulted in a five day stay at the Royal Northern Hospital in London, a building which was demolished in the mid-1990s to make way for residential housing – the demolition works being delayed after the murdered body of 24-year old Michelle Folan had been found buried in a shallow grave in the hospital grounds and whose 46-year old husband, Patrick had strangled her after she had filed for divorce in 1981.

Fotheringham only played a handful of games as he had his career cut short after suffering a horrendous fracture of his right leg and after four matches of his comeback – in the reserves against Luton Town on the 8th October, 1960, he suffered another break of the same leg. During the time he was laid up with injury, explained his grandson, he had managed to teach his wife to drive their Austin A40, him removing the front seat so he could get his huge frame in it. On a much sadder note, some years later he was involved in a horrific car crash which he managed to survive, only to die two weeks later from a heart attack. He was only 43.

As for Vince McNiece – he never did get his move to Arsenal nor any other big club and finished playing in 1964 and went over to Denmark where he managed B1903 København in 1973 – who were one of the teams that merged to form what is now F.C Copenhagen.

Swindin's idea was to build the team around Mel Charles, another player that was signed after the transfer deadline, therefore making him ineligible to play – who strangely he went into an auction for after stating earlier in the season after losing out on Bobby Collins – that wasn't his way. However football, along with society, was changing rapidly.

As regards the post-deadline transfer merry-go-round the *Daily Mirror's* George Harley ran with the back page headlines 'Arsenal Let Big Jim Go' adding, "Arsenal cannot play Charles in any First Division match because they are in the running for the championship and talent money. Hearts cannot include Fotheringham in their Scottish League side because they too, are chasing championship honours. Yet big Jim, one of the tallest centre halves in the game, was willing to go anywhere to get back to first team football."

As for Mel Charles, Swindin told Harley, "He will be a tremendous asset to Arsenal", however, unbeknown to the Yorkshireman at that time – the signing of Charles would be the start of his undoing.

In addition to a £40,000 fee paid to Swansea Town – they received transfer-listed right-half Peter Davies – who Swindin had earlier valued at £500 and former England youth left winger, 19-year-old David Dodson, who had at first dug his heels in and refused, before finally agreeing to the move in early July.

Charles would come to regret his high-profile move to Arsenal and what history will tell you is that Charles suffered some bad injuries – so much so the press labelled him 'The Knee', and that he couldn't adapt to the changes and complexities of what was a rapidly-modernising game. Chuck the fact that he had a poor relationship with Ron Greenwood into the mix, and there appeared a huge problem.

I had got into work around 7:30am with George Swindin still playing heavily on my mind. Well him, Arsène Wenger and the wanker who pulled out of Duckett Road in a black Mazda just minutes earlier, causing me to spill coffee everywhere.

Swindin was one of the few goalkeepers that went into top flight management – with Gil Merrick of Birmingham, Willie 'Iam' McFaul of Newcastle and Nigel Adkins of Reading being the only others in England that immediately spring to mind – although on the continent both Dino Zoff and Raymond Goethals had made great careers for themselves after hanging up their gloves.

When Swindin was told his contract wouldn't be renewed in March 1962, it was revealed that he had spent around £300,000 on players. He seemed to have a scattergun approach in his recruitment process and appeared to just buy for buying's sake rather than diligently undertaking the task. However the club; as strangely as it sounds, were restricted by the £20-plus maximum wage, with nearly every club in Britain capable of matching the wages, meaning the name 'Arsenal' and the perks that go with it were the only major draw – something which was highlighted by the fact that a player like non-league Peterborough United's then 25-year-old schemer Dennis Emery couldn't be persuaded to join the club, meaning that Arsenal had missed out on some of the best – one of who was indeed Denis Law.

Law told the *Daily Express* on 15th March, 1960, "It's Arsenal for me", much to the dislike of his club's Chairman with the paper running the headlines – "Denis Law is talking himself out of his dream transfer to Arsenal. The 20-year-old Scottish international, Britain's most highly priced and extensively quoted footballer, was last night under fire by his club, Huddersfield Town. A Town official said: 'Law is giving the impression that he is conducting his own transfer to one particular club. You would think it is all cut and dried and the other clubs are merely wasting their time in contacting us'."

Arsenal had been tracking him throughout the 1958/59 season; however Law getting injured during Arsenal's abysmal capitulation during the Christmas period of 1958 hung fire on any bid and it wasn't until the following spring when a £50,000 bid looked like getting him.

The *Daily Express'* Harry Langton wrote on 28th March, 1960 after Arsenal had toiled to get a 1-1 draw against what was a nine-man Leeds United in front of a paltry crowd of just 19,735, "Ten years ago Arsenal were still being described as the best team in the world. Against Leeds they were being booed by their own supporters. The Arsenal of old would have swept in with an unbeatable bid for Denis Law – who is now a £53,000 Manchester City player. Arsenal 1960 merely printed a sniping attack on newspapers in their programme, while giving their version of their failure to sign Law – What a come down."

Arsenal had made tentative enquiries about Albert Quixall, lost out on Bobby Collins, and failed in a bid to get John Grant of Hibernian and Phil Woosnam – a player they again bid for in 1960 – and passed on the chance of signing Gordon Banks. What has also rarely been said was that while Heart of Midlothian were dealing with Arsenal in the transfer of Fotheringham, George Swindin was in South Wales doing his damnedest to stop Spurs from gazumping Arsenal for Charles – and being asked to leave the room during the transfer whilst Spurs' Bill Nicholson spoke with the Swansea manager Trevor Morris. What history will tell you is that Arsenal got their man while Spurs did no more and raided Hearts for Dave Mackay – and with the fact that Swindin missed that move entirely, could conclude that he had been the one with problem with his eyes, and not Mel Charles.

"What are you on with?" asked Kirsty as I trawled through the ITN Archives looking for Charles' gaffe in front of the camera, where he supposedly told the world that he needed clitorises removing from his eyes.

"What, he actually said that?" asked Kirsty.

I nodded.

"He obviously meant cataracts," she said.

"Obviously," I replied.

"He sounds a brick short of a load," she quipped.

I then mentioned the Denis Law transfer that never happened as she handed me a coffee before sitting on the corner of my desk.

"You're right into this, aren't you?" she asked.

She was right I was. After raiding Hearts for Dave Mackay, Tottenham would become the best side in England during the following few years and attract brilliant players to the side such as Jimmy Greaves from AC Milan, Cliff Jones from Swansea Town, John White from Falkirk – even pushing Fulham to the brink whereby they had loads of worried and desperate fans outside Craven Cottage in August 1964, after the club's high-profile albeit failed bid for the legendary Johnny Haynes. Tottenham were going places; Arsenal however, were not.

I then I told her of the failed transfer bids after the great captures of Docherty and Henderson, adding that Swindin had also tried to recruit lesser players such Alan Fox of Wrexham, Jackie Plenderleith of Hibernian, Charlie Livesey of Southampton and Eric Tomkins of Hereford United, all of which were as awe inspiring as the players that did go to

Highbury during that time such as Billy McCullough from Portadown, Billy Rudd from Manchester United, John Hughes from Bangor, Alan Skirton from Bath, Roy Drake from Barnet and Alan Morton from Peterborough United, with the latter's transfer being somewhat contentious.

"Posh Accuse Swindin – You have taken our best boy," wrote Harry Langton of the *Daily Express* on 4th February, 1959. "Arsenal manager George Swindin has infuriated his former club Peterborough United by taking their brilliant youth prospect, Alan Morton. Swindin has persuaded Morton, a 16-year-old inside forward on the fringe of international youth honours, to have a trial at Highbury. Peterborough manager Jimmy Hagan, who succeeded Swindin as boss of the giant non-League club last year, said last night: 'Swindin has taken this boy away just when we were going to get some benefit out of him. He will be 17 next month and we were hoping to sign him as a professional – I understand Swindin has been warning other clubs about poaching his players – and now he comes along and does this to us.'"

Hagan went on to deny that Morton was discovered by Swindin while at Peterborough and added, "We are trying to build a team to get into the League without paying out a lot of money for players and then this happens."

Arsenal could have also had Chacarita Juniors' 22-year-old Argentinian international left winger Roberto Brookes for £9,000, as he wanted to come to Arsenal, but the club passed on him after sending him an air ticket and giving him a trial in September 1959.

There was very little footage of Arsenal's failed Parallel season; therefore I had to build it up from the following season along with various football reports.

Swindin dropped major bollock in not getting Law, with Arsenal's move coming shortly before the 16th March transfer deadline and during the weekend where they were beaten in a friendly by lowly Leyton Orient – 2-0 in front of just over 18,000 at Highbury.

Arsenal had had first refusal on Law after Swindin had seen him at his scheming best during a 5-1 mauling of West Ham United in a F.A Cup Third Round replay at Upton Park in January, and in front of just over 22,600, which was confirmed on 14th March, 1960 by Ken Jones of the *Daily Mirror*, who sensed the masked comments being made by chairman Sir Bracewell Smith. "Despite a smokescreen statement I expect Arsenal to be ready to part with a new record fee to take Law to Highbury," he said.

Jones described Denis Law as a boy among men. "Law is that soccer phenomenon these days – an artist who will fight," whilst further adding, "Arsenal manager George Swindin continued his almost endless trek to and from Huddersfield when he watched Law for the umpteenth time on Saturday in a game where they beat Hull 1-0. These are the vital points that will almost certainly put the Gunners out in front of a six-club battle for the youngster, who in three years has become one of the most controversial players in the game. Arsenal have first refusal – Law wants First Division football, and in London. Manager Swindin has players to exchange if Huddersfield won't make it a straight cash deal – and Law is a firm friend of Arsenal's Scottish international wing half, Tommy Docherty."

Everything pointed to a move to Arsenal, although what has also been rarely said was that fellow Scottish international striker David Herd was being lined up as a £25,000 makeweight – meaning that he would not only have to move up to Yorkshire – but would also have to drop down a division. It was something that was a sign of the times in British football, and something that would soon be stamped out after the maximum wage was abolished.

Jones further added, "Docherty, as Scottish skipper, fathered Law when he played his first international two seasons ago and he told me last night 'Denis is a great player – he is a performer in the Arsenal tradition, and it would be wonderful if he came here to play.'"

The very next day it was a completely different story with Jones stating, "Manchester City are now red hot favourites to clinch the crazy cash race for Denis Law, which will make him the most expensive piece of soccer merchandise in Britain, and which all points to a dramatic last-minute twist to a transfer serial that only twenty-four hours ago looked certain to end with Law moving to Arsenal."

Arsenal's Ron Greenwood had been present up at Huddersfield's Leeds Road ground to enter what became an auction, whilst Swindin was at Highbury watching the possible makeweight in the transfer – David Herd hit an equaliser after 72 minutes against Leicester City in front of a whistling and jeering crowd of just under 28,000, with Bob Pennington of the *Daily Express* describing the match of 'fumbling, farcical football' as he put it, and candidly stating, "On the evidence of this game Arsenal would find even Denis Law's dad an improvement in certain positions."

To make matters worse, up in Huddersfield Manchester City kicked up an offer of £53,000 with Arsenal unwilling to match it. Maybe if Swindin would have been there it may have happened; however, it didn't and the rest is history.

On another note I had interviewed a few people for the new colourisation department and we had whittled it down a shortlist of six – well seven when I had received a knock on my door the other day from one of ITV 7's bright young things.

Becky Ivell was a 20-year-old girl that I'd set on as one of the 'out and about' reporters. I didn't really have any dealings with her as such, as there was a pecking order where I told Abi what I wanted and she made sure it got done. It transpired that she was after moving to London from her home in Southampton and that she would like the chance of a full-time job as opposed to the odd couple of days.

"And you fancy working on the colourisation instead?" I asked.

"No – I'd prefer to do it as well as," she replied.

"That'd make it a seven-day a week job," I explained. "Sometimes working twelve hours a day."

"I want a future," she said.

I told her that I'd think about it and mentioned it to Abi.

"Why not?" Abi had said. "She seems keen."

I gave her the heads-up on the job and told her that she would be joined by a Becky Sparshott and a Ekaterina 'Cat' Ulchenkö – the latter of who had been on the sales counter of Carphone Warehouse and knew mobile phones inside out, but who could have easily be cast as some Eastern European spy in a James Bond movie – and it would be here that a masterstroke would occur as this particular morning I had them colourising segments from the ITN archive, one of which was monochrome footage of Denis Law's transfer from Huddersfield Town, when some suits from ITV turned up – one of who was the Deputy General.

"Lee – we've got some suits in reception," buzzed Faranha.

The entourage of five came upstairs and were shown into my office where I was just completing some more copy as regards George Swindin – with the George Eastham saga blowing the Denis Law saga completely out of the water.

"Haven't you finished that yet?" smiled the head of sport.

"Nah," I replied. "Anyway, I've got something I want you to see."

I took them through the open plan office and around to the new colourisation suite where my newly appointed team – labelled by everyone internally as 'The B.B.C' – were hard at work converting their 'fifty shades of grey'.

They were hooked.

"We've only done a small amount as I've just set this department up, but they have a huge list of things to do, a lot of which should be ready for the launch," I said. "The public will soon be able to see the likes of Tom Finney and Johnny Haynes – and all in colour."

They couldn't believe it.

"It's time consuming," I said. "But this is one of the routes I'm wanting to go down."

"So how much is this going to cost us?" asked the big boss.

"Nothing as such – I'll just factor in the man hours," I said before giving them a wink, "I'm hoping that you'll want us to colourise some old programmes for you such as Doctor Who or Z Cars."

"They are BBC programmes," said the director general.

"Yeh – I know," I smiled.

They still couldn't believe it all and it was then I gave them a rough guide to the art of colourisation whilst telling them of my previous billion botched attempts at it.

They had initially come over to see what we had got lined up as regards doing them some extra programming, and went back to their head office with something else to think about.

Cue: Reception calling me that an irate Tottenham supporter-cum-lead singer wanted to see me.

He was a bit pissed with me that our corporate law firm had had YouTube take down the 'Live at The Warehouse' clip with them on it – in fact with everyone on it – and all the ITV Sessions footage.

"If you want me to piss you off further I could also sue you for breach of copyright," I told him before adding, "I own the footage, not you."

There was, however a compromise – a compromise weighted heavily in my favour I should hasten to add – and that was White Lion Street – well, it would be eventually, and that being the case I dragged Abi off set and got her to listen in.

"I'm in discussions with ITV's head of entertainment and some other suits as regards an extension of our Sessions programme and also about a music label."

"What, a record label?" he asked.

"Yeh – that's what I just said, didn't I?" I told him. "We've got the facilities here for the time being but I'm hoping that in the New Year I might have a proper recording studio on White Lion Street."

"So you are going to offer us a deal?" he asked.

"Maybe," I replied, "However, I have to have one of my lawyers present as I don't want shafting."

"Nor do I?" he said.

"Good, then we've got something in common," I said.

"A record label?" shrugged Abi on him leaving. "We don't know anything about producing records."

"It can't be that hard, considering some of the wankers that have been successful at it," I said.

I got back home to Emily teaching some kid the fiddle and I wished that I hadn't.

"Aw, don't be mean – she's only just started," said my wife.

"It sounds like it," I replied. "Anyway who is she? I thought you weren't taking on any new pupils."

The answer surprised me in that it was the daughter of ITV's development director. It also transpired that she was also teaching the daughter of ITV's director general and that being the case, ITV were trying their hand at world domination. My world, that is.

I picked up a remarkably placid Sammy and went into the kitchen to make a coffee. "If your mum asks you if you want to play the fiddle – tell her no," I told him. "Or ask to play the guitar as she can't play one of those."

"I heard that," shouted a voice.

"Good," I replied.

I answered another one billion emails and by 8:00pm I was knackered. I really needed to delegate some more work as I was starting to lose control of everything.

"Can I help?" asked M.

"Not really," I said, before telling her that I needed to restructure LMJ as every time I seemed to be coping, ITV threw me another bone.

"Just say no," she smiled.

"They've just offered us a thirty-eight week extension of the Sessions programme," I said.

"Well, don't say no to that," she smiled.

"And that idiot from Electric Ladyboy wants to sign up with us if we get the record label going," I said.

"Well, don't say no to that as well," she said.

"And I've got your Stuart and his mate coming down from Lime Street on Friday night and I've got to prep them on what I want."

"Well yer can't really say no to that either," she twanged.

"I'll probably just have to cut sex out," I winked.

"You do that and I'll definitely start nagging you," she smiled.

We had a bit of a meal and watched Jeanette on TV who we both thought was getting better every show, although she had kept on putting the trip to China off, which meant that even though we had shot most of the footage for 'The Rape of Nanking', we still couldn't complete it.

Thursdays were beginning to be a right ball ache as the Live at The Warehouse show meant that I was tied to one place at a certain time and that I was dealing with a lot of people; however, this Thursday was going to be a bit worse as by 8:20am I was alerted to an article in *The Sun*. 'Sports Media Mogul and Love Rat', it read. '25-year-old marketing executive from Bristol, Nicole Averiss reveals her steamy relationship with ITV 7 producer Lee Janes and explains the story behind the TV star he left her for'.

Fucking epic! I thought. I couldn't make this up – What next, a spot on 'Good Morning Britain'?

"Have you seen it eh, eh, eh," chortled ITV's head of sports. "Keep this up and we'll have twenty million viewers for the channels launch."

"You're in the papers again, Lee," smiled Faranha, as she brought me a coffee.

I had been on UK TV once and American TV once and for a period totalling 28 minutes, yet I was in the lousy papers every stinking day. The only good thing about this story was that Emily was very well aware of it. Well, I thought she was until it was relayed to me that Nicole had told the world that I wanted to marry her.

"Is it true?" asked Emily.

"No," I replied.

"Well it says here that Jeanette advised you to dump me and marry her because she loved you and that I was just some woman who was having an affair on her husband," she said. "This isn't nice, Lee."

It wasn't, and I sloped off into sanity and the surreal world of ITV 7 where the crew were putting together three documentaries – a three-part programme on violence on the terraces; Ajax Amsterdam's domination of European football in the early 1970's; and one on ex-Queens Park Rangers player Stan Bowles.

"How is she?" asked Kirsty.

"Don't ask," I replied.

"Okay, then I fucking won't," she snapped.

I had got decorators working in a room at the back of The Warehouse, which was once a store room but which was now being converted into a pressroom as ITV wanted me to smooch with reporters from the tabloids, and tomorrow I would have the place packed to the rafters obviously wanting my take on the 'Nicole-thing'.

Meanwhile at Stately Wayne Manor I had a pissed-off wife to deal with and that being the case I had to drive back home only to be greeted by a reporter from the *Daily Mirror* backed up by his photographer at our door. Our lives certainly weren't our own any more.

"Can you give me a take on *The Sun's* story this morning, Lee?" asked the hack.

I told them to come in and wipe their feet and I'd give them some background before adding, "You misquote anything I say and you'll have a major problem."

Emily wasn't at all happy about having the press in her house in light of what had just been said about her, in that she was basically some old trollop that had been having an affair on her husband and who I'd got pregnant.

With Sammy copping forty-winks – seeing as he kept me up half the night howling like a Banshee – I invited my wife to sit with me. "Come on M – Let's clear this up," I said whilst patting the sofa.

"I have only ever loved two women," I told the reporter. "And that is Jeanette and Emily."

I wasn't lying as that was spot on.

"I have only ever asked one woman to marry me and that's Emily," I said.

My wife looked at me – rather strangely, if I'm being honest.

"With Jeanette it was a mutual thing, as opposed to a 'Will you marry me' thing," I explained. "I asked Emily to marry me more or less exactly where your photographer is standing and she said 'Yes'. Emily is the loveliest woman you could ever meet and I love her a lot. I also still love my wife and will do until the day I die, but it is a different type of love, but a love all the same."

"You mean sex?" asked the reporter.

"Don't be sordid, pal," I said. "I'm telling you a story about the two women I love – don't you ever make it dirty."

The reporter apologised on the spot.

"My wife threw me out as we were having problems, which wasn't helped by my infidelity. I was wrong and I lost everything I loved, which just goes to show that shagging around isn't the best way to keep a marriage together. I immediately went off the rails and went wild – why not? I had everything at my disposal, however, here is the thing – Jeanette along with a close family friend – female I may hasten to add – reigned me in and helped me understand what I had done and what I was doing. Jeanette because she loved me, the family friend because she is a bossy cow – but all the same, if it were not for those two people I wouldn't be here now."

The reporter and Emily appeared very interested in where this was going.

"As all the world knows, I crashed at Yasmin Cowley's place for six days and eventually moved in with Nicole. Nicole was really nice – and I say this with all honesty, but there was something missing from our relationship which Emily gave me. Emily loved my children whereas Nicole didn't want what she saw as baggage. Did Nicole love me? Yes, I'm sure she did. Did I love her, in all honesty I thought I did, but if you have ever loved someone properly then you know the difference between loving someone and liking them."

Emily then linked my arm as the reporter watched.

"It is true that Jeanette advised me to marry Nicole but at that time she didn't know Emily. Jeanette and Emily are now best friends so I suppose you could draw your own conclusion of who was right and who was wrong."

I then shrugged my shoulders. "That is the true story," I said. "Lies and intentional misquotes may sell papers, but they also hurt people – and it is mostly people that don't deserve hurting."

The reporter shook my hand and after drinking a coffee, left happy. They had been given a scoop of sorts, and for nothing.

Mine and Emily's life was becoming a Soap Opera, which was not helped by this tabloid frenzy and on Friday morning in the new press suite I had exactly twenty-three press men and photographers wanting some exclusive, especially as there had been a second mini-riot during Live at The Warehouse the night before. Whereas Electric Ladyboy had set the precedent for the ultimate riotous performance, 'Red and White' with their lead singer Joe '90' Atkin, complete with glasses, were the ultimate in cool. They were all smart-looking lads from around the Angel and Essex Road area of north London – who I thought looked the Smiths but who sounded absolutely nothing like them. For me they were absolutely awesome and had the crowd up on their feet from the word go, but had my wife absolutely red-faced with their song 'Emily, Please'.

It sounded a bit like a cross between the Super Furry Animals 'Something 4 the weekend' and the LA's 'There she goes' yet it didn't as the thumping drums and whirring Danelectros gave it more kick without losing the melody. I'd never heard anything like it and the fact that the lead singer was asking for an Emily to turn around and 'get on yer knees Emily please' so he could knock one out would have probably pissed me off if I could have actually made out the words, however I couldn't. As it happened though, Emily did – and she went the colour of beetroot.

"For me," Emily had said at the press conference which I had urged her to attend, "They are one of the most exciting bands in the UK who could well have the pull of Oasis."

"Pull?" asked a press man.

"Don't you start," blushed Emily. "I've had enough innuendos to last me a lifetime."

"Don't you find it a compliment?" she asked.

"Of course I do, but I'd rather you ask me another question," she replied.

I got out of the conference to a couple more suits from ITV who were being escorted around The Warehouse by Faranha and Annie, the latter of who had just told me that we had just had a BACS payment for the fly-on-the-wall series – even though the two 16-year-old cameramen were still in Liverpool copping a McDonalds. It turned out that the suits had been down to Nubeon's studios off Old Kent Road and didn't like what they saw and wanted it filming here.

"Aw come on," I told them. "I can't have them shooting that shit up here."

However shooting that shit up here was exactly what was going to happen. ITV as ever called the shots and I went absolutely ape shit with Sooty for not getting his house in order after he'd been forewarned. Now it meant I had to deal with loads of adult actresses along with Sooty and his pervert boss from Cheshunt with the 3kg medallion hanging around his neck swanning around up here.

"You can create a studio, can't you?" asked the suit.

"Yeh – course I can," I told them, "But it's hardly fucking fly-on-the-wall if it's going to be up here."

Cue: Red and White and Electric Ladyboy at 1:00pm, and the deal.

"Ten songs a piece and I'll put you an album together; however, they have to be good. I don't want any shit. I want you to run with a similar sound – impress me and I'll do another three albums for you over two years."

"Do we get a fee up front?" was always going to be the first question.

"I'll sub you all a two hundred quid a week basic wage, I'll pay you five grand a piece now and you'll get twenty-five percent royalties ...... net."

Cue: Annie Dixon.

"Sort them their cheques, and get Jaime to sort them studio time – but make it at night as I can't be listening to that racket all day," I said.

Cue: Fox Fab Four.

"Any of you want to play at being an undercover reporter auditioning to be a porn star?" I asked.

Sinead was the first with her hand up.

"Done," I said.

Now Joe frigging 90 from Red and White had my mobile phone number he was being a right pest and even wanted to sing to me down the phone, and in one instance while I was picking Stu and his mate up from Euston Station.

"Pinky and Perky!" I said, as Stu came over and gave me a hug before introducing me to his mate.

I took them to our house where Emily had made them some tea and packed them a couple of boxes of essentials for the flat before I gave them the third degree.

"Trust is a big part of this," I told them. "It is the chance of a lifetime, so any of you fuck me about and that's it."

Stuart knew more than anyone that I meant it, however the other part of the dynamic duo was more interested in ogling his mate's newly famous big sister. "Oi, Scouse Billy," I said. "Are you listening?"

I got nods from both of them and drove them up to Wood Green Tube station and to the flat, which I had to say had been described a lot better than it actually was – although both lads thought it was brilliant. The place was freezing until I kicked up the heating, and that being the case it smelt a bit damp.

"Make sure you both phone your parents and let them know how you are," I said. "And make sure you come into The Warehouse at ten o'clock sharp looking nice and presentable – that means shower, shave and looking smart."

I had no idea what Jonathan thought of it all as he'd hardly said a word since getting off the train.

That Friday night was no different to most Friday nights, apart from the fact that Stuart was on the phone texting me to say how great everything was – and that Jeanette and Paul had called round and that being the case, I had to be on my best behaviour – with the main topic of conversation being Sooty and Libby.

"She's actually filed for divorce," Jeanette said.

"Yeh – I know," I said.

"Has Sooty said anything to you?" she asked.

"No," I lied, before offering Paul a red wine.

Paul may have liked to be a part of the King's Cross sewing circle, but I didn't and while he listened to my wife and ex-wife yapping I sought solace in watching Winnie the Pooh with my kids.

"Why do they call him Winnie the Pooh, Dad?" asked my lad.

"Because he stinks," I replied, which sort of had them both giggling.

"Monday night," Emily said – sort of out of the blue.

"Yeh – what about it?" I asked.

"We are having a meal over at Mr. and Mrs. Marsden's," she replied.

"Well, that's something to look forward to," I lied.

"Don't be horrible," she smiled, before continuing yapping to Jeanette.

"How do you think we'll fare against Blackburn tomorrow?" asked Paul, as regards Brentford's chances.

"It's a hard one to call, Paul," I said. "At the minute the results are all over the place, but Brentford are looking okay so I'd call a home win. As for us – half the time I have no idea which team is going to turn up, but Newcastle are due a battering even though their form suggests otherwise. If was a betting man – I'd stick fifty quid on both us and Brentford winning."

Mmm, he did, and got a fairly nice return as he coupled my information with Manchester City and Chelsea winning, but that was in the future and this was now and the very next day I had two Jack Russells humping my leg in anticipation of seeing a few porn stars get battered along with Ginge showing them how to work a Canon XF305 High Definition Camcorder.

"I thought the cameras would be bigger than this?" Stu asked.

"These are portable ones," explained Ginge. "You can't go using a great Match of the Day type camera while you are crawling up and around round some bloke's arse."

"He's right, albeit rather crudely stated," I said. "And you're not filming pornos, you're filming the goings on in the studio."

Saturday morning in The Warehouse was a lot quieter than normal and this day only The B.B.C, my two PR people and Kirsty over at ITV 7 were in.

"Kirsty – Stu and Jonathan," I said, introducing the dynamic duo.

"Yeh, what about it?" she replied.

"We are on about sending her to charm school," I lied.

However, what was to happen when Georgia Clayton came out of her office with a load of mail was going to have a bearing on someones or someone – that someone being Stuart. Georgia walked across to me in a big jumper, short, black checked skirt, opaque tights and no shoes and slumped at the side of me showing me some mail. To me she was just a bright young thing with a pretty face, but to these two adolescents she was some blonde-haired temptress.

"Who are the two lads?" she asked.

"Stu and Jonathan," I said, as I read the mail. "Stu's M's brother."

Now here would be a story!

Chapter 26

Jeanette's Tales – Take 9

I should have warned Lee about Sinead exactly the same as M should have, however we didn't – why? Because me and M liked her, as she was the only one of the ITV 7 team that really had anything to do with us, although Les and Oliver did say hello when they saw us.

Sinead had only been at The Warehouse a week when she part-exchanged her Peugeot 307 for some red Porsche. But that wasn't anything new as Karen had nearly run over three press men and a dog trying to reverse her brand new and very big Ford Mustang into her parking space. I have no idea how that happened as it certainly wasn't the quietest of vehicles.

Sinead milked the attention and loved her photograph taken and that being the case she was never out of the limelight and was the unelected leader of Force Fox Four or Foxy Fab Four or whatever they liked to call themselves.

One particular morning she pulled up as a couple of paparazzi flashed their cameras and asked the same daft questions as they always generally asked; however, this time she got out of the car both heavily made-up and in the shortest red dress you will ever see and by short, I mean short. Even the normally unshakeable M was taken by surprise. "What's that – a top or a dress," she whispered.

Next morning Sinead was 'The Lady in Red'; however just off Old Kent Road, she was 'The Lady in Bed' as her undercover reporting that was being filmed by M's little brother and some other lad I was to come to know as Jonathan, and under the direction of all people – Sooty, was a little raunchy to say the least. That being the case it was only a matter of time when Lee had a knock on his door late one night. It was Sinead's husband, Tommy.

"I expected her being here," he had told Lee on being invited inside.

"Why?" Lee had asked. "She's never been here."

Whilst Lee had been asked an array of questions, M had kept schtum. M was like that – a great ally and confidant, unfortunately Lee was completely in the dark as regards Sinead, and unbeknown to him he was being recklessly grilled by her husband, who with Lee being in the papers on a daily basis with reports of him being frantically pursued by every available female, he thought that she was part of his fan club.

"What, you think I'm giving her one?" Lee had asked.

"She has a problem," Tommy had told them both. "She can't help it. It's some borderline personality disorder that she has. It's not bad, but she sort of attracts a lot of attention."

"What, like a nymphomaniac?" a totally engrossed M had asked.

"A bit like that," he had said.

He then went on to tell them that she had some fixation on Lee, which then sort of pissed M off.

"You never said that," she had told Lee.

"Probably because I can't say I'd ever noticed," he'd innocently replied, although the total gob shite that he was, he did say that after he'd thought about it, that she did do a lot of bending over and stretching in front of him.

Tommy had left around 10:30pm and that was when M came clean and my ex was less than happy. Well, he was then but he wasn't after he'd raided the contents of the two camcorders the two young lads had brought back from Nubeon.

"She was brilliant," said Stuart. "She didn't mind us filming her."

"You can't tell your mum and dad about this," whispered Lee cagily looking around. "Or anybody."

They were both under his spell and were nodding like a pair of rear-tray poodles.

I had met Stuart a few times, and as I've said, he thought Lee was some godlike person and like most who meet him, was in complete awe of him. However, what Stuart didn't realise is who he actually was down here and that was Lee's younger brother-in-law and protégé, and brother of LMJ's biggest star – M. And that being the case he was being closely monitored by one Georgia Clayton who made no secret of the fact that this bright young lad could be key to her future.

On getting out of the studio after filming some rubbish about a ghost in Cannock Woods I had a word with Lee – firstly about the crap programme I was doing and then about the Georgia thing.

"She's a pretty girl," he said, "And he'll be back home in two weeks."

"I thought he had a girlfriend?" I asked.

"He does," he replied, still looking through the fly-on-the-wall film footage. "Paige."

"Exactly," I told him. "Look after him."

I might have well have been talking bloody Swahili, as the next thing I know she's waggling her arse past him and that being the case I had a word with Abigail who nipped it in the bud, by sending both lads over to the editing suite where Lee's mate Ginge was downloading all the film, and where Les Crang and Oliver Norgrove suddenly appeared and who Abigail bollocked to get back over to Fox Force Three as they were a woman light, as one of them was now in Lee's office and that being the case I let M know as I couldn't bloody keep track on everything around me. Grrrrrr.

M never bollocked Lee, which is probably one of the

other thousand reasons he liked her better than me. She told him off but half the time he was too thick to see that she was telling him off. That is what I meant by the fact that Emily is clever. Lee liked the dippy, helpless little waif, and that's how she played it – or him rather.

I thought I'd try the helpless waif on with him by asking if I could buy the house in Clerkenwell, as with all this money coming in I could just about afford what would be a rather large outgoing. It was really wrong of me but I also egged Paul on into thinking that we could both be involved and then I mentioned it to M.

"I can't see why he wouldn't," M had told me. "All he wants is for you all to be okay."

Therefore I asked – not to okay me to buy it as such, but for him to ask a zillion questions in could I afford it? Was I sure about this and was I sure about that? And doing lots of umming and arring before knocking it back and keeping the things the way they were as that would mean him still being in my life … Oh yeh, and that he certainly didn't want Paul around all the time and that he was going to dump M and come live with me. I had it all nicely planned until he told me to give him a few days and he'd sign it over. Grrrrrrrr.

I had really got the hump and if that Georgia waggled her arse anymore she take a kick up it. Saying that, nobody waggled her arse more than Sinead and she waggled it straight over to me and told me that she'd just had a right telling-off from Lee. "I nearly got a spanking," she said. "God, I love him."

Grrrrrrrr.

I walked over to Lee's office with my intention to issue him a bollocking; however, before I did he glanced me a smile and asked if I fancied doing the narration of the fly-on-the-wall.

"What about Sinead?" I stomped.

"What about her?" he asked.

Grrrrrrrrrrrr. Pig Thick!

345

"Are you okay?" he asked.

I was bloody dizzy thinking about everything and I told him so.

That night me, Paul and the kids drove up to a flat near Wood Green Tube station where M's little brother was staying. As for M – her and my ex-husband had been invited over to my kids' headmaster's house for dinner, which had really, really pissed me off. Calling at the flat wasn't unexpected as M had told their Stuart that we'd be dropping by and on seeing him both my kids were ecstatic, but I wasn't as the place was a dump. "I can't bloody believe he's put you in a place like this," I said.

The thing is, my idea of a nice house and both lad's idea of a nice house were totally different, however after one hour and fifteen minutes they certainly got my idea of a nice house and everything was jiffed down, sparkly and tickety-boo, whilst Paul had a bad back after I'd made him cart a load of rubbish down three flights of stairs. I then made them some tea which I knew they'd appreciate and made sure they ate every last bit before I left.

I got two "thank-you Jeanette"s as we left and I let Sil' know that they had been seen to, which she thanked me profusely for, although I did hear a whisper through the grapevine that I had been a bit bossy, making them both eat their greens and tidy up their bedrooms. I tried to get to the bottom of where these rumours emanated from and found that it was that bloody Georgia Clayton, who I heard had been round with her mate after I'd left.

Grrrrrrrrrrrrrrrrrrrr.

I got in Tuesday morning to be whisked into make-up where Chris dolled me up for a few camera shots before getting chucked into a temporary studio that looked like some French boudoir and the next thing I know I had Lee and Abigail whispering to each other and looking through the camera for fifteen minutes and doing a bit of deliberating. "Nah, it looks shit," he said and then they had some conflab. Me? I was stood there like bloody Clem.

"Hold on a minute," I said with my arms on my hips. "Why am I done up like a kipper in some tart's chamber and you two are whispering?"

Mmm. The answer was nice in that I looked too nice. I think? Or was that bad?

The next thing I know I'm being asked to walk around this studio whilst those two are still whispering and looking through the camera. The next thing I know Lee says he's done and Abigail is on her mobile phone whilst Faranha is dragging me upstairs to their office and where I see Georgia Clayton making eyes at young Stuart who is just loading up his rucksack for a Tube ride down to the Elephant & Castle – however, this time I'm going with them.

"What?" I asked.

"I need you videoed on a Tube," Lee said. "Just sit there like you have a pole up your arse and read a magazine or whatever and cross your legs a bit – just act normal."

That was it, I gave him a right bollocking.

"I love you," he winked, and that was it.

Did I do it? Yes.

I hated the Tube and even more so as I had some young lad filming me, however signing autographs for a few people was quite nice whilst they inquired what I was doing.

"Some fly-on-the-wall documentary for ITV," I proudly told them.

We got down to the Elephant & Castle and had to walk towards Nubeon, which I certainly wasn't happy about with as it was miles and I'd got a short-ish skirt and heels on – and I had my handbag with my purse in it.

"Just make sure the video cameras don't get nicked," Lee had told me.

Grrrrrrrrrrrrrrrrrr.

I had the two lads following me all the way into Nubeon where I immediately had some fat tanned pervert drooling all over me. Apparently it was Sooty's boss.

"What, you actually work for him?" I asked.

Lee had given me a list of do's and do not's and I was taken into some wardrobe where a couple of girls were and they showed me this, that and the other, even though I couldn't understand a lot of what they were saying as none of them were English. It was hardly awe-inspiring and I thanked god when I got out there only to hope that god would let me back in when I saw what was happening. I wasn't that under the door regarding anything regards sex as I'd spent over 11 years with Lee, however it was extremely seedy and when I got back I played merry hell with him. Well, I would have done but he had Karen Beckley in his office.

"What's he in with her for?" I asked Faranha. "In fact I thought she was going to do the Nubeon-thing?"

Huh – it turned out that she was busy talking about some old footballer called Stan Balls in one of the nice warm studios all morning and not freezing her pips off in some lousy garage off the A201 roundabout, whilst being subjected to some young bit of fluff being wrongly sent to an insane asylum in Uttoxeter and accosted by its owner. I had no idea why they had used Uttoxeter? In fact I didn't even know where Uttoxeter was?

M was straight on the phone to me asking for every detail, one of which was had I seen Sooty's new girlfriend? Seeing as I was having to watch all manner of things whilst I had some Baron Greenback lookalike breathing down my neck and touching my legs, I had to be frank in that I did not. I did ask her how the dinner went over at Mr. and Mrs Marsden's and all she did was laugh and say, "Don't ask."

Aghhhhhh.

All the way home I had Uttoxeter on my mind, and I have to be honest in that it was the first thing I pulled up on Wikipedia when I fired up my laptop.

Chapter 27

The Teacher's Pet

The kids' head teacher Ted Marsden had invited me and Emily over to dinner, me knowing only too well that there would be a catch.

Ted wasn't an Arsenal supporter or even a football supporter, telling me that he preferred Formula One and golf. His wife though, appeared to have a minor craving for Olivier Giroud and once I arrived I felt a similar feeling aimed at me, as I had the inside of my thigh rubbed on a couple of occasions and when I told M on the way home in the car, she had said something similar.

"That wasn't me," I said.

It wasn't; I'd had to work my way through Mozzarella, rocket and balsamic vinegar salad starter whilst I endured what I assumed was her angling to undo my flies.

"And it wasn't you rubbing your hand up my legs?" she asked.

"No," I said.

"Huh – right," she said.

"Huh – right – what?" I inquired.

"I thought it was," she said.

"And?"

"Well, I sort of let him," she said.

"What made you think it was me?"

"Because you always touch the inside of my legs under the table when we are out," she said.

"Not in my kids' teachers' house I don't."

349

"Well, yer did tonight," she twanged.

"Didn't you notice an expression or summat?" I asked.

"You mean something dear," she corrected me.

"Yeh – something then," I hastily replied.

"No – because you always pretend it's not you."

She also mentioned that it had gone on a little bit through the Dover Sole main course and definitely more so during the cheesecake, which she explained nearly got her twitching.

"You were really good," she said.

I felt extremely violated and was like a coiled spring when we pulled up outside the house, with my first instincts being to go back and throw a brick through their window, however Emily showed me the ladder he had allegedly made in her tights and I needed to relieve exactly three minutes 32 seconds of pent-up frustration before she told me that she was indeed only kidding.

"What – it didn't happen?" I asked, whilst totally out of breath.

"No," she smiled, her certainly not out of breath.

"God, we are going to have to do that one again," I said.

"Did you like that one, then?" she asked.

"It was well up there with the dirty Scouse Easyjet air hostess who keeps on saying 'Speedy Boarding' and the French student who was forced to sell her body to help fund her boyfriend's commitment to ISIS," I said.

"I'll get twins at this rate," she winked.

More sleepless nights and misery, I thought.

I had no idea where she had bought the cabin crew outfit from and I was going to ask her until she mentioned the filming of the double feature at my kids' school.

"They are doing Scrooge aren't they?" I asked.

"Well, why do they want Sammy then?" she asked.

"What they want him?" I inquired.

"Yeh," she replied. "Ted was on about it for a good ten minutes while he had his fingers in my cheesecake," she smiled.

"I wish you'd stop it," I said.

"Spoil sport," she winked.

Life was great and I was truly looking forward to Christmas, although I wasn't looking forward to being conned into producing three thousand DVD's and pissing away a load of wasted man hours at my kids' school, the latter of which had been pencilled in for Thursday afternoon.

"So tell me again, why do they want Herbert?" I inquired.

"To be baby Jesus," she told me.

"Jesus wasn't in Scrooge."

"No, Year One and Two are doing the Christmas Story and Year Three are doing Scrooge," she explained. "Jamie's a wise man."

"Christ, who did the casting on that one?" I laughed.

"Joanne Peters," she said.

Wow, I was impressed.

"He was learning his lines on Sunday," Emily added.

"Oh yeh," I recalled. "'I come bearing Frankenstein?' I wondered what he was on about."

"Harmony's Mrs Cratchet," she smiled. "She's really good."

Well, if I wasn't looking forward to doing it before, I certainly was now.

Tuesday morning was a weird one as I had a 9:00am meeting with one of the bands from the Sessions programme, who were looking to cop a contract – The Queen & Pistol, who were headed by Ross Bain – who, incidentally was another Arsenal nut. They were pencilled in for the rescheduled Christmas edition Live at The Warehouse along with Electric Ladyboy, Red & White, C.G.G, a pretty young thing called Sami McDowell and Binh Binh Pham a band whose lead singer was known as DeeMan, who was north London's equivalent to James Brown when it came to moves, but nothing like him in the delivery of his lines, with his rather haunting 'Play with Air' song being something very, very strange. I say strange as you needed a fucking degree in English Literature to understand it and it was Emily who explained that the song was about a man clutching on to his last moments of life.

Back to the Queen & Pistol – these were an aggressive four-piece band from Walthamstow who at times made Electric Ladyboy look quite reserved, but everyone who had heard them knew that they were going places.

I had my corporate lawyers in with me when they arrived at 8:59am and I had them signed by 9:12am on a two album a year, three-year contract with 25% royalties, plus I wanted them to use some of their music for some series that ITV were looking at doing, which was the ultimate sweetener.

The White Lion record label wasn't a subsidiary of LMJ as such, it was just that we owned 75% of it, with four suits from ITV owning the other 25%. We were the main backer, and they were in it to make sure that we made money. I also had Chris Windley from make-up get his rather corpulent art designer boyfriend 'Yogi', to draft me up a logo for the brand, which was based upon the Royal Air Force-style Mod Target.

Cue: Scott Tighe up at BBC Radio Merseyside.

"Job here if you want it," I told him. "Producer-cum-engineer – White Lion Records."

"Records?" he asked.

I told him that I'd signed up a few bands through the new company and that the intention was to convert an old factory on White Lion Street into the next Abbey Road. "I'm being backed by some senior executives from ITV," I said.

I wasn't really – as it was me that was financially backing them, but it sounded better the other way around and I'll give Tigger his due; not once did he mention money, just when could he start?

I had a few interviews booked in for around lunchtime – for the position of head of marketing for both the TV programmes and the record label; however what was to happen was a bit strange, in that ITV's head of entertainment phoned me and asked for a favour.

"We've got a half-hour spot free on the day before Christmas Eve," he said. "You got anything funny we could use?"

"What time is it going out?" I asked.

"Prime time – after Coronation Street."

"Possibly," I told him, "Do we have a budget?"

I heard him laughing at the other end of the phone, but he did, and quite a nice one actually.

"Well, get your advertising space booked because this will blow them away," I said and I got Abi in the office and told her what I wanted, and that was of any daft footage we had from the screen tests, bloopers or whatever and to get it edited down for a thirty minute showing on the 23rd – Oh yeah, and to get ITV to raise an order.

"What are we calling it?" she asked.

"Really Live at The Warehouse," I said.

I managed to settle on two marketing girls, both of who Les Crang thought were absolutely red-hot – Jet Marchione and Connie Nugent, before I nipped out to the Coffee Shop to meet Emily and Herbert, both of who had just been out doing a bit of Christmas shopping.

"There's a lot to be said for shopping online," she told me. "It's been mad."

"How's buggerlugs been?" I asked.

"He screamed his head off at Father Christmas," she said. "He definitely didn't like him."

"Did you buy much?" I asked.

"A pair of shoes and a handbag – oh, and a dress."

"So it wasn't a wasted shopping trip then?"

That made her laugh but not as much as when I told her of the outtakes that were going to get made into a 30 minute programme to go out as prime-time Christmas viewing.

"You've definitely, definitely got to do the screen tests," she chuckled.

She wouldn't shut up about it and appeared really excited, but not as much as when I got back in and copped everyone standing around the editing suite watching her playing some piano and Jeanette and Abi firstly dancing in front of the camera and then singing – and I'd told her that I'd use it. That resulted in one hell of a scream down the phone. I could understand why as well, as on playing it back a few times it was extremely good, but for the life of me I couldn't make out when it had been filmed.

I had a meeting with Sooty later that evening who introduced me to the girl he was now sharing a flat with.

"So you and Libby are done for good?" I asked.

"I've not been this happy for ages," he lied.

"What about the kids?" I asked.

He nodded, "Yeh, they're a bit upset."

I knew exactly how upset they were when I got in around 8:00pm, as Emily was watching TV with them.

"Hello," I said. "What are you two doing here?"

I got a kiss plonked on my lips by my wife who whispered that they were really upset and that their mum would be putting their house up for sale.

"You're joking?" I said.

She told me she wasn't and explained that my two god-daughters would probably also be moving from Colliegate School.

"Where is she now?" I asked.

"With Jeanette," she replied.

I couldn't really fathom it out. Sooty and Libby had always been there but now they were not. I was supposedly the unstable part of the not-so-dynamic duo and here I was sitting his kids while he was doing whatever he was doing and she was in free-fall and on about selling up and taking her kids out of private school.

Emily took some prawns out of the fridge and chucked them in a pan whilst I sat down with them.

"How are the ferrets?" I asked.

"We fed them," said Zooey, "And Auntie M let us bring them in the house for ten minutes."

"Will we have to live in a flat?" asked Mia.

"What makes you say that?" I asked.

354

"Just that mum and dad were shouting and that dad said that he would see her on the street before he paid her any money."

I glanced over at Emily who returned it. I didn't like it but there wasn't much I could do apart from doing what we were doing. I could have lied, and told them everything would be alright, however I'd known Sooty all my life and if he had decided that he didn't love Lib anymore, well, there wasn't a great deal to be said. If you fancy someone, there's always a chance of a reconciliation – but if you don't, there is no chance whatsoever, and Sooty had just told me that he hated the sight of her and was just glad to get shut. They stayed at ours the night and Libby picked them up the next morning and gave me a look that suggested that I was somehow involved in her downfall.

Chapter 28

Madjeski

What a week this would be. We had battered both Newcastle United and Galatasary and Aaron Ramsey was coming back on form and scored what was one of the best goals I've seen in a long time. Yeh, and then he got himself injured. I found out that Sinead, who I had just tied to a 12-month contract was some can't-say-no nymphomaniac and that Georgia Clayton was apparently weighing up moving in on young Stuart and that being the case, I had orders from the top – Emily and Jeanette – to give him a talk. Oh yeah, and I was invited down to the Madjeski Stadium to meet with some director of Reading F.C who was a colleague of one of the partners at the corporate law firm that we were using.

Jeanette had been on some mad mission up at The Warehouse and was doing quite a lot of foot stamping, but what else was new? I don't actually know what was on her mind as she didn't tell me, which was a strange one; however Wednesday's showing of our re-branded Inside True Britain was really good, and got some extremely positive reviews from the press, along with a load of fan mail from people that were either into the occult, ghouls, goblins, witchery or whatever, or who were indeed just sad bastards. 'The Black-Eyed Child – The Ghost of Cannock Woods' I had to say was brilliant even though everyone who had come in contact with it had thought it pants. Jeanette was superb, as was the writing of the script and the editing.

"I told you it would be good, didn't I?" I said after dropping off the kids.

"Have you had a word with Stuart?" she asked.

"What about?"

I had a load of superlatives slung at me, the door slammed shut in my face and it reopened before I was told "sorry" and that she loved me and did I want to come in for a coffee? These were becoming a bit regular if I'm honest, as was cuddling up to me on the settee.

"Are you okay?" I asked.

"No," she said.

"Why, what's up?" I asked.

She never told me and just huffed and puffed and complained that she had to put up the tree.

"What tree?"

"The bloody Christmas tree, you idiot."

That meant I was not only tasked with putting the tree up but dragging the thing out of the loft, and then had two eager kids insistent that I stay with them until the fairy got put on the top and that they sung me 'Silent Night' around it with the house lights off and the Christmas Tree lights on. This immediately brought back thoughts to last Christmas – the Christmas that I had spent on my own – not just Christmas Day but the period running up to it and the period after it. It was a period that I had my kids kept away from me for 23 days and it broke my heart, and now here I was with Jeanette cuddled up to me and both kids sat around the tree singing.

"Do you miss home?" she whispered.

I did, I missed home; however, back during the time I was really missing it Emily had helped make me a new one and in the process helped me find not only myself, but a way back into my kids life and strangely Jeanette's, and I wasn't that stupid in that I didn't know where this was all leading. At the moment everything was nice and after I let the kids sing me 'Away in a Manger' I got up to leave.

"What, you're going?" asked Jeanette.

"We really need to talk," I told her.

Tomorrow however, I was to have a bitch of a day as ITV's head of sports and director general came in unannounced and both eventually managed to find a chair.

"How do you work in here?" asked the big boss, whilst looking around at the shit tip that was my office, and at the piles of nappies, toys and other rubbish that was scattered around it.

"My wife likes me to feel that I'm at home – In fact, both my wives do."

"Yeh but I've been to your house and it's spotless," said the head of sports.

"M just chucks all the rubbish in the ironing room when she knows you are coming round," I lied. "Anyway – what's up?"

I had got to know ITV's head of sports fairly well and saw him around three of four times a week and kept him up on what we were doing. Providing a full weekend of football was relatively easy, if you take into account 09:00am – 6:00pm is all about the day's matches – with me really wishing that football would go back to being played on a Saturday at 3:00pm – with the mornings being taken up by chat and highlights from around Europe and South America along with profiles on players and what have you forming the other bulk of programmes; however the documentary angle is what ITV were interested in and over the course of a few months we had raided the ITN Archive and literally hammered it, and up to date had produced the guts of 532 hours of documentaries and I told them so.

"You what?" asked a rather aghast director general.

"It's not shit either," I said. "We need to clean up, add narrative and in some instances colourise a bit of it, but at the moment I reckon we are pretty much good to go."

532 hours meant 532 pieces of individual film that could be marketed and sold as many times as possible – and the money which could be made out of that could be endless, as it could theoretically be made into 532 individual DVD's

which you could saturate the market with at £10 a pop which if you sell 100,000 a piece equals £532 million gross – all in all, it is a billion pound business if you take into account the advertising. And as for ITV's outgoings – mine, Abi, Les, Oliver, the Foxy Fab Four's and The B.B.C's wages, our twenty roving reporters plus a bit of administration – £4.5 million tops. Would you invest £4.5 million to get a billion pounds return? As I said, sport is a big, big business – but football blows all other sports out of the water! Like I said, ITV knew what they were getting. Me – Cool, eh?

"Tell it me again," asked the director general, therefore I did adding that if the marketing was done right, the opportunities and money to be made was endless.

"You mention the money – is that why you do it?"

"I love football," I replied. "But I can't say that the money isn't a welcome bonus."

There was a catch coming that I hadn't envisaged and that was that ITV demanded that I not only produced the ITV 7 channel, but that I hosted its prime time results service.

"Are you asking me or telling me?" I asked.

"Would you do it if I asked?" asked the head of sports.

"Do I have any choice?"

There were two shakes of their heads, followed by a nod of mine, however this was not something I wanted, nor was having to be a guest on The Jonathan Woss Show.

"What?" I asked.

I'd had thousands of hours of programmes on my CV but as already stated – only 28 minutes of air time on TV and they wanted me for an hour long interview in front of a celebrity studio audience, which included – and get this – professional footballers, managers, coaches and their wives or girlfriends and I suppose boyfriends, now that the F.A. say being gay isn't a horsewhipping offence.

They were adamant about it – 20th of December 8:00pm – 9:00pm. I couldn't believe it.

I got out of the meeting two hours later to find that I had to have a chat with Stuart, who I have to admit, had been absolutely brilliant, as had his mate. I loved potential and those two cameras never ever stopped rolling.

"Video everything," I had told them. "Keep everything in focus as we'll blow in and out of it and edit it ad-hoc. Pretend you are being nosy – sort of undercover cops."

They had – even in The Warehouse, as Abigail told them that I'd like some off-the-cuff filming.

Cue: Stuart and the chat, however Jeanette had turned up and decided that she would like to sit in on it.

"It's for M – and Sil's benefit," she lied.

"And you're not just being nosy?" I asked.

"Certainly not," she lied – Again.

"Then it'll be a one-way conversation and I'll get to know nothing as he'll certainly not talk in front of you."

"Why?"

"He just won't, that's all."

She huffed and puffed and asked if I could video-link it into another office. Well, she didn't really as she hadn't thought of it, but she certainly would have if she had known it was possible.

It transpired from Emily that their Stuart had been seeing his girlfriend Paige for just under three months; however, since he'd been down here a week, Georgia had been taking a lot of his attention. In my eyes there wasn't anything wrong with that, but in others' eyes however – there was.

I had him in and asked him a few questions about general stuff – The camera-work that he'd been doing – The goings-on down at Nubeon – Was he enjoying London? Just general stuff, and it was him that popped the question. "Can I ask you something, our Lee?" he asked.

"Sure," I said.

"How old you when you first – yer know?"

"Yer know?" I smiled.

His face went bright red.

"A bit younger than you," I replied.

"How younger?"

"About four years younger."

"What – yer were twelve?" he asked, rather aghast.

"Yeh I had a lot of dirty aunties," I lied, which set him off laughing.

"So," I asked. "How's Paige?"

"I'm thinking of packing her in," he said.

"Why, don't you like her?"

He nodded. "Yeh, course I do."

"Paige's dad is that man who's been working with your dad at Hamilton Square, isn't he?" I asked.

He nodded.

"And that's the man that I sat and had a coffee with the other week and who was saying all those really nice things about you?"

He nodded.

"That's quite nice," I acknowledged.

He sat in thought as I passed him one of my secret stash of biscuits.

"You definitely can't tell your M about these," I winked.

His smile, like his two sister's lit up the room before he finally confided in me. "Did you know my mam and dad won't leave us on our own?" he said.

"What about Paige's mum and dad?" I asked.

He shook his head.

"So you've not 'yer-knowed' yet?" I winked.

Again he shook his head.

"What – so are you wanting to? Is she wanting to?" I inquired.

"I don't know," he said. "We never get any time to ourselves."

I nodded.

"It's just down here everything is different."

"Down here you have your own independence, but up at home you have people who love you," I said, "I know exactly what you mean."

"Do you?" he asked.

I then told him something very few people knew in that when I was fifteen I got a sixteen-year-old girl pregnant and her parents made her get rid of it. "When I was seventeen I also got a girl from college pregnant," I said. "She was sixteen as well."

"Did she keep it?" he asked.

I shook my head. "Remember what Jeanette told everyone at our wedding – about my dad. All I ever wanted to do was to have kids, but people kept on taking them away from me."

He was eagerly listening when I hit him with the big one.

"When me and Jeanette got together she wasn't always the bossy cow that she is now," I told him. "She was a right livewire and we were all living what you would think is this great life – Remember Bondy's flat we went to?"

He nodded.

"Well me, him and Sooty were making thousand's ripping off companies that made DVD's and CD's as we were making really high standard copies of them and churning them out as the real deal. At the time Bondy, Libby – and Jeanette were into a bit of gear – nothing nasty, but not good all the same. Jeanette got pregnant and we ended up flying out to Bangladesh to see Bondy's brother get married. Jeanette was coked-up half the time and refused to take some anti-malaria tablets because along with the stuff she was taking were making her throw up and she became really ill. The baby was born early and died, and I had another one taken off me. Jeanette blamed everyone but herself for it and became really depressed. She never did coke again."

He was gobsmacked.

"I've never been as upset in all my life."

The lad sat glued to his chair before asking, "What was it?"

"A boy," I said. "We called him Lee."

Does our M know?" he asked.

"Yeh, your M knows," I told him.

He just sat there in thought.

"To make something so beautiful and to have it taken away is the worst feeling ever; you think your mum and dad are being old fashioned and perhaps they are," I said. "However, in reality they don't want to see you hurt, as I would imagine Paige's parents wouldn't like to see their daughter hurt."

"So what are you saying?"

"I'm not you – you're your own person," I said. "It's you who decides what to do and no one else."

"Yeh – but my mam and dad don't know anything?" he said.

"Yeh, they do Stu – they gave your M her freedom and everyone ended up getting hurt – but there's a much bigger story," I told him, before handing him a calculator from my drawer. "How old is your dad?"

"Forty-seven," he replied.

"What about your mum?"

"The same."

"And how old is your M?" I asked.

"Thirty-three next month."

"Then do your sums and ask yourself why your Granddad Bill and your dad never spoke," I said. "And I don't mean because of the Foxes – I mean well before that?"

He looked at me and did his sums.

"Your dad loved your mum, and for two, maybe three years he was kept away from her – Your dad loved your mum, like he loves you, your Lucy and your M," I said.

"They were fifteen?" he asked.

"No Stuart – Your mum was fourteen when she got pregnant and for nearly three years your dad was kept away," I said. "But I'll tell you this – The man never ever walked away or shirked his responsibilities and here you all are."

He just looked at me as his eyes welled up.

"Your dad ranks up there with the best," I told him. "As does your mum."

"How do you know all this?" he asked.

"Because your sister is not only my wife but my best friend," I said. "When you look for a partner, you make sure it's the right one."

"Paige?" he asked.

"Georgia's nice but she's a fairly worldy eighteen-year-old," I told him. "You're a bonny lad with the world at your feet. You take the opportunities that are being offered and you will have everything. Paige likes you because you're Stuart Orr from Birkenhead – the reason Georgia likes you is totally different."

He listened, but I don't know if he really took it in.

"Paige is pretty, as is Georgia. But Paige knew you before all this and Georgia didn't. Paige might not be the one but she deserves a chance," I told him. "But what I can guarantee you is that Georgia is definitely not the one."

He never said anything to that.

"Paige deserves a phone call," I winked. "And maybe if her parents are okay with it you could both come down one weekend."

His eyes lit up at the suggestion.

"You have a responsibility to yourself though," I said.

After I'd got that out of the way I managed to get down to the coffee shop where Emily was trying to ram the pushchair through the glass door. "It's rubbish this door," she moaned. "It always tries shutting itself before we get in."

"That's so no customers can escape before they've spent all their money on the gaming machines," I replied.

We ordered a couple of drinks as I got slung Herbert who was looking not too bad and even glanced me a dangerous half-smile, before I rammed the dummy in his chops just in case it became a dangerous half-groan.

"Have you had a good day?" she smiled.

"Nope – have you?" I asked.

She had been listening to music all morning and writing down notes for the Sessions programme so she told me she hadn't.

"Should we pack it all in?" I asked her.

364

That took her by surprise and I got that lovely smile aimed over at me. "Is everything okay?" she inquired.

I then told her that they wanted me as a TV presenter for ITV 7 as well as its producer and explained that I'd be on The Jonathan Woss Show in front of a live celebrity audience the Saturday before Christmas.

"I think yer'll be great," she twanged.

"I had a word with your Stu," I said.

I got another nice smile back for that. "What did you tell him?"

"What you wanted me to tell him," I said.

"What, really?" she asked.

"That's what you wanted isn't it?" I asked.

It certainly was, and not only did I have Sammy on one knee I now had his mum on the other with her arm around me.

"Should we put the tree up tonight?" she asked.

Not again, I thought.

"Why, do we have a tree?" I asked.

"No – but I'll get one," she smiled.

Well, that's something not to look forward to, I thought.

"I've bought you a present," she said. "You'll really like it."

"A schoolgirl outfit or another job lot from Gossard?" I inquired.

"You wish," she winked. "But no, definitely none of those."

I got back to The Warehouse and had Sinead to deal with, well I had after I'd seen the frigging so called edited fly-on-the-wall footage.

"Look you can't go doing this shit – never mind on camera," I told her.

"Why, isn't it any good?" she asked.

Well it was really good, I thought, but I certainly wasn't telling her that.

"You're going to be a high-profile TV presenter – once the papers get hold of this ITV will make me cancel your contract," I told her.

"One of them asked me out?" she said.

Mmm. That was interesting, I thought.

"Which one?" I asked.

"The man that wears the suit," she said.

"They all wear suits – that's we always refer to them as suits," I said.

She then gave me a description that told me it was one of their heads of marketing.

"He's quite cute," she said.

"I'll take you word for it," I said, "But do me a favour – stop having sex with everyone."

Cue: Jeanette.

"You still here?" I asked. "Who's picking the kids up?"

"My mother and dad are down," she said.

Good, I thought, *at least I won't have to have her cuddle up to me on the sofa.*

Then reception passed me a phone call which went around ITV 7 team before it got to me.

"What?" I asked.

Reading F.C wanted me to have a meeting with a few of their directors prior to them sacking their manager and when that information was relayed via the ITV 7 team they were all ears and even more so when I told them that I had my UEFA Pro Licence and F.A Coaching Diploma.

"Since when?" asked Oliver.

"Since three years ago," I said. "Me and Sooty both did it."

"So they are wanting you to manage them?"

"Don't be a frigging idiot," I told him.

They wanted me to have the meeting at The Madjeski Stadium, however that was never going to happen as getting to Reading at any time from north London was a ball ache in itself, so I told them to come over to The Warehouse where

I could also let them see all the footage we had on the enigma that was Robin Friday.

Meanwhile there was some hot debate between all the members of Fox Force Four in who was or wasn't going to do the narration on 'The Curse of The Owls' documentary; however, there was no way on this earth that Kirsty was doing it wearing a biker jacket and those lesbian boots she always wore.

"Kirsty – you're doing it," I said, and I summoned Chris Windley to make her look beautiful.

"Why, can't I just wear these?" she asked. Well she didn't ask, it was more of a demand.

"It will be a great documentary and I want you looking pretty," I told her.

"Why, what's up with me how I am?"

"You look a bit tomboyish that's all," I said.

"I can't very well effing ride my bike dressed like Sinead or Karen, can I?"

She had a point but I certainly wasn't going to tell her that.

"I bet you'll look lovely," sniggered Kim.

She did a bit of 'teeth grinding' and booted the waste paper basket over before she succumbed to my request and I had Chris whisk her away for a makeover.

"I know it's panto season, but don't be going fucking overboard," I told him.

We had worked hard on this documentary and it came as a bit of a surprise to everyone of how good Sheffield Wednesday actually were and the extreme bad luck that stopped them from being the team they should have been. They had one of the most respected managers in the game in Harry Catterick and one of the most tragic but well-loved figures in the prolific centre-forward that was Derek Dooley.

"If we can get Kirsty to play ball, it could be as good as the Sammy documentary that we did for ESPN," I said.

About thirty minutes passed before we were graced with Kirsty's presence and to be honest I wouldn't have recognised her. Well, I wouldn't have if she had kept her trap shut.

"Wow – you look great," I said.

She did – I wasn't lying. Saying that, she struggled like hell to walk in those heels, and she definitely wasn't happy wearing tights.

"I feel clumped up to hell in these chuffing things," she said. "I couldn't wear this shit every day."

"I bet your boyfriend would like it," I smiled.

"What boyfriend?" she replied.

"There you go – Wear your 'nice lady' clothes and you might cop a date."

"Go bollocks, Lee."

I loved her – and I had to giggle to myself as I watched her trying to negotiate her way around the desk in those stilettos. She looked like she'd just rode twenty miles on a horse.

She might not had had the glamour of, say Sinead, Kim or Karen, but she was on cue with everything and to the dot, but more importantly – the camera loved her – a bit like it did with Emily, really.

Our roving reporters were proving to be a pain in the arse as we had dumped around six of them including Dave Moggy – but him leaving was a totally different reason to the other five. In the end I had settled on nineteen, including the rather pretty and diminutive Abygaile Gibbs and the rather astute, albeit pedantic reporter that was known as 'Atwood', the latter who I'll get to later.

I got out of work around 6:30pm and home to a wife who was doing a bit of deliberating and scratching of her head whilst looking at what was a massive tree that had been dumped in the kitchen.

"You chop that down yourself?" I asked, as I clambered over it.

"It's a bit bigger than I thought," she said.

"What is?" I winked.

"Shurrup you," she twanged.

She was right, it was absolutely frigging colossal and filled up half the lounge, and after I'd managed to get it up, I had what felt like a thousand pine needles down my back.

"I've ordered a similar tree for Hamilton Square," she said.

"That's nice," I lied, as she passed me a yellow drink.

"What's this – banana?" I asked.

"A Snowball," she smiled, as she clinked my glass with her glass, which looked like it was full of pig's blood.

"What have you got?" I asked.

"Port," she said.

Mmm. Why had I got Snowball and she had Port? I thought.

I certainly knew the answer to that straight after I'd tasted it.

"Jesus – it tastes like raw eggs and meth's," I said post-gulping of the stuff.

"My mam always used to make 'em for my dad when he put our tree up," she smiled.

"I'm surprised he's still with her if she made him drink that," I said, as I spat it in the sink before trying to get it off my teeth. "It's definitely a bit on the rich side."

"Don't you like it?" she asked.

"It's a bit heavy going if I'm being honest, M," I said. "Why can't I have Port like you?"

"I'm not giving you my Port," she said, as she pretended to both sip and saviour it. "It's all mine."

"Oh yeh?" I replied.

"I really, really love Cockburns," she winked, after giving me the double entendre. "It gives me a tingle in my tummy."

That was it and ten minutes later – after a special love on the couch, which included the relatively new rule number one followed by the utilisation of half a roll of Andrex, she thanked me profusely and hoped that it would find its way to helping ruin our life even more by producing another screaming lump of misery – we slung some lights and a few baubles around the tree.

"It looks a bit sparse," she said, sort of hands on hips.

369

"Probably cause it's one size down from a Giant Redwood," I said. "You could stick another million baubles on it and it'd still not be full."

All the same she got out the step ladders and pissed about with them for another hour and made it look really nice, and whilst sitting back on the couch, legs crossed with her Cockburns and admiring it, there was a bit of lip wobbling before she said that it was the best tree ever and I got a cuddle very similar to the cuddle I received the other day. I was just glad she never brought Sammy and the ferrets out to give me a rendition of 'Silent Night', and rather stupidly, I mentioned it.

"What, you put Jeanette's tree up?" she asked.

At the time I innocently nodded, however I really, really wish that I had lied.

"She's currently keeping Paul at arm's length, started going to The Warehouse whenever she can and suddenly being nice with you," she said. "And now you are sat around together listening to your children sing carols after you've put up her Christmas Tree."

It wasn't a telling off as such, it just sort of felt like one.

"What's the matter?" I shrugged.

"And when you had your tea there the other day?" she inquired.

"Lamb steaks," I said. "And corn on the cob."

"And possibly a cuddle on the settee?" she asked.

Jesus, what's she got – CCTV? I thought.

"I'm your wife and I really love you, yer know," she said. "She had a try at doing the self-same job and failed."

"Yeh – I know."

"Come on Lee, you're not an idiot, love," she said.

Mmm. It was definitely now sounding like a telling off and I wish I'd found time to have a word with Jeanette as Emily was going to do exactly that.

Chapter 29

Jeanette's Tales – Take 10

I knew I had made a mistake as soon as the phone rang that night.

"You are really out of order Jeanette – really out of order," she said. "I would never do anything to hurt you and you've done exactly that to me."

It was M.

I would have argued my case but I knew she was right. I had known what I was doing and tried to do it subtly. I now wished that I had gone all out – the whole bloody hog and tried harder, as at least then I would have known I had failed. This wasn't a failure, it just felt like it was. A seedy half-arsed bloody failure.

I didn't even apologise as I thought it would have been no good and while she waited for a response I just mumbled, "Okay M."

And that was it. M's termination of her friendship with me.

So what now of the children? They adored her.

I wanted to phone Lee but he was really busy and when I got in to The Warehouse I felt sneaky, underhanded and dirty, but what I didn't know was that life outside the 'Me and Lee Show' goes on and while Abigail had me doing a lot of Autocue work for the fly-on-the-wall series which she had edited herself, M came into The Warehouse and immediately set about doing some work opposite one of the writers – a young girl called Roz Kendall, who had just begun penning a re-write of The Milly Dowling story for me to present.

I didn't get a 'Hello' or 'How are the children?' Nothing. She just set about her work for the Sessions programme and put on some earphones before Becky Ivell, who was the latest addition to the ITV 7 team asked her if she'd like a drink.

"I'm fine, love," she smiled. "But thanks anyway."

For two hours we sat close to each other and not one word passed between us and it took her actually leaving before the deadlock was broken.

"Nothing changes as regards the children," she said. "I think they're amazing. If you want me to pick them up or take them here, there or wherever, I'm always here."

I nodded and she put on her coat and left to pick Sammy up from crèche.

I called on Libby that night who was extremely pleased to see me, and as soon as I saw her I burst out crying and told her everything. Libby had just been dealt one hell of a blow in that Sooty had moved into a flat in Chiswick with his girlfriend, but she took the time to listen to me. I didn't want Paul – I wanted Lee. I made a mistake by kicking him out and I wanted him back, but now he had M.

"I thought you and M were both good friends?" she said.

"We were," I told her. "But I've messed it up."

"Did you do anything?" Lib asked me.

"Nothing – Just a cuddle – It was nice," I replied. "Twice."

"Well that's hardly an X-certificate show of emotion," she said. "He gives me a cuddle every time I see him."

I laughed at that and laughed even more when she casually mentioned it was generally as she was leaving.

"It didn't mean much to him," I told her, "But I was there if he wanted me."

"What, you told him that?" she asked.

"No," I said.

"Then what's up?" she asked.

"M knew what I was up to," I explained. "I've been keeping him at mine as long as I can and she knows this."

"So there was no kissing or 'you know what' as part of this cuddle?" she asked.

I shrugged my shoulders. There wasn't – just me linking his arm and putting my head on his shoulder whilst watching me on TV and the kids singing carols.

"And that's it?" she asked. "Definitely no kissing?"

"No," I told her. "It wasn't seedy, it was nice."

"So how did she get to know about it?" Libby asked.

"That idiot will have dropped it out – possibly while she's trying to get him to give her another baby," I snapped.

"What, they're trying for a baby?" Libby asked.

"A girl," I told her.

"How can you try for a girl?" she asked.

"If Lee wants a girl, he'll get one," I said.

I stayed until around 11:00pm and was going to get the kids up to drive back over to Clerkenwell, but I couldn't do that as it was cold and so we stayed over and after I dropped off the kids at school I had a lousy day in the Chelsea Bridge store, a till jamming the cashier's hand which culminated in two broken fingers, three shoplifters – all foreign, Paul trying it on with me in the manager's office and a forced stock take, which would keep me there until 9:00pm. And Lee wasn't picking up.

I rang M at around 3:00pm and called in a favour, which I hated doing.

"Don't worry," she said. "It's sorted."

And that was it; however, whereby Lee generally dropped them off and I gave him his customary bollocking hoping that he would just tell me to shut up and then ravage me, I had to call to pick the kids up from theirs – or have them stop over and Lee drop them in school, "If that's what I would like," she had said.

I'd never taken a telling off without it being a telling off and this felt strange. Lee never told me off, but Paul did – most of the time for stringing him on, and sometimes on a weekend when I'd complained of an headache, which itself is a lie as I've generally fantasised about being M long before Match of the Day comes on, and that being the case the last thing I wanted to be was some performing seal for someone who had no idea at all how to throw a fish. God, I'm awful aren't I?

Picking the kids up felt strange as M pandered around after them as she always did and told me that they had done this, that and the other and never once had she gone against my wishes.

She was still the same M, but different. Different with me that is, and without having to do a thing she was pushing me out to sea. I had always fought like hell to put my point over; however M never did. She just made it and boy, how I envied her.

I used to scream and shout at Lee after we'd moved to Southgate – and he'd moved the business down to their first offices off Euston Road. He was always coming in late and I used to issue bollocking after bollocking – and Lee? He just used to stand there and take the lot.

"Okay Jeanette," he'd say. "Point taken."

With M he came in at all hours and got food and a drink placed in front of him with a bit of pampering topped off by a kiss. He may have not liked the greens on the bloody menu but I know from eavesdropping on the conversation between him and Sooty that he adored everything else. I never heard Lee say it, but I certainly heard Sooty say it while I was down at theirs and it drove me mad.

"Yeh but you're divorced," Libby had said.

"Yeh but I didn't want to be," I'd replied. "He tricked me into it."

He hadn't really. I'd tried angling for him to kick off thinking that me and Paul were looking to tie the knot at a future date and smugly relayed that information to him. The next thing I know he's asked her to marry him and they're having parties up in Liverpool and the next time I saw her she's wearing a million-pound engagement ring. I lied when I said mine was as nice. Hers might have been the proceeds of some Hatton Garden ram-raid, but all the same, it is bloody awesome and that was another night Paul ended up getting it in the neck and I cried myself to sleep.

"Why do you always argue with the boy, Jeanette?" my dad used to tell me. "He gives you everything you want, yet you still want more."

My dad never said a lot, but a lot of what he did say was right including what he said about M on meeting her. "She is a beautiful young lady – I hope it works out for them."

"I bloody don't," said my mother.

My mother soon changed her tune when she'd met her. "What the hell is she doing with him?" she asked.

"Probably the same as I was," I told her.

Whilst the M and me thing was going on, I am sure Lee never had a clue as he never changed his attitude towards me once and was continually praising me, which I am sure would have pissed M off – I think.

A few days later The Warehouse car park was full of reporters as Lee had been approached by some football club and Sky Sports News were there with their version of Fox Force whatever, who I had to say looked nothing like ITV 7's. It turned out some second division club who wore the same type of shirt to Stan Balls had supposedly been sounding out Lee as their director of football. I don't know how true it was, but he had been in his office talking to some lawyers, one of who was a director of the club, and when Les Crang said that both Nigel Adkins and Andy Crosby had been sacked, the phones in The Warehouse went haywire.

Kim Stowe went out to see the reporters and answered a few questions for them.

You would never get any change out of Kim, as like M she was one thousand percent behind Lee, and being faced by what was a barrage of questions she answered them one after the other without breaking sweat. "Lee's commitment and contract is with ITV," she said. "His ambition is for ITV Seven to be the premier sports channel in the world."

I bet Sky Sports were really glad of Kim's answer, as we trawled through all of their reports and not once did we find that comment; however ITV, god bless them, had included it in its snippets of sports as part of their nightly news.

I tried to compliment Kim on her showing, however like Karen and Kirsty, they had their own team and I wasn't part of it. ITV 7 were a really professional setup which was further specified when ITV sold Lee's six-part series 'The Curse of The Owls' to NBC for an absolutely staggering six-figure sum.

"Don't you mind?" I heard Kirsty ask him.

"It's their shout – not mine," he said.

ITV 7 would get to air it; however NBC now had the rights – but the precedent was set. Lee was now ITV's moneymaking machine.

Chapter **30**

A Nuclear Fall Out

The fly on the wall documentary was being put together when I got in early. Ginge and Abi had pieced it together and I'd borrowed Roz Kendall from London University to help give me some copy for Emily to do the first narration, however Emily didn't seem that bothered and it was then she told me that she had indeed had words with Jeanette.

"Nothing went on," I said.

"I know," she replied, "but that's not the point; she knew what she was doing."

"And what's that?" I asked.

"Leave it, love," she said. "This is between me and Jeanette."

I had always thought that things were a bit close for comfort and distancing myself from my ex wasn't a problem, but since the wedding we had become close again, and I mean close as friends and nothing more. Jeanette had said nothing and was still the same Jeanette, but I had noticed that the phone calls outside of the kids had suddenly stopped between the pair.

Karen was due to interview both Stevie Kell and Kevin Whitcher, the latter of who is editor of The Gooner fanzine in one of the studios for one of the documentaries about violence on the terraces, whilst Kirsty was due to do the narration on a six-part documentary on Brian Clough – her being adamant that we shouldn't use the 1972/73 footage of

Derby County's 5-0 thrashing of Arsenal, that I'd also used as part of the 'Parallel's' documentary.

"It makes Arsenal look rubbish," she said.

"At times we were rubbish," I told her. "But you can't take anything away from Derby County and Brian Clough – they had a good side and he was a fantastic manager."

The game at the Baseball Ground was Bob Wilson's first game back since his injury in the 1971/72 F.A Cup Semi Final against Stoke City, and in all honesty he had a right stinker, being culpable for at least four of the five goals he conceded and I could never understand how he never got made the scapegoat.

History will tell you that the 1972/73 team was unlucky in both the pursuit of the League and the F.A Cup; however as with the 1958/59 team, the good ship Arsenal was being driven towards the rocks at an uncanny pace by the man at the helm, and once through the rocks would spend the next few years floating around in the doldrums and close to relegation until a new man with new ideas was put in charge.

After the pummelling at Derby, there were signs of unrest and there had been a big team meeting to discuss what was going wrong, with journalists in the tabloids tipping that the brilliant Double side would be broken up further, with Frank McLintock, Charlie George, George Graham, Peter Marinello, Eddie Kelly and strangely reserve left back Sammy Nelson all being tipped to leave, with Everton, Leicester City and Stoke City apparently interested in Graham.

The issue with 28-year-old George Graham was a conundrum. Graham had only missed the 2-0 win against Birmingham City at Highbury on 26th September, 1972 and like Jon Sammels – strangely, the man he replaced during the near all conquering 1970/71 season, had become a bit of a target of the Highbury boo-boys, with captain Frank McLintock telling Harry Miller of the *Daily Mirror* after the home game against Southampton on 30th September,

1972, "He is either loved or hated by the fans – he is that type of player."

Graham had been dropped for the 2-0 win at home to Birmingham and was a substitute against Southampton, coming on to replace Ray Kennedy after 63 minutes and crashing home the winning goal five minutes later.

Graham played in his side's tempestuous 1-0 defeat at Bramall Lane at the hands of Sheffield United, which wasn't helped by the dismissal of Alan Ball on 68 minutes after a cynical if not brutal challenge on United's Trevor Hockey; however, four days later as the club prepared for their league match against Bobby Robson's high-flying Ipswich Town, a team who *Daily Express* journalist and 'man of the people' Desmond Hackett duly described as one of the most underrated sides in the country, Arsenal offloaded one of its Double season bit part players. Central defender John Roberts was sold to Birmingham City for £140,000, a move which would come to haunt the club come the end of March, as Frank McLintock and Jeff Blockley would both sustain injuries leaving the club with only one fit central defender in Peter Simpson. The exact same thing happened in the 1958/59 season, when the 5'7" Tommy Docherty was dropped back into defence to play as makeshift centre-half.

In a hard-fought match against Ipswich it was Graham who broke the deadlock in a somewhat dramatic fashion as he unleashed a 30-yard drive on 62 minutes to both beat the impressive goalkeeper David Best and claim the winning goal.

On 18th October, 1972 Graham was called up for Scotland against Denmark in Copenhagen; however one day before that, Arsenal were due down at Home Park in Devon to play a testimonial match for ex-Arsenal and Scottish international goalkeeper Bill Harper in front of a crowd of just over 18,000.

Mee used this game to run the rule over goalkeeper Bob Wilson, who had missed his club's impressive start to the season. Wilson's comeback as a half time substitute in the

1-1 draw strangely coincided with 33-year-old ex-Arsenal player and inside-right from the 1958/59 season John Barnwell getting the sack as assistant manager and coach of Hereford United and after just three months in the job. The man who sacked him? None other than ex-Arsenal player Colin Addison – who had played with Barnwell at both Nottingham Forest and Sheffield United and who over his career had managed a string of clubs as diverse as Atletico Madrid to Merthyr Tydfil.

On another 'Parallel' note, the man who had given Graham his seventh international cap was none other than Tommy Docherty, who would shortly resign as Scotland manager to take over the hot seat at Old Trafford.

A day later the elegant midfielder that was George Graham impressed in his country's 4-1 win, with Norman Gillier of the *Daily Express* describing the game as a live exhibition of naked football graced by the elegance and silky skills of Graham, who along with Leeds United's Billy Bremner dominated the midfield, so much so the score could have been near doubled as his side was denied by the woodwork three times.

Arsenal were second in the league and one point behind leaders Liverpool after the club's contentious 3-2 win at Selhurst Park against bottom of the league Crystal Palace on 21st October, 1972, with Graham still in the side and for the first time that season featuring Eddie Kelly who was looking rather dashing with his newly-acquired Hispanic-looking moustache, but a side which was still minus the suspended Alan Ball.

The televised match concluded that all three Arsenal goals should have been disallowed by Portsmouth referee Harry New, with the *Daily Express'* Norman Gillier stating that Palace had been burgled of two vital points, with the most controversial being goalkeeper Paul Hammond's save after 28 minutes from a penalty by Charlie George, whereby he palmed it onto an upright before smothering it; however, the referee ruled it had crossed the line.

Next up were Malcolm Allison's under-performing Manchester City at home in the league and the exciting Sheffield United away at Bramall Lane – again – in the League Cup. Graham played in both the 0-0 draw against City and the 2-1 win to dump United out of the cup to gain a bit of revenge for the league defeat, however before the home game against Joe Mercer's Coventry City on 4th November, 1972, Graham was dropped as Alan Ball returned to the side from suspension. What also happened was that Peter Simpson was relegated to the reserves to play at Plymouth to make way for the new signing and soon-to-be capped England international Jeff Blockley – the player who's eleventh minute mistake led to Sheffield United's decisive goal in early October. This created some mutiny within the rank and file and the goings on suggested Bertie Mee was losing the dressing room. It appeared that he was sacrificing two of his Double team to justify his £420,000 outlay and the inclusion of his two luxury signings. What should also be noted that neither George Armstrong nor the now-fit Bob Wilson were included in the team, even though the latter pulled out of the Scotland squad stating that his knee still wasn't 100%. Mee had deflected his decision to include Jeff Blockley in the team by stating that Peter Simpson wasn't fully fit, however Simpson told Norman Gillier, "I think I am match fit and I am really sick and disappointed about this decision. I stalked out of the ground today after Bertie Mee had told me I was out. I will not be content with reserve team football as there's only one way your form goes in the reserves and that's downhill. I shall give it a few weeks to see what happens and if I am not back in the first team I will have to give serious consideration to my future. This is the worst thing that could have happened as far as my chances of playing for England go."

As for George Graham being dropped, Graham himself said, "What staggered me was that Bertie admitted that I had been playing well. I cannot even remember what I said to him I was that stunned. All I can think is that my style doesn't appear to fit in at the present time. I don't want to involve the club or myself in any bad publicity as that has never been my way. I never create any fuss when I am left out but this time I feel I owe it to myself to say something. I know somebody had to make way for Alan Ball and I can see the clubs position on this – but why did it have to be me? I have just had a very good month, what with playing well for Scotland and snatching two vital goals in our last two home matches. Now I'm dropped?"

What should also be noted that these were all popular players within the club, and it would be the start of a player revolt, similar to what Brian Clough endured during his short tenure at Leeds United; however, what is worth noting is that Clough was the new boy in class. Bertie Mee, however, was not.

Lowly Coventry City arrived at Arsenal and went back to Highfield Road with two points courtesy of a Brian Alderson goal after 11 minutes and a brilliant solo goal by Tommy Hutchinson on 75 minutes, whereby he ran 40 yards with the ball outpacing and outmanoeuvring three defenders – including Jeff Blockley, to strike home.

After watching the match *Daily Mirror* Journalist Mike Ramsbottom inferred that leaving Peter Simpson out had been a huge mistake; however Bertie Mee was never one to be told so, and after a midweek friendly at Highbury where Arsenal won 1-0 against Racing Club of Paris – a fixture in which Sammy Nelson got sent off and went AWOL for a few days afterwards, and a team they had also beaten 1-0 in a friendly in the 1958/59 season – Mee reinstated Simpson before reverting to the exact same line-up he'd picked for the Coventry game to play in the match against Wolverhampton Wanderers at Molineux.

What history will tell you is that after the Coventry game, George Graham would never pull on an Arsenal shirt again. Mee had frozen him out in a similar manner to what George

Graham, the Arsenal manager some 23 years later would do with possibly the clubs most exciting player at that time, Anders Limpar.

Arsenal travelled to Wolves and came back with an impressive 3-1 win courtesy of a brace by John Radford and a goal by Peter Marinello, however Arsenal had to wait late in the game to take the two points with Wolves' manager Bill McGarry totally unhappy with the space that his side had given Arsenal, with Jack Steggles of the *Daily Mirror* stating that he was unwilling to talk publicly about their defensive shortcomings and turned his back on reporters after the game.

McGarry had been a feature of the 1958/59 season and had suffered as part of the Football League's clampdown on violence on the pitch the very same day that saw Arsenal's Len Julians get suspended. McGarry was captain of Huddersfield Town at the time and they had been playing a Yorkshire derby match at Leeds Road against the team who would become Arsenal's Fifth Round F.A. Cup opponents that season, Sheffield United.

McGarry was sent off as United came away with a 2-0 win, however manager of The Blades, former reserve wing-half for Arsenal, Archie Clark – the man who had replaced Villa-bound Joe Mercer and who had signed on at Highbury, at the same time as Eddie Hapgood, had said that after the right half's dismissal both teams lost their heads, and that some of Huddersfield's tackling was vicious.

The Huddersfield manager eloquently returned comment, "The sending off of McGarry was unbelievable. Bill was on the ground and only extricating his legs from a tangle with one of the Sheffield players. It was a surprise decision and after that, the match cut up rough."

The Huddersfield manager at the time? None other than the legend that was Bill Shankly, who at the end of that season would become the manager of Liverpool, the team he still managed and the team that were currently suffering an erratic run of form but still sitting proudly at the summit of

Division One on 11th November, 1972 – and still only one point in front of Arsenal.

Whereas Arsenal had beaten Wolves, Liverpool had crashed to a 2-0 defeat at Old Trafford.

In another 'Parallel' moment on the said day, Huddersfield Town were involved in another tempestuous game – this time away at Swindon Town, where seven players were booked and their goalkeeper Gary Pierce was sent off – after arguing with referee Tom Oliver as regards a twice taken penalty. Gary Pierce? He would eventually play for Wolves in the 1974 League Cup Final where John Richards would score the winning goal.

Richards had scored a brilliant equaliser in the match versus Arsenal to cancel out John Radford's just as impressive volleyed opener, as well as seeing another shot cannon back off the woodwork.

Jack Steggles said of the game, "Wolves were drawn like bees to pollen and Arsenal skilfully made the most of the situation: twice they pulled Wolves defence towards the near post, then dropped the ball on the other side of goal for the unmarked John Radford to apply the finishing touch. Then Arsenal stretched the defence wide, leaving Peter Marinello free to take Charlie George's glorious through ball for their third goal."

Although Bill McGarry had refused to speak to the press as regards his team's defeat, it was clear he had not been as reticent with his players, claimed Steggles. "Their faces showed they had been on the receiving end of a verbal lashing. And rightly so. For unbelievably bad marking and covering gave Arsenal the luxury of more time and room than they are normally accustomed to getting."

The game at Wolves however just papered over the cracks as did Arsenal's home win over an out of form Everton the Saturday after – a team who had been minus striker Joe Royle, who had been side-lined with a slipped disc.

A couple of fitness issues messed with the dynamics of the defence, but brought Peter Simpson back into the line-up at the expense of captain and groin strain victim, Frank McLintock.

The run up to the game had had Alan Ball in the papers reacting to criticism by pundits Jimmy Hill and Jack Charlton, the former who said that he didn't shoot when given the opportunity, with the latter eloquently stating that he couldn't shoot anyway, and who is a player that just pushes the ball on.

After 36 minutes of the Everton game he pushed the ball through to John Radford whose mishit shot deceived goalkeeper David Lawson to give another 1-0 to The Arsenal.

Next up was a midweek League Cup match against Norwich City, who after their 2-0 win at home to West Bromwich Albion, were now 31 games unbeaten at Carrow Road. However, the Tuesday night match wouldn't be at Carrow Road – it would be at Highbury.

Arsenal had not done well in the League Cup since they got to the two finals in 1968 and 1969. In 1969/70 they got knocked out by eventual League Champions Everton 1-0 at Goodison Park; in the Double year they went out against Crystal Palace losing 0-2 at home; and the season prior lost 2-0 away to Sheffield United – with all these defeats strangely coming in replays after 0-0 draws.

Norwich were a credible sixth place in Division One when they travelled to Highbury and had already beaten Arsenal at Carrow Road 3-2 earlier in the season, with Arsenal's tormentor that day being their £30,000 signing from Partick Thistle, Jimmy Bone, who had made his full debut for Scotland in the summer, and had scored his country's second goal in the recent 4-1 mauling of Denmark. Arsenal's other tormentor that day was Terry Anderson – a player who was signed as a 15-year old by Arsenal manager George Swindin in 1959, but who after a mere 26 appearances was sold to Norwich for £15,000 by Billy Wright in 1965.

The *Daily Express'* Pat Gibson had described Norwich that day as totally aggressive, totally ambitious, and totally committed, whereas Arsenal were not. As what generally happens with Arsenal is that ex-players generally do well against them and Anderson had netted the first with only two minutes on the clock and the winner after 85 minutes.

"Arsenal obviously expected superior skill to bring the yapping terriers to heel, but once their football had been strangled by the denial of space Arsenal found that the First Division new boys were more composed than themselves," explained Gibson. "Eventually it was only the inspiring Frank McLintock, his muscles already exhausted by the relentless running of Jimmy Bone, who kept them going."

Arsenal however, were unlucky not to equalise in the last couple of minutes as John Roberts headed against the bar, but it was Norwich who took the points.

As for Terry Anderson, four years after playing his last game, on 24th January 1980, he went on a training run in Great Yarmouth and never returned. His body was found one week later, having drowned.

For the League Cup Quarter Final game Arsenal were without the cup-tied Jeff Blockley, therefore the not 100% fit Frank McLintock lined up alongside Peter Simpson, giving a 'Double feel' to the defence, which was further shored up by Peter Storey marshalling the front, but which was still minus Bob Wilson between the sticks.

Over 37,500 watched on as Norwich schemer Graham Paddon hit a hat-trick to claim a 3-0 win for The Canaries and dump Arsenal out of the cup. His goals came after 17, 27 and 51 minutes; however there was more to this story as Bertie Mee now had a scapegoat.

"Cup slaughter by Norwich as Barnett slips," exclaimed the *Daily Mirror's* Harry Miller.

"Arsenal had dominated the early stages – only for every raid to be met by a dense forest of yellow shirted Norwich men, with giant centre half Duncan Forbes always in the thick of the action. The first two goals followed appalling errors by Arsenal goalkeeper Geoff Barnett. The first was a goal from nowhere and it left Barnett wringing his hands in despair. Paddon picked up a pass from Doug Livermore, thirty yards out. Arsenal looked absolutely in no danger as he hit a low and not particularly hard shot, but Barnett, with a clear view of the ball, let it go underneath his body and into the net."

Barnett was badly at fault for Norwich's second goal as Paddon inflicted more damage, and when it looked as if he might have run the ball over the goal line, Paddon pivoted and hit an acutely-angled shot that went between Barnett and the near post – quite reminiscent of Steve Heighway's goal against Bob Wilson in the 1971 F.A Cup Final.

Arsenal tried to press to get back in the game and Norwich right back Geoff Butler cleared shots off the line from Eddie Kelly and John Radford, whilst Kevin Keelan brilliantly finger-tipped an Alan Ball shot round a post whilst another drive by Ball managed to beat Keelan only for him to see it skim past the upright, however early in the second half Arsenal were running out of ideas and it was then Paddon took a cross from substitute Trevor Howard, and drove it past Barnett.

Miller added, "Few sides work harder at their game than Norwich and their performance was something special. They are no aristocrats. Their game is simple and direct. You can criticise them, but they proved yet again that you just cannot ignore them. The longer the game went on the more ragged and ruffled Arsenal became, with Arsenal's marking in the latter stages of the game almost non-existent."

Paddon had been Arsenal's tormentor, just has Gerry Queen had been two years earlier in the self-same competition and on the self-same ground. However, as good as Norwich had been, and although they would make the League Cup Final by beating an exciting Chelsea side over two-legs, their form would become erratic and as such, their season would implode. As for Geoff Barnett, he was catapulted back into the reserves and was only ever called upon for five first team matches over the next three seasons and duly left the club in January 1976.

Next up was Brian Clough's Derby County at the Baseball Ground, where Bob Wilson probably played the worst match of his career, and post-game what was to be one of the turning points of their season.

The 16th November, 1972 will be etched in Derby folklore, as Arsenal were truly destroyed by a team which were as good as Arsenal were pitiful, but it was also a game which finally spelt the end of George Graham's career with Arsenal. After the 3-0 and 5-0 mauling's there was still no place for the goal scoring schemer, which told you only one thing – Mee didn't want him.

Graham told the *Daily Mirror,* "I cannot accept the fact that I am not good enough. I expected to be in the side."

What was stranger still is that Wilson kept his place yet Peter Marinello who had finally displaced George Armstrong had been dropped and wouldn't feature again apart from a substitute appearance against Bradford City in the F.A Cup Fourth Round.

Nearly a month later, an Arsenal Reserve side, fielding both Graham and Marinello, would thrash Leicester City's reserves 6-0, with five goals coming from Charlie George, and on reporting to the training ground on the morning of 19th December, 1972 Mee told both Graham and Marinello of his decision to sell them.

Graham explained, "I feel terribly saddened, but when the club itself agrees that you don't have much of a future with them you only have one alternative."

Bertie Mee was a hard man to figure out, as captain Frank McLintock would soon find out.

To really love Arsenal, you really do have to appreciate their history!

That aside, I thought the ITV 7 team were absolutely brilliant and none more so than Les who, due to his connections with London University had helped make the re-branded Inside True Britain a great success. After just two months, The Warehouse was alive with people everywhere, and outside a firm was finally erecting a huge neon sign to advertise the place. It had been a long time coming, but it was well worth the wait.

Since the birth of Sammy everything had been one huge blur, and I was often asked by Emily – and her mum come to that, if I could keep it up? ITV asked me to do something, and it got done. I never told them 'No', even though this fly-on-the-wall documentary was causing problems in that it could affect the man who I had always considered my best friend – Sooty.

"Are you sure you want to do this?" asked a rather concerned Abi.

I nodded a 'Yes'.

The six-part series would be going out on air for its first showing late Sunday night on the 28th of December and I rang one of the suits at ITV to let them know of its content.

"Even though we've toned it down through editing, it could still be a bit sensitive," I told him. "And it's quite possible that after its first showing that the National Crime Agency could become involved."

Within 30 minutes I had not only ITV's development director on site, but its director general with me explaining that human trafficking plays a part in who actually sits on the casting couch.

"It's not totally illegal," I said, "as all the actresses are up for it, but it is possible that they are initially misguided into what they will be doing before they actually get here."

Both Jeanette and Sinead had done a brilliant job in getting some of them to talk, with the latter very inquisitive as regards the x, y and z of it all, so much so she wasted no time in being auditioned for a semi-raunchy ten-minute scene with one of its female stars who went by the stage name of 'Cristiana Vai'.

I knew once this went out live that Nubeon could be closed down, that is how hard-hitting the documentary was. We had three girls openly admitting that they were lied to, to get them into the UK – and on false documentation, and I sought a bit of guidance from our corporate law firm who told me that this could most definitely be the case.

That Friday afternoon my thoughts were with Libby and her kids, however. My first instinct was to call her, as has much as she had pissed me off over the years, I did still love her and I wanted nothing more than to get things back to the way they used to be – however I eventually thought better of it and left it alone, although I did inform Emily that circumstances could well change down Holland Park before the New Year.

"I definitely want to do some of the narration then," she said.

"Yeh, I thought you might," I told her.

The two suits had watched some of the footage and were extremely happy, although the director general did give me a bollocking for doing the filming down at Nubeon's studios after he specified that the studios off the Old Kent Road were deemed not fit for purpose.

"It's the real deal," I told him.

"Yes, I can see where you are coming from now," he said before adding, "By the way, who's doing the camera work on this?"

That made me smile and I gave Faranha a shout to get Stuart and Jonathan in my office so he could meet them both.

"They are with Ginge filming that documentary Karen Beckley's doing," she said.

"Give them a nudge," I said, before explaining to both the suits that I was investing in the future.

"What – they are students?" asked the development director.

I nodded as the door opened and in walked the dynamic duo.

"Stu – Jonathan, these are the people who help run ITV," I said. "They've just been commenting on your camera-work down at Nubeon."

"Hello," they both said in unison.

"And you must be Emily's younger brother?" asked the director general.

Stuart nodded.

"They are both at Liverpool College but Stu has been working part-time with BBC Radio Merseyside," I explained.

"Well this must seem a bit different," he said. "So what's it like working for your brother-in-law?"

"Amazing," he replied.

If I wanted a PR manager, Stuart was definitely that and after a couple of handshakes they left my office to go back down to where Karen was interviewing Kevin Whitcher.

After the two suits left I went into the editing suite where Les was working on piecing together the Brian Clough documentary and making a right cow's arse of it, that was until I put the piece in the right time-frame for him.

"You make it look easy," he said.

"You have to remember that I've been doing this stuff for years," I told him.

He then told me that he and Claudia - his partner, were now not an item anymore.

"How do you mean anymore?" I asked. "You were hardly an item back in September."

That much was true. I remember her locking him out of his apartment in Bow and he'd tried borrowing a ladder to get in through the window and the thing had slipped which left him dangling from a window frame. What was ironic was that he was stark bollock naked bar a pair of socks, which led me to assume that there was a lot more to the story than he actually told me – Especially as they were Chelsea socks.

Around lunchtime I was informed by Faranha that three thousand DVD's of my kids' Christmas play had arrived at their school and an elated Ted Marsden was on the phone.

That had been a strange day as both Jeanette, Emily and Sammy had sat together in the third row watching, whilst my lad in his Arab garb delivered the line of lines, "I come bearing Frankenstein."

And that was after hours of his mum and M coaching him. He did raise a few giggles though – well more than a few giggles really as Mrs Peters nearly fell off her chair, which led me to believe that she had known exactly what she was doing when she cast him. Any idiot can say gold or myrrh – that's dead easy!

Herbert's stage debut was just as indifferent, as he screamed his frigging lungs out at three shepherds, the innkeeper, his stage-mum Mary, and his rather gullible stepdad, the latter who himself ended up roaring his eyes out after the miserable albeit immaculate conception had made him fluff his lines in front of a packed house. Baby Jesus then treated us all to the grand finale where he had pee dripping through the bottom of the manger.

"I told you to put a nappy on him," I told his mum afterwards.

"They didn't have Pampers back then," she replied. "It has to be realistic."

"A six-year-old girl giving birth to a thirty-pound new-born, twenty bearded midgets running around Bethlehem and a British Friesian cow that can talk," I smiled. "I can certainly see where you're coming from."

"Shurrup you," she twanged.

My daughter, however was a cracking Mrs Cratchet and didn't half dish out a bollocking to Mr. Cratchet for giving a Christmas Toast to the mean and odious Mr. Scrooge, who strangely was a coloured lad called Benny Green, which immediately had me thinking of Grange Hill.

"You've done a great job," explained Ted. "I can't thank you enough."

"Don't worry, you can falsify my lads' exam results to help get him into Eton," I replied.

That made him laugh. I've no idea why, as I actually meant it!

The strange thing was that whilst we filmed it I noticed that very few words were passed between Emily and Jeanette, which wasn't like Emily at all. She hadn't said much about it, and it was one of those moments where I knew there were more things that she wasn't telling me.

Cue: Annie Dixon.

Money plays its hand in everything you do and not just on some days, but every day. Annie had continually been on at me to move LMJ's around a bit as we were starting to accumulate quite a lot of the stuff.

I had invested a lot of my own money into the purchase and redevelopment of The Warehouse and its infrastructure, which had set me back just over a million quid. Chuck in all the furniture and all the high-end gadgetry and you could add another third of a million to that amount. As I owned the studios lock stock and barrel, she advised me to have it overvalued and restructure a payment plan where I got my investment back and whereby LMJ then owned The Warehouse and its infrastructure. As I often did, I ummed and arred a bit, that was until Savills called and gave the nod that £9.6 million was a sensible valuation.

"You're fucking joking," I said.

"No. That's straight up with no overvaluing or anything," Annie replied. "That's what the property is worth."

I called my corporate law firm whilst my financial director set a payment plan in motion. I was to be paid a total of £11.04 million including interest over a period of 12 months starting from 4th January, 2015.

There was a couple of other things, one of which was to do the exact same thing once the purchase of the old factory down White Lion Street went through, with the other being that I had to start taking money out of the company in wages.

"ITV pay me enough," I said.

"That's not the point, Lee," she said. "I suggest LMJ match the wages with ITV."

I felt like I was bleeding the company, but in all honesty I wasn't even making a dint in its finances. I would be earning in excess of £80,000 a week – which was as much as a top-tier premiership football player. It was also much lower than some really crap premiership players as well!

I got back in around 7:00pm that night to my wife and her mum doing some baking, whilst Mike was on the sofa trying to get Sammy off to sleep, who once he saw me come through the door woke up and commenced grizzling.

"You been busy, love?" Emily smiled, as she came over to me and plonked me a kiss on the lips whilst getting all flour over my cheeks and then informing me that there was a nice Casillero del Diablo Pinot Grigio chilling in the fridge. "My mam brought it down for you."

"Nearly ten quid, that cost," exclaimed Mike. "Our Frank distils his own and it only works out at two-bob a bottle."

"Yeh, I tasted some at that anniversary party," I said. "Its price tag's certainly no exaggeration."

I looked around for my kids.

"They're upstairs," smiled Emily. "Writing their letters to Father Christmas."

"They've been at it the last forty minutes," explained Sil'. "Jamie's a bit stressed wondering how Father Christmas will get down the chimney as that long gas fire is in the way."

"Didn't you tell him he was magic?" I asked.

"I did," said Sil', "But he was adamant that his Granddad Mike should move it."

Mike and Sil' had been coming down at least once a week, with Mike's van being loaded to the hilt on its return with bits and pieces destined for Hamilton Square. They had also been down to check in on their Stuart and his mate and appeared quite impressed that both the lads and the flat were all in order. Jeanette and Paul were nipping up there every other day and Emily had popped her head in a few times and that being the case there was nothing untoward to report.

As regards the job they were doing for LMJ, I had told a bit of a white lie in that they were doing some backdrop camera-work, which could have meant anything really, and that being the case I never got asked any intricate details. In reality both young lads had provided me with not only 75% of the camera-work for the fly-on-the-wall series, but at the same time had got a few valuable lessons in life.

"I'd love a bird like that Cristiana," young Jonathan had told me.

"No you wouldn't kid," I'd replied. "Get yourself a proper girlfriend."

"Like Paige?" Stu had said.

"Something like that," I'd winked.

I'd dropped them off some spending money and a pair of Oyster cards and they thought it was brilliant. Life can be like that at sixteen. Both lads had been great and when I sat at the side of Mike and took misery guts off him I told him so.

"Both their names will be on the end credits," I explained, before opening my briefcase and eventually digging out two envelopes.

"What's this?" Mike asked.

"It's the start of their future," I said.

I'd had my law firm draft up two contracts, which would give them their first proper jobs along with a couple of cheques for two grand a piece. "They'll be working for ITV 7 on a weekend and LMJ throughout the summer," I said. "But finishing their two-year college course is a must. They bollocks that up and these will mean nothing."

Mike still couldn't get his head around it.

"He's growing up, Mike," I said. "He is a really, really good lad."

Me saying that put a lump in both his parents' throat and it was then I mentioned my talk with him, which I didn't know was a good thing or bad thing as I also mentioned getting Paige's parents to give Emily a ring if indeed she and Stu both came down one weekend.

"Lee's right, dad," Emily said. "If Paige's mam and dad are okay with her coming down, so should you – I'll make sure that there are guidelines and that they are adhered to."

"I don't know M," he said. "I don't want him ever having to go what I went through."

"You're not the only one that's been through things like that, Mike," I said. "Your life eventually got turned around when you started seeing your daughter – I would have swapped two or three years out in the cold for what I got."

Mike just gave me a blank expression.

"I had my first baby die on me," I said.

That was a total shock as Emily had told them nothing, and Sil' being Sil' immediately wanted to know more about this and it wasn't me who told the story – it was my wife – and she told it exactly how it was.

Later that night Emily sat cross-legged on the bed whilst I told her what was happening at work. She had a fair idea of how good things were, but not that much of an idea as regards the money element of it. So long as there was enough in the pot for food, bills, fuel and the odd twenty or so pairs of shoes, she was happy.

I loved Saturday mornings – It was a case of no work, having my kids and football; however, this day would be different. This day my wife and kids were heading up the M6 to Hamilton Square whilst I had to do a live interview at 8:00pm as part of The Jonathan Woss Show, with me promising that straight afterwards I would drive up to Liverpool so we could all have Sunday lunch together before a trip over to Anfield with Bill, where the sort of in and out of form Arsenal would be taking on a definitely well out of form Liverpool.

Hamilton Square had been a relatively easy project for Mike, and it was a damn sight easier purchasing and renovating it than getting furniture delivered, as Emily had been going bats one morning due to the bed company saying that the said beds she had ordered and paid for wouldn't be in stock until January.

"So – I'll just pick a couple up from Ikea," I told her.

To me a bed was a bed, but to her it was not and although I got a peck on the lips for my suggestion I was duly informed that we were most definitely not getting the beds from Ikea.

I had been woken up by Herbert screaming out his lungs at 5:00am, who pointed out the fact that I should be a more responsible and attentive father and that he shouldn't have to wake me up and have to wait for his bottle made up as he was absolutely starving.

"I bet you're glad you're not breastfeeding him," I said to his mum as she made her presence known in the kitchen, whilst Rosemary's Baby was trying his level best to rip the teat of the bottle with a pair of choppers he didn't yet possess.

"He's definitely teething," she smiled.

"Tell me about it," I replied. "If he chews any harder he'll have milk everywhere."

Later that morning I helped Mike load up the van with bits and pieces and waved off Emily and my kids in the Mean Machine and kept my fingers crossed that The Jonathan Woss Show would be cancelled. Unfortunately however, that never happened and after getting to ITV's studios I was grilled by its head of sport and a well-known football journalist from the *The Telegraph* as regards the outcome of tomorrow's game.

"On paper we should batter them," I said. "However, Arsenal being Arsenal will probably bollocks it up – Especially this Arsenal side."

"So what do you reckon?" asked the guy from *The Telegraph*.

I was sick of forecasting two-all draws but that is what I said along with, "They just seem a bit incapable of being able to keep a clean sheet or maintaining a lead."

Cue: Jonathan Woss.

I had certainly never met the man and my first instinct was that he was a damn sight bigger and chubbier than I had imagined and that if I were being brutally honest, he could have done with a trip to Tony the Barber's on Grays Inn Road for a shave and haircut. He gave me a sort of itinerary of some of the questions he would be asking and I gave it a glance knowing full-well that this interview would be nothing like the said itinerary, which it most certainly was not.

"So Lee," he said, as I sat down in front of his so-called celebrity audience after I had walked on amidst manufactured audience participated clapping. "I understand that you're a big Arsenal supporter?"

"Yeh, something like that," I replied, before adding something what Stevie Kell once told me. In that he, just as I did, thought that all Arsenal fans are really special people. Well, proper Arsenal fans, and not the fans who think Arsenal was founded in 1996, which had some of the audience laughing.

"An old mate of mine once said that is easy for any fan to become a Manchester United fan, Liverpool fan, Chelsea fan, or even a Real Madrid or Barcelona fan – you just buy the shirt and there you go, you're a United or a Liverpool fan and so on. You will probably never go to a match and will shout the loudest in the pub when the game is on the TV and as Roy Keane said in his biography – the team you have chosen will probably prop up your life like some form of crutch as they will use the success of their football club to fill what is probably an unfulfilled life."

I could sense a few mutterings in the audience before I delivered Stevie's next mouthful.

"You know you will also change your team when they become rubbish."

That bit got me a few claps.

"If you are an Arsenal fan, you know what you are getting into when you choose them – you know you are in it for the long haul – oh yeh, and it will cost you a fortune. When you choose Arsenal you are a special person because you understand what being a football supporter is all about. You know they will throw away three and four-nil leads and on occasion get dumped out of a cup by the likes of Wrexham, York and Northampton, but you will also know that they will always have their day as well, and there will be exceptional times like, the double-Doubles, The Invincible's, cup Doubles, beating Real Madrid, Inter Milan and Bayern Munich in their own backyard, and winning the title on the final game of the season at Anfield or White Hart Lane. That is why Arsenal fans are special – because it not easy, and yet they still chose to do it."

A few people in the audience stood up which was followed by a few others and by a few others and suddenly they were all up clapping me – and these weren't my words, they were Stevie Kell's and I told the audience exactly that.

"And you will be watching them at Liverpool tomorrow?" asked Jonathan.

"I'm driving up after the show," I said. "I'll be at Anfield with Emily's granddad who is one of the old school Liverpool supporters who saw both Billy Liddel and Bob Paisley play and who stood on the Kop singing 'She Loves You Yeah Yeah Yeah' whilst on their way to winning the title in nineteen sixty-four."

"You speak with an affection for football," said Jonathan.

"Football is such a beautiful sport when you take away the politics and agendas," I said. "It really is."

I was then asked about ITV 7 and how I got involved and it was then that I explained about Emily having Sammy and that I'd had the business I helped create sold from under my nose and how the big bosses at ITV had been supportive of me.

"I was told you had job offers from America?" he asked.

"Yeh, that's true," I said. "NBC and Fox Sports – they were really nice people, however I have a family that I love and the offer would have had to have been out of this world for me to move to New York."

"Wasn't it a good offer they made you?" he asked.

"Yeh, it was an extremely good offer," I said, "But they could have offered me twenty million a year and I still wouldn't have taken it."

It was then mentioned by the host that I had two families, in Emily and Jeanette and that I had in-laws but no parents, and that between the three parties they made sure that they made up for the fourth. Someone had done their research well and I told him so, which raised a few laughs.

"I've never met anyone like Emily," I said. "She is one in a million."

There were a few mutterings and blowing of hankies in the audience.

"And of course you mean Emily Janes from the Live at The Warehouse?" he said.

"The Emily you see on the show is exactly the Emily I see at home," I explained. "Bright and bubbly and always smiling – well, to me that is – and certainly not to the firm that she recently ordered some beds from or the plumber that put the bath in the wrong way round."

That certainly produced a few laughs.

"Your baby Sammy?" he said.

"Emily named him after the Arsenal player," I told him. "Jon Sammels."

Just then a huge screen behind us was kicked up and my family were there waving to me from a living room in Birkenhead – not the living room in Emily's mum and dad's house but the room at Hamilton Square – ITV had a camera in the new house.

"Hurry up home," twanged Emily. "Yer've got another tree to put up."

"Are we on telly?" asked my lad.

Everyone was laughing, and even more so when I told them about his acting debut where he fluffed his lines. "Both M and Jeanette had him rehearsing this one line about a million times – and he still told the audience that he came bearing Frankenstein."

The rest of the show was a blur, but I have to say that I really enjoyed it. I thought I was going to get dragged over hot coals as regards my past life, but that never happened and on getting out of the studios my phone was red hot.

"The house looks nice," I said.

"You were fantastic," said Emily. "We are all dead proud of you."

Those seven words meant everything to me.

Chapter 31

Jeanettes Tales – Take 11

It had been frosty outside as well as inside between M and myself, and even at the kids' Christmas play there wasn't a lot of dialogue, even though the laughter had been raucous and the two plays as enjoyable as anything we'd seen. I thought Lee may have said something to her but he hadn't. I think with his workload he was kind of oblivious to everything and all Friday he had been in and out of meetings to the point that I had missed him until he popped up on our screens on Saturday night. The man who was in the newspapers almost every day was a special guest on The Jonathan Ross Show. Although he loomed large in the tabloids, none of the public really knew who he was as his TV career on screen lasted less than half an hour; however, that Saturday night they certainly did. I had Libby and her two over as Paul had been to Cardiff to watch his beloved Brentford and we both sat in awe as he showed its host exactly what being a TV personality was all about. There was no show on show as such, just pure one-hundred percent charm and charisma, and it was the main reason why I had fell in love with him all over again, and on seeing the scene of our two kids on the living room floor of their new house in Liverpool talking with their dad on video link, I cried my eyes out.

What I was to do next, though I would quickly come to hate myself for as I told my mother that all four of us would be going to their house Christmas Eve, knowing full well that Lee would be robbed of their presence the following day.

"Okay Jeanette," he had said.

He never argued the case but I knew I had hurt him, as more than anything he wanted to see the kids open their presents. Me? I just wanted him to be upset, so M would be upset. It is what is called being an utter bitch.

My Saturday night's Sessions programme went out and I was in three newspapers on Monday morning as it was I who had promoted part of the new north London Sound that everyone was talking about, with the Queen & Pistol being dubbed as possibly one of the greatest bands since Blur and Ross Bain, who was its front man saying quite a few complimentary things about me. However all that was on my mind was hurting my ex-husband and my lost friendship with M and all the way through my interview with the journalist from the music press that is all I was thinking about.

"Hiya Jeanette, how did it go?" Lee asked, as he saw me walking from the press room that both M and myself had helped create and across the open plan office.

"Really good," I lied.

His smile lit up the place, but it always did and it wasn't until around 1:15pm when there was laughter coming from over at the editing suite that what I had done really hit home. Abi, Ginge, Faranha and Lee were watching some of the footage that had never been seen before – of the so-called bloopers and screen tests and of course me, Abi and M singing into the camera.

"I'm sorry Lee," I said, "I really have to go out and do something."

I jumped in the car, braved to the rush hour traffic and drove into King's Cross and on to Frederick Street and banged at the door hoping like hell for M to answer it.

"Can I come in?" I asked.

"Yeh, of course you can," she replied, looking a bit concerned. "Is everything okay?"

I told her that it wasn't and I set about pleading for another go at our friendship by telling her that I was truly, truly sorry in that she felt that I had undermined our friendship by making her feel that I was purposely clinging on to Lee.

She immediately took in what I had said and gave a nod of her head before changing the subject, "You were good on TV Saturday night."

"And so were you," I told her. "I'm so sorry, M."

"How's Libby?" she asked.

"Still hurting," I said.

"Well, you've just seen how easy things can change," she said.

When I said Emily was clever, I never understated it – she was – very!

"That undercover work you did on Nubeon has gone down like a bomb," she added. "I have to go in and narrate on it tomorrow evening."

"Do you want me to have Sammy?" I said, as I picked him out of his chair and gave him a cuddle.

"Well, he has missed you," she said. "We all have."

"Thanks M," I said.

And that is all it took – it was as easy as that, however the hard part was how to not be an utter bitch without being one and that meant possibly telling my mother that our Christmas plans had changed; however, I now had M on my side whereas just recently I had not.

My parents now lived in Bakewell, which was a couple of hours from Liverpool and that being the case M suggested we go to their house Christmas night, and get this – stay over.

"How would Lee feel about Paul staying over?" I immediately asked.

"About the same as I would you staying over," she smiled. "Strange."

I went home feeling absolutely brilliant, however what would happen was that Paul thought that it was a truly rubbish idea and him staying at theirs wasn't a subject that was up for debate. In fact he wasn't that well up for stopping at my mother's either. My mother thought I could do a lot better and her thinking that he was another Lee in that he'd just stand there and just receive a lashing from her a wicked tongue – well, he wasn't, and he had put her straight on a couple of occasions. Therefore he and my mother were never the most amenable of pairings.

My mother had said something similar with regards to the boyfriend that I had who I'd dumped for Lee. He was from a rather well-to-do family and he drove a nice new car, which his father had bought him and which he wasted no time in trying to get me into as my mother didn't like the look of him and, as that was the case he never got past first base in our house as she marshalled the space he occupied like some prison guard.

When I dumped him she was so relieved and then nearly had kittens when she saw Lee turn up at the house in a Jaguar sports car.

"Is that yours?" she asked, as he walked towards the door.

"No, I stole it," he winked, before passing her a really nice compliment.

He'd passed the first of many tests she had set for him.

I used to watch how he played her, and how he nullified her caustic remarks with his smile. He thought she didn't like him, but she did. He got the preferential treatment regardless of her sniping, and it was only when his affairs started did she lose the former to give more of the latter and boy did she bloody give it him. Anyone would think he'd had the affair on her.

"Okay Kate, point taken," he would say, before being verbally battered and bruised by another twenty lashes of her tongue.

In the early days I told her to butt out; however my mother was always one of those who ground you down over a long period of time, which was more or less what Lee had said to me during one of our last one-sided arguments prior to me kicking him out.

The reality was that he had hurt my mother and she took it personally.

Monday the 22nd was a strange day in that I had to complete the documentary on what was a really upsetting story of the murdered girl, Milly Dowling and M had to do the narration of the fly-on-the-wall documentary and then get changed to do the rescheduled Live at the Warehouse. Therefore it was agreed that she would have the kids in the morning and I would have them at night. What I was also going to have was another unannounced visitor in the ladies' toilets – this time, though it was Ross Bain. His band had been setting up on Stage 4 for the Warehouse show and he had asked if I minded him using the mirror as he had something in his eye and the lighting in the ladies was better.

I'd spoke to him on set but that was about as much as I had done, and he seemed quite nice, and that being the case I tried getting what was a coarse hair from his eyebrow out of his eye, and he thanked me with a peck on the lips before introducing himself a little bit more.

Ross Bain was certainly no Lee, but he was also certainly no Paul either, and although nothing major happened, it certainly could have and certainly would have if it hadn't been for me panicking a bit, thinking someone could walk in on us. If you ever get chance to date a guitarist, then try it as one thing they are great at is using both sets of fingers! And when the Queen & Pistol went live that night Ross Bain was wonderful, but at nine years my junior and me with two kids, maybe a tad too young, but all the same I was extremely flattered, and even more so when M had finished the show and had called to pick Sammy up.

"That Ross Bain asked me if I'd give him your number," she told me.

"You haven't told Lee, have you?" I inadvertently asked.

"What's it got to do with Lee," she said. "It's you whose number he wants."

I smiled.

"In the meantime he told me to give you this," she said, and passed me a yellow post-it note with a mobile number on.

After M left I deliberated about ringing the number – well for less than ten minutes anyway and sent him a text. 'My number – Jeanette x'.

My phone immediately rang and for the next ninety minutes I was in conversation with him on a variety of subjects from music, to art, TV and films, which concluded would I like to be taken out to see one?

"I'm divorced with two children," I told him.

"I know," he said.

"And I'm nine years older than you," I added.

"And?"

"And I want to be taken seriously," I said.

"You will be," he said.

It took me ages to get to sleep that night as all I was doing was thinking about him. Ross Bain, one of the faces of the new north London Sound.

Chapter 32

Good Neighbour Sam

I'd gone to Anfield to watch Arsenal squander yet another lead and watch a 10-man Liverpool equalise nearly ten minutes into injury time. It was another frigging déjà vu moment in the life of the poor sod who follows Arsenal and was a stark reminder of 17th April 2011 at The Emirates, where Liverpool had similarly equalised a staggering 12 minutes into injury time to tie that particular game.

You think the 1958/59 and 1972/73 seasons were frustrating? 2014/15 was getting just as bad!

I'd have settled for a draw before the match and certainly during the match as we played shite, however to concede like that and against ten men was disgraceful. That being the case I had a face like a dog's arse when I got back to Hamilton Square, which was partly offset by a smiling wife at the door holding a rather miserable-looking lump of my DNA in her arms.

"Wave to daddy," she told him.

She may have told him, but it was certainly not in his remit of things to do and he just glared at me bit.

The house had a really new smell to it and was looking really good; however it was really big and as it was constructed over five floors it was a right hike upstairs to summon the kids for their tea.

Emily loved it, not so much because of the gargantuan-sized kitchen it possessed nor the three bathrooms with the mega-sized baths and showers, or the solid wooden floors that had cost as much as a three-bed terrace to put down, but because to her Birkenhead was home, as her family lived there.

"I could stay here forever," she told me, as I took misery guts off her and tried placating him with some brownish-looking gee that looked as about as appealing as it tasted.

She made me some food, which included a nice pie that her gran had made up.

"What's that?" I inquired.

"Gooseberry," she smiled.

"Sound," I replied. "I could definitely stay here."

As much as I wanted to stay and veg-out until well after Christmas, the next two days would be very busy, as I was needed to do some more editing on the behind the scenes programme before signing it off, complete the re-branded Inside True Britain programme and do the rescheduled Live at The Warehouse, where I knew there could be a frigging riot as the Electric Ladyboy were due on set and were the most troublesome and confrontational set of individuals you could ever meet.

"You smash the set up and I'll fucking bill you for it," I had told their grinning lead man.

I had told the Red & White's and the Cockney Green's the same, however no-one had seen anything of the Queen & Pistol's Ross Bain, who I was told by Ginge had recently been having a bit of thing going with Karen. And Sasha from PR. And Jen Steward the cleaner.

"What, all at the same time?" I'd inquired.

"Nah, Karen was like his girlfriend for three days," explained Ginge. "Sasha was just a one night thing."

"What about Jen, as she's like a million years old?" I asked.

"Yeh Karen went batty when she found out," he said. "So did Sinead, but he hasn't gotten around to doing her yet."

I'd asked Emily about Ross, who immediately told me that he was indeed quite the ladies' man.

"He's quite an old ladies' man as well," I said. "He's been at Jen Steward."

"Wow," was all she could say before she dropped out the big one. "He semi-propositioned me as well, but I threatened him with you."

"You're joking?"

She shook her head. "He's like a male version of Sinead but not quite as good looking."

"How does he do all this raping and pillaging?" I asked. "He's only been to the Warehouse about three or four times."

It was a weird one that and I came to the conclusion that he must wait around outside to pick them up. I immediately put kicking his arse on my ever-growing list of things to do.

I knew Emily didn't want to leave the new house and whereas I took my two kids back first thing Monday morning she stayed a few hours longer. My first point of call was to Paul's sister over in Southgate – Chrissy, who I had met a couple of times and who I have to say was both always smiling and who was a really nice lady who the kids liked immensely. She had even watched over Sammy a few times.

I finally got into the office and had a fight with the Christmas tree in the foyer after Georgia Clayton had left two sacks of post on the floor,

"It's Christmas cards," she laughed. "There are loads of them."

I looked in on the gallery of The Warehouse where, under the supervision of our studio and lighting boss Jaime Hudson, five temporary studios had become one and where tomorrow night there would be none as it would be packed to the rafters for the Christmas edition of Live at The Warehouse and that being the case she was currently giving a couple of the lads from Binh Binh Pham a bollocking for dropping all their gear all over the place.

"Put them over on Stage One," she snapped.

Jaime was a behind-the-scenes girl and Arsenal season ticket holder who ran The Warehouse giving us timetables of what and when to do it. She was very efficient and made sure that everything ran like clockwork – even though their drummer – Glenn Abbott moaned and groaned as he wanted a more central position.

On another note, Jeanette had been pissing in my ears as regards what they were actually doing for Christmas and it was a case of 'is she or isn't she?' At the moment her best laid plans involved her mother's in Derbyshire, however that could easily change as I knew from Paul that he wasn't that keen. I obviously wanted the kids to wake up Christmas morning at mine, but I wasn't that selfish or stupid to think that it was ever an option. I loved them all and therefore I would do whatever it took to work around her and whatever mood she was in, which over the weekend I had to say had been a bit strange.

Monday morning it wasn't much better and while I was sat at the editing suite cobbling together the behind the scenes programme she just upped and left.

"What's up with her?" asked Faranha.

"No idea," I said, whilst getting down to the nitty-gritty of finding something stupid I could find one of the ITV 7 lot doing.

The next thing I knew it was around 6:00pm and home time. I was absolutely 'cream-crackered' and after fighting through the lousy Christmas traffic I got into the house only to fight my way past a great seven-foot skeleton on castors in the kitchen.

"Where did he come from?" I asked, as I got planted a kiss from my wife who had poured me a Perrier water from the fridge.

"He's that PPI man that called a few months ago," she lied. "Maybe now is time a good time to bury him."

"Are you sure it's not Per Mertesacker?" I asked as I took off my jacket. "It certainly looks like him."

"No, definitely the PPI man," she lied.

"Where's Herbert?" I asked.

"Bed, thank god."

"That sounds ominous."

"He had a mega throwing-up session in the car."

"When?"

"About junction 20 of the M6," she replied.

"I hope you told him off."

"Definitely," she lied. "I threatened to leave him outside Greggs bakers at Poplar Services but he said now that we're famous he would tell Esther Rantzen."

"Why, does he actually know who she is?" I asked.

"Yeh, Luis Suarez's mum," she lied.

"So what about the PPI man?"

"He needs wrapping up," she said. "It took me ages to put him together."

The PPI man was really a Christmas present for my lad who had been nagging like hell for a skeleton since he'd watched 'Jason and the Argonauts'. Oh yeh, and that Emily had told him that they are made up of 206 bones, although I did pull her up on that point.

"They are," she said.

"What about Sherilyn Fenn?" I said. "She definitely didn't have that many bones."

"Who's she?" she asked.

My lad was dead-interested when I mentioned the fact that a possessive surgeon amputated her arms and legs and had her stood on his telly like a vase.

"It can't have been a flat screen telly Dad or she would have fell off," he had quite rightly pointed out.

"No, it was one of them old ones that Mrs Sosk has," I'd told him.

"Can we go see it?" he'd asked.

"What?"

"That woman with no arms and legs on Mrs Sosk's telly?"

I then had to curb his enthusiasm by informing him that Sherilyn Fenn was an actress in some rubbish film called 'Boxing Helena' and that Mrs Sosk didn't really have her stood on the telly like a vase.

We spent the evening wrapping presents – well, I didn't as I hated wrapping presents – I watched Emily do it and she was as crap at it as she was the ironing, although she strangely enjoyed it.

"Have you bought me anything?" she inquired.

"No," I lied.

She then sulked a bit until I told her I was fibbing and explained that I'd bought her one of those nice commercial irons for her to take to Hamilton Square.

"I hope you are kidding," she said.

"It was either that or a pair a diamanté mules I saw in that posh shoe shop near Covent Garden, but I knew you'd already got a pair similar to them and that you definitely needed an iron."

"I'd prefer the diamanté mules," she sulked.

"I know."

"Will you buy me them, then?"

"Maybe," I said.

I got a cuddle on the sofa and just as I was about to slip into second gear, Herbert woke up and started screaming the place down.

"He definitely doesn't want a sister," I told her.

"Well, he's definitely getting one," she said, and within two minutes she had nipped upstairs and covered his dummy with half a tube of Araldite and was back downstairs and casually walking over to me in a pair of diamanté mules that she'd just happened to find in the bottom of my wardrobe.

"You fibbed," she said.

"How did you find them?" I asked. "I'd hidden them."

"Not very well, though," she winked.

"Really?"

"Sammy's real dad came to the house and he found them and made me put them on for him," she lied. "And he – yer know."

The relatively new rule number one was immediately implicated with speed and precision with her hoping that Mr.

Stork would be arriving with another lump of misery in around nine months' time.

"I really hope we get one," she smiled.

"Well, it's not for the lack of effort," I told her.

It wasn't, it was great. I was turning up to a different wife nearly every night. Saying that, the other Wednesday's session was a bit weird as the night before we had watched a film titled 'The Magdalene Sisters'. On getting through the door I nearly had a coronary. I thought Vanessa Whitlock was in the house. Never heard of her? Then google her – dead scary. However that was then and this is now, and just to keep me on my toes Emily gave me another seizure.

"You what?" I asked.

"I asked Jeanette and Paul to spend Christmas night with us," she repeated.

"Tell me you're joking."

"Okay then, I'm joking," she replied.

"You're not, are you?"

"Nope."

"I see her nearly every day already," I said. "I definitely draw the line at having her listening at my bedroom door."

"She wouldn't do that," Emily smiled.

"You want to bet?"

"But she'll be with Paul," she said.

"So what, that won't stop her."

That news put me on a right downer which was made worse by Jack Lemmon being on TV in a film called 'Good Neighbour Sam', and his blonde-haired wife had to trade places with Romy Schneider. Never watched it? Then do. It's about as complex as my life was getting.

I found out next day that Jeanette staying was a long shot, and thanked god that Paul had kicked that idea out to touch. I didn't want them staying as much as he didn't, and after a really long Monday which involved Emily doing a great narration for the fly-on-the-wall and the rowdiest Live at The Warehouse Show ever, with the Queen and Pistol blowing everyone away, I would be able to cop a few days off. However, prior to that I had to break up a fight with half of Electric Ladyboy and the Red & White's.

"What is it with you lot," I said. "I don't go around battering other football fans – can't you just get on?"

I also needed to have a word with Ross Bain, especially as I'd seen him talking with Emily; however I now had Sami McDowell jockeying for a bit of attention, but she was not really what the White Lion label or the so-called north London sound was really about. Needless to say she did a bit of pressuring which culminated in me telling her that I'd think about it, however I'd thought about it already and got pulled into another football discussion with the most infamous of football players, which was picked up on camera and made the early pages in *The Sun*.

'ITV 7 going for viewers' it read. 'Joey Barton being lined up for main pundit?'

That was a right load of bollocks. I'd spent a few minutes chatting to him about the house up at Hamilton Square, how well he played in the 4-4 draw against Arsenal, and how crap Alan Shearer's face was for TV. I had said absolutely nothing about a job with ITV 7, however my phone was red-hot the next morning as not only had 18.3 million viewers tuned in to Live at The Warehouse, I now had a load of ex-players' agents haranguing me for a spot on the new channel. I also had Sami McDowell offering me some quid pro quo arrangement about me signing her up for White Lion. It sounded great as she was extremely fit, but I had to pass on it as Emily was doing a great job of occupying that side of things.

Just as I thought I could begin to relax and chill out, ITV's head of sports graced me with his presence.

"Don't you have your own office to go to?" I told him. "You're here more than I am."

He laughed at that – asked me what we were up to Christmas Day and that ITV were on about dumping Adrian Chiles.

"You must have been talking to Kirsty then?" I said.

He laughed at the suggestion and more so when I told him that I always felt that he was out of his depth and should have stayed in radio. "He's certainly got the fucking face for it," I said.

I knew with ITV 7 kicking up, it would spell the clanging chimes of doom for ITV's main anchor, as you only had to glance at its core team, any of who wouldn't have been out of place in some fashion shoot or commercial, but the thing was – they all knew their stuff.

Chapter 33

Jeanette's Tales – Take 12

I'd had a right humdinger of an argument with Paul the day before Christmas Eve. It wasn't about one thing, more to do with a few things, one of which was me being invited to The Garage over in Highbury on the 27th as a V.I.P of sorts to watch the Queen & Pistol. Well, not so much the invite, but the way of the invite as M had picked up the kids and taken them to see Father Christmas while Paul had called around unannounced and walked in on Ross Bain sitting on my couch.

"Who the hell are you?" was his first impression.

I was just glad he never turned up five minutes earlier as he would have had the shock of his life as the lead singer had an amazing sleight of hand and while I was trying to hold on to my bra at one end he was trying to give me some internal at the other. I thought I'd been dragged through a hedge backwards after five minutes. My hair was all over the shop, my make-up all smudged, my blouse half-unbuttoned and my tights around my knees.

"Stop it," I told him.

I may have told him, but it certainly didn't stop him – He was like a bloody whirlwind.

I finally managed to hold him off and told him in no uncertain terms that this wasn't how it worked. I wanted wooing. That certainly wasn't wooing, it was more having a game of trying to hide the bloody sausage with Squiddly Diddly.

"Come on, you know you want to," he told me.

No, I didn't. I was quite happy baking mince pies until he knocked on my door and it was only Paul's car pulling up outside that had made him stop.

I got back from a minor refurbishment and straightening myself up exercise in the bathroom to see Paul showing him the door.

"So, what's going on?" he asked me.

I told him nothing, but that fact that Ross had got half my make-up and lipstick on his face told its own story.

"So why's he got half your make-up on his face?"

See?

He dished me out a bollocking, thought about leaving, but before he did he asked me what really happened. I think he had been around me too long and was starting to turn into me, because that is what I always did with Lee.

I didn't give him what he wanted, but told him that it may be a good idea if we had some time apart. Ross thought that was an extremely good idea and when he saw Paul's Mercedes leave he was back at my door doing everything but pee up the thing; however, I did what I thought was the right thing and told this particular alpha male that I wanted taking serious and treating with respect, and although I admired who he was, during our two previous encounters he had done neither.

M turned up a couple of hours later with the kids including her beautiful baby, and I gave her the edited highlights of The Ross Bain Show with this week's special guest star – me.

I found it strange that she found it quite amusing and then totally pissed me off by mentioning his three-day fling with Karen Beckley. And then pissed me off again by mentioning Sasha. I was just about to offer him complete forgiveness when she told me about Jen Steward.

I didn't know any Jen Steward. Why didn't I know any Jen Steward?

"She's one of the women from the contract cleaning company that come in," she said.

I didn't know her, but that was no surprise as I generally went to The Warehouse when I wanted and left well before any of the brush and mop brigade came in.

"She's about forty," M told me. "She drives that mini with the Union Jack on the roof."

I still didn't know her, but I'll give M credit where it was due, she let me know her feelings in that Paul was a damn sight better option than Ross, however as much as Paul was good with the kids and wanted nothing more than set up home, provide for us all and bore me to death for the rest of my life, I was one of those women who suffered from a bit of Stockholm Syndrome as every now and then I yearned for a bit of selfish affection from the alpha male and that being the case I told M that I'd drive over to Liverpool with the kids after the Queen's speech to be in the company the most alpha of males I had ever known. And his wife, of course.

I let Paul know my plans and had him a bit of a fluster as he still wanted to know about Ross – oh yeh, and that he didn't want to go to Liverpool.

"Tough shit," is what I said to the latter, however what I said to the former was – well, a bit not nice really, as I told him about the brief encounter over at The Warehouse and Ross phoning me and then coming over this morning as part of his pre-planned, albeit failed fertilisation project.

Did I like him? Yeh, most definitely; however, when I got asked the question I answered it rather differently.

We were joined by Libby and her two kids around 2:30pm, which I have to say was really lovely, as we opened some wine and put some food on, which set the tone for the rest of the day as all the kids were plonked in front of TV watching 'The Lion, The Witch and the Wardrobe' whilst we were sat chattering around the table. One thing I've never mentioned about M is that she can talk for England, but after she has a drink she becomes quite untouchable and has more rattle than a can of marbles; however never ever could she be described as boring to be around as she has a refreshing honesty and charm about her, as Libby was soon going to find out.

Lib was feeling a bit sorry for her and rightly so as Sooty was being an arse. However after her first glass of wine M mentioned that Lee had had his corporate lawyers running the rule over the first instalment of the fly on the wall series, and it could be that Sooty's boss could end up in trouble. It is also worth noting that the 'Lee bit', is generally included in these conversations, which is probably another reason why I tended to hang on to her each and every word.

"So what are you saying?" asked Lib. "Tim could end up running it?"

"No, I don't think so," replied M. "Lee reckons that if his boss gets arrested that Nubeon will fold as they'll probably put some sort of seizure on his assets."

"Well that's not going to do either of us any good, is it?" replied Lib.

"I don't fully understand it," she said, "Lee could tell you better, but he did say that if Nubeon goes under that the Rumanian girl will probably dump Tim and that he'll – well, sort of go back to you with his tail between his legs – I think?"

"And that's good?" Lib snapped.

I interceded as I certainly wasn't having Libby having a dig at M, and I immediately asked her the question of did she want him back or not?

"Yes, of course I do," she said.

"Well shut up then, you silly cow," I told her, whilst at the same time giving M a wink.

On M's second glass of wine, she kicked up the subject of his Rumanian bit on the side and rather candidly added, "She was knocking off one of the technician's and Tim got dead jealous and sacked him."

That was a bit close to the knuckle and even more so when she bloody involved me. "Sinead told us, didn't she, Jeanette?"

420

Shit, I thought.

"Sinead?" asked Lib. "Who's Sinead?"

"She works for ITV Seven, but she has some compulsive disorder when it comes to sex," she blabbed. "Her husband once came to our house looking for her – he thought she was having some fling with Lee, but she was down at Nubeon with Tim."

Double shit, I thought.

"So Tim and this Sinead?" asked Libby.

"Oh, nothing went on, she just fancied his girlfriend," she added, whilst nonchalantly sipping at her wine. "She is pretty though."

By now Libby was grinding her teeth down to dust; however M still wasn't done.

"She said Tim tried it on with her, but she knew that Lee would be narked, so she started dating one of the actors," she explained, before sort of including me – again. "Which one did she say it was, Jeanette?"

Triple shit, I thought.

Libby was not a happy bunny; however before she could interrogate me, M side-tracked her by continuing the conversation. "Lee said that if it all goes pear-shaped down there he would be more than welcome up at The Warehouse."

"What, so there's a job there if he wants one?" inquired Lib.

"Oh yeh," said M, "Lee told me he'd offered him a job again after you had been round at the house, but he said he was really happy doing what he was doing."

Libby was all over the place with this and asked her repeat each and everything she'd just said, and she did, but this time with my son sat on her lap.

By 5:00pm we had gone through a few bottles of wine, when Lee came to the house to pick M and Sammy up, however our two wanted to go over as well.

"Dad, can we go to your house?" asked my son.

"You can for me, but then your mum will be on her own," he said.

Mum will definitely not be on her own, I thought as I'd had around six text messages in my phone to tell me that my company was requested forthwith, and that being the case I said, "Yeh, I don't mind", which Lee picked up on straight away.

"Are you okay?" he asked.

"Yeh, why shouldn't I be?" I replied.

He just shrugged his shoulders and by 5:40pm the house was empty, but that was soon to change as ten minutes later Paul did the bad penny act and was at the door. Grrrr.

Chapter 34

It's beginning to look a lot like Christmas

This time last year was the worst time I had ever known; I was alone and hurting, now 12 months on life was fantastic.

It is wonderful what can happen in a short space of time, and last night I brought home four pieces of wonderful, as one of those said pieces of wonderful had had far too much to drink and that being the case, I had to retrieve the Mean Machine from Clerkenwell immediately after I'd got back to Frederick Street, and trying to get a cab at this time of year and that time of day was a job in itself. Did I mind? Nope.

Even though they had picked up two trophies, if you can class the Community Shield as a trophy, Arsenal were still annoying the hell out of me— but there you go, you can't have it all!

The kids got into the house to find a million wrapped-up presents beneath the tree, and all my lad wanted to do was open them.

"You can't open them yet," I said.

"Well, when can we?" he asked. "My mum is going to Grandma Kate's and you are going to Granny Sil's?"

He had a point.

"Father Christmas will take them to Hamilton Square for you to open," I lied.

Well hardly, Emily had arranged Mr. Man in a Van off Donegal Street to run them up there along with all the rest of the presents, one of which included young Stuart's.

"Don't worry, when your mum comes over Christmas Day they will all be there for you," I assured him.

"I want a dog," he said.

"No you don't," I told him.

That night, Emily semi-sobered up and made us some supper, whilst we watched an updated version of Scrooge starring George C. Scott on DVD, which absolutely petrified my lad.

"Do ghosts come every Christmas?" he asked.

"Only to mean horrible people," I said. "Mrs Peters has got half a dozen due tomorrow night."

"Behave," quipped my wife, as she summoned us to the breakfast bar to tuck into some pre-Christmas fayre of pork pies, Italian ham and loads of other stuff whilst she poured me a white wine.

"M, what's Father Christmas bringing you?" my lad asked.

"A baby sister for you, I hope."

That got my lad's head ticking, wondering how he'd get that on his sleigh and down the blocked up chimney at Hamilton Square.

"What's he bringing you, Dad?" he asked.

"I have everything I need in this room," I said. "I'm happy with that."

"So you won't want your present off me?" Emily smiled.

"Why, do I deserve one?" I asked.

"Yer know yer do," she twanged.

"Well, if you insist," I smiled, whilst fighting to open a jar of Piccalilli. "Just make sure it speaks French and can iron."

"Shurrup you," she twanged.

As we were eating we had a knock on the door and Sooty graced us with his presence.

"What do you want? I gave your missus all our old rags the other day," I lied.

My kids loved their Uncle Sooty, as he spoiled them as much as I spoiled his two, and that being the case they both left the breakfast bar to greet him.

"I've got two tickets for the QPR game," he said, whilst giving my kids a hug. "Corporate box in the East Stand."

"Oh yeh," I replied, as I passed him over a glass of wine.

Sooty had not been at our house since Sammy's christening as he was all over the place, and one place that he had never been was The Warehouse – and if I'm being honest, I didn't think he had even seen Emily's show even though we had been on air since the 13th of November.

Emily took her plate over to the couch to make way for him to sit across from me at the breakfast bar.

"I can't believe how well you've done," he said, whilst looking around.

"Timing, Sooty," I said, shrugging my shoulders. "And Emily of course."

He then went on to tell me about him speaking to Libby less than half an hour ago as regards both Nubeon and the fly-on-the-wall documentary.

"I gave you the permeations of what could happen when I put forward the idea," I said. "I even advised you to get your house in order before the cameras started rolling. You've been around the block enough times to know what happens when you play with fire."

He glanced me a nod.

"Come on Sooty – you've had a go at it, now do the right thing and bugger it off," I told him. "You're better than all this."

He gave me another nod and I knew then that he was angling for me to re advertise a 'situation vacant', however he wasn't getting it that frigging easy.

"Mia and Zooey have missed you," I told him. "They've been here quite a bit."

"I have them," he said. "I've missed yours as well."

"Well, you aren't seeing them again – we've only just got Jamie to stop saying 'summat'."

Emily never said anything but I knew that she wanted me to say something, therefore I said it. "Libby would have you back tomorrow," I told him.

"Yeh, right," he quipped.

"Dump the actress and the job and go back to your wife," I said.

"The actress?" he said. "That's been done since Thursday."

Mmm, I didn't know that, I thought.

"I saw you on Jonathan Ross," he told me.

I knew exactly what he meant by that. Jonathan had a brief from his producer to inquire into my personal life, and I don't just mean Emily and Jeanette, but what all the tabloids were writing about me, with my newfound financial status causing something of a stir in certain circles – mainly Sooty and Lib's.

"I read somewhere that you are earning around a million pounds a week," Jonathan had said.

"Your figures are slightly out, but we do okay," I had replied – and remember Emily's mum and dad and all her other family were watching this.

"So is it you who actually owns The Warehouse and all the studios and offices?" he had asked.

"I do at the moment," I had replied, "However, come New Year LMJ Media will own it."

"So you've sold The Warehouse to the company that you own?" he had asked. "Could I ask how that works?"

"They will own the property and I will be paid eleven million pounds over a period of a year," I had replied.

"Are you comfortable talking about money?" he had asked.

"I'm comfortable talking about any subject that I'm familiar with," I'd told him. "However football is my passion."

Sooty then referred to the self-same questions before he asked me one.

"I get paid by ITV and LMJ," I told him. "If you are after a job, you'd be working for ITV Seven through LMJ as we bill them on a cost-plus – your contract would tie in with that, and not the other programming."

"How come you've got so clued up all of a sudden," he asked.

"I've always been clued up," I smiled. "It's just that you always wanted the reins of the financial stuff with me left to my own devices."

"Yeh, but you never offered any ideas," he said.

"Yeh, because it's frigging boring."

"So what job would I have?" he asked.

"To be honest Sooty, I've not thought of it as such; however, I will need a sort of general manager for ITV Seven."

"And I'd report to you?" he asked.

"Something like that," I replied, "But Abi would be your direct boss."

That he didn't like, nor the fact that Annie Dixon and Jaime Hudson would outrank him as financial and studio directors respectively – Not that he actually knew who they were, however.

"It's a great way of getting back into sport and getting your life back on track," I told him. "And you've already got plenty of money,"

"Not as much as you, I haven't," he said.

"Well, that's a first then," I laughed.

At around 8:00pm he left and I got M to tip the wink to Libby by way of a phone call who thanked her before she was passed over to me, where I got the one hundred thousand dollar question of what kind of money I'd offered him.

In between the 'Sooty and Clean Sweep Show', Emily's mum had called and put their iPhones on Facetime so she could see her grandkids, the tree and of course her daughter, who nine months ago was pregnant, estranged from her husband and without a job and driving back home to their semi' in Birkenhead. And I thought my life had changed!

The kids were all getting excited, bar Sammy, as his head hit the feather as soon as we had got in, obviously trying to catch up on some beauty sleep before the clock struck 4:30am and he could bawl out his orders and have us all racing around after him. I wasn't wrong either, as at 4:26am the main man sprang into life, and it was I who he'd summoned for execution, by the way of one heavily-soiled nappy. Strangely I'd not dropped off until late as I'd had an effervescent wife sitting cross-legged on the bed immediately after the relatively new rule number one had been executed, and rattling on about the White Lion label amongst other things, and how did I rate Ross Bain of all people – as a person? He was a talented 23-year-old kid with the world at his feet and if he took his chance and looked after what he'd got, then he could have everything. However, I hadn't put my ex-wife into the fucking getting everything category.

"He's bonkers for her," Emily told me.

"Yeh, he was bonkers for Karen Beckley until she gave him a kick in the bollocks for diddling Sasha," I recalled before bringing up a question. "So where's Monty Python in all this secret little soap opera?"

"She told him that she wants time apart," she said.

"I bet that took some of the shine off Brentford's three-two win at Cardiff," I said.

Therefore whilst I applied Sudocream to Sammy's arse, my thoughts were on his underhanded fairy godmother who had obviously been waving more than her magic wand. I didn't mind Ross, but his lifestyle was not something that I'd want my kids involved in. Was I bothered that Jeanette could become his next thing? Not really, as I now saw her as a nagging friend or sister as opposed to a nagging ex-wife.

"What do you reckon?" I asked the whining lump of misery as I rammed the bottle in his chops before I told him to "steady on" as he was gulping at it as though he'd had ten days in the Sahara on the back of a camel.

Emily surfaced at 5:15am and told me she hadn't heard me get up, which was a great stinking fib as I saw her quickly shut her eyes after I'd opened mine and I pulled her up on it so much so, she offset it – or she thought she'd offset it by asking my thoughts on Sanchez's role in the team now that Giroud was back firing on all cylinders.

"Do you think I'm daft?" I asked.

"No," she smiled as she kicked up the percolator. "I was just wondering."

"No, you weren't – you were being deflective," I told her. "And don't think I've not noticed that this is becoming a regular habit – You might be cute, but you're getting dead sneaky."

"You still love me though?" she smiled.

"Not when I was chiselling shite from around his arse half an hour ago I didn't," I winked.

She plonked herself at the side of me and gave me a hug and told me that she was due on.

"Due on what?" I asked, as I tried ripping the empty bottle out of Herbert's mouth even though he was clinging on to it like some dog on a bone.

"On, on," she said.

"Uh right," I said. "Something to look forward to in nine months' time I suppose."

"I'll mark it on the calendar, eh?" she smiled.

"Yeh, first of September 2015 – cancel rest of life," I said.

"Oh, that's terrible," she said.

"Don't worry I'll keep my fingers crossed for you."

"There's loads of text messages flashing up on your phone," she said.

"Probably condolences," I winked.

"I do love you, yer know."

I did know, as I got told it all the time.

My lad descended on us a couple of hours later, still adamant that the presents under the tree seemed quite a lot to be transported via sleigh to Birkenhead. He also appeared quite concerned as regards the time element as he mentioned both the traffic and the time it took to drive up the M6, along with the fact he has to drop off toys to a billion other kids, so much so I thought he was becoming a bit stressed.

"Why do you think nobody ever sees him?" I asked my lad.

"Because he's not real?" came his quick-fire reply.

"No," I lied. "It's because he's that quick, and of course he's a bit magic."

"Like Harry Potter?"

"If you like," I said.

"You called Harry Potter a gimpy four-eyed turd," my lad eloquently reminded me.

"Yeh, that's because the DVD player got jammed while he was in it and it took me over an hour to get him out as you were kicking off that you wanted to watch something else."

"Does he really support Stoke City?" he asked.

"Who?"

"Harry Potter."

"Definitely," I lied.

I dropped both kids off at their mum's and told her of my lad's concern regarding his presents, so much so he was debating whether or not I should just put them all in a van and drive them up there myself and not have to rely on Santa. She gave me a smile and a big hug, which I thought strange, and then told me that they would be going up to Bakewell around tea time.

"Well, drive carefully," I said.

On getting back to the house M was in 'mad mode' and cleaning everything in sight as Mr. Man in a frigging Van had just left, and as that was the case, there were pine needles everywhere. As for Herbert – he was chewing at his dummy before he copped sight of me and then spat it out.

"What – you think I'm going to pick it up for you?" I asked.

"He's getting dead manipulative," Emily noted.

"How do you mean getting?"

"Libby says he's getting right like you," she smiled.

"Well so long as he not like her, he'll be fine," I said doing my bit to help with the housework by picking up his dummy and flicking on Sky Sports.

"Are we going up in your car or mine?" she asked.

"We'll not get in mine for all the shite that you're on about taking up," I said.

"We need to be up by four because we've got a delivery from Tesco's due," she said. "My mam's already got the turkey and the goose."

ITV's head of sport rang me to ask if I could get him a few tickets for the QPR game while I was loading up M's Range Rover.

"What am I now – your tout?" I said.

He wanted around five and I told him I'd get Stevie Kell to sort it, before he told me that the ratings had come in for the Reality behind The Warehouse programme, which I'd obviously watched a billion times before, but not while it had actually been on TV.

"Twenty million," he said.

"What, for that thing?" I asked.

"I'd been a bit preoccupied with M's perfect Christmas, Sooty's love life, worried kids and baby-making in that I hadn't looked for any feedback, although there were a few text messages that suggested that it was actually nice viewing.

"They are all on about it," he said.

I got in the house and told Emily what he had said, which was met with a bit of a sad expression.

"I forgot it was on," she said.

"It's on my Dropbox," I told her. "I'll cut a DVD if you want."

"It's not the same though," she said.

"How do you work that one out?"

"It's not telly for one," she said, nudging me before putting a coat and bonnet on Herbert, which I have to say he definitely didn't like.

431

"Let me put it on," she said. "Yer head will get cold if I don't."

It was great seeing how rigid he went and the faces he pulled when he didn't want to do something.

"If you put that thing on me I'd be dead pissed off," I told her.

The journey up the M6 was on par with the last million journeys up there; however M putting some carols on and listening to the radio was quite nice, so much so that Herbert never groaned or grizzled throughout the journey, although he did remove his hat and spit out his pipe a few times.

On arriving at Hamilton Square, something happened that made me realise exactly who I was and more to the point in what I had. Mike had met the van driver and put all the presents around the tree for us, but what was to put a lump in my throat was that young Stuart was with his dad and that being the case when I got out of the car he raced up to me an gave me the hug of all hugs before emotion took over and he began crying.

"What's up with you?" I asked.

The motorbike was what was up with him. And his dad. And his mum when I eventually saw her. Everyone likes presents and even more so big presents; however, the easiest thing to do when you have money is to stick some in a card, however there's very little thought that goes into that, and even less thought when the recipient is spending it. Thought had gone into every present that we had bought, but more so with Stuart.

"He's washed it twice already," smiled Mike.

"You can ride it if you like," I said.

"It's not insured and I haven't got a helmet," he said, before his big sister threw him a present and said, "Catch".

It was insured, and he'd done his crash-course in scootering – or Ross Bain's younger brother had rather, and that being the case I watched him fire it up and do a couple of laps around the Square and reminded him of both the trust I had in him and the responsibility to himself. "Just be careful on it," I said.

The goose and turkey had made its way around as had Bill and Edie, and the sight I was soon to see put another lump in my throat whilst I watched M, her mum, grandma and young Lucy in the huge kitchen in the basement baking. I had never had that before, but I had it now and whereas young Stuart had shown me true emotion, I was feeling exactly the same.

"'You alright, love?" M inquired.

I nodded as she came over, pecked me on the lips and got flour on my face – again, before asking me to hang a huge flat screen TV that had been delivered a few days ago so she could see the show she'd missed the night before.

Mike had already put the bracket up so it was only a ten-minute job to hang the thing – that was if you happened to have been built like frigging Dolph Lundgren, as it weighed a ton. After forty minutes of sweat and toil it was done and I was just glad a download from Dropbox and cutting a DVD didn't take that long as my career would have certainly been quite different.

I didn't watch the show with her family as I was busy dealing with a Tesco's driver and van who refused to park outside the side door as we were on a junction, but I certainly heard the laughter.

"Somebody sounds happy," I said, as I carted the twenty-eighth box of shopping into the house and which took as long as it did to put up the TV. I had never worked this hard on a Christmas Eve and I let that be known, so much so that I was poured a Chardonnay and told to go put my feet up and watch TV in the lounge. Oh yeh, and change Sammy as he had shit himself again. I delegated the last job to Mike who had just come back from rehousing Giroud and Arteta over at theirs and had got bitten in the process.

"That Giroud is a bit keen," he said. "The little bugger was hanging from my lip."

"What – you were kissing him?"

"Yeh – I'll not bloody do it again," he said.

I never thought Mike would be the type of guy to kiss a man-ferret, although I could see him kissing Steve Mungall or Jason Koumas, knowing the way he talks about them both.

Hamilton Square was supposed to be our house, however that Christmas Eve there was never less than ten people in it, and whilst all the in-and-outing was happening, the reporter from the *Liverpool Echo* knocked on the door and asked if I had five minutes to spare, so much so he spent thirty minutes talking to me and two hours talking to Bill and Mike on a variety of subjects ranging from me and Emily to Liverpool and Everton or in Mike's case, Tranmere Rovers.

The house became empty at around 10:00pm give or take a minute, and Emily slumped at the side of me and suggested a bit of 'yer-knowing'.

"I yer-knowed you last night," I said. "And this morning."

"So you can yer-know me again," she replied. "I like being yer-knowed."

"I know you do – it's getting to be a full-time job just recently – even though we weren't supposed to be trying for Herbert a sister."

"I want her to have blonde hair and blue eyes," she said.

"I'm Lee Janes, not Josef frigging Mengele."

That raised a giggle but she ended up getting what she wanted, that was apart from her coming back from the bathroom a little bit upset. She wasn't pregnant.

"Will you tell me what you told me again," she asked.

"You will get pregnant and Sammy will have a sister," I said, whilst she cuddled up to me in bed.

"Promise?"

"Have I ever let you down?"

She shook her head whilst looking at me. "It's been mad today, hasn't it?"

"Wait until tomorrow," I winked. "It'll be even madder."

Sammy was up on the dot and wasted no time in complaining that Father Christmas hadn't left him much.

"He's too young to notice, plus he's got loads of stuff already," his mum said.

He obviously thought different as he moaned like hell as none of his bottles were ready or in the right place.

"Look," I told him. "It's a different house and I haven't got a sequence going yet."

I then went on to explain that it can be the same with new players at football clubs.

"Who are you talking to?" asked Emily, as she came down into the kitchen just as misery guts slung the rusk on the floor that I'd been trying to placate him with.

"Herbert – and I can't find the milk."

"Well, we definitely brought it as I fed him yesterday," she said.

"Yeh but there's like a million cupboards and it's like trying to find a needle in a haystack," I told her, more or less immediately before she found it.

"That can be the cupboard for the baby – or babies once you get your act together," she said.

"I'm starting to feel a bit dirty and used," I lied.

"Well, get used to it as I'm upping your programme to two dates a night," she said.

"Thanks for the notice."

"Anyway, where's my present?" she asked.

"You had it the other day – those shoes," I replied.

"No I didn't – I saw you sneaking them other presents in the house," she grinned.

I argued my case, but even so five minutes later she was ripping them open, which was greeted by the main reason I fell in love with her – her smile.

"I thought I couldn't go wrong with cheap imitation jewellery," I said. "Thirteen quid from Select."

"I love it when you lie to me," she said as I got a nice kiss and a cuddle from her. "And thank you so much, they are lovely."

"Okay then, you fat horrible cow," I lied, "where's mine?"

This was to be reminiscent of the time I handed her her engagement ring as she pulled a present from under the tree and passed it me and then sat cross-legged on the wooden floor whilst watching me open it. "I hope you like it," she said.

She had outshone my present of a pair of diamond earrings by buying me a watch; however this was a bit special. Not just because of the fact that it was an expensive watch, but more to do with the fact of how she bought it. The money I earned I considered was ours and never just mine, it was the same with Emily. We worked as a team, however when Emily finally got paid out from the sale of her house, part of the team told a white lie in how much she had got after it had been transferred into our account. She had kept back a chunk of change to buy me a watch, as the one I had was absolutely nothing compared to this.

"It should fit as I measured it against your other," she said.

"And you bought this me from your house money?" I asked.

She nodded her confirmation.

"It's really nice," I said.

"It's to say thank you for all the nice things you do."

One of the nice things I did drove into the Square a few minutes later and was hammering at the door. "Mam says do you want any breakfast, as she's got the bacon on?" said Stuart.

This was to be a Christmas like no other and a Christmas Day fry-up at 7:30am was something else. Ten minutes later we were over at Mike and Sil's and it was mad – with Sammy in awe of everything around him, which got me thinking that – *maybe part of the reason he was such a miserable kid, was that with just me and his mum it was, maybe just a little bit too quiet for him.*

Sil' made it obvious that she was keeping tabs on her daughter and her menstrual cycle as much as her husband was keeping tabs on his son and his motorcycle.

"Don't worry love, just enjoy the fun trying," she told her.

We sat around the table, as we always did and I thought it was fantastic. Emily never ever sat on her own chair, but shared mine or sat on my knee and as I have often said, at times I actually wondered if she was trying to climb inside me, so much was the affection that she showed.

We left them after an hour although we were minus Sammy, his granny obviously disguising the fact that she wanted more activity on the 'trying to give her a granddaughter front', with her daughter whispering to me, "I think my mam wants you to put the goose in the oven."

I had to admit that being on The Wirral was something else. I loved the vibrancy of London and the fact that you could get anything at any time, which I suppose you could over the river in Liverpool, but the people here were what made it so special, and I was married to the best one of them all. I watched her in between checking both ovens whilst running up a flight of stairs and meticulously setting the table in the huge dining room. Me? I was tasked with peeling a billion sprouts, which I knew was a pointless task, as I for one wasn't that keen, but did I mind? Nope.

I'd had the kids phone me up to inquire whether Father Christmas had been, and Emily had made sure that her iPhone relayed them the fact that he had. "Granny Sil' and Granddad Mike have got you quite a few as well," she had told them.

That wasn't a lie, as a right pile of them had been deposited in the room last night, which was on par with the great pile of ironing I shut the door on before we left London.

It was thought that Bill and Edie would renege on their decision of dinner at the house – by everyone else but me that is, and as I thought they were the first round, with Edie immediately getting involved down in the kitchen.

As with Emily, I could listen to her grandfather talk all day. Some people are like that, in that nothing they say can ever bore you.

"Our Sil' says you and our M are trying for another young 'un?" he smiled.

I told him that I wasn't that fussed on the 'saying that we were trying' bit and told him that if it happened, it happened, and anything that came out of it would be more than welcome.

"Edie would love a girl," he winked.

"So would your Sil'," I said.

"When our M was a little 'un Edie pushed her for miles in her pushchair," he said. "The most beautiful girl you could have ever wished for."

I smiled at his comment before passing one of my own. "She still is."

"We are both so happy that she has found what she was looking for," he said. "We do all love her a lot."

"I know," I said, feeling slightly emotional. "And so do I."

I was just glad Mike, Sil' and Lucy had arrived as I was starting to well up a bit.

"Where's our Stuart?" I asked them.

"Showing his bike off down at Paige's," Mike replied.

As a gesture, I asked both father and grandfather to cut both birds, as I knew that's what they did at their homes year upon year.

"Don't you want to cut them yourself, Lee?" asked Bill.

"No, I'd prefer you both to do it. I'll have plenty of time to do that when our kids get older."

Dinner was brilliant as was the bit of present-opening beforehand.

Chapter 35

Jeanette's Tales – Take 13

My first Christmas with Lee was absolutely fantastic and was like a fairy tale. If you wanted fun he gave it you by the bucket load; however my last Christmas was one of the lowest points in my life, so much so I possessed thoughts I never knew I could have, and it was only the kids that kept me going. I had thrown him out a few days prior. He had hurt me and now it was his turn to be hurt. There was no way that he was ever coming back into my life. I made a point of never crying in front of him, and after he left I went through every emotion possible.

"Is Dad coming back?" Harmony had asked.

How do you answer a question like that?

I'd done the screaming and shouting and hurled a few things at him and he was gone.

"Tell me," I'd said. "Tell me the truth, I want to know how many and who they all are."

He had sat there and told me each and every one. I had asked why? And how could he do this to me? And he told me the truth, and it hurt, therefore I hurt him.

"Don't think you're getting access to the kids, because you're not," I'd screamed.

I wouldn't pick up his calls nor answer the door. I made the point of never letting him back into my life. It would be a lie to say that Lee rarely showed emotion, as he did, however outside of Arsenal he was certainly never the screaming or shouting type. I wanted a response – I always wanted a response, however when I screamed and shouted he just stood there and took it.

I kept him away from the kids for a couple of weeks before he told me that him being denied access wasn't right and if we didn't speak though a counsellor or mediation or whatever he would force the issue through his lawyers.

"Please don't make me do it, Jeanette," he had said.

I still remember it as though it was yesterday and I sat in mediation with him with the sole intention of giving him nothing; however, he put all his cards on the table and told the woman doing the mediation that he was willing to pay all my bills and make sure both Harmony and Jamie were very well-provided for.

"Whatever has gone between us," he had said, "is between us. I will not have the kids go without as they are everything to me."

The woman doing the mediation told me afterwards that she had never seen anyone like him before and that his brutal honesty was quite refreshing, so much so if I hadn't have been there I'm sure that she would have possibly made a play for him. I walked out into the street that afternoon knowing that I would be financially secure and free of a man that I had loved like no other, and now here I was driving down the M56 on a Christmas night and over to his and his wife's new house in Liverpool along with two very excited kids. Twelve months on and I was driving over to see the man that I had thrown out. My mother couldn't understand, yet strangely my dad could. Paul had gone absolutely ape shit last night as I had told him about my plans, which were plans that didn't really include him. He obviously blamed Ross, but he wasn't the reason, he was just a guy that had helped give me a bit of a reality check to who I really was. As for Ross? Did I want him? Maybe, but certainly not like he wanted me.

I pulled up at some traffic lights and the kids pointed to the huge black door on what was a house that wouldn't have looked out of place in London or Edinburgh. I indicated and parked up the car and looked up at the bright lights which emanated from each and every window of the property. Lee came out and walked across to the car to greet us and both kids were absolutely ecstatic as he picked them both up and gave them a hug before turning his attention to me. "Where's Paul?" he asked.

"Long story," I replied.

I walked inside the house to be met by M, who wasted no time at all in giving me a hug and relieving me of my coat and handbag and pouring me a drink as both kids shot into a room to be met by what was a mountain of presents.

"Crikey, I'll never get that lot home," I said.

"Don't worry, my dad will take them down," M smiled.

There was Christmas wrapping paper everywhere as both kids read the tags and opened present after present after present after present and whilst this was going on M gave me mine.

"What's this?" I asked.

"Open it," she said, therefore I did.

It was lovely and I thanked her for it.

"I've not got you anything," I said.

"Yeh yer have," she smiled. "You're all here."

I spent the whole of Christmas night in their company with both Lee and M telling me to just treat the house as it was my home, however as it got later and later I knew that there would be something that I certainly wouldn't like, and that thing would be bedtime.

M had already given me a guided tour and I had even been in both kids' bedrooms whilst Lee had tucked them in, with Jamie being rather insistent that the skeleton, who he called Mertesacker, would sleep with him.

"What did you buy him that thing for?" I asked.

"He wanted one after he had watched an old DVD and M had told him about the different bones as part of their make-up," Lee said.

"Mam, did you know that bit is the sternum," Jamie had told me. "That holds his ribs together."

Twelve months ago he could barely read, now he had a book or a comic in his hand every day and he was always inquiring about one thing or another, and it wasn't so much his dad who was helping him, it was M.

"He's a really bright lad," she had said.

She had also said the same of Harmony, who absolutely loved her, so much so at times it made me feel quite inadequate in that they quite often spoke of things that I had little or no knowledge of.

Lee went to bed around 11:00pm whilst M and I drank wine and chatted about a whole range of subjects – the kids, mainly, but she did inquire to how I was feeling as regards the Paul and Ross thing and she hoped that I wouldn't feel uncomfortable come bedtime. Paul and Ross were the last thing on my mind, as yes, I felt uncomfortable knowing that I'd not only be in the same house as my ex-husband and his new wife, I'd be in the bedroom opposite to theirs, knowing full well that she wanted nothing more than to get another baby.

"I do a bit," I told her.

She told me she understood, but I don't think she did. Well, if she did, she went a strange way about showing it as there was an awful of noise from across the landing on her closing the bedroom door.

I got up early next day and had a bit of a nosy around the house and walked into the kitchen to find Lee in a pair of grey joggers and sweatshirt talking to Sammy. "See, your Auntie Jeanette's come to see you," he said.

I had got to Liverpool fairly late so I had just popped my head in his bedroom to see him asleep in his cot, however now post-kiss on the cheek from my ex-husband I was being handed him while he poured me a coffee.

"M still in bed?" I asked.

"Nah, she's took the kids round to see Giroud and Arteta," he replied.

"What, the ferrets are up here?"

442

"Yeh, Mike built them a hutch at theirs," he said. "You want to see it – It's massive."

Another thing was bugging me was that it wasn't even 7:45am – on Boxing Day and they were all up and about.

"What time did you all get up?" I asked.

"Me – about five o'clock with Sammy and M and the kids about an hour later."

"Six o'clock?"

"About that," he said. "They'd been in with me and M since three – Mertesacker had scared Jamie a bit, when he woke up."

"So do they get in with you regularly?" I inquired.

"No, not really," he said. "He's just in a strange house and he was a bit scared."

I should have told them that the bloody skeleton on wheels had scared me, I thought.

I looked at little Sammy smiling back up at me and without thinking brought up the subject of the pre-planned 'new addition' leaving out the fact that they were a bit too noisy for my liking.

"It's not pre-planning Jeanette, more if it happens, it happens," he told me. "However, saying that there is a bit of pressure being put on us by Sil' and Edie – and on me by M."

That last bit pissed me off straight away.

"How do you mean, M?"

"She wants the baby."

"What, and you don't?" I asked.

"I would have preferred to have waited a bit until I knew I was financially secure," he said. "M knows that."

"How secure do you want to be?" I asked. "You told loads of viewers on the Jonathan Ross Show that you were earning millions and that you were due another eleven next year, plus the lump you got for the old business and what ITV pay you."

"Frigging hell Jeanette – you're starting to sound like Libby," he said.

He was right, I was.

I took Sammy up into the room where all the presents were and which had been totally tidied up. The place was spotless to the point I thought that they'd either had the cleaners in through the night or that she had some compulsive cleaning disorder. I still couldn't believe how early they all got up.

M and the kids came back from her parents and she immediately made a fuss over me. I had just had over an hour on my own with her husband and there was no envy nor insecurity. If it had have been me I would have been climbing the walls, but with her – nothing.

Chapter 36

Fly on the Wall

The Queen & Pistol's aggressive bass and tub-thumping rhythm set the introduction for the fly-on-the-wall documentary that would bring down Nubeon. Human trafficking, lies and deceit were the foundations from how it had been constructed. One of its top actresses, Christiana Vai explained to reporter Jeanette Janes how it all worked, which was echoed by another six actresses including Sooty's Rumanian ex-girlfriend.

The camera-work was unique, the music spellbinding and Nubeon's owner – nothing more than a suntanned, bling-wearing ponce.

Our undercover reporter Sinead McAnenny sat amongst the girls being auditioned and during short clips of her with another actress as part of the audition she explained what the director wanted her to do. It was pure journalistic dynamite, and one of ITV 7's new anchors showed the world exactly who she was. Beautiful, intellectual, but obviously leaving out the fact that she was sex mad. "They treat the girls terribly," she explained into the camera. "The whole setup is morally very, very wrong."

She then went on to explain that the owner is offered girl upon girl and that false promises are made in that they are lied to about exactly what they will be doing.

"It was exactly the same with me," added Sinead. "I passed the audition and was cast alongside of one of the male actors and was shouted and screamed at through direction before I was prodded and poked around with by what was some essentially some dirty old man."

Obviously she never told them that she'd actually quite enjoyed it and that she had gone out on a date with him, but there you go. This was supposed to be hard-hitting and not a re-run of the 'Darling Buds of May' with Del Trotter and his fat wife.

The papers were full of it the next day and Sinead was the real star. 'The ITV 7 girl – Sinead McAnenny goes undercover to lift the lid on female exploitation and human trafficking'.

There were camera's everywhere when I got into work and Sinead's no holds barred question-and-answer session was really something else. "So how far did you actually go?" Jeanette had asked her.

"It was supposed to be simulated sex," she replied, "However it was anything but."

The phones were red hot and ITV were very pleased as the attention this documentary had was unbelievable, however I now had Mike on the phone.

"Did our Stuart camera all that lot?"

"And Jonathan," I replied.

He was quiet, with my initial thought being that he was a bit narked with me.

"So what do you think about all this?" he asked.

"I think your son has done a wonderful job in helping bring what is quintessentially a criminal empire that exploits young girls, such as his girlfriend, to light and I would hope that you and his mum are very proud of him," I said – obviously keeping my fingers crossed that he'd fall for that.

Both Jeanette and Sinead posed for the camera and had numerous questions thrown at them one of which was a personal one to my ex.

"There's a rumour going around that you are seeing Ross Bain of the Queen & Pistol indie band," said one reporter.

"I met him through my work at The Warehouse and I was invited to a gig at The Garage in Highbury, but apart from that he's just someone I know from the job I do," she said.

That convinced me as much as it convinced them and on the same reporter pulling Ross Bain up on it he had a juicy story. 'Sex Pistol and his Queen – Ross Bain dating TV presenter Jeanette Janes'.

However, what was going to happen shocked me – not as much as Queens Park Rangers' Nedum Onuoha going to ground like some flaccid daffodil after Olivier Giroud stuck his face in the Nigerians, which led me to the conclusion that either moving to Manchester had softened him up – or that if that if he is a prime example of a 6'2 Nigerian then the Italians could quite easily relive their glories of 1936 and quite possibly have a new country to invade.

"Kate?" I asked on answering my phone. It was Jeanette's mum.

"I'm sorry to bother you, but I'm a bit concerned about our Jeanette."

Sorry to bother me? She had never been sorry to bother me before, so why now? And what was she concerned about Jeanette for?

"It says in the paper that this Ross Bain fellow is twenty-three," she said.

"He is," I replied. "He's a very talented lad."

"Can't you stop it?" she asked.

"Jeanette's thirty-two," I said, "And she's also her own woman and she listens to me about as much as you did."

"What happened with Paul?" was her next question.

"I don't really know, Kate," I replied. "You should really ask Jeanette as I feel a bit uncomfortable talking about her behind her back."

"You didn't feel uncomfortable doing other things behind her back," she argued.

Why do I always leave myself open to this? I thought, and after the conversation I rang Jeanette.

"Your mum has just phoned me in regards to Mr. Queen and Pistol."

"You are joking?" she replied.

No, I wasn't and I relayed all the questions that had been thrown at me during the ten minute Q&A session.

"So what do you really think?" she asked.

"Paul was very good with the kids and with you," I said. "Outside of those two things you are your own person and it has got nothing to do with me."

"And you told her that?" she asked.

"I did."

There was a bit on quiet at the other end of the phone – well, for a few seconds anyway.

"I can't believe she's actually gone and phoned you," she said.

I couldn't believe it as much as the next phone call I had – this time from 'Jilted frigging John'.

"I'm sorry Paul, I'm no agony aunt," I said. "This is between you two – or three rather."

However what would happen later on that week was really strange as the Queen & Pistol were recording part of a new album for the White Lion Label and during a half-hour intermission they were chatting with studio director Jaime Hudson who wanted them in Temporary Studio 5 for a photo shoot when Paul came marching into the studios and floored Ross, before apologising to everyone and then walking straight back out.

"Did that really happen or did I imagine it?" I asked Chris from make-up.

Ross obviously thought it did, as it had been an absolutely awesome smack in the mouth and he let us know exactly how much it hurt and that being the case he had Mr. Make Up artist all in a flutter. "Oo it was really nasty, that was," said Chris in his ever so effeminate voice, whilst the rest of the band did a bit of sniggering.

I then let Jeanette know that Monty Python had just walloped the new love of her life, but not before Karen asked me if we'd caught it on camera. It was twice in as many weeks that he'd hit the deck after being on the receiving end of both a size six stiletto and a knuckle sandwich.

"You are joking?" asked a rather aghast Jeanette when I told her.

She had begun saying this quite a bit.

"Yeh a smack in the mouth," I said, absolutely loving it. "If he pisses you off, you'll definitely be able to give him a clout as he went down easier than Emmanuel Eboue."

Georgia Clayton brought me part of the stash of hate mail that ITV had sent me over as regards the fly-on-the-wall documentary.

"Did we get any nice letters?" I asked.

"Yeh, they were all for Sinead."

On another note we were beginning to gear up for the start of ITV 7 and Les Crang was getting a bit nervous as that was the fifth time this morning he'd gone to the toilet.

"You got a bird in there?" I asked.

"No, I had a Cornish Pasty from the chuck wagon outside and I reckon it was off," he replied.

"Off – off where?" I asked.

"Off – out of date."

Sooty had been due to start at The Warehouse on Monday the 29th, however he had been helping detectives from the Metropolitan Police with their inquiries and had therefore been locked up for a couple of days. I had told them that I thought he was the real brains behind the operation and that that suntanned pervert from Cheshunt was his stool pigeon. He wasn't really – it was a white lie. Sooty had just made sure none of the titles they shot ended up as part of the free porn streams on the net as well as seeking out new avenues for sales.

He finally rolled into The Warehouse a day late and was a bit taken aback at the surroundings he was in. I gave him a guided tour, explained how everything worked and took him into my shit tip of an office where any impression I had initially made was firmly flushed down the pan, and it was

449

then I formally offered him a three-year contract as general manager of ITV 7.

"No shagging the staff or arguing the toss with me and a hundred grand a year," I said.

"I was on four' at our last company," he said.

"Yeh and you fucking sold it," I said.

He signed the contract and I introduced him to Les Crang who introduced him to everyone in the team. We were ready to go.

...

Chapter 37

Jeanette's Tales – Take 14

I walked into The Garage that night and there he was as bold as brass, looking like a cross between Jon Sammels, the player that Lee did that documentary on and Stevie Marriott of the Small Faces. He'd had everybody applauding after each and every song. At the start of the show he appeared very laid back, however as it went on he became a real live wire. He was bloody brilliant.

I'd gone with both Abi and her partner Ronnie, the latter who was a really lovely girl but whose name was really Liza Biggs – so you can see how she got her nickname! We all thought they were great and a reporter from the *London Evening Standard* took a few photographs of us with the band themselves, one of which – of just Ross and myself – would eventually make its way into *Hello magazine*.

We had seen quite a lot of each other; however, our respective ideas of a relationship were completely different and as such he was pushing for the status quo to be broken and that being the case he asked afterwards if he could stay over. I told him that I thought that it wouldn't be a good idea and that we should get to know each other a little better first, which he obviously said, by him staying over we most definitely would.

I got home only to find Paul at my door, who I let in and who I ended up having a long drawn-out conversation with, which concluded with the fact that I didn't want him in my life anymore. And that was that – our relationship was ended.

I phoned M early next day, firstly to ask about the kids and secondly for someone to chat to. As it happened, Lee had been up and out early as the launch of ITV 7 was getting closer and there were lots of loose ends that still needed tying up.

"I'm a bit worried about him," M told me. "He's been complaining about his eyes again, so much so we went to the hospital last night."

That didn't sit with me very well, especially as while they had been watching over my daughter, son and godson, I had been out having a good time.

"Is he okay?" I asked.

"He has a leakage behind his right eye that's not quite bad enough for laser surgery and he needs glasses," she said. "He's also been complaining about having some really bad headaches."

Lee was never one for complaining about his health so I knew it must have been bad, and as M sounded extremely concerned, I told her that I'd be round in ten minutes.

I got there to find my two eating toast and marmalade and sat in front of the big TV whilst little Sammy was sat in his chair watching their every movement. As for his mum? She was laughing whilst talking on the phone to his dad.

"Dad's got to wear glasses," said Harmony.

"Only for work though," I said, before smiling over at M.

"Look in that," M said rather excitedly pointing to some Jiffy bags on the breakfast bar.

I opened one of the bags only to see some magazine, with what looked like a drawing – of Lee and M – I think – on the front cover – with M knelt on a sofa similar to the one I'd picked that was in one of the studios with a rather evil and manipulative looking Lee grasping at her necklace.

"What's this?" I asked.

"Uh, not that," M said. "The other jiffy bag. That's what ITV's head of sport commissioned some artist to do for the front cover of some internal magazine."

"It's a bit raunchy," I noted.

"Yeh – I know," she said. "Lee thinks its ace."

He might have, but I bloody didn't.

I then opened the correct Jiffy bag to see mine and M's face on a box set DVD titled 'ITV Sessions – The North London Sound'. I had seen us both on TV but it seemed very strange seeing us as part of a DVD collection.

"It's all happening, isn't it?" she smiled as she got off the phone.

"How is he?" I asked.

"A bit narked as he's had to go into work," she replied whilst at the same time pouring me a coffee.

"It's definitely over with me and Paul," I told her.

"And you and Ross?" she inquired.

"I think that is definitely on," I said, whilst checking the contents of the DVD but getting slightly side-tracked by the flipping ITV brochure. I then told her about last night and the conversation that I'd firstly had with Ross and then Paul. M was never overly opinionated, and just listened.

The kids had never met Ross and to be honest, I didn't really want them to until I knew him a little bit better; however that statement is yet another one of those bloody double-edged swords, as to know him better I had to see him, and as it was me who had the kids – that was the problem. There was another problem in that Paul's sister Chrissy often looked after them, and now that avenue would be certainly be closed. And with Libby concentrating on trying to make a go of it with Sooty, all I had was Lee and M, and it would be highly doubtful that my ex would undertake babysitting duties whilst I appeared to be making a fool of myself by chasing around after a man nine years my junior.

"I'm always here for you," M smiled.

It was as though some telepathy existed, whereby she knew exactly what I was thinking.

453

"Do you think I'm making a mistake?" I asked her.

"We all liked Paul, but it's not us who was with him – it was you," she said. "If Paul would have been the one you would have taken it to the next level as a kind of natural progression, but you didn't, and that being the case he obviously wasn't."

She made everything sound so very straightforward.

"What about Ross?" I asked her.

"He's both attractive and talented," she smiled, "But from what I've seen of him he'd not be someone that I'd like to pin my hopes on – Then again, I've made loads of rubbish decisions, so I'm hardly the best person to offer any advice."

I knew she was right, but it was something that I intended having a go at, not at least for the excitement factor, something that my employers would be completely trying to snuff out as when I got over to the Chelsea Bridge store I found out that I was being moved to the Lewisham Way store in New Cross – and on a permanent basis. This move had Paul written all over it. A 12-mile round trip over to south London with some really unsociable hours thrown in for good measure. When I finally got him to pick up his phone I went ballistic with him and ended up getting it back in Spades. "You'll be doing one day a week at the Lordship Lane store in Dulwich as well," he said.

I was a right miserable cow for the rest of the day, which was compounded further when I went out to my car and found it had been clamped and that's when I hit the dial on the Batphone.

"Calm down Jeanette," Lee told me. "Where are you?"

"Outside The Flower of Kent pub in New Cross," I told him. "I'm not familiar with the area so I parked my car outside some workplace on Florence Road and I've been clamped."

Within thirty minutes Lee pulled up outside the pub, and by that time I was a gibbering wreck and god knows what he thought as it all came out. His solution was simple, however. "Pack the frigging job in," he said.

I sat in his car whilst he paid the fee over the phone to have the car unclamped and then bollocked both the guys as they did it – that was until one of them mentioned that he was a Charlton Athletic supporter. He then stood talking to them both for a good fifteen to twenty minutes and ended up shaking both their hands.

"Did you forget they clamped my car?" I snapped.

"He follows Charlton, home and away," he replied. "You've got to admire that."

"Really?"

Lee nodded. "They're a strange side at the minute though."

I was going to ask him why, but I thought better of it, however he just shook his head and said it anyway, and started prattling on about some mercenary Belgian businessman called Roland Duchatelet who owned the club and who was odds on to sack the manager and replace him with an ex-Israeli under-21 manager called Guy Luzon.

"Neither of those lads have ever heard of him," he said.

"Join the club," I said.

"I told them if Luzon goes to their club, they will certainly get the best out of Tal Ben Haim and most probably look to sign Alou Diarra," he added.

I looked at him whilst he pondered in thought and just shook my head.

"I think one of their problems is that there's no stability at the club – the majority of their players are journeymen."

"Really," I said.

I eventually got out of the car and drove back with the intention of picking up the kids from their dad's but ended up having supper with them all. It had been a truly lousy day.

That night I phoned my mother and informed her of my current status. She always wanted to know my problems, but never ever had a clue how to help me deal with them, and in reality just added to them. It was the same when me and Lee first split up. She wanted to know every detail, but all she did was give me one of those 'I told you so' conversations, which never really help anyone. She was even worse when I had him back and stinking unbearable after I'd chucked him out for good.

"So this Ross Bain fellow?" she asked. "Is it permanent or just one of your whims?"

She had asked something similar about Lee, however Lee immediately won her over the same as he did with M's parents. However Ross was certainly no Lee and to say my mother was a hard one to please is an understatement.

"It's nothing at the moment," I told her. "We are just friends."

"What does *he* say about it?" she asked.

"Lee doesn't have any say in anything I do," I lied.

"Yes, he bloody well does," she argued.

Ross phoned me later that night and asked to come round, however I told him that I needed some time to think.

"Think about what?" was his immediate reply.

"I don't want to be made look a fool," I replied. "And by fool, I mean I don't want to be just another notch on your headboard."

He laughed at my comment, and then he told me that he loved me.

"You've only known me two minutes," I replied. "And you're all over the place – I can't go following you around the country like some bloody groupie."

The last bit was true. I used to moan like hell when Lee was working all hours when we were first together and even more so when we were in Southgate, but at least he came home. Ross had showed me his itinerary for the next 12 weeks and for a lot of that time he would hardly be in London. Another obstacle was the financial side of things. He shared a flat over a shop on Blackstock Road. I'd never been in it as such, although I had dropped him off outside it after I'd watched him at The Garage.

"Do you want to come in for a coffee?" he had asked, which roughly translated meant do I want chasing around the sofa for a few hours.

"Not particularly," I had told him.

As Lee was in the process of getting his corporate lawyers to transfer the deeds of the house and mortgage into my name, coupled with the fact that I had my own wealth, I felt a bit edgy in that I would suddenly become something of a sugar mummy (or bloody dummy), as what he currently earned only just covered his rent.

"We'll make it big next year," he had told me.

I didn't doubt that for one minute, but what I had, I had fought for, and I didn't fancy anyone free-loading, and that had included Paul.

I was due in The Warehouse to do some narration on a couple of episodes of my show the next morning, followed by eight hours down at the store in New Cross, which meant that I had to rely on M to watch over the kids, which was something that I had mentioned to Ross during what was our near-on two hour phone conversation.

"I'll watch them," he said.

"Lee would go mental," I said.

"Why?" he asked. "I get on with him."

"They are his kids and he's very protective of them," I told him. "And they don't even know you."

That however would soon change as early next morning he came knocking on my door bearing gifts – a bunch of flowers for me and two belated Christmas presents for the kids.

"Who is he?" asked Harmony.

"Ross," I replied. "He's a musician who works with your dad."

"I don't work with him," Ross replied. "He just tells me what to do the same as he does everyone else."

"He doesn't tell me what to do," she replied. "Nor mum, nor my brother, nor M."

"That's because you are all special to him," he smiled. "I'm not quite that special yet, but I'm working on it."

He then had Jamie to deal with. "Who are you?" he asked, as he wandered into the kitchen.

"I'm Ross," he replied.

"He's a musician who works for dad," said Harmony.

"Yeh – so what's he doing here?" he asked.

"Yeh, so what are you doing here?" I smiled.

"I just thought I'd call in to see what you both looked like as I've heard so much about you," Ross told my kids as he handed over the two presents.

Harmony ripped open hers to uncover a really nice silver flute whilst Jamie got what he initially thought was a clock.

"What's this – a clock?"

"No, a speedometer to put on your bike," Ross smiled. "It tells you how fast you are going."

"I can't play the flute," said Harmony. "But I can play the violin and the piano a bit – M teaches me."

"Well I'm not that good on piano either – but I can play the guitar," he said.

"Both presents are really nice," I told him.

He got a "thank-you" off Harmony, however I was minus a son as he was now trying to figure how he was going to attach the speedometer onto his bike.

I made him some breakfast and watched him as he ate, whilst at the same time chatting to my daughter, who had suddenly become her father's PR manager. "Dad supports Arsenal – Who do you support?"

"The same," he smiled, "although I certainly don't know as much about them as your dad does – in fact I don't think anyone does."

"Who's your favourite player?" she asked.

"I quite like Aaron Ramsey, although Theo Walcott is a player I like a lot too," he said. "But to be honest I've been a bit busy of late to go see them so I just catch them on TV."

It was quite nice watching him talk to the kids; however I wasn't so sure how Lee would react, but that would come later.

The Warehouse was a hive of activity when I got there around 9:30am with Jaime Hudson rushing me straight down to a studio to do the narration of a 1960's band from north

London – The Dave Clark Five. Exactly 45 minutes later I got pulled up by Lee, fresh from bollocking the DPD driver for depositing a load of DVD's at the front desk. "Was Ross Bain around at yours this morning?" he asked.

"Is that a question to something you don't know, or something you do?" I replied, knowing full-well that M wouldn't have said anything – although my kids certainly would have.

"Jamie asked me if I'd put a speedo on that that Ross man brought for him this morning," he said. "I didn't have a clue what he was on about until I inquired further. I thought he was on about a pair of trunks."

That bit made me smile.

"I think he's trying to woo me," I told him.

"So, he's not wooed you already?" he asked.

"It's none of your bloody business," I replied. "But just for the record – no, he has not."

"I'm just asking as he has a tendency to do a lot of wooing," he said.

I would have liked to have thought Lee was a bit jealous, but he wasn't – he was just concerned that I wouldn't be made to look an idiot, something that my mother was on the rag about during the majority of last night's phone call.

I managed a cup of coffee with M and all three kids over at their coffee shop around lunchtime, where I got told that she was to be interviewed as a special guest on BBC Breakfast by Sally Nugent prior to the launch of ITV 7, while the shop's owner was rather proudly putting up some framed photographs of Arsenal playing some Greek side.

"What's he on with?" I asked M.

"ITV 7 are using this as one of their venues for the pre-match chats with fans," she smiled. "I think Kirsty and Kim are hosting it on Friday evening."

"So where will the other two be?" I inquired.

"I think they'll be up at some similar place in Manchester," she said.

"Manchester?"

"Yeh, I think so," she said whilst at the same time trying to dislodge an empty bottle out of Sammy's hands and having both my two laughing at him. "Let go – you've drunk it all."

"Ross is in Manchester on Friday," I said.

M shrugged her shoulders, not knowing what I was implying.

"And Karen will be up there," I added.

"So," she replied. "Karen's in London all week and so is Ross – It doesn't actually mean they'll be together."

"Yeh I suppose so," I replied.

"So what are you doing about the job?" she asked me.

"I still like it, but it's made it hard for me being moved," I said. "Why, what would you do?"

"I'm not you, Jeanette – only you can answer that," she replied.

"Crikey, you're starting to sound like Lee," I said.

I got that lovely smile aimed over at me as she passed me over Sammy. "Here, go to your Auntie Jeanette."

I had half an hour with them all and drove down to New Cross where I was met by two policemen escorting some shoplifter off the premises.

"He's the third one this morning," said a girl on the till.

I definitely had to think about handing in my notice.

Chapter 38

2015

The Live at The Warehouse show was initially pencilled in to go out on New Year's Day, but it was ITV's idea to have us shoot it live a day earlier on New Year's Eve instead, which meant that the amount of celebrity guests we would have hoped for possibly wouldn't materialise as they would be busy with their own lives, therefore I had another idea. However, so as not to get in front of myself, I'll rewind back a day.

I had been in three meetings with ITV as regards one thing and another, so much so I didn't know whether I was coming or going and that being the case Emily had called into the optician's to pick up some glasses as I'd recently been struggling with my eyesight on top of having some blinding headaches. On meeting my wife and offspring over in the coffee shop, I immediately noticed a smirk emanating from her chops, which suggested something untoward. You sort of notice things like this when you've been married as long as we had!

"Hiya love," she smiled.

I looked round just in case Eamonn Andrews was lurking in the background with a great red book, however he wasn't so that certainly couldn't have been what she was grinning at. "I've picked up your 'feed you to the pigs' glasses," she said.

Mmm, she's still on about that, I thought.

We had watched Guy Ritchie's 'Snatch' a few nights ago, and Emily had pointed out that the 'bins' that I had picked out reminded her of the ones Alan Ford's 'Brick Top' character had worn in the film. "You're not going to feed us to the pigs when you get them, are yer?" she'd twanged.

They were nothing like them – they were Gucci; however what she pulled out of her handbag were anything but.

"What are these?" I asked.

"Yer glasses," she smiled.

It certainly said Gucci on the case but that was about your whack, as they were like quadruple-glazed so much so my eyes looked ten times bigger than they actually were.

"They are what you ordered," she smirked.

"M, these definitely can't be mine," I said whilst sort of deliberating and holding them up to the light. "I'm sure the frames I ordered were different and I can't see a frigging thing through them."

"It says Gucci on 'em," she smirked.

"What's that got to do with it? It says 'Warm and friendly welcome' on the door of this place," I replied, whilst pointing over at its owner who was now arguing the toss with a couple of Greeks over at one of the card tables.

"What do you reckon, Herbert?" I asked.

He didn't say a great deal and just looked over at me and then screamed the place down when I put the glasses on him.

"What's the matter with you? You look like 'Brains' out of 'The Thunderbirds," I told him.

Brains or no Brains, he was less impressed with them than I was.

My sneaky wife eventually came clean and passed me my real glasses. The pair misery guts had just slung on the floor had been a substitute pair she'd picked up earlier from one of those charity shops as a joke, but saying that even the real glasses took some getting used to as it felt like someone was sucking my eyes out of their sockets. Emily said they made me look "dead intelligent", but I still noticed her grin at me a couple of times and tell Herbert that "Daddy was going to feed him to the pigs if he didn't stop chuntering."

"Anyway – how's he been?" I asked.

"Fairly sociable until he woke up," she said.

"When was that?" I asked.

"About half-four this morning," she replied. "It's going to be dead rubbish when he learns to click his fingers – he'll have me running about all over the place."

Emily slung Herbert over to me and I rammed a bottle in his chops, however he immediately noticed that it wasn't as warm as it normally was.

"Your mum can't be expected to have it spot on all the time," I told him.

"Thank you dear," she replied.

I then gave her the runners and riders as regards the three meetings I had been in and that an Arsenal programme had been bought by NBC. The fee wasn't as much as the Sheffield Wednesday one, but all the same it was still a tidy six-figure sum.

"Which Arsenal one?" she smiled. "You've done about ten of them."

"Parallels," I replied. "The throwing away of the Double's."

"That was the first one you started writing after Sammy was born," she smiled. "In fact – aren't you still on with it?"

She was right – and yes I was – I had kept on being side-tracked.

She then brought up the time after Sammy had just been born when I'd been sat at the breakfast bar downloading newspaper articles from the national press archive and piecing it all together.

"Look how far you've come," she said.

"How far 'we've' come," I said.

I just loved seeing that smile.

"You were fascinated that Arsenal were plagued with injuries back then like they are now," she said. "Can you remember?"

I loved the way she could converse with me about football and I glanced her a smile back.

"You also said that that season was a defining one for The Tottenham Hotspurs," she said.

"Tottenham Hotspur," I corrected her.

"They signed that man who looks like Norman Rossington out of 'A Hard Days Night'," she smiled. "Whilst Arsenal bought Ray Charles from Swansea."

"Mel Charles, dear," I corrected her. "Although he may have well-worn sunglasses after he'd had the clitorises removed from his eyes."

That made her laugh, however she was right – and it should have definitely been the other way around. Tottenham signing Dave Mackay was nothing short of a master-stroke by their then-manager Bill Nicholson.

Charles had been wanted by Tottenham but Tommy Docherty and George Swindin had sold him the concept of The Arsenal, leaving Tottenham to plunder Heart of Midlothian for what wrongly seemed at the time for some broken-down player for £17,500 less. What was strange was that Arsenal had chased Charles all season, but bought him after the 16th March transfer deadline, making him ineligible to play in the run-in for the league title. What was stranger still, and possibly a first in football, was that Charles had appointed an agent in the guise of a solicitor and ex-Queens Park Rangers player Neil Harris to help push the transfer through. These were changing times. Harris had had to retire from the game in 1947 due to a head injury and was brought in as Arsenal and Swansea were at an impasse – which was basically due to the then-Swansea Town manager Trevor Morris, who, rather than put the player on the transfer list, had been whoring him out to all and sundry, with Newcastle United more than interested in lining him up alongside fellow Welshman Ivor Allchurch. Charles however, only wanted to move to one club – The Arsenal.

Trevor Morris appeared as strange a man to figure out as Bertie Mee. He had publicly slighted Arsenal and Welsh international inside-forward Derek Tapscott when Arsenal had offered him Swansea early in the 1958/59 season as a make-weight as part of the Charles-deal. He then wanted Charles to go to Tottenham, Newcastle or anyone else as opposed to Arsenal and had even slung several reporters out of Vetch Field who had tried to get to the bottom of the story. He could have been construed as being bitter, as his playing career consisted of only one appearance for Ipswich Town before the Second World War broke out, and which a broken leg during a wartime match against Bristol City had put paid to any future career after the war. He also had the ignominy of managing the relegation of both Cardiff City and Swansea Town in 1957 and 1965 respectively; however, his military record was quite something else. He had served in R.A.F Bomber Command and piloted the lead aircraft in a squadron of Lancaster's on D-Day as well as flying countless bombing raids over occupied Europe, even being awarded the D.F.C.

It would have been interesting if Mel Charles had gone to Spurs though, as it would have been highly doubtful that they would have achieved the success they had without the brilliant Dave Mackay, a player who Jon Sammels had regarded as the best British player of the 1960's. "What a signing for Spurs," he had told me. "All his teammates idolised him."

That night we were to be graced with young Stuart and his girlfriend coming down from Liverpool followed by Emily's mum, dad and Lucy the next day. I'd promised Stuart that they could both go to the Live at The Warehouse show and that being the case Emily had had to call Paige's parents to sound them out about certain ground rules. Now here was a story, and one that shows you just what a small world we live in.

As I've said, I had briefly met Paige's father over at Hamilton Square, however it wasn't the father who Emily had been speaking to, but her mother, who after speaking to her for a few minutes wished to speak with me. It transpired that not only had I known her – she had also been the best friend of the girl I'd got pregnant when I was fifteen years old. The fact that I couldn't believe it wasn't in it. I was absolutely staggered.

"I bet you can't remember me?" she had said.

I remembered exactly who she was as you don't forget things like that. I hadn't forgotten her best friend's father either, as he had knocked the living daylights out of me, so much so my mum had gone around and played merry hell with him, which was most unlike her.

"What are you doing over on The Wirral?" I had asked.

"I met my husband in Sheffield and we ended up getting engaged," she'd replied.

The telephone conversation however, had intrigued Emily to the point that I knew at some time I was going to get the standard twenty questions; however, for me the Stuart-Paige thing now had a bit more substance to it than it had before, and as such I felt I needed to watch over them a little more than I would have normally done, and I promised her mum exactly that.

"Separate bedrooms, mate," I had told Stu, whilst he was on his way down. "You in our Jamie's – Paige in Harmony's"

"Did her mam tell our M that?" he whispered.

"No, she told me," I'd replied.

On them both arriving at the house one of Emily's first missions was to have Paige show her the contents of the photos on her mobile phone, which of course included photos of her mum and dad.

"Yer mam is really pretty," said Emily, whilst casually glancing over and giving me a wink.

I would have asked for a look, but I decided against it and did a bit of editing on a documentary we were doing about football violence. Not the football factory type stuff, but more humorous than anything. Nearly every football fan has a story to tell you about something such as this. Sooty once told me that whilst outside Elland Road he and a few other Leeds supporters had chased this Wolves fan into some street where he turned on them and pulled out some great dagger. Sooty was only fourteen at the time. It was an absolutely stupid thing to do and god knows what is mum and dad would have thought, even more so if the lad had actually used the knife. Stevie Kell had told us another about some Liverpool fans going mental in the tube station after a match against Arsenal whereby they were just needlessly slashing innocent people with Stanley knives. Everyone knows that football once-bred this form of tribal mentality, but it wasn't something that I fancied glamorising on TV therefore I went the way of away-day humour more than anything, and that's where you have to rely on the real football fan – the football fan that follows his club both home and away and through thick and thin. The meeting at Highbury corner early Saturday morning for the bus to pick you up, or in some cases, jumping on the old Inter City Specials, which sounded a hell of a lot better than they actually were, and which were in fact pure squalor. Half the broken down carriages never had any lighting and the train ride itself – although it never stopped at any stations, always took twice as long to reach its destination.

Gaz Lawrence sat in the studio and told us the story of his mum packing him and his brother off, telling us how she ever afforded it, he'd never know. "I'm sure she must have pawned stuff," he'd said.

Brian Allan was another one – a West Ham United supporter for near on 55 years, he had seen it all. He sat and told us of some young Hammers trying to take the piss out of an older thick-set supporter called Jock who worked in the printing industry, and who this particular day was stood in the ground wearing a donkey jacket which said 'Press' on the back. The young lads found it highly amusing and kept on 'pressing' his back before he turned round and gave them the 'Scarborough warning', which they found more amusing than anything. The next press was greeted by something a little bit north-westerly – a 'Glasgow kiss', which brought blood gushing from one of the lads faces. Jock did no more than casually turn around and continued watching the match.

I could listen to the old school supporter all day long!

Even though Stuart had come down to London with his girlfriend it didn't stop him from hanging from my shoulder like a parrot and asking me a million questions, one of which was about the premises on White Lion Street. From the blur that was our life – everything had moved at pace, however the purchase of the factory on White Lion Street wasn't one of them, and my corporate lawyers were now having to deal with more than a few obstacles, the main one being that the company that owned it were now in administration and the appointed liquidators were continually moving the goalposts on the 'agreed' price. Stuart on the other hand knew that there could be a flat or apartment in the offing as part of the development, and as such he wanted to see it?

"Go on maps google," I winked.

"Yer know what I mean," he smiled.

I did. I knew exactly what he meant and I promised him that I would run them around there in the morning, especially as his dad had been looking over the architect's plans, and it was then Paige pulled up a stool at the breakfast bar and sat opposite me.

Oh shit, I thought.

"My mam said that you were really clever at school," she said.

"Maybe," I replied. "But I was also lazy and disinterested."

"She said that you went to Sheffield University to do a degree."

"I did," I told her.

Emily smiled over at me, before Paige asked, "Do you think I look like my mam?"

I didn't like the sound of that, I thought.

"A bit," I replied. "Although it was a long time ago."

"She didn't realise who you were until she saw you on The Jonathan Ross Show," she said. "She couldn't believe it."

I quite liked that, but not as much as the next bit.

"My mam said — 'I can't believe it — he used to go out with your Auntie Julia'," Paige added.

No, definitely not that bit!

"Mam says Auntie Julia had a right argument with her dad afterwards," she said.

Yeh — that bit!

"I didn't know your auntie went out with Lee," Emily smiled.

"Yeh, my mam said all the girls fancied him."

That night in bed I had a minor interrogation from the wife. Emily's way of an interrogation was hardly a lamp in the face and thumbscrew job, more a way of a gentle coaxing.

She was due to present New Year's Eve Live at The Warehouse as Little Red Riding Hood and that is what I got treat to, and I have to say it didn't sit with me very well. It was hardly a case of 'What time is it Mr. Wolf' or 'Grandma, grandma, what big teeth you've got', more a case of me feeling like some sex offender before, during and after I'd done the deed.

"I thought it would take you back to your schooldays," she smiled.

"It definitely did," I told her. "It was a bit Fred West-ish, if I'm being honest."

It was, and I had to wonder what exactly went through her head during the day, as I could never have thought up half the things she said whilst at the other side of the bedroom door. Not that I ever minded, however.

"You once said Fred West looks like Gordon Banks," she smiled.

"He did a bit," I replied, whilst watching her as she hung up the red outfit, whilst also yacking about this, that and the other — one of which was her hoping that Mr. Stork would shortly make a call, before slipping into her Arsenal shirt and reverting back to the Fred West conversation — or Gordon Banks, rather.

"He was the best goalkeeper in the world, wasn't he?" she asked.

"In his time he was," I smiled. "Although Bob Wilson rated Peter Bonetti higher."

"You said he looked like Fred West as well," she smiled.

"All goalkeepers are a bit strange," I replied. "None more so than the idiot we've got in between the sticks at the minute."

"You said we've not had a great goalkeeper since Lehmann," she said.

"We?" I asked.

"Yeh – I like Arsenal just like you," she smiled. "I just don't shout and swear at the TV like you do."

"Jens Lehmann was as mad as a hatter as well," I told her.

"That's not him who had the pony tail, is it?"

"Nah – that was Seaman," I said, the subject of which was the catalyst for rebooting up the Mr. Stork conversation.

"I do hope I get pregnant this time," she said.

"Well, it won't be for the lack of trying," I smiled.

"Can I ask you a question," she asked.

"About football – certainly," I said.

"No – it's not about football," she replied.

Shit, I thought.

"Did you and Paige's mam ever – yer-know?"

"I was only a kid in school," I said.

"And?" she replied.

"Exactly that – I was only a kid in school."

"Would you have fancied me, when I was at school?" she asked.

"M, I think you're the most beautiful woman I've ever seen, so it goes without doubt that I'd have fancied you back then."

"I wish I'd met you when I was sixteen," she said, whilst sat cross-legged on the bed and looking over at me. "Instead of – yer know –putting my mam and dad through what I put them through."

She appeared to dwell on that particular subject quite a bit.

"We might have lived in some semi in Liverpool, eh?"

"I doubt it M," I smiled. "I was always going to move to London – you needed to do what you did for me to find you."

"Why are you so nice to me all the time?" she asked.

"Probably because you're perfect," I replied.

I got a cuddle for that and she snuggled up to me and began talking of her life's if's and if nots and it was as though she were the only one who'd had any baggage, and her having it in some way made her appear inferior.

"I really upset my mam and dad."

"And are they upset now?"

"No, are they heck," she smiled.

"There you go, then – everybody's happy."

I then mentioned Gordon Banks and a part of the Parallels documentary where Arsenal were looking at buying him from Chesterfield. On 13th December, 1959 they ran the rule over him and watched him play in his clubs 1-1 draw at Saltergate and against the club who would capture the hearts and imagination of the public that season, Norwich City – a club from Division Three managed by ex-Arsenal player Archie Macaulay. Norwich would make it all the way to the F.A. Cup Semi-Finals, knocking out both Manchester United 3-0 and Tottenham Hotspur 1-0 on their way. Strangely during the 1972/73 season they did a similar thing in getting to the League Cup Final after beating the likes of Leicester City, Arsenal and Chelsea – but losing to Tottenham Hotspur 1-0.

As regards Gordon Banks, Arsenal eventually passed on him, which was an extremely bad decision by the club as they never adequately filled that position until Bob Wilson came of age – and even then it was fairly momentary. I've said it before, the man Bob Wilson *is* often clouds the judgement surrounding the goalkeeper that he actually *was*. He had two great seasons – 1968/69 and 1970/71; however, what should be noted was that Arsenal were a very defence-minded and organised unit around that time. Wilson had quite an unorthodox technique and was extremely brave; however on the downside his positioning could be erratic and his distribution rather woeful, with Peter Storey being openly critical about his dramatics. In 1978 whilst on the BBC's 'Football Focus' Liam Brady was asked the question of how did he rate the programmes presenter – as a goalkeeper. "He was quite old when I was there and by then he was making quite a few mistakes," Brady had innocently stated.

Bob's face was a picture after that statement.

Bertie Mee had been tracking Peter Shilton since the late 1960's, something that Wilson mentioned in one of his many biographies, and on 28th January, 1971 Alan Williams of the *Daily Express* ran a piece on Shilton wanting out, firstly quoting President of the Football League and Chairman of Leicester City Len Shipman, who snapped, "He has signed a four-year contract and the whole structure of soccer agreements in the future depends on the stand Leicester City intend to take in this matter. As far as I am concerned circumstances could develop whereby Shilton has to sit in the stand for 12 months. Any attempt by him to force the club to let him goal will fail. I am a hundred per cent behind manager Frank O'Farrell."

It was rumoured that Arsenal had tapped him up.

Shilton responded, "If Mr. O'Farrell is hinting that I have been tapped up by a big club then he is barking up the wrong tree. I have not been tapped by any club."

On 25th August, 1972 Norman Gillier of the *Daily Express* wrote, "Leicester and England goalkeeper will be the next £200,000 player to move. And Arsenal are favourites to sign him. The club will sell him to the highest bidder once manager, Jimmy Bloomfield has satisfied himself that Mark Walllngton is ready for a permanent first-team place. Arsenal can swing the Shilton deal by offering one of their transfer-listed trio – Charlie George, Eddie Kelly, or John Roberts in part exchange. Bloomfield wants a midfield anchor-man to go alongside Keith Weller and ex-Gunner Jon Sammels and Scottish Under-23 international Eddie Kelly fits the bill. Arsenal considered going after Shllton when Bob Wilson broke down, but manager Bertie Mee and coach Steve Burtenshaw have been so pleased with the form of reserve Geoff Barnett that they have held off. They are still big admirers of Shllton though, and realise that at 23 he could give 10 years' service for around £200,000."

History will tell you that never happened and over the next 10 years Shilton would be firstly signed by Stoke City for £325,000 – a world-record fee for a goalkeeper at that time – and would later be the subject of a £275,000 bid from Manchester United as Stoke were in dire financial straits and needed to sell – however, United rather strangely couldn't afford Shilton's wage demands. He was eventually signed by Brian Clough at Nottingham Forest in September 1977 and under his wing he won two European Cups, a European Super Cup, a League Championship, a League Cup and the 1977-78 PFA Player of The Year amongst other things, and became one of the greatest goalkeepers in the world.

As for Jack Kelsey, he was a brilliant goalkeeper but got badly injured in February 1959 during a F.A. Cup Fifth Round replay, who after five minutes broke his arm and didn't feature until late October the next season, which was the reason they got dumped out of the F.A Cup and one of the reasons that their form during his absence was so patchy. Banks' presence in the side could have given the club an extra ten to fifteen points a season, and would have quite possibly helped earn the club a trophy along the way. At the end of the 1958/59 season Chesterfield sold him to Leicester City for £7,000 – Leicester's manager? Matt Gilles, a man who would spend part of the 1972/73 season staring down the barrel of a gun as the soon-to-be sacked manager of Nottingham Forest.

To sum Arsenal up in one word I quote author Jon Spurling: 'Parsimony'.

The next morning I awoke to Herbert screaming his lungs out across the landing and rather than get up with him I put him in bed with us, which was a huge mistake as he decided now was the time to have a shit.

"I really do think you do these things on purpose," I told him.

"D'yer want me to get up with him?" Emily asked.

"Nah – stay in bed like you normally do," I replied.

"I don't always lay in bed," she smiled.

"Yeh you do – you've not got up with him since Halloween – and that's only because you were excited at scraping out that pumpkin for him."

"That scared him to death," she said.

"I know – he cried for a solid three days after that – It got that bad that if he'd had teeth I would have had them wired together."

"I still want another though," she said.

"Well, at least we now know that when you stick a dummy in his mouth he stops whining."

"He right likes that Bongela," she said. "Stick some of that on and he's quiet for ages."

"I noticed," I said, as I picked him up to take him downstairs to have his arse jet-washed. "He was as high as a kite the other night. You're only supposed to put a bit on his gums – You grease up his dummy up like you're using K-Y jelly."

That brought a bit of laughter.

I changed his backside and gave him some breakfast whilst at the same time kicking up Sky Sports hoping that Arsène Wenger was looking to bolster the side with a proper defensive midfielder and defender during the January transfer window, when Paige joined me and duly took over baby feeding duties, which pleased Herbert immensely now he wasn't looking at me.

"Stuart said that you get up early," she said.

"It's a bit earlier than I like, but yeh, most days I'm up before six," I told her before asking her if she had slept well?

"Yeh – it's lovely down here."

I switched on the coffee machine and stuck some bread in the toaster as Emily came into the kitchen and gave me a peck on the cheek for kindly doing the abysmal deed of changing Baby-Face Finlayson.

"Are you excited, M?" Paige asked her.

"Excited?" she shrugged.

"For tonight – you are on TV."

"To be honest, it's not that exciting anymore," Emily replied. "I love the Sessions programme as that's music and something that I like and which I can do anytime but as the Warehouse is live, we have to work around it as opposed to the other way around, and as Lee has to work on it too, it makes things a bit awkward with Sammy."

Paige looked over at me and I nodded a confirmation. "It's quite fun to do, but we're both out late and always knackered," I said.

"I'd love to be on TV," she smiled.

"I'm sure you would," I replied. "However, real life is much better."

"Stuart said that you never really wanted to do normal telly – just football," she said.

"It's a long story but I took on a huge workload to initially win favour with ITV, however mine and M's home life has suffered quite a bit," I explained. "It's not hard work like say your dad does – but it's really stressful in that the hours can be long and everyone seems to want a piece of us, whilst all me and M want to do is enjoy each other and our family's company."

Emily smiled at what I'd just said.

"Once the sports channel kicks off I'm hoping that I can relax a bit," I added.

Stuart graced us with his presence around two hours later and I ran them over to the factory on White Lion Street, which I was hoping would become a nice investment for the future. Paige had caught Georgia Clayton-syndrome in that she now understood exactly who she had got, and that certainly wasn't some snotty-nosed chav from Birkenhead, but a possible heir apparent to some media business. "How long will it take you to rebuild?" she asked.

"Mike and your dad are great guys," I said. "I'm sure they'll be able to turn in around for me in a few weeks."

I could see she liked that, as did her boyfriend.

We walked up the six flights of stairs to where the flat would be and they seemed more than impressed, which to some could have appeared quite strange in that they could see the bigger picture. The thing is with youth is that it has an exuberance that everyday life tends to batter out of you as you get older, and that being the case, it is sometimes hard to envisage something that is not immediately staring you straight in the face.

After the viewing I dropped them off at the nearby Angel tube station as it was their intention to go and get some breakfast and as I pulled up outside the house after getting caught in a traffic jam, I immediately copped sight of Libby standing at the front door along with both her kids.

"I've got no change on me," I told her.

"Ha, ha – very funny," she said.

"Yeh, so what do you want?" I asked as I let them in.

"Where's M?" she asked.

"She's left me and run off with Mertesacker," I lied.

"What, the skeleton?" smiled Zooey.

"Yeh – she likes tall skinny blokes with shiny white teeth," I replied, before coming clean in that she was actually at Euston waiting for her mum, dad and sister.

"I've come to ask you a favour," she said.

"What?"

"Could the kids stop at yours Friday night as I'd prefer to travel to Manchester with Tim rather than him be left to his own devices in the city?" she asked, with me obviously thinking trust and lack of it was giving her cause for her concern. However, that is where I would be wrong.

"They can for me Lib, but I'll be out all day so it's really M's call – Don't forget that she'll have mine as well," I said, suddenly realising what I'd said. "Anyway, what's the matter with asking their elusive fairy godmother?"

"She'll be in Manchester too," she mumbled.

"What for?" I inquired.

She shrugged her shoulders and sort of deflected the question by giving me one of her own, in was I nervous about the launch of ITV 7?

"Not particularly," I replied. "Why, is Jeanette?"

"I wouldn't have thought so," she replied.

"Then why will she be in Manchester?" I probed.

Libby shrugged her shoulders – again.

There was a lot she wasn't telling me, the bulk of which involved Jeanette and her new beau, Sooty, Libby, Les Crang, Oliver Norgrove, Kirsty, Abi and her 'bloke' and Becky Ivell going to watch Electric Ladyboy over at the Retro Basement Bar on Sackville Street. In fact, I was just about the only one who hadn't been invited.

"That sounds all very nice and cosy," I said. "You lot out on the raz' while me and Emily are lumbered with all the kids."

"I thought you liked us?" said Mia.

"I do," I said. "I just don't like sneaky, underhanded mums, dads, ex-wives and gimpy lead singers."

"What's a gimpy lead singer?" Mia asked.

"Ask your Auntie Jeanette," I said.

Lucy was pushing the pushchair onto the street as I waved Libby and the kids off, with both Emily and her folks following her.

"What did Libby want?" asked M.

"If I fancied partaking in the 'egg under the hat' trick," I replied before giving Sil' a peck on the cheek and Lucy a hug. "She asked if we could have her kids at the weekend."

"We'll be in Birkenhead," she shrugged.

"Yeh – and she'll be in Manchester – with the Sex Pistol and his Queen," I said as I winked over at Mike.

"Well, I don't mind," Emily smiled.

"I frigging do," I said.

477

That afternoon I drove up to The Warehouse which I knew would be packed to the rafters as we had sent out an extra 500 tickets and made sure that I had seven bands (five of who were under contract to us) lined up to play out the old year, one of which was Ross Bain's alter ego, the Queen and Pistol. I had hired in my version of 'Pan's People' and had a scaffold erected for them, which was just being chucked up as I got there.

Jaime Hudson had some sheet in her hand and was busily directing traffic.

"You're not going to Manchester at the weekend are you?" I asked.

"Yes, why?" she replied.

"Who else is going?" I asked.

She didn't tell me as she got busy giving one of the bands a bollocking for chucking all their gear all over the place before getting side-tracked and then bollocking one of the guys from the temporary works company erecting the scaffold. I would have hated to be her husband as she looked pretty intimidating when she got into an argument with one of the 'Ladyboy's. "I don't care who you think you are, but in here, when I say one, two, three, jump – you do it."

There were a few superlatives in that lot, so much so even Kirsty would have been a bit red-faced.

"Oi potty mouth," I shouted, as I saw the Pocket Rocket skulk across the upstairs landing. "Which F.A. Cup match are you reporting on?"

"Manchester City," she replied. "Why."

"Where's Becky Ivell going?"

"Tranmere versus Swansea," she said. "Why?"

Well, they had a reason to be in the North West, I thought.

I sought Sooty out who was doing the rosters for the weekend's games – I say weekends as our launch would coincide with the Third Round of the F.A. Cup and meant I had two lots of six hours in front of the screen, however as I was its anchor I needed to know where everyone else would be. Sooty however, had only ever dealt with a few people at a time and was still trying to get his head around what was ITV 7 and The Warehouse.

"I'm all over the place here, mate," he said. "We've got nineteen reporters plus the three K's, Sinead, Les and Ollie."

"Yeh – seventeen cup matches Saturday and ten on Sunday – what's the problem?"

"Half of them want to be somewhere else," he said.

Running the business side of a business is relatively straightforward; however, once you start employing staff that is where any business can fall down. I therefore called a team meeting down in the press room for five o'clock sharp and had Sooty bring in the rosters, Abi the scheduling and Faranha the details of the accommodation.

"Who's not here?" I said, looking around.

"Atwood," said Kirsty.

"Go get him," I said.

Sometime later he came in through the door with a huge grin on his face.

"I called a meeting for five o'clock – it's now seventeen minutes past."

"I got talking to one of the press men outside the building," he smiled.

"And?"

"We were talking about the Southampton-Arsenal game," he said.

"Then go and have another fucking chat with him – you're out," I said.

"You can't do that," he exclaimed.

I could and I did. I then made it known to the rest of the staff as regards what the pecking order or structure in ITV 7 was, in that it was Abi who picked the vehicles and Sooty who directed the traffic.

"What game was Atwood supposedly covering?" I asked.

"The Stadium of Light on Sunday," said Sooty.

"No problem," I said. "Abygaile Gibbs is doing the Blyth Spartans – Birmingham game Saturday – let her stay over and do the Sunderland – Leeds match."

I looked over at Abygaile who glanced me a smile back.

"Are you okay with that?"

"Yeh, no problem," she said.

They had the best jobs in the world; however the idea was – never to bollocks it up.

Chapter 39

Jeanette's Tales – Take 15

The New Year's Eve show at The Warehouse had been excitedly riotous, so much so the newspapers were full of it leading up to the launch of ITV 7 on Saturday. Seven bands played all through the night and the party atmosphere had been nothing short of electric. ITV only showed an hour and a half of viewing, but the actual seven hours were absolutely brilliant and one young girl came up to me and said, "I can't believe how fantastic everyone is."

All the bands intermingled with the crowd and the fact that Lee finally made his presence known along with his glamour gals of ITV 7 went down like a bomb. The fact that Lee had invited a few press people and their partners didn't hurt either and I was asked on numerous occasions about my relationship with Ross, both by the press men and by the show's host – my ex-husband's wife and my best friend – M.

"Here's Jeanette Janes and Ross Bain, everyone," she had smiled to loads of applause. "Come on Jeanette, let's have the low down of this relationship everyone is talking about."

However it wasn't me who began to fill in the blanks, it was Ross. "I love her a lot," he said. "However I've been told that I need to get my act together before I truly win her over."

"That's not totally true," I replied into the mike.

"She's a beautiful lady," said Ross, "Who has a lovely family, and that being the case she needs to know that I'm not the shallow and unreliable type."

He then kissed me in front of everyone including the 17.1 million viewers sat at home watching, and the photograph of that said kiss was in the papers and all over the internet the very next day, but that was nothing to what he had said immediately after. "I'd marry her tomorrow if she'd have me."

As nice as it was, I could have crawled under a bloody table and died!

I didn't think that anything like that could have ever been topped; however I would be wrong. M cajoled Lee into standing alongside her and she went about her PR job and pecked him on the cheek and wished him luck for Saturday and for a baby in nine months' time. "He keeps promising me," she smiled.

That night M invited both myself and Ross back to Frederick Street, however I passed on it. "Thanks M," I said, "but I'm trying to work at being a bit more of my own person and it's not fair that I keep on hanging on to you both."

She knew exactly what I meant and she gave me that lovely smile, a hug and a kiss – and on tippy toes 'like I was some giant', however strangely – this time it never actually bothered me. "We all love you and we're all here for you," she said.

I knew that, and I appreciated every word. As for Lee, he walked over to me and gave me a hug and wished me a happy New Year and shook Ross' hand before saying, "Just remember who she is."

"I know exactly who she is," he replied, and later on that night I let him find out – and afterwards I had him sat up talking to me into the early hours of what his plans were, and if I wanted, he'd like me to be included in them. I'd say he sounded like Lee had when I first met him, however that would be untrue.

I got up early the next day and rather than let Lee or M bring the kids around I drove over to theirs to pick them up and there was Lee sat at the breakfast bar conversing with M over a coffee, whilst little Sammy was being fed by Lucy.

Whereby I used to phone first and not even come to the door, I had started a process of actually getting out of the car and knocking – and then knocking and just going in – however M had said, "You don't have to knock, Jeanette – just come in."

"Where's everyone else?" I asked.

"My mam and dad are still in bed and our Stuart and Paige have took the children over to St. George's Gardens so they can ride their bikes," she smiled, prior to pouring me a coffee.

"I didn't think they could ride their bikes down there," I said.

"There'll be no-one around this morning," Lee said. "It's the quietest day of the year."

"Aren't you going up to The Warehouse this morning?" I asked him.

"You must be joking – I've got Jaime Hudson up there supervising the clean-up," he said. "I'm not in until Monday."

"If you are wanting us to have the children," said M. "It's not a problem."

M always seemed to know what I was thinking; however, this was a hard one, as Sil' and Mike had watched over them last night while they stayed over and they were due to stop with their dad and M up in Liverpool Friday until Sunday, and I knew that M had some spot on BBC Breakfast at MediaCity in Salford and that Lee would be really snowed-under. There was also the small fact that I was their mum and that I should look to be responsible.

"You're in Manchester at the weekend," said Lee. "We're only an hour and half away if you want to see them."

"How do you know I'll be up in Manchester?" I asked.

"It's the worst-kept secret up at The Warehouse," he replied. "Even Libby tried palming her kids off on us."

I couldn't help smiling at that.

"You're getting very sneaky in your old age," he added.

"Don't mind him, Jeanette," M smiled. "The children will be fine and you know where we are."

M was brilliant and I suddenly had four days to myself; however what I wasn't to know is that Sainsbury's were short of a stand-in manager on Tottenham Court Road and did I want it? Who asked me? Paul.

"What's the catch?" I asked.

"None," he replied. "Just report in Saturday at eight."

"I can't do that, I've got the weekend off," I said.

"Then report in Monday at eight."

The phone call ended.

Wow. I was impressed.

I got back in to Ross drinking tea and watching the rerun of The Warehouse on my laptop.

"Where are the children?" he asked.

"Their dad's – I have four days off."

I don't have to tell you what the rest of that morning and half of the afternoon comprised, but I'm sure you can guess. Afterwards we had a shower and went over to The Woodbine pub on Blackstock Road, where under some duress, I watched Arsenal lose 2-0 away at Southampton before I was treated to seeing the flat where he actually lived. To sum it up it was far worse than the place I had shared whilst in university.

"The lad I shared with has gone back up north," he said.

I looked around whilst he cobbled together some food, and it was then he invited me to stay.

I disliked squalor and this was exactly that. He was a soon to be 24-year-old living the life of someone who was here, there and everywhere with people coming backwards and forwards and in and out of his life, but just recently his ship had come in, in that Lee had given him his first contract.

"You need to look after yourself a bit more," I told him.

"I have you now," he replied.

"You won't have if you don't start looking after yourself better," I said.

I spent the evening taking cleaning stuff from my house over to his flat and doing the best I could to make his place habitable. I also changed his bed and slung the bloody awful sheets and quilt and replaced them, and by 10:00pm that night I had some order. It was hardly perfect, but certainly good enough to stay the night.

Blackstock Road, if you have never been is quite a vibrant place and I got woken up by traffic very early the next day and made my way back to Clerkenwell, where the house was empty and it was then I had my first pang of guilt. I was putting my own enjoyment before my kids and I rang Lee to ask how they were.

"What's up with you – have you shit the bed?" he asked.

It was only 5:40am.

"No, I just wondered how they were?" I asked.

"They're fine," he replied. "Do you want me to get them to call you when they get up?"

"Please," I said, before passing comment on Arsenal losing yesterday.

"It was an embarrassing performance and none more than the goalkeeper," he said. "I thought Wenger would have learned after the Manchester United game."

It transpired that they had driven up to Liverpool in preparation of Lee going into ITV on Saturday.

"I hope it all goes well for you," I said.

"I'm sure it will," he replied.

And that was that.

Chapter 40

The Launch of ITV 7

Early Friday morning I dropped the kids off with Sil' as I had to drive Emily into Manchester as she was a guest of BBC Breakfast over at MediaCity. I told her I'd be a couple of hours while I called in at the old Granada Studios to introduce myself and look around the facilities, however just as I was in with some suits my wife rang me to tell me that she had finished.

"I've done – can yer pick us up?" she twanged.

"That was quick – how was it?" I asked her.

"Okay," she replied. "The presenter is from Birkenhead."

"Yeh – Do you know her?"

"No, she's about twelve years older than me – my mam knows her family though."

"So, did it go okay?" I asked.

"So-so – she wanted to talk about marriage and relationships – that kind of stuff. She was really tall as well."

"I bet she had big feet?"

"Dead long legs," she laughed.

I picked her up and we drove down the M62 and to Liverpool and through the tunnel and on to Hamilton Square in between listening to her 'rabbit on' to her mum about the twenty questions that at been thrown at her and some prat on TalkSport who was trying his utmost at winding up some Arsenal supporters.

The house on Hamilton Square was as homely as the one in King's Cross, but far more elegant and as such I had a study to work in; however I didn't realise how much time I would be spending in it as I set about tightening up the schedule in between hoping that none of the team would let us down.

That evening we would be filming pre-match talks with football supporters at coffee shops in both London and Manchester, which was linked by satellite to a camera in the study where I'd be on hand to pre-empt or ask questions. I would then do a first edit and send it over to ITV.

Emily popped her head in every now and again as did the kids, but at around 5:00pm she urged me to come away from my desk and rest my eyes. "You can do something too much, yer know," she smiled.

She was right and I followed her down into the kitchen where my kids sat at the far end in front of the long gas fire, watching some cartoon or other on the self-same TV that I'd had to mount on Christmas Eve, including Sammy who was in quite a genial mood seeing as he had his brother and sister sitting either side of him.

I received yet another call from Abi who had just arrived on site in Manchester. "I certainly don't think they like us up here," she said.

That was strange as I'd had that self-same feeling when I'd drove over this morning, and I'd copped a few snide comments directed my way about there being 'a bit too much London in Manchester' and that being the case I felt it would become even worse once the rest of the team arrived.

The more time ticked on the more edgy I became and I began asking myself what felt like a billion questions in my head of was this right and was that right? Or should I do this or should I do that?

Emily poured me a coffee and came over to sit with me. "We should plan to get away in June or July," she said. "ITV Seven will be off air and there will only be the Sessions – and that's all pre-recorded."

I smiled at her suggestion.

"Two weeks this time," she said. "All of us."

487

"Dad, are we going on holiday again?" asked my lad.

"I think it's a great idea," I said.

"Then leave June or July free," she said as she gave me a peck on the lips. "I mean it."

"I want to go back to Morocco," insisted my daughter.

"No matter where we go, we'll have a great time," said Emily. "Come on let's make some tea and we'll try and decide on where to go."

"I want to go to Greenland to see the penguins," stated my lad as he got up off the couch.

"There aren't any penguins in Greenland, you divvy," argued my daughter. "Penguins live in the South Pole – Greenland is near the North Pole."

"M, penguins do live in Greenland, don't they?" he asked.

"No," Emily smiled. "Your sister's dead right on that one. Polar bears, reindeer and Arctic foxes live there though – and Greenland sharks and killer whales swim off the coast."

"I definitely want to go to Greenland then," he said.

"I don't," I said. "We need somewhere nice, warm and sunny – not cold, wet and dangerous."

"What about Egypt?" asked my daughter. "One of my friends has been there."

"Egypt is warm, wet and dangerous," I said.

"It's not wet," argued my daughter.

"It will be if I chuck you in the sea," I said.

That got her laughing.

Emily kicked up her laptop and the kids went surfing for holiday destinations in between mixing what looked like some fish batter.

"What are you making?" I asked.

"Pancakes," she smiled. "Why – you want some?"

"No, I'm fine," I replied.

"My gran's made you an apple pie," she smiled.

"I'll definitely have some of that then," I replied.

Whilst M was making up the batter my daughter asked if she could have maple syrup on hers whereas my lad most definitely wanted chocolate sauce on his.

"I've never seen you make pancakes before," I noted.

"M makes us them all the time," said my lad. "She makes them really small, like those in a diner."

"A diner?" I smiled.

"Yeh – you and M went to one of them when you were in New York and M had them for breakfast," he said. "M put a smiley face on one with sauce and sent a photo over to us on her phone and told us that she wished we were there with you."

I was amazed.

"Dad, can we go to New York?" asked my daughter.

"Not for our big holiday, but me and M could probably take you for a few days in summer if you want."

"That would be dead cool," said Emily. "We can go up the Empire State Building."

"Is that what King Kong climbed up?" asked my lad.

"It is," said M.

"I hope he's not there when we go," my daughter replied.

I had my apple pie, answered a few texts and then went back into the study to see Fosis face looking at me through my monitor. "Is that your house?" he asked.

"Yeh – the one in Liverpool – Anyway, where's Kim and Kirsty?"

"They play cards with Turkish George, Man with one eye and Man that look like woman."

"Yeh right," I said.

"It is true – they take all their money."

I didn't like the sound of that so I rang Kim.

"He's pulling your leg," she said, as Fosis shifted his great face out of my monitor. I then saw that the place was packed to the rafters.

"Jesus, how many are in there?" I asked.

"It's mad, Lee," said Kim. "We are good to go if you want."

489

"Yeh – whenever you're ready – Get them talking about the FA Cup – but one at a time."

However, I would be immediately pulled in as what I thought was some form of adjudicator; however that's where I would be wrong.

"Lee, there's a Hull City supporter here who wants your take on Sunday's match," said Kirsty.

We exchanged peasantries before I passed comment. "I quite like Hull City as I've had a lot of nice moments recently when I've seen them play against Arsenal, and Steve Bruce was not only a severely underrated player – he is a really nice guy."

"What do you think our chances are?" asked the Hull fan.

"Hull did really well at the Emirates early on in the season, but after Arsenal's weak showing on Thursday I think you'll see a different team."

"Do you think we'll lose?" he asked.

"I do, mate – two or three-nil."

"Okay Lee," he replied.

The high regard the lad showed me hit a nerve.

"Put the lad back on Kirsty," I said.

I looked at the guy with his yellow and black scarf around his neck and said, "Look – I never bet on Arsenal – ever, as I must jinx them or something. Put twenty quid on an Arsenal win with Alexis Sanchez to score and if Hull don't get anything result-wise, you should get some form of compensation – about two and a half hundred quid if you put it on in the right place.

Boom! That was it – Fosis place was alive and it set the precedent for the other coffee shop with Karen giving me a shout from Manchester as regards Manchester's United and City.

"Two easy wins," I replied. "Although City will make hard work of theirs."

"What makes you think that?" asked the guy.

"They don't take lesser opposition from the Championship seriously and expect a walk in the park – Look at what happened last season against Wigan."

It was supposedly conversations from within the coffee shops, however I was being brought in nearly every time.

"I'm sorry Lee," smiled Kim. "Another question."

"Do you reckon if I put money on Man City, Man United, Chelsea, Arsenal, QPR, Southampton and Palace winning, I'll get a score?" asked another guy.

"I wouldn't have thought so as one of those will let you down," I said.

"Which one?" he asked.

"Well I certainly don't fancy QPR," I said.

"What – you think Sheffield United will win?" he asked.

"I never said that," I replied. "I just don't think QPR will win."

This went on well into the evening and it was Kirsty who eventually halted the proceedings. "Oi – I'm having to drive to Manchester tonight and be up at stupid o'clock in the morning, can we wrap this up."

"Sure," I said.

I looked at my watch and saw it was 9:20pm and I then realised I had to be a lot more regimental with my timings, however what I'd got on my final edit, was pure dynamite and I sent it over to ITV around midnight for them to further edit it and put it in its correct slot.

"I bet you're shattered, aren't you?" Emily asked as I climbed alongside her in bed.

"Knackered."

I got a cuddle followed by a 'yer know' and the next thing I remember is Sammy waking us up around 5:00am.

Emily put the pillow over her head as I sat up in bed.

"Well, today's the day," I said.

"I hope it goes well for you, love," said the voice from under the pillow.

"Me too," I said.

I walked into the bedroom across the hall and looked into the cot. "What's up?" I asked him.

He didn't say a deal, but I assumed he wanted his backside changing and some breakfast, and that being the case I pulled him out of his cot and walked down the few flights of stairs and into the kitchen where I turned both the lights and the fire on before slinging him on his mat and changing his arse.

"You should have had a lie in," said his mum, as she came down into the kitchen and kicked up the percolator. "You'll be busy all weekend."

I glanced her a smile as she kicked up ITV 7 on the TV and told me that there was nothing on it yet, just adverts for it starting at 6:00am. The music was good though.

"Who's doing the music?" she asked.

"Red and White's rip off of Bowie's 'Heroes'," I replied, as I juggled with a nappy and Sudocream as Little Lord Fauntleroy was continually trying to boot me. "Stop it, will you – or I'll be here all day."

"What's he doing?" asked his mum.

"I don't think he wants his nappy on."

"He obviously takes after his dad," she smiled.

My phone rang just as ITV 7 was about to start. It was a withheld number. In fact, I'd had around seven missed calls from a withheld number – and at various times throughout the night.

"Yeh?" I asked.

It was Les Crang.

"What are you doing withholding your number?" I asked. "You know I never answer them."

He gave me some garbled message.

"What?" I asked.

He gave me another garbled message.

"Corporate Law firm?" I asked. "Why, what's gone on?"

He just told me he was 'dead sorry' and could I just make the call.

I did, and rang them immediately, and they got back to me within half an hour and told me that half my staff were in Bootle Street Police Station, after what had been a riotous night out in Manchester.

"What's wrong?" asked a rather concerned wife.

I just shook my head and gave her the edited highlights of the 'When Electric Ladyboy go wild in Manchester' show.

"Crikey," she replied.

"Crikey indeed," I said.

I rang Sooty at the Midland Hotel, to find that he had been banished to another room, as Libby had got the hump with him. I then informed him of last night's goings-on.

"Where's Abi?" he asked.

It was a good question, so I rang her to find out. Fortunately, however, she and Ronnie had left with Jaime and her husband before it had all kicked off, so at least I had a couple of staff on hand, however there was something else that she let me know.

"How do you mean Ross Bain was fighting? He couldn't fight his way out of a wet paper bag," I said. "So where's Jeanette?"

"Jeanette okay?" asked Emily.

"Abi said she's not in her room," I replied.

I rang the corporate law firm and it appeared that she had been locked up and would be helping the police with their enquiries, along with Les, Ollie, Karen, Sinead, Becky Ivell, Ross Bain, Chris Windley and three of Electric Ladyboy. There would have probably been four – but their idiot singer had sustained a suspected broken ankle and was in hospital. It also transpired that the police were very interested in the footage that we'd filmed.

"We filmed?" I asked the brief.

"Yeh – there were three cameramen from your company filming it – the officer in charge mentioned that one was a coloured lad."

I rang the said coloured lad in question to awake him from his slumber. "What were you doing in Manchester – and with one of my cameras?" I asked.

"Three of your cameras," he replied. "Young Jono and your Stu were with me."

"What – M's brother?"

"Yeh – how many other 'your Stu's' do you know?"

"Where are you now?" I asked.

"Birkenhead."

"Birkenhead?" What the hell are you doing in Birkenhead?"

"I stayed at Jono's mum's – she did us a great supper – she puts potatoes and onions in her scrambled eggs."

"Really," I replied.

"And she did these really spicy sausages," he added.

"Never mind that," I said. "Who gave you the okay to take the cameras?"

"Stu asked me, and I asked Jaime – and she said it would be a good idea," he said.

Mmm. It was quite a good idea, I thought.

"We signed all the equipment out," he added.

"Were they good?" I asked.

"Fucking awesome, Lee," he said. "They smashed the place up."

"Are all three of you okay?" I asked.

"Yeh – sweet," he said.

"Well stay in Birkenhead, as Becky was supposed to be covering the Tranmere Rovers game and I'm not sure when she'll be out. Ring Abi – and she'll sort you."

I hung up the phone, strangely smiling to myself.

"So, our Stuart was in Manchester?" Emily asked.

"Yeh – they filmed last night's set."

"Mam never said anything," she replied.

"Mam probably didn't know," I smiled. "Frigging brother-in-law certainly didn't."

I drove over to the Granada Studios whilst talking at length with young Stuart about last night's events and parked up my car to be met by what looked like around 30 people.

"Lee – what's your take on last night's episode in Sackville Street?" asked a journalist.

"Is it true that half the ITV Seven team were there?" asked another.

Wow, this was bigger news than I thought, I thought.

"We had a camera crew filming it," I told them. "I'll let everyone see the footage after I've done here. I should be done at six – I hope."

I walked into the studios to be greeted by ITV's rather worried head of sport.

"What are you doing here?" I asked.

"We came up last night," he said.

"We?"

"Yeh – me and the wife," he replied.

"You know that we are a bit light in the studio?" I said.

"Yeh," he replied. "We were in that Retro Basement Bar with Abi and her girlfriend and your studio boss, but left before it all kicked off."

I nodded.

"So who's missing?" he asked.

"Everybody," I told him.

That bit really pleased him and it was the first time I'd ever seen him kick off, and after watching him try and attack a coffee table and punch a door he seemed to calm down a bit before succumbing to some form of anxiety attack.

"Steady on," I said.

"Steady on – You're on live in under three hours and there's no one to man the studio."

"Well, that's a lie – we have Kirsty, but Abi's sent her over to cover the Tranmere Rovers match – It was either that or have one of our cameramen do it."

"There's a thought," he replied. "Is that do-able?"

"Not while Swansea have fucking Wilfried Bony and Bafétimbi Gomis in their side, it isn't."

"You mean that Ginge kid," he said.

"Yeh, if he reports on that, those two will be worth two hundred million apiece after the game."

"Will Bony be playing?" he asked.

"I doubt it," I replied. "It'll cup tie him for when he joins Man City."

A bit of football talk eased his panic – that was until we got into the actual studio which I have to be honest, totally knocked the spots of SkyTV's set up – it was really that good. I looked over at the five big cameras and then around at the five empty desks, as did the head of sports who then started biting his nails again.

Abi came over to me pecked me on the cheek and gave me the nod in that I had some moral support – Eddie was here – as was the ex-football player that we had done a documentary on – the documentary that had helped propel me to where I was now. In an empty fucking studio ready to tell the world that I can't be trusted in putting a sports programme together.

"He's travelled up from Leicester," she whispered.

Although I had spoken to Sammy (Jon Sammels) fairy regularly – mostly via text message – I had never actually met him, and the first thing he did was to shake my hand and thank me for all the nice things that we had said about him.

"That's alright," I replied. "You deserved it."

We somehow got talking about Brian Moore, and I mentioned that if the ITV's current head of sport kept on panicking like he was, he would have a head as sporty as that of the iconic TV presenter.

"I can't tell you any worthwhile stories about him," explained Sammy, "as I had only met him a few times during interviews with him down at ITV studios, but what I can tell you is that in the football world he was regarded as very knowledgeable, well respected and was someone who everyone loved."

"Sounds a bit like you," said Sooty, as he walked onto the set.

"Where have you been?" I asked. "I've been here an hour already."

"Lib wouldn't let me back in the room," I said. "I had to get concierge to open the door."

I introduced Sooty to Sammy.

"Sammy?" he replied. "What, *the* Sammy?"

"The very one," I said before I explained to Sammy exactly who Sooty was. "It was his decision to do the documentary on you."

"No it wasn't," Sooty argued. "He told me that if we didn't do the Sammy documentary that he'd not do the World Cup one."

Eddie laughed and told Sammy about first meeting us both. "Terrible with each other, they were," said Eddie. "You couldn't turn your back for two minutes."

Sammy smiled at what he had just heard.

"I knew your old manager Jimmy Bloomfield, very well," said Eddie. "A lovely man – It was tragic that he died so young."

"Jimmy deserved to have played for England," said Sammy.

"A lot of players did that didn't," said Eddie.

I told Sammy that Jimmy Bloomfield was part of a two-part programme we had been doing and according Bob Pennington of the *Daily Express* he was actually due to get his international call up to play against Wales post the selectors meeting on 26th November, 1958, but it never happened – he got passed over.

At the time England were looking at axing Bobby Charlton and Pennington had written, "This could mean a first England cap for Jimmy Bloomfield of Arsenal as the Arsenal inside forward was watched by England team manager Walter Winterbottom in the 0-0 draw against West Ham where he hit peak form."

Bloomfield had also been instrumental in the dismantling of a rather boring Nottingham Forest seven days later, where in front of a crowd of over 49,000 they beat them 3-1 with

Desmond Hackett stating, "The slow handclap blemished the Highbury arena as Forest played Arsenal offside so often I lost count. However top of the league Arsenal the team most likely to win the championship were able to spank their resentment with a win that was sheer teamwork. While Forest trimmed out lacy, attractive patterns that got them nowhere Arsenal stroked out firm, decisive moves that demanded the best of this so sturdy Nottingham defence starring Jack Burkitt and Bill Whare. And the man behind this Arsenal aggression was their rather under praised inside-left Jimmy Bloomfield."

While newly-capped England international Danny Clapton and Scottish International Jackie Henderson failed to pull out the well-known Arsenal "wings for victory effort" as Hackett had called it, Bloomfield kept the ball close down the middle while adding that he had never seen Vic Groves lavish so many quick-witted passes.

An own goal after 25 minutes set off the scoring, whereby Bob McKinlay had been hassled by David Herd into a 40-yard back pass which if it had been at the other end would have been a contender for the goal of the season, which was followed by a Bloomfield pass to Henderson who played Herd in on goal after 28 minutes and with just over a quarter of an hour left on the clock Jimmy Bloomfield centred for Henderson who headed home.

He had scored a dozen goals for Arsenal during the 1958/59 season; however, he lost his place in the side to firstly Len Julians and then John Barnwell.

Arsenal had paid Brentford £8,000 for the powerful and industrious inside forward a few years earlier, and like Sammy – his first signing whilst manager of Leicester City, he won caps for England at Under 23 level, but never at full level, and strangely – like Sammy again – had also played for a Football League XI.

Losing his place in the side came after he had torn a cartilage during the 2-2 draw in the F.A Cup Fourth Round at Layer Road – against Benny Fenton's Colchester United, where Arsenal – being Arsenal – lost a 2-0 lead with 10 minutes to go, much to the frustration of their 4,000 following supporters.

Fenton had been one of those many players who had his career interrupted by the Second World War and born in West Ham, he had started out as a wing half with his boyhood club, and a club who his elder brother Ted would end up managing.

After the war he had a spell with Millwall before he joined Charlton Athletic to play in front of 40, 50, 60 and 70,000 crowds and in the same side as the legendary Sam Bartram – described by many at the time as the finest goalkeeper never to play for England. Fenton, however was signed too late to play in the 1947 F.A Cup Final against Burnley, which courtesy of a goal late in extra-time by Scottish-born winger Chris Duffy, his side won 1-0.

Described by journalist Brian Glanville as a man who was the 'quintessence of Cockneyism' and who was known for his innocence of expression – "What, me ref?" – told reporters after his side's comeback from 2-0 down, "Weren't they magnificent? I wish all Britain had seen us – I was worried in case we let ourselves down. How wrong can you be?"

John Morgan of the *Daily Express* had said that for 75 minutes Colchester had held Arsenal, then within two minutes they were two goals down from the sort of patterned Arsenal moves that might have produced a flurry of earlier goals were it not for the brilliant goalkeeping of Bedford-born Percy Ames.

Vic Groves blasted Arsenal in front after receiving a pass from Danny Clapton and then two minutes later he had out jumped everyone to head Arsenal further ahead on 77 minutes after he had latched on to a cross from Gerry Ward.

Fenton admitted that he thought the floodgates would open, however Colchester's £6,750 signing from Plymouth Argyle – centre forward Neil Langman, picked up a loose ball on the half-way line, brilliantly dummied stand-in centre half Tommy Docherty, raced for goal and belted a left foot drive past Jack Kelsey.

In all the excitement Benny Fenton raced to the touchline and dropped to his knees to celebrate; however more was to come. A minute or so later Colchester's huge Glasgow-born inside-right, Sammy McLeod stroked a superb pass over to winger Peter Wright who hammered the ball across Arsenal's 18-yard box, and as the Arsenal defenders dithered, recent £4,000 signing from Liverpool and ex-Charlton Athletic inside-left John Evans – a player who scored a goal as part of The Addicks' 5-2 mauling of Arsenal in February 1951, coolly placed the ball past Kelsey. Colchester, who were currently lying fifth in the Third Division, had scored the equaliser.

Morgan added, "This was Colchester's finest hour. So ecstatic it left Fenton moist-eyed with pride, wondering who to cuddle next, such was his tremendous joy. And even if, in Fenton's words, 'Arsenal nick it' in Wednesday's replay at Highbury, there is this comment which should be a lasting tribute to a fine football match with never a foul worthy of the name to mar it."

Arsenal did nick it the following Wednesday – with a resounding 4-0 victory, as the rather acerbic Desmond Hackett wrote, "Arsenal firmly and mercilessly put Colchester out of the F.A Cup and in the process put them back where they belong – in the Third Division. It was as one-sided as a Soviet parliament. The story of the match can be told in eight words: Kelsey did not have one shot to save."

As hundreds were locked out after arriving late due to a tube malfunction on the Piccadilly Line, a crowd of nearly 63,000 watched on through the fog as two goals from David Herd – one a volley, a finely taken goal from Len Julians and a penalty by Dennis Evans after Vic Groves had been rugby tackled by Percy Ames, eventually saw them off. However it was the back page of the *Daily Mirror* that truly caught the feel of the era that was to come.

"A mob of football fans who were locked out of the Arsenal - Colchester Cup match last night, because a London Underground hold-up made them late, stormed a block of flats overlooking Arsenal's ground in an attempt to see the game," it read. "Nearly 500 fans were held up on their way to the match – a replay at Highbury, when a signal fault brought chaos to the Piccadilly Line Tube service. When they reached the ground and found the gates were shut, the fans made for nearby Aubert Court, a six-storey block of Islington Borough Council flats in Avenell Road. As the football crowd streamed in on the ground floor, people living in the flats fought their way out to get the police. When the police, including some on horseback, arrived at the flats, some of the football fans had smashed doors to get out on the roof of the block of flats."

As for Jimmy Bloomfield? Arsenal treat him disgracefully and tried to make him a makeweight as part of George Swindin's failed attempt to sign both George Eastham and Phil Woosnam and much to the displeasure of the Highbury hierarchy, Bloomfield penned a piece in the *Daily Express* on 14th October, 1960 stating that sadly he would never play for Arsenal again.

Bloomfield wrote, "I have finished with Arsenal. The friendly match against Northampton last Monday night was my last voluntary appearance in the first team. I am sorry to reveal that Arsenal put me up for transfer this week in a desperate attempt to clinch the deal for George Eastham. After that I just, don't want to know any more as far as Arsenal are concerned. When I reported to the ground on Monday to go to Northampton, the manager George Swindin, called me into his office and asked if I would be willing to see Charlie Mitten, the Newcastle's manager, with a view to joining them. I was staggered and very hurt to think Arsenal would consider parting with me. However, once a club wants to part with you the situation between club and player is completely changed."

As has been said, George Graham was quoted as saying something similar in autumn 1972.

One day later the *Daily Express* ran with the heading, "Swindin gets Team Vote".

Tommy Docherty said, "Mr. Swindin commands your admiration. This man lives, eats, and breathes Arsenal" – whilst Jack Kelsey added, "Mr. Swindin is absolutely straight with us – he tells us what goes on and if you have a bad game he says so, however the next minute it's forgotten. This is a man's man."

Tommy Docherty had been in a similar boat to that of Bloomfield in that he was being touted for sale in a bid for the club to generate funds for the Eastham-Woosnam deal, however he had point blank refused to join Blackpool. David Herd and Danny Clapton were also being freely advertised for sale, something the ex-Arsenal board member Jimmy Joyce, who had resigned some three months earlier, had been livid about. Bill Holden of the *Daily Mirror* had interviewed Joyce after a somewhat heated shareholders meeting – his piece headed, "Arsenal Chairman in Rumpus – Meeting closed as ex-Director tries to speak".

Joyce, who had resigned from the board after 12 years' service, had asked permission at the meeting to raise several points criticising the way some of Arsenal affairs were being run and later said that he had not been given the opportunity to state his case. "I was just shot down by Sir Bracewell," he said.

The meeting had focused on the possibility of live football being shown on ITV, and Arsenal's firm opposition to it – This and the fact that the said Arsenal Chairman, Sir Bracewell Smith, had just accepted a position on the board of an ITV company, and as such the club's opposition to live football on ITV had suddenly been dropped – and without the board's consultation, which had been the sole reason why Joyce had tendered his resignation.

"It was I who introduced George Swindin to the board as a possible manager when Joe Mercer turned the job down –

I introduced Ron Greenwood, his assistant and fought for three years to get new, properly-qualified medical staff at the club," Mr. Joyce told the journalist, the latter of which would include Bertie Mee, meaning that Joyce himself has to be applauded, in that without his input there would most probably never have been an Arsenal 'Double' in 1970/71.

"There is a clash of wills between myself and Sir Bracewell," he added, "and I believe that it is quite dreadful that players such as David Herd, Danny Clapton, Jimmy Bloomfield and so on should be offered in part exchange transfer deals."

Bloomfield was wanted by several clubs – Sheffield United, West Ham United, Chelsea, Sunderland and Birmingham City, however Arsenal were quite insistent that he form part of a transfer deal – for either Eastham or for Woosnam, with Swindin also focusing on a huge move to bring Alec Young down from Heart of Midlothian, who history will tell you ended up going to Everton.

The whole saga was a sorry mess.

Bill Holden of the *Daily Mirror* said on 7th November, 1960, "Arsenal yesterday agreed to sell former Young England inside forward Jimmy Bloomfield to Birmingham for £26,000 triggering off what could be the most sensational week ever of big soccer transfers.

Today the Gunners themselves could clinch the transfer of Phil Woosnam, 28, Welsh international inside forward from West Ham for a fee of £30,000. Woosnam, who is keen to join Arsenal, said yesterday: 'I would like to get a move settled by the middle of this week'."

Arsenal had already offered £40,000 for George Eastham, and two of Newcastle United's directors, Lord Westwood and Alderman W. McKeag were in London – reportedly trying to actually get a player to sign for them, as very few top players at that time fancied them, the club having failed to get Mel Charles, Jimmy Bloomfield, David Herd and in this particular instance Phil Woosnam.

Holden wrote, "Woosnam himself made one concrete decision yesterday. He told Reg Pratt, the Hammers chairman, that he would not join Newcastle."

A change of plan?

Bill Holden of the *Daily Mirror* said a day later, "An Arsenal bid for Phil Woosnam of West Ham yesterday fell short of the amount wanted by roughly £4,000. The Gunners offered Jimmy Bloomfield valued at £26,000 plus £10,000 cash for the Welsh wizard inside forward. West Ham decided the Arsenal bid wasn't big enough."

Bob Wall, Arsenal's secretary told Holden: "Negotiations are still continuing for Woosnam – and for George Eastham of Newcastle."

£9,000 was the amount that was holding back both transfers to the club – £2,000 more than the amount of money that took Gordon Banks from Chesterfield to Leicester City and in today's money the equivalent of £187,000.

Holden added, "Arsenal hold the key, but until they cut out the haggling, the crazy merry-go-round will go whirling on."

Nothing much changes then?

A dizzy Bill Holden of the *Daily Mirror* wrote on 9th November, 1960, that Bloomfield will be going to Birmingham City, however the player himself preferred West Ham, the latter of who were now telling Arsenal that the Phil Woosnam deal was £40,000 cash only, saying, "It seems certain that The Gunners will eventually get their man – They hope to have him in time to play Chelsea on Saturday, although there is no sign that the George Eastham saga is any nearer its end."

A day later Bloomfield was in Birmingham whilst Bob Wall was still negotiating with West Ham for Woosnam telling the *Daily Mirror*, "West Ham hold a board meeting tonight and we expect no developments until Friday."

Friday came and the *Daily Mirror* ran with the heading, "Hammers Silent on Woosnam" coupled with the fact that

Arsenal were still trying to use Bloomfield as some makeweight to capture the player even though a fee had been agreed with Birmingham.

An even dizzier Bill Holden wrote on 12th November, 1960, "Bloomfield Deal Shock – Arsenal hold up 'Brum' move – He was offered a job."

Holden added, "The Arsenal inside forward, yesterday refused to join West Ham in part exchange for Welsh International Phil Woosnam, He has said he wanted to go to Birmingham. But Arsenal, who had agreed on a fee with Birmingham have slapped a shock ban on this deal."

Bob Wall, Arsenal secretary, told Holden: "Bloomfield refused to sign for West Ham and said he had an offer to contribute to a Midlands newspaper if he would join Birmingham. Therefore I have refused to complete his transfer to Birmingham. This might be just a temporary measure, or it might be permanent."

Meanwhile, a Mel Charles goal wasn't enough for a Bloomfield-less Arsenal, as Chelsea came to North London and in front of over 38,000 battered them 4-1, heaping more pressure on George Swindin.

The Friday after Ken Jones took hold of the reigns of the Arsenal reporting for the *Daily Mirror* and reported the clubs £47,500 capture of George Eastham. "Eastham joins Arsenal today and goes straight into the stiffs", it read. "Now Newcastle are expected to spend some of the money right away on inside forwards Charlie Cooke, 18 of Aberdeen, and Mark 'Pancho' Pearson of Manchester United."

These were another two players that didn't fancy going to Newcastle.

As for Bloomfield, Bob Wall told Jones, "The situation regarding Bloomfield remains static – It has nothing to do with Eastham."

Bloomfield was finally sold to Birmingham City on 19th November, 1960. He would go on to play in their European Fairs Cup campaign of 1960/61, where they beat the likes of Újpest Dózsa, 3-2 at St. Andrews and 2-1 over in Hungary –

Kjøbenhavns Boldklub (later FC Copenhagen), 5-0 at home, and drawing 4-4 in Denmark – Inter Milan, winning 2-1 both home and away – and losing in the final against Roma, drawing 2-2 at home and losing 0-2 over in Rome.

He also helped them get to the 1963 League Cup Final, where they beat Joe Mercer's Aston Villa – a side which also included George Graham – 3-1 at home, in which he scored a goal to make it 3-0 after 66 minutes, and drawing 0-0 over at Villa Park.

Jimmy tragically died from cancer, aged only 49. Back to the 1958/59 F.A Cup match with Colchester, what should also be noted is that the player who had helped set up the equaliser against Arsenal in the first match, Sammy McLeod – emigrated to Australia and sadly died at the very young age of 39.

As for Phil Woosnam, a player who Rodney Marsh compared to Matt Le Tissier, describing him as both intelligent, two-footed and stating that he was a wonderful passer of the ball who could go past a defender on either side – he never went to Arsenal and stayed with West Ham before being sold to Aston Villa in November 1962, with Joe Mercer paying a fee of £25,000 for the 30-year old. This was eight months after Mercer was being again tipped for the Arsenal job after the *Daily Express* ran the story of "Swindin to Leave Arsenal – Arsenal manager George Swindin was told by chairman Denis Hill-Wood yesterday: 'I'm sorry, but the board have decided we must part at the end of the season'."

This came just two months after Swindin had tried to buy three England internationals in a £100,000 deal that would include Southampton winger Terry Paine, Huddersfield Town's left back Ray Wilson and Bolton Wanderers' newly capped inside left Freddie Hill.

Although Billy Wright was being heavily tipped for the job – as he had been offered the job of coach in November 1961 after Ron Greenwood took up the post of manager with West Ham United, the *Daily Mirror's* Ken Jones

506

reported on 14th March, 1962 that Mercer along with ex-skipper and Northampton Town manager Dave Bowen were both candidates for the post, with 46-year old Swindin being heavily tipped by the *Daily Mirror's* John Bromley five days later to go to Newcastle United. Swindin however, was going to be another man that Newcastle didn't get.

Swindin had blown around £300,000 on transfers but had missed out on several big names such as Denis Law, Jimmy Greaves, Cliff Jones, Dave Mackay, Bobby Collins and Johnny Byrne, the latter of who was bought by Swindin's one time assistant Ron Greenwood in a deal worth £65,000 and who Greenwood would favourably compare with the Argentine and Real Madrid striker, Alfredo Di Stéfano. The Byrne transfer was around the same time as the Arsenal board were deliberating getting shut of Swindin.

Swindin did have one fan however, that of his wife Stella, who made the front page of the 14th March, 1962 edition of the *Daily Express* stating, "There's been so much talk about Billy Wright coming to Highbury that it's been most undermining. George has worked very hard since he took over at Arsenal four years ago. It seems a pity that someone else should reap the benefit. Just think of the load of rubbish there was at Arsenal when George took over."

One wonders what Sir Bracewell Smith or Denis Hillwood's take on that was?

Ken Jones of the *Daily Mirror* reported on the 24th May, 1962, "George Swindin stepped back into soccer yesterday as manager of Second Division Norwich City just two months after the shattering blow of Arsenal's decision to replace him with Billy Wright. Swindin is gambling with one of the hottest seats in the game."

"Hottest" being the fact that the Norwich City chairman Geoffrey Watling was as ruthless then as Roman Abramovich is now and had dispensed with five of the backroom staff during the last seven months, including former manager and Glasgow Rangers striker Willie Reid – and after just five months in charge.

Swindin would guide Norwich City towards the summit of the Second Division; however on the 10th November, 1962, after watching his team batter Trevor Morris' Swansea Town 5-0 at Carrow Road, he left to join Cardiff City on an extremely lucrative deal but without a contract – his decision as it had been at Norwich, and not the clubs, stating through the media that he would never ever be shoved around by another club again. However this would be a decision that would come back to haunt him as his tenure in South Wales would become a nightmare, as at one time prior to his sacking, he had seven first team players out with broken legs – something quite unheard of at any club, ever.

Post Jimmy Bloomfield debate, Sammy asked me, "Can I ask you a question?"

"Yeh – sure," I said.

"Malcolm Allison didn't really say all those things in that documentary you made about me, did he?"

"He did," Eddie nodded. "I was there when he said them."

Sammy appeared taken aback.

"He was a brilliant coach but he needed guidance," added Eddie.

He was right. Allison in his own right was as 'successful' as Bertie Mee was without Don Howe, or Howe without Mee. The winning formula he had with Joe Mercer had been first rate.

Allison upset the equilibrium at City just as Mee had done at Arsenal, and whereas City had bought Rodney Marsh – Arsenal had bought Alan Ball – both great players – but possessing different dynamics for the teams that they joined. Whereas Ball liked the play to run through him, Marsh helped stall Manchester City's all action rampaging style, which had made them so successful by hanging on to the ball too long, often showboating.

Sammy, like most old players, reminisced by mentioning City's blonde-haired, mop-topped, non-stop, box-to-box midfield Colin Bell – the player who was both labelled as world class by Allison and nicknamed Nijinsky due to his immense energy on the pitch, and a certain match up at Maine Road in December 1970.

Sammy explained that they had used some form of OPTA type stats – sort of high definition sports performance data, to determine how much ground each of the 20 outfield players covered, which was quite unheard of at the time, and on seeing the results everyone assumed that it would Bell who had covered the most ground – however it wasn't – it had been Sammy.

"It's strange how City rarely beat Arsenal with you in the side," I told him.

As we talked he explained that John Barnwell had been his mentor – a player who he regarded as a very intelligent and skilful player.

I then told him more about the 'Parallel's' programme that ITV had just sold NBC, and that Barnwell had been mentioned a few times within it – especially during the 3-2 win over Manchester United on 28th February, 1959.

Barnwell had put two goals past Harry Gregg on 24 and 28 minutes and in front of a crowd of over 67,000 with the *Daily Express'* John Morgan candidly inferring that United were lucky in that they never left Highbury with a proper spanking. "The flattering 3-2 score line indicated nothing of the soccer lesson they were handed by George Swindin's master Gunners and a last-minute goal by right winger Warren Bradley gave the score a false touch of respectability," he said.

It is worth pointing out that on that day Arsenal had ended United's 12-game unbeaten run, with Arsenal's first goal coming from 24-year old David Herd after 12 minutes – a player that Matt Busby would eventually sign for £35,000 in July 1961 and who played a big part in helping United overcome the Munich tragedy by regaining honours, as they won the 1962/63 FA Cup, scoring two goals in the final itself against Double-chasing Leicester City and being part of the team that won both the 1965 and 1967 League championships.

Bloomfield and Herd leaving Arsenal to find success — History repeating itself?

"Dazzling Docherty, brilliant Bowen, backed by a defence now ranking with Arsenal's best, so domineered this game that Jim Standen did not have a save to make in the first half," added John Morgan as regards Arsenal's performance, further supposing that only good times lay ahead for The Gunners. What he didn't know however, was just how long they would have to wait.

Swindin revealed that Standen — a replacement for Jack Kelsey who was out for the season, was doubtful up to the last minute as his knee was not quite right.

'Parallel' moment with the 1972/73 season? Injuries and injured first team keepers with knee problems?

Just a few days before the United game, Arsenal had used 19-year-old Peter Goy as goalkeeper in their hard fought 1-0 win over Leeds United at Highbury — a team that would come to haunt them throughout the following decade.

Just over 30,000 watched the game with Ross Hall of the *Daily Mirror* saying, "Crippled Arsenal, with five first team men out of action, battled back to the top of the First Division last night. These glorious, never-give-up Gunners grabbed the vital points with a superb, heart-tingling display of guts and gameness. They are now one point ahead of Wolves, who have two games in hand."

He went on to state that the display summed up the terrific enthusiasm that was driving what he termed 'this new Arsenal' to the top — a club spirit that surely rates with the best pre-war standards. "But it was victory at a heavy cost," he said. "For skipper and left half Dave Bowen finished the game limping badly after taking a nasty knock on the ankle."

David Herd hit what would be the winning goal after 28 minutes taking a superbly timed and angled pass from Tommy Docherty and from 30 yards out unleashed one hell of a shot past the Leeds and ex-Sheffield United goalkeeper, Ted Burgin.

"They were a really exciting side that season," Sammy told us.

"That team should have gone on to greater things," I said. "As should the Double team."

I then had a nod from Abi that the cameras were ready for rolling. The time talking with Eddie and Sammy had flown. I therefore walked over to the five empty desks where my teamsters should have been at, but weren't, whilst one of ITV's make-up artists came fluttering around and offered her advice on removal of the shine from my face.

"What shine?" I asked.

"On your head."

"I don't have a shiny head," I told her.

"Yeh, yer do," she replied.

"Oi – Do I have a shiny head?" I asked Abi.

"Not particularly," she smirked.

"There you go – now piss off," I said, to a bit of laughing coming from behind the cameras – and just as ITV's head of sport came back in – and who was still panicking until I told him that Emily had text to tell me that Sinead, Karen and Becky Ivell had been released half an hour ago and that Kirsty was currently over at Prenton Park trying to dislodge Ginge from in front of the camera.

"What about Les and Ollie?" he asked.

"Just going through some formalities," I said. "Stop worrying."

I then got the nod that the programme was about to start – and I saw the intro come up on the screen with Sammy's 35-yard strike against Manchester United – for the first time ever seen in 'glorious technicolour' followed by an array of similar struck goals as part of the montage. This was really the 'Me Show starring Me'.

10, 9, 8, 7 and so on, and then boom!

"Good afternoon Great Britain, I'm Lee Janes anchoring for ITV Seven's afternoon of football which I'm hoping will be one hell of a ride for both us here and all the viewers watching at home," I said. "We've a couple of teething problems in that we are currently a bit light 'staff-wise' as all the team went out on the lash in Manchester last night and got arrested, but who are now making their way over to the studio's as we speak, so at the moment it's just me."

I gave a slight pause.

"What – you think I'm kidding?"

I then had camera number one turn to Abi.

"Abi Tyson in the red dress and earphones is the show's producer and apart from Emily is the one that keeps me in check. She's been with me years and is like my little sister and knows as much about football as anyone," I said.

I then had camera one pick out Sooty and summoned him over.

"This is Mr. Sooty, who I can assure you doesn't need any archive of facts, figures or stats in front of him regarding football – he's the general manager, but I'm sure he can stand in until the rest of the team arrive."

I then had camera four pick out Eddie.

"That guy over there is Eddie Mardell – a top, top journalist who currently does a couple of days a week for us. He helps give us copy and mentors a few of our writers and he's here to lend moral support and watch me cock it all up," I said, which got a few more laughs from the floor.

"Thank you," smiled Eddie as he took a bow.

Then camera four picked out Sammy.

"Now here's one of the most iconic football players of the sixties – a player who was part of one of the most exciting teams of his era, and who scored one of the three of the most important goals for his club – ever, and against the European superpower that was ... Leatherhead."

There was a load of laughing coming from the floor.

"I bet you thought I was going to say Anderlecht or Ajax didn't you?" I winked.

"I did, if I'm being honest," replied Sammy.

"This is Sammy or Jon Sammels rather, the ex-Arsenal schemer, who hit what was the winning goal in the European Fairs Cup Final and whose goal against Manchester United which you've just seen on the intro was one of the Goals of the Season in nineteen-seventy – even though he did tell me his goal against Liverpool was better," I said. "Saying that he told Kevin Whitcher that his goal against Southampton was even better than that."

"That was one of my goals you couldn't find," said Sammy.

"Yeh, yeh, yeh – I'm not perfect," I winked. "He also shot a dog, but he'll probably tell you it was Eddie Clamp who did it," I said.

There was more laughing coming from the floor, which added a bit of levity to the situation.

"That's untrue," said Sammy.

"I could imagine Eddie Clamp shooting a dog," I said. "I've got some footage of him in a game against Manchester United in October fifty-eight where he goes straight through Albert Quixall – he was a right animal."

"What, you have TV footage of that?" asked Sooty.

"Course I do," I replied. "The first thing I did when I signed the contract with these was raid ITN's archives."

There was more laughing from the floor.

For the record, Eddie Clamp had been a no-nonsense and tough tackling right half in the brilliant Wolverhampton Wanderers side of the 1950's and the eventual 1958/59 League Champions and who had been George Swindin's last signing for the club – at £34,500. He was capped four times for England during 1958 and had been one of the few players to threaten to wallop Ron Harris. He also played a major part in Wolves' failed attempt at the first Double of the century, where they beat Blackburn 3-0 in the 1960 FA Cup Final – a Blackburn side that had included current Wigan chairman Dave Whelan, former Scotland manager Ally McLeod and former chairman of the Professional

Footballers' Association Derek Dougan, the latter who would later on become a Wolves legend.

I then further explained about the setup, and more importantly about my missing so-called football experts.

"ITV Seven is part-produced from Bounds Green Studio's in north London – which you'll probably know as The Warehouse, where we put together programme upon programme and have been doing so for the past few months," I said. "What started out as me, Abi and Eddie has grown into a really good team of people, and as we also shoot other programmes of a completely genre there, we have sort of grown into one big family. That being the case, a few of the said family came up to Manchester yesterday to lend support to another part of the family – who in this instance were one of the bands that are contracted to us – Electric Ladyboy, who if you haven't seen live – well do as it's an experience. Last night they used some pyrotechnics that set the place on fire and created a riot when all the sprinklers came on – and around a dozen of the said family have had to help with the police's enquiries."

There was more laughing coming from the floor, before I got all professional.

"Okay Mr. Sooty," I said, whilst sitting on the desk. "Let's go – what's first up?"

"Seeing as Sammy is here we can do Leicester City versus Newcastle if you want," he replied.

"Okay," I replied. "What do you reckon?"

"Newcastle have got rid of Alan Pardew, but for what?" shrugged Sooty. "The club have a brilliant infrastructure for success, but I just can't see it happening anytime soon."

Newcastle United's continual failure to get good players?

I gave him a nod.

"Just look at their side – There's no-one there that inspires me," he said.

"There's nobody in their line-up that you would fancy in the Leeds squad?" I asked, whilst at the same time letting all the world and its auntie know that he followed the once 'Mighty Whites'.

"Yeh, 'course there is," he said. "But who would any of the top five teams in the country want in their first eleven?"

"It's a good point – 'You reckon Leicester will do them?" I asked.

"Why do you?" he asked.

"I'm asking you," I said.

"Yeh, but I don't want you to make me look stupid," he grinned.

"I don't have to do that – you can do that on your own," I told him.

There was more laughing from the floor.

"So?" I asked him.

"So they need a decent manager to get the best out of what they have and if not, to get better players to the club," he said.

"And John Carver can't do this?" I smiled.

"You know he can't."

"He was a great footballer," I lied.

"No he wasn't," argued Sooty. "He only played for Gateshead."

"He didn't – he played for Cardiff City as well," I said.

"What – a couple of games?" he asked.

"No, thirteen," I said. "A leg injury did his career."

"You've been researching this to make me look rubbish," he argued.

"I didn't even know you'd be here," I said.

"Come on then," Sooty said. "If you were Mike Ashley, what would you do?"

"Take up jogging for a starter," I said, as more laughter emanated from behind the cameras. "They need an inspirational manager – however, sadly for the United supporters that isn't what's going to happen."

"You reckon they'll keep Carver?" asked Sooty.

"Nah – what I'm hearing is that they've got Steve McLaren lined up for the job."

You could have heard a pin drop after I'd said that.

"Where did you hear that?" asked Sooty.

"It's my job to know – that's why I'm on here," I winked. "It's Ashley's idea of a big name manager."

Sooty then asked me my thoughts.

"When Keegan arrived both as a player and as a manager during his first tenure at the club, there was a real buzz about the place. The clubs supporters need something like that again, and I'll tell you now – neither John Carver nor Steve McClaren will provide it."

"Okay – taking up jogging aside – what would you do if you were Mike Ashley?" smiled Sooty.

"Make a ten million a year offer for Jose Mourinho – let the Premier League know that you mean business. Inspire the supporters and show them that you actually care."

"Mourinho would never leave Chelsea for Newcastle," Sooty argued.

"Maybe not," I said. "However, and here is the point – Newcastle may not have Abramovich's Roubles but at least he'd see what real football supporters are – his team playing to packed houses week in week out and in a proper stadium. Newcastle don't have the one season wonder type of glory boys or tourists passing through their turnstiles, they have real people and people who care."

"And as your backup plan, when your Mourinho bid fails?"

"Approach Ajax for Dennis Bergkamp," I said.

"Yeh but he wouldn't be able to fly out to places like Zenit or Galatasaray to manage the games," Sooty argued.

"Ask any Newcastle United fan if they would mind him not being able to travel to Champions League qualifiers," I winked. "I think they'd take that."

"Do you reckon he'd make a good manager?"

He'd inspire the players he had, and he'd be able to attract quality, anyway Fantasy Football aside, what's your prediction?"

"A Leicester win," he said.

"Sound," I replied.

"Go on then – what's your prediction?"

"A Leicester win," I replied.

"You can't have that as I said it."

"Well, I can say it as well," I said.

"Well, elaborate on why then?" Sooty argued, amidst laughing coming from the floor. "You can't just copy what I said."

"Okay then – Leicester will win one-nil with a goal by an ex-Arsenal player," I said, whilst at the same time winking at the camera.

"Which ex-Arsenal player?" he replied. "They haven't got one."

"Really?" I asked.

That immediately had him scurrying around looking at some notes.

"Who – Matthew Upson?" he asked. "He's injured."

"No."

"Well there is no other ex-Arsenal player," he said, whilst meticulously trawling through more notes.

"Their big Argentinian forward," I told him.

"The only Argentinian I know that's ever played for Arsenal is Nelson Vivas," Sooty said. "And he was about three-foot eight."

"What about Leonardo Ulloa?" I said.

"He scored against Arsenal a couple of times, but he's never played for them," he said still checking the notes.

"He played for Arsenal Sarandí," I told him, "And possibly part of the squad that won the 2007 Copa Sudamericana, however I'd I've to check on that."

"Arsenal Sarandí?"

"Yeh – we did some boring documentary on the competition for another TV station that we can't mention on here," I smiled. "They beat River Plate in the semi-finals after penalties and Club América from Mexico City in the final on away goals."

"Jesus, that was a poor competition," noted Sooty.

"I know – you fell asleep three times while editing it. Abi thought you'd died."

More laughter came from behind the cameras.

That competition may well have been poor, but the start of ITV 7 was anything but – We were setting a benchmark. We were about to take over from Sky.

The End

James Durose-Rayner

BBC Breakfast Interview on 'Marriage'

Sally Nugent with Emily Janes at MediaCity, 2nd January, 2015.

SN: Thank you for coming on the show, Emily.
E: (Smiles, crosses legs) No problem.

SN: So, what is it like being Emily Janes?
E: If I answered that properly it may make me sound conceited, and I'm not like that. Well, I certainly hope I'm not.

SN: So you're married to TV producer Lee Janes, the man the press often label Mr. Arsenal – How did you two meet?
E: (Smiles) It was at some presentation that the firm that I then worked for had. He came up to me, asked me my name, and as you do we got talking, a few text messages were sent and returned – you know – that kind of thing.

SN: And you were married at the time.
E: Yes, I was married.

SN: And Lee?
E: He was separated.

SN: From Jeanette Janes?
E: (Nods)

SN: Did he know you were married?
E: For the past eighteen months my marriage had been breaking down; however it's not something I am really comfortable talking about on national TV.

519

SN: Were you in a violent marriage?
E: (Shakes her head) Controlling.

SN: And Lee?
E: Controlling? God no.

SN: When did you first think that you loved him?
E: I've always loved him.

SN: Always?
E: (Smiles) From the first time of seeing him.

SN: What was it that you liked?
E: (Laughs) His smile, his kindness, but perhaps most of all the fact that he's such good fun to be around.

SN: Do you have a song that you remember that takes you back to you first seeing each other – an 'Our Tune' kind of thing?
E: (Smiles) Yeh, sort of. Lee had 'Shine Eight' in his car and I liked it so much that he gave it me. Well he didn't really, I just never gave it him back. In fact, I think it's still in my car now!

SN: 'Shine Eight'?
E: It's a compilation of songs. The Lightning Seeds' 'Sugar Coated Iceberg' is on it. That's Lee in a nutshell – dead cool and dead sweet. (Thinking) That was the first song we ever danced to – at some wedding party we gate-crashed over in Cockfosters.

SN: Can he dance?
E: (Laughs) Yeh, badly. But he's definitely great to smooch with.

SN: I read somewhere that he asked you to marry him?
E: Yeh, he did.

SN: Had you known each other long?
E: (Shakes her head) No, not long. Five months, I think.

SN: Wow.
E: (Smiles) Yeh, wow.

SN: How did it happen?
E: It was really nice. It had been mentioned a couple of times, but I was really taken aback when he asked me.

SN: You were shocked?
E: (Smiles) Not shocked as such as we were getting on really well and everything seemed to fit. Happy, elated. I think those are probably the right words.

SN: You say 'seemed to fit'?
E: Sometimes you just know when something is right.

SN: Do you ever argue?
E: (Smiles) We may form different opinions or have differing points of view from time to time, but no – we never argue.

SN: Can you give us a 'for instance'?
E: Me making him eat certain foods and him not wanting to, or Lee wanting something ironed and me hating it – you know, that sort of thing.

SN: What food does he like?
E: (Laughs) Everything that's bad for him. My mam and my gran are a dead bad influence.

SN: With both your workloads, do you manage spend quality time together?
E: (Smiles) Yeh, all our time together I would say is quality time. I think Lee would tell you the same. Sometimes we manage to get out for some time on our own and we'll have a meal or drop in at a bar off Euston Road where we used to

go when we were courting and where the likes of Ross Bain, The Dee Man and Pedo Pedro used to hang out.

Laughing from behind the cameras.

SN: (Shrugs and smiles) I've got to ask you who that is?
E: Pedro? Peter La Greave. He's the little front man with Electric Ladyboy.

SN: Surely he doesn't know you call him that?
E: (Laughs) Yeh he hates it. He used to be with this rubbish boy bad who auditioned for the X Factor and who used to have twelve- and thirteen-year-old girls chasing after them.

SN: And these are one of the North London bands that are tied to your husband's White Lion label?
E: (Nods) They are really good. They are playing in Manchester tonight.

SN: It's a strange name.
E: (Smiles) Yeh, it's a very strange name, but the story surrounding it is really funny.

SN: How so?
E: Pete – Pedro – ran this Arsenal blog. Well it wasn't really, as he is this die-hard Tottenham Hotspur supporter. He just ran it with its sole purpose being to sleight the club and wind up Arsenal fans. Obviously Lee knew this and when they were first introduced on the 'Sessions' programme I had introduced them as 'Electric Ladyland' – you know, after the Jimi Hendrix album. However, before Lee signed off on it he dragged me back in front of the camera and had me reintroduce them as 'Electric Ladyboy'. (Laughs) I told him – 'Lee yer can't do that'. He did though. Pedro went absolutely ballistic when he saw the programme.

SN: I'm not surprised.

E: Lee even dubbed over one of his interviews on the Sessions programmes and started talking in a Chinese dialect. I'd asked Pedro about one of their songs and as he told me how he'd come up with the idea Lee dubbed over his voice (Chinese dialect) Ah so, great mistress. I watch Kung Fu with David Carradine for mah inspiration. (Normal, smiles) I asked him about his upbringing and Lee started talking for him again (Chinese dialect) Ah so. I am from Beijing great mistress but I can't eat with chopsticks as ah am left handed (Smiles) Lee kept this going for ages and had everyone in stitches. He ran a bit of it as part of the bloopers programme that was shown at Christmas.

SN: (Laughs) What's he really like - this Pedro character?
E: (Shaking her head) If you ever meet him, he is one of the most highly-strung individuals you could possibly meet (Smiles) He came barging into the studios the next morning after the Sessions programme had been aired and after Lee had changed his bands name and started shouting and swearing at Lee. (Laughs) He was dressed like one of the gangsters out of Kubrick's 'Clockwork Orange' complete with bowler hat and brogues. He thought he looked dead cool and kicked over a couple of waste paper bins and emptied the top of a desk on the floor whilst Lee just sat on the corner of the self-same desk watching him kick off, both grinning and winking over at us. By this time Pedro's head was ready for exploding.

SN: What happened?
E: (Laughing) I can't.

SN: Go on, Emily.
E: (Shaking her head, Laughing) Lee did no more and picked him up by the collar and while he was hung, dangling there Lee says to him, 'Oi March the flipping Tailor calm down and get that lot cleaned up before I give you a belt round the earhole. (Laughing) The next thing we see is Pedro hoovering the office, and still wearing

that daft bowler hat. He had all the office laughing. It was really funny. Pedro got his own back on Lee when we were over in Germany though and caused a riot at The Warehouse. In fact, they always cause a riot wherever they go.

SN: Do they get on?
E: (Smiles) Yeh, sure they do. I don't think any of the band realised how well they would take off.

SN: So, what do you both do on your days off?
E: On a weekend we do things with the children; however when ITV Seven kicks off, that will certainly change.

SN: Do you see that being a problem?
E: (Smiles) No, we work as a team, so I know that it won't be a problem.

SN: A team like Arsenal?
E: I flipping hope not – I don't want to be in fourth place come May.

Laughing from behind the cameras.

SN: So you both manage to get out?
E: A bit, but with Lee it tends to be nearly all work-related. Just the other week we were out with Brian and Elaine Allan – as we missed their Ruby anniversary. Both lovely people, however Brian is this old school West Ham United supporter and afterwards I knew as much about the likes of Trevor Brooking, Bobby Moore and Phil Woosnam as anyone.

SN: Phil Woosnam?
E: He played as an inside right for West Ham. I think that's a number eight. Arsenal tried to buy him several times between 1958 and 1960. Sammy – Jon Sammels, the Arsenal

footballer once wrote to him as a young boy and asked him the question of how he managed to fit playing football in with teaching, along with asking a few other tips on football.

SN: He was a teacher?
E: A physics teacher at Leyton High School, yeh. Sammy met him in New York in the late 1970's but never got the chance to thank him for replying to his letter. I think Sammy regretted that. Lee loves to hear stories such as that.

SN: So, do you know much about football?
E: (Laughs) I know a lot more about it since I met Lee, that's for sure.

SN: I still can't say that I've ever heard of Phil Woosnam.
E: He had a look of Samir Nasri. He played a big part in helping the United States get to host the 1994 World Cup.

SN: Do you have a favourite football team?
E: (Smiles) It has to be Arsenal as I've had so many lovely times watching them, although I have a soft spot for Everton too, as when I went out to Germany with Lee the other month, I met a lot of their supporters and their Chairman – all of who were extremely nice people. And of course I'm from up that way too.

SN: You're from Liverpool?
E: (Shakes her head) The Wirral.

SN: It's a small world – So am I.
E: (Smiles) Yeh it is.

SN: So, what do you do for a quiet night in?
E: (Laughs) Maybe a bottle of wine and a good film – if I get my way. Or if Lee gets his – a Spaghetti Western or a definitely 'not good film'. He watched seven or eight

episodes of 'George and Mildred' the other week. I think George Roper's his hero!

SN: There was an amusing story in the media about Lee catching you singing football songs.
E: (Smiles) Football songs? No sorry, I don't know that one.

SN: You were singing it in Spanish.
E: (Laughs) Oh, god yeh. I was teaching Lee's daughter to sing 'Guantanamera' in Spanish to her baby brother – you know the one.

SN: (Shakes her head) No, but you can tell us.
E: (Sings) Mi verso es de un verde claro, y de un carm n encendido, Mi verso es de un verde claro, y de un carm n encendido, Mi verso es un ciervo herido, que busca en el monte amparo – Guantanamera, guajira guantanamera. (Talking) When Lee came in and heard us he started singing the chorus along with me – in English – sort of. 'You only sing when your winning – You only sing when you're winning'. (Laughs) The great nit thought that they were the actual words.

SN: So, you can sing and you speak Spanish?
E: (Laughs) His mate Sooty – the pig – got me to sing to him at our wedding. Lee nearly died of embarrassment, the poor thing – and yeh, I speak a few languages.

SN: The story in the Daily Mirror the other day – was that true?
E: (Shrugs) Which one? We're in the papers almost every day.

SN: The bed.
E: (Smiles) I don't know that one either? (Shrugs) Me going mad with the firm who we'd ordered some beds off? Setting the beds on fire?

SN: I was going to say the broken bed, but I'll certainly take the setting the beds on fire story.

E: (Laughs) When we first moved in together we had been homeless, but Lee had got this house off Grays Inn Road, not too far from King's Cross station. He'd had tenants in but they'd left it in a right mess. Lee had it cleaned-up and decorated and he'd dragged all the beds outside and set fire to them. He used a bit too much petrol. Well, that's what the three crews of firemen said!

SN: So I gather that it was a fairly big fire? E: (Smiles) Yeh, it was definitely up there. Next door's fence and shed caught fire and as it was full of paint, creosote and stuff the neighbours had to be evacuated. Lee's children loved it, his little lad saying – "Can we do that again, dad?" As for the broken bed, yeh, that was Lee's rubbish attempt at DIY!

SN: How did it break? E: (Laughs) I definitely, definitely can't tell you that.

SN: So? E: (Laughs) As we had nowhere to sleep after he'd burnt next doors shed down, Lee went and ordered these beds from IKEA online, and ours was this really massive one. He was dead proud of that – that was until they arrived in bits and he had to put them together. From the fourth day of putting ours up it was continually dropping to bits – that was until he had this brainwave. The bottom of the bed – the bedstead thingy was sagging, so he propped it up with some books. It was like that until my mam and dad stopped to look after the ferrets while we were in Morocco, and dad pinned it together.

SN: You have ferrets?

E: (Laughs) Yeh, they are so cute – Giroud and Arteta. Lee bought them for the children after they had seen some at school.

SN: Do they bite?
E: (Laughs) Well, neither me nor the children have ever been bitten.

SN: So, can you remember what books they were?
E: (Smiles) Books? Yeh I can, actually. They were all research as part of Lee's Sammy documentary and a documentary of the 1970 World Cup. A bio on Bob Wilson from 1971 – Back Home by Jeff Dawson – Sammy's bio – Jon Spurling's 'Highbury – Arsenal in N5' – Bertie Mee's bio – Terry Neill's revelations of a football manager – A bio of a player called The Doog who had a Village People-type moustache and who sat on the ITV panel during the 1970 World Cup – and The Worst of Friends, which is a fictional football book by Colin Shindler (Smiling and advertising to the camera) All of which fit perfectly beneath the bedstead of a Hemnes supersized bed from IKEA.

SN: So how do you cope with all the media attention?
E: Mmm. Some of it can be a bit intrusive and there has been some instances where Lee has had to really lose his manners, however there are some instances when it is quite nice – that I certainly don't have a problem with.

SN: So, Lee is protective?
E: (Smiles) With his family, yeh very.

SN: Does he get angry?
E: (Laughs) Only when Arsenal are on TV. I think that's mainly frustration.

SN: There's a sixties' feel about the programmes that you do, and of course surrounding this music the press have labelled as the 'North London sound'.
E: (Smiles) Yeh, you're right – there is a bit.

SN: Could you explain?
E: When we first started living together Lee was doing several documentaries – but it was his Sammy documentary that was taking the majority of his attention. Sammy was very different from your players back then – such as Bobby Charlton, Nobby Stiles, Jimmy Greaves, Alan Mullery and so on. He was Arsenal's first pin up – the beautiful, well-spoken boy who looked like a cross between Keith Moon of The Who and Steve Marriot of the Small Faces and who had the model girlfriend on his arm. George Best may have been the darling of the media, but he was in Manchester. Sammy wasn't. Sammy was in the centre of what was 'Swinging London'. Lee's documentary captured the moment beautifully and the music was something else. He'd even incorporated Sammy and his then girlfriend Angie's 'Our Tune' if yer like into it – Tim Hardin's 'If I were a Carpenter' – the song he wrote and sang live at Woodstock. The sixties was an era when football and fashion began moving hand in hand. It was really inspiring and when Lee started recording bands and rigging out the studios, some pattern was forming, but Jeanette needs to take a lot of credit for this.

SN: Jeanette Janes?
E: (Smiles) When I first saw Jeanette, I thought 'Wow – she looks good'. She had a style and aura about her which was very much 'Miss Sixties' and a lot of the girls in the studios and on the ITV Seven set have been influenced by her, especially as she introduced them to Milan – her wardrobe guy.

SN: Does Lee use him?
E: (Laughs) No. But a few of the bands do. He's really good.

SN: Do you use him?
E: (Winks) No, Lee makes me shop at Primark

SN: What, really?
E: (Smiles) Nah – I'm kidding.

SN: One last question Emily – what do you want for 2015?
E: (Smiles) Just for all my family and friends to stay healthy.

The End

James Durose-Rayner

To be continued in

The Queen of Cups

ITV seven

Lightning Source UK Ltd.
Milton Keynes UK
UKOW04f2001071215

264302UK00004B/99/P

9 781785 076084